Kükuchi
Her Life and Times©

A Historical Fiction

By

Sipho Ernest Mahlobo

PHYSICAL ADDRESS:

61422 Motel Road,
Mqedandaba,
Estcourt,
KwaZulu/Natal 3330

ACKNOWLEDGMENTS:
Grateful acknowledgement to:
June Jordan Literary Estate Trust
Copyright 2005 for the lines reprinted
Page 185
www.junejordan.com

Kükuchi is a work of fiction.
The main characters are entirely fictional.

***

This book is dedicated with love to
My Loving Siblings
Sylvia Khululiwe Dlamini 1944–2018
Sibongile Priscilla Dlamini 1952–2019
Cebo Norman Mahlobo 1955–1977
Busisiwe Mahlobo 1957–1957

A writer should stir things up.
- Henry A Giroux -

CHAPTER 1

Prologue

Flashes of anxiety keep Kükuchi awake all night. The seven-year-old girl is looking forward to the promised picnic with Musa, away from the sometimes tedious but still fun work at her grandmother's chicken farm.

It's a foggy morning when they finally head west toward Pasiwe, a rocky hill overlooking the rural communities of Mandabearni, Moyeni, Ngonyameni, Makhekheni, Mnyangweni, Tatane, Maqabaqabeni, and Mqedandaba. As they climb, the chubby toddler rolls her eyes, while butterflies flutter in her stomach.

The smart girl's curiosity rises and then falls like the tide, as she secretly wonders if Musa has brought her to the mysterious Pasiwe to harm her. Little children often disappear without a trace, not to mention the plight of girls living with albinism on the continent of Africa, who quickly learn to trust no one.

However, once Kükuchi and Musa approach the top of the fog, the sweet aroma of the earth wafts through moist air, urging them to continue. By the time they reach the hill's crest, the sun has risen, making the view around the Drakensberg much clearer.

***

Kükuchi sighs in relief when they finally reach the west side of Pasiwe. Glancing out of the corner of her eye as they walk across the soggy grass, she feels a rush of fear upon spotting a shed snake's skin nearby. At that moment, Musa makes a gesture that draws Kükuchi's attention to an adult black mamba slithering like lightning into the dense brush. She looks at Musa, who seems more captivated by the curled-up skin than the mamba that just disappeared.

> "We must go back home now; there are poisonous snakes here…" Kükuchi whispers.
> Musa smiles and says, "Look at this pretty dry skin. Don't you want to take it with you?"
> "The snake's skin? No, Musa."

Kükuchi directs her wandering eye at the imposing Drakensberg. The sight gives her a strange sense of intimacy and foreboding, as if she could easily touch the 'Devil's Tooth'. Her grandmother, Salu to everyone, used to cook up a variety of blood-curdling tales about the 'Devil's Tooth', which she reserved for her night-time fireside storytelling, always under moonlight.

Salu created some of her creepy folklore, inspired by African and Eastern mythical creatures. Sometimes, when she ran out of new ideas, Kükuchi's grandma would borrow a few stories from murder mystery writers like Arthur Conan Doyle and Agatha Christie. Salu used to be an English teacher before she reluctantly became a farmer.

Kükuchi leans against the rocks covered in mould, quietly admiring the peacefulness of the Drakensberg plateau. The sight of the Injesuthi River, flowing gently like a silvery serpent, leaves her in awe. She imagines crocodiles and alligators swimming in the waters, while nearby, hippos nod their heads, hiding their predatory shrewdness. As she watches the tributary streams flow into the Buffalo River, Kükuchi recalls a verse from Ecclesiastes that she recited passionately during their busy Sunday School sessions: Ecclesiastes 1:7, 'All the rivers run into the sea; yet the sea is never full; to the place from which the rivers come, there they return…'.

Once settled, Kükuchi lets her inquisitive eyes sweep westward, hoping to see Salu's land and dwellings further away below. Salu frowned at the idea of the excursion, blaming Musa for exposing a child to danger. Kükuchi smiles when she spots Salu's farm amid the rolling hills of Pangweni, her farmhouse hidden behind a patch of thick forest. A few meters from where the two have parked, jets of fresh spring water delight a group of playful monkeys, fooling around and rummaging for snacks.

Musa giggles incongruously and says, "Forget the animals. Do you see all this land down there? That is Moyeni. Look over there. That is Cathedral Peak, located towards Bergville. You can see Champagne Castle on this side of it, right?"

"Yes…?"

Musa motions for Kükuchi to turn around. She points at Maqabaqabeni and Mqedandaba. From there, they can see vast stretches of white-owned farmland extending from Estcourt to Winterton to Bergville.

"What do you think?" She sounds Kükuchi out.

"Think? I don't know, Musa…"

"This beautiful countryside, which you see beyond Moyeni and Maqabaqabeni, was stolen from the Africans by European settlers. I brought you here so you can see the land that belongs to you. The English people and their families arrived in this area from England in 1820. They destroyed our Hlubi and Ngwe Kingdoms and claimed all the fertile land they found. They forced our young boys and girls like you into indentured slavery and left us with rocky, barren plots suitable only for goats and hedgehogs."

I know how Snakes think.

As for Kükuchi, she briefly thinks about asking Musa if she's sane, but decides not to. Questioning Musa about anything is like poking a rattlesnake with a tiny stick. Back home in White City, Khulu, her other grandmother and Salu's older sister, once whispered to Kükuchi, 'Musa has worms in her head.'

Musa continues her political lesson, saying, "You owe it to Bashaye and all our ancestors to get our land back. Promise you will fight for our country when you grow up."

"Fight…? You say the Europeans stole our land. How did they steal it?"

"One day, when you become a teenager, I'll tell you how the Hlubi and the Ngwe lost all the land around here to foreigners. Even the Zulu people lost their country after the British murdered King Shaka."

"My mistress at Donaldson told us Dingane killed the king."

Musa retorts, "Your mistress knows nothing. King Shaka was ambushed and murdered by the

Europeans because they feared a repeat of their Haitian humiliation."

"What? But our mistress read that in a book."

"One day, I will teach you how the Haitians, who are black like us, defeated the armies of France and England. Do you want to know how that happened?"

"No, Musa. I don't know those people."

"When you grow up, you will learn many things about the people you don't know."

Kükuchi is hardly impressed with Musa's stories about the British. After reminding her about the picnic, Musa says, "Okay, let's walk down and seek shelter with the Mdakane family. We'll picnic with them because I've brought enough chicken pies to share around. Besides, they are the only Africans with fresh running water from the taps."

Then they detour toward the brushy area vacated by the mamba. There, Musa pulls out a withered skin recently shed by a cobra and says, "I thought we would find the skin of that mamba we saw earlier. But this one! It belongs to a spitting cobra, no less. I'll take it home to show our grand one to Salu."

A dome of leaves representing a cobra's home attracts Musa's curiosity. She crouches and quietly motions Kükuchi to look. Kükuchi bends cautiously to peek. Several cobra hatchlings are wriggling like worms inside the nest.

Musa smiles delightfully and says, "I'll be returning to fetch the babies. These are cobras! Tonight is my diamond night?"

"Please, Musa, it will be dark. The baby's mother is dangerous. She will kill you."

"Oh no. I know how snakes think; I work for them in Mayfair."

I am a woman now.

Many years have passed, and Kükuchi's memories of the Pasiwe expedition are fading fast. Even though time has blurred her recollections of her youth, nothing could erase what Musa planted in Kükuchi's mind about the land down Drakensberg Basin and the British.

Back in White City, her township home in Johannesburg, Kükuchi was lying lazily in bed, considering whether or when to kick off the blankets and prepare for school. While she grew up to be funny and personable, Kükuchi had slowly developed a streak of bad temper that had become her trademark in her township. Some people thought she was somehow mentally disturbed or even 'possessed', all of which was made worse by negative perceptions about people living with albinism.

After slipping out of her blankets, she stood stiff as a lamppost in the middle of the bedroom. Evil thoughts started to fill her mind again, and she began murmuring her carefully chosen curses, yelling at anyone by name: a friend, a relative, or any neighbour whose name she could recall. When she 'reached' Khulu in her head, she said, 'No, not that one'. Khulu was Salu's elder sister. Kükuchi carried on with her mindless swearing until she reached the name 'Toby', at which point she paused, smiled, and said, 'Not that one'. The two girls had been wearing a thong and shorts since infancy. When the random drawing of names from her warped mind finally carried her to 'Salu', she paused, ruffled her ginger hair, and said lamely, "Salu? Not Salu."

However, Kūkuchi spared no one else, not even Musa, or her elderly neighbours next door, or her teachers at Donaldson Primary. Not satisfied with her vile monologue, she paced aimlessly, stopped to spit on the floor, and whispered, "And as for you, Uncle Dodo, may the demons in those pigs drive you to the river to die."

Kūkuchi's wild curses were often loud enough to fill Khulu's space, echoing beyond their neighbours and past anyone who cared to listen. While quietly taking note of her granddaughter's outpourings of madness one morning, Khulu felt Kūkuchi had crossed the line.

"Kūkuchi!" Khulu yelled. "What are you doing...?"

"I am up, Khulu... ready to wash."

"You're up and cursing like a demon! Is that what you learn at your Sunday school? Are you inviting Satan into this house?"

Kūkuchi grinned, stretched out, and let out a lazy yawn.

***

As the muffled but increasing sounds of the school grew louder, Kūkuchi began to move a little faster. She stepped closer to the window, peeked through the curtain, and softly rubbed the foggy glass with her fingers. Thick frost covered the narrow patch of grass, sending icy chills through her bones. When she lifted her troubled eyes, she saw the lonely peach tree's remaining leaves drooping with dewdrops.

On the dusty street opposite, commuters rushed to catch transport — taxis, trains, and buses — to get to work in town. She threw a cynical chuckle across the tiny bedroom and pulled the curtain. Khulu shouted again, "Stop fooling around and hurry up. You will be late. The kettle is boiling. You must wash your body."

Kūkuchi glanced at the frosty autumn morning again. In her mind, something about the onset of winter did not fit in with school. If she could help it, those Mamas from the Women's League would shut her school forever. She would then stay home and spend time with Toby. She relished the company of friends under the Yellowwoods, where the girls spread gossip and conspired on their raids of Mr Tatenda's 'Fish and Chips' outlet.

Kūkuchi stepped back and sat on the battered dressing table, her ironic smile slowly disappearing as her mind rushed back to the significance of her day. Friday had finally arrived, bringing her long-awaited break into her teenage years. She had always wondered where her family would be when she grew up, secretly craving a better life for Khulu and herself. She knew she had to do something to escape deprivation and despair, a common feature of life in White City and Jabavu. She rubbed her eyes delicately and then nudged carefully towards the door to steal a look. Her grandmother had continued pounding away on her sewing machine while keeping a careful eye on the incwancwa (soft porridge) simmering away.

Kūkuchi seems unaware that the clock's hands are moving. When Khulu angrily yells for her to hurry and get into her uniform, Kūkuchi says, "Khulu, you remember Salu telling you about the day Musa took me to the top of the Drakensberg?"

"That was not the top of the Drakensberg. Do you know what the top of the Drakensberg looks like? Your grandma told me you and Musa climbed a hill and then came back."

"Okay, Khulu, forget what Salu said. Let me tell you, even now, Musa refuses to explain how the British took the land in the Drakensberg. Last time we were there, she said she would tell me about the people from England when I turn thirteen."

"What good is that to you? The Europeans deny they took any land from anyone."

"Do you want to hear what else Musa said about those people from England...?"

"No. I don't want to hear. You must get ready for school."

Kükuchi whispers, "Musa says whites are settlers in our country. Did you know that, Khulu? I spoke to Salu and she agrees with her."

"Never repeat such things. Do you want us to go to jail?"

Disappointed with Khulu's response, Kükuchi hurried to the bedroom to grab her crumpled bottle-green beret from Khulu's suitcase. By the time Khulu returned to sewing, Kükuchi had already started again. "Tina told me about settlers. She said her mother always says, even in Rhodesia, they have their settlers from England."

"Voetsak!"

Kükuchi pulled her beret comically over her head to make herself look like a hedgehog without its prickly spines.

"But you said you hate that beret."

"I said I'll put it on one day. What did I say about that day, Khulu?"

Kükuchi thought Khulu might remember something about her birthday.

"Do you know what I am today, Khulu? I am a grown woman now. Musa must return from Mayfair, tell me about our history, and bring my gifts because it's time." When Kükuchi saw Khulu's eyes watering, she dropped the subject and left her alone. Khulu looked uncomfortable because she had no birthday present for Kükuchi, except for a few tears she tried to hold back.

In the background, one could catch a hazy glow of colourful sounds, a droning echo of Putco buses, and more screeching taxis fighting for quick gaps on the narrow streets of White City. A few yards away, Donaldson Primary buzzed with the angelic voices of its girls' choir, where they were rehearsing O'Carolan's 'English Country Garden' for their Provincial Competitions. Mr Zondi had made a name for himself as one of the top composers and music conductors in the Transvaal.

Kükuchi was ready for school. Two thin slices of bread lay on the table waiting for her to finish *eating the* soft porridge. Because Khulu had run out of white margarine and supplies, she would later struggle down the muddy streets, as far as Phefeni, to collect money and excuses from her pinafore debtors. On her way back, she would stop at Tatenda's shop for more brown bread and white margarine. Kükuchi entered Donaldson barely a minute before the sound of the second bell. School dragged on, during which time she spent her free time inviting her girlfriends to their spot outside the schoolyard. She wanted her friends to get a sneak preview of her secrets. At that time, she believed quite naively that her girlfriends would each open up and reveal all about the goings-on behind the walls of their homes once they heard her story. She had it all laid out, beginning with her birthday, of which she would toss a strong hint about the gifts she expected.

CHAPTER 2

State of squalor

Twenty kilometres south of Johannesburg was White-City, one of the shantytowns built for Indigenous Africans by successive colonial regimes. The apartheid racists, who relied on brute force as a method of social engineering, later incorporated White-City into the sprawling settlement they named 'Soweto.' Despite its promising name and fancy white walls, White-City was an embodiment of pain and secrets, a dark hole where clever resourcefulness often proved helpful.

Kūkuchi started to resent the squalor surrounding her life the moment she realized that life was tough for her as an African girl. She saw that white girls and boys, in their secluded, leafy spaces, were having a good time at school and home. In the past, little black girls didn't openly question such differences because everything around them—whites and blacks living in separate worlds in the same country—looked as natural as the blue skies. When Kūkuchi's eyes began to notice the differences between natural skies and white wealth, she understood that everyone in White-City was getting the short end of the stick.

This realization fuelled her hidden anger toward white people, which grew into mental anguish. She began taking out her frustrations on those close to her in various aggressive ways. By her first day at Hebe-Hebe, an unregistered private school in Moroka, she had perfected the art of bullying, yelling, and defying, which often helped her get her way. Because her mind was constantly racing, Kūkuchi was confused, and the authorities found her behaviour troubling. Living with albinism added to her mental pain. She had to deal with cruel remarks and awkward reactions, people hesitant around her, and visibly uneasy about getting close enough to hug her.

Our stove is busy

One of the episodes in Kūkuchi's memory is related to how she had to endure the humiliation of begging neighbours for a stove to cook food for Khulu and herself. Khulu sometimes found it hard to save enough money to buy a bucket of coal from local peddlers. When things become desperate and they run out of firewood and coal during winter, Kūkuchi sits on the kitchen wall to enjoy the warmth from the neighbours' Welcome Dover stove. White-City is a semi-detached neighborhood with walls so thin that you can hear entire conversations next door.

Khulu often dispatched Kūkuchi to their middle-aged neighbours, Papa and Mama Maseko, for favours. The elders were retired teachers originally from Piet Retief. Each time she sent Kūkuchi to the couple, Khulu reminded her to say politely, 'Khulu is asking for a favour; to use your stove to cook supper'.

In that situation, Kūkuchi endured sitting in the neighbours' kitchen, quietly suffering as Mrs Maseko openly criticized her for interrupting their focus on the Zulu drama playing on their rerun.

One afternoon, while she was messing with Mrs Maseko's stove, Kūkuchi simmered with anger as the old woman scolded her, "You must learn manners and behave like a decent girl. Do we have to put up with your loud voice every morning? Who taught you to use such wicked language so early in the morning? You are an evil child..."

Kükuchi quickly responded, "You know what Salu says? She says you like sticking your nose into other people's business."

"Khulu says that about me?"

"No, that is Salu from Estcourt. She is the one, not Khulu. Don't you know Salu is Khulu's sister?"

Mrs Maseko heaved a sigh of pain. She retorted, "Next time your Grandma from Estcourt gets here, I'll fix her."

"You can't fix Salu. She'll fix you first before you even try."

Mr Maseko promptly said, "Mama Maseko here is joking. Is that not so, Mama?"

"Yes, Papa. Mama is joking."

Kükuchi added, "So, you won't tell Salu or Khulu what I just said? You must not do that, Mama. Otherwise, I'll stop telling you things people say about you."

"People?"

"Yes, Sister Mohale, the nurse, says that I shouldn't be called names just because I am a girl living with albinism. She says, "People with albinism are human beings too."

Mrs Maseko rested her arms on her broad figure and shouted, "Me? When did I call you names?"

"I don't know. Ask Sister Mohale. Papa Mkhize once told me people in White City like gossip just as much as chewing chappies."

"You are not what people call you, Kuchi," Papa Maseko put it gently. "And you are a very clever girl. Your teacher told me you are the smartest in your class..."

"Does that mean I can come every night to cook on your stove?"

"No," Mama Maseko quickly responded, "Your teacher also told us you are the worst kid at your school, and one day your principal will send you to Phomolong, where girls like you eat *morogo* and rough porridge every day."

"I'll go there and break all the windows. Tell the principal that's what I'll do."

Meanwhile, Mr Maseko ignored Kükuchi and focused instead on his Zulu drama. Mama Maseko began again, expressing even greater dissatisfaction with Kükuchi's entire family, while the girl she was targeting kept making faces and wiggling her tongue at her. Eventually, the older woman stopped when she realized her scolding wasn't getting anywhere.

As Kükuchi walked out, Mrs Maseko yelled, "You can't even say 'thank you' after using my stove. You people are the greatest leeches of White-City. Next time, buy coal and use your stove to cook. No more favours..."

From that day onward, Kükuchi stopped using the word 'favour' when talking to Mrs Maseko. Sometimes, the elderly couple refused Khulu's requests, saying their stove was 'busy'. Knowing she could go to bed hungry if she didn't find a stove to cook on, Kükuchi had to get creative; she would enter the elderly couple's kitchen without knocking, whistling a strange tune, and head straight to the furnace as if she owned the place. After Kükuchi repeated her act three times, Mrs Maseko locked her doors every day at noon to keep Kükuchi out.

One afternoon, Kükuchi desperately tried to get into Mrs Maseko's kitchen. The elderly woman yelled, 'Our stove is busy, go away.' Clutching her pot of chicken giblets, Kükuchi kept insisting and demanding to see if the stove was free. The Maseko couple ignored Kükuchi's lengthy ranting. Finally, Kükuchi sneaked around to the back of the house and climbed through the window while the elderly couple sat comfortably, listening to the Zulu drama on their *rediffusion*.

Once inside, Kükuchi realized that the stove was far from busy. She shouted, "You are the greatest liars in White-City. This stove is not busy! You call one lousy boiling kettle busy…?"

Her wayward granddaughter's misbehaviour quickly caught Khulu's attention. Before she could visit her neighbours to apologize, Mrs Maseko had already gone to Moroka Police Station to file charges against Kükuchi. In a panic, Khulu asked Mr Mkhize for help to calm Mrs Maseko down, who had already filed a case of burglary and attempted murder at the station. Mr Mkhize was a resident of White City, a fatherly figure to Kükuchi and Khulu, and the only trusted male neighbour. He rushed to Moroka and offered to discipline the wayward child himself. Everyone was satisfied, including the bemused police officers. Mrs Maseko returned home with a smirk and joined Mkhize and Khulu on their long walk home.

Kükuchi Lacks Melanin

One Sunday, a church pastor named Bandile Gumede stood on the terrace after his uplifting service, smiling broadly as he greeted the congregants who filed out of the pews, shaking hands, occasionally cracking jokes, and laughing loudly in front of the women and small children. However, as soon as his eyes met Kükuchi's, he pulled away from shaking hands and hurried back to his vestry. His sermon focused on the holiness of God and how He uses all kinds of people for His purposes. Kükuchi wondered why the pastor acted like a thug toward his congregation at the sight of a girl living with albinism.

At a young age, while other children played with mud, Plaster-of-Paris, or engaged in kick-the-can and jump-rope games, Kükuchi focused on studying her body—her face, legs, and arms in front of a mirror—trying to find ways to cope with the effects of being different. Her situation worsened as she entered adolescence. She believed that the white skin she dreaded made her stand out everywhere she went, leading her to see everyone as a potential threat. She also thought, influenced by callous neighbours, that enemies might have cursed her. This belief began to take hold for her, affecting her connection with society. She began to openly respond to teasing and ridicule with foul language and threats of violence against anyone who confronted her.

Her despairing moment came the day she did tasks during preparations for the funeral of a relative's baby. The grandmother of the dead baby banned Kükuchi from her kitchen. She instructed the rest of the party to ensure she stayed away from her cutlery and food. Kükuchi was hurt. She went home in tears. From then on, she stayed away from funerals and family gatherings.

Kükuchi lacked melanin, which meant that her skin failed to absorb the sun's rays when exposed to sunlight. Overexposure resulted in her falling sick for days. Her face would break out into blisters, and her eyelids would swell. Like most people living with albinism, Kükuchi was always in danger of impaired vision due to the lack of the same melanin pigment during development. Her eyesight was troubling. Although she resented the idea, circumstances compelled her to use reading glasses.

Many people, including relatives, avoided discussing Kükuchi's albinism, squirming uncomfortably if anyone dared to bring it up. Sister Mohale was the notable exception. While she refrained from directly mentioning her albinism, Mohale was willing to share sensitive 'girlie' topics with Kükuchi. A nursing sister at Baragwanath Hospital, Sister Mohale, lived up the street from Kükuchi's home, and her large house stood out like a tulip in the prairie. As a nurse, the white township superintendent had granted her permission to own a home in her name as a single mother, complete with running water and an indoor toilet.

Mohale helped Kükuchi through her biological transformation, with some things emerging and others growing larger. She was becoming a woman and nurturing erotic and nuptial fantasies. Sister Mohale always affirmed Kükuchi and encouraged her to believe in the strength within herself.

Kükuchi was destined to face the trials and tribulations of being a Black woman. Furthermore, her white skin added an extra burden to her fragile psyche. Over time, small dark spots on her skin would become insignificant compared to the challenges she was meant to face in her male-dominated society. On top of that, the weight of her dysfunctional family became a noose around her neck. Yes, lurking in the shadows, something was slowly developing, like rising damp, concerning the strange relationship between women in her family, most of whom had a streak of stubbornness.

Sister Mohale was all over the place. Mkhize once said of her, 'If you reveal a secret to Mohale, you are like a man carrying sugar beans along the street in a bag with a hole.' Kükuchi appreciated everything Mohale provided, who also gifted Kükuchi a floppy grass hat to screen her face, which the fussy girl hid permanently in Khulu's wardrobe. Mohale paid Khulu regular visits to deliver Kükuchi's skin liniments, eye drops, sunscreens, hats, and newspapers.

More often, Mohale stopped by for a casual chat with Khulu to add some colour to local gossip about their neighbours and people who had gotten themselves arrested for meddling in politics. After delivering Kükuchi's prescription one day, Mohale asked Khulu to lend her five shillings. As usual, Khulu obliged, taking a few coins from her pinafore cash. By month's end, Mohale swore, "You are wrong, Khulu. You gave me half a crown, not five shillings."

Khulu later quipped, "Mohale should have been a lawyer, not a sister in that big Bara Hospital because lawyers are liars."

***

One day, Mrs Khuzwayo, who lives next door to Sister Mohale's mansion, hangs herself. Up and down the streets of White-City, people know that her husband regularly uses fisticuffs on her when drunk. In the company of other people, a safe distance from her husband, Mrs Khuzwayo always smiles and keeps her secrets of abuse to herself. Whenever Mohale and other concerned women appeal to her to use her head and leave the abusive marriage, her face beams incongruously. Still, she puts it in her silky voice, 'Oh, you worry too much about me.'

The residents believe Khuzwayo murdered his wife and then staged a suicide. Khuzwayo does not wait for the verdict. He disappears from White-City long before the funeral, escaping the swift and fatal street justice that usually happens in such cases.

Kükuchi feels both troubled and happy for her because she believes Mrs Khuzwayo has gone to heaven. Miss Lumka, her twenty-year-old Sunday school teacher who also teaches privately at Donaldson Primary, often assures them that those who suffer on earth go to heaven when they die.

A few days after the burial of Mrs Khuzwayo, Kükuchi steals away at night into her Donaldson classroom, determined to hang herself, too. She is not scared of dying because she knows she will go to heaven and stay in a big house like white people. The school is always eerily dark, and the silence chills at night. Kükuchi shatters the windowpane and goes inside. As she is figuring out how to secure herself with a rope beneath one of the rafters, Kükuchi says, "God, what did I do to you? Everyone stares at me as if I were dirty and mad. Does that make you happy? Why did you make me white like this? Why didn't you make me look like Toby?"

Kükuchi pauses, pondering on the stillness of her school and the whispering murmurs of the soft wind sweeping the roof. Then, unexpectedly, a woman's voice that seemed to spring from the small window along the long corridor whispers eerily, "Kükuchi! What do you think you are doing?"

The principal, Mrs Posa, is tall, lean, and strict. Her attire is formal, cut with precision to cover the knees. She walks with military emphasis on the concrete hall across the length and breadth of her school. Whenever she approaches, all classrooms in her path suddenly fall silent. Despite her wayward behaviour, Kükuchi is terrified of her principal, which explains why her ginger hair stands on end when she hears the admonitory voice. She holds her breath, listening more intently. She knows the principal's voice all too well, but she does not think it wise to respond. Instead, she leaps through the window the way she came and disappears into the night.

Trembling like an aspen leaf, Kükuchi emerges from the shadows of her school-yard feeling queasy. She hides her bright face behind her jersey when she sees hazy figures walking her way.

Kükuchi later denies ever having been anywhere close to the school that night.

"Don't you think I know your face even in the dark?" Mrs Posa crows.

"It could have been anyone…"

Mrs Posa proceeds to punish Kükuchi for breaking into her school's classroom and participating in strange Satanic rituals. Later, the story about Kükuchi's break-in reaches Khulu's ears, but the girl denies everything, challenging Posa to prove she saw her in that dark classroom.

***

Kükuchi came out top of her Standard Two class. Then, an unidentified person gave her a trendy, bottle-green beret. It was a uniquely precious gift with great emotional significance for her. However, with time, she discovered that her cherished gift had come from Musa. Despite the disappointment, her beret lifted her spirits in ways she could not explain. Walking with spring in her step, she spotted her beret and greeted everyone with a broad smile. Her high spirits took on a mysterious tone. She began to create her fantasy from her dreams, flying high above the Natal Midlands among the white clouds, towering over every hill and stream.

Kükuchi later told her grandmother how important she was, as she could fly with the clouds above the Drakensberg. After listening with extreme concern, Khulu dashed to the bedroom to pray for Kükuchi, "Almighty, please get rid of these demons in Kükuchi's body and send them to those pigs next to Blake's funeral parlour. Maybe they will run to the Klipspruit River and drown. Please, God, this child is possessed."

Early next morning, Khulu staggered up the street to Mkhize's home to seek advice about the demons stalking Kükuchi.

Mkhize was a township consultant on *muti* matters. He peddled illicit identity passes and death certificates from his two-roomed house. A strong rumour was that he owned a baby-brown gun that kept local *Tsotsi* troublemakers respectful towards him. The Apartheid authorities ignored Mkhize's illicit activities as he kept his nose out of overt struggle politics. When African police needed cash for a 'cold drink,' they paid local shops, such as Barberton Brewers. They made a quick visit, ostensibly to warn them to be careful about engaging in illicit activities. While at it, they touched Mkhize's house and put it to him tongue-in-cheek, "We know you are a law-abiding Zulu man. Be careful of township lawbreakers, Mkhize."

Khulu said, "Mkhize, Kükuchi has delusions. She thinks she can fly over the Drakensberg. I prayed for her all night, but the pigs did not run into the Klipspruit stream. What must I do?"

Mkhize said, "Pigs? You are speaking strange tongues, Khulu. You know God is a very busy man. How can you waste his time praying for Kükuchi all night just because she thinks she can fly above the Drakensberg? I told you long ago that I am worried about this child. As you have told me, she walks in her sleep and dreams strange dreams. What is puzzling is that one day, she counted my groceries in a split second and told Mr Tatenda he had short-changed me. Imagine! I would have lost one-and-six."

"So, why are you worried about her, Mkhize?"

"She's too clever. I think there's an ancestor whispering answers in her ear. I've never met a child with such rude answers. The other day, she told a black police officer to go to hell. I believe she hears voices. She's strange, like the Albertine tornado. With all these dreams, our departed ones call her a Sangoma."

"A *Sangoma*? I don't think that one will agree to be a *Sangoma*!"

"It's not up to her, Khulu. I wish to carry this child to Mtubatuba to our Great *Sanusi,* who will show her the correct Ubuntu ways. I have seen her sandy eyes. She belongs in the wilderness, up the stony hills, open spaces, springs of ancient rivers, down the Drakensberg basin. That is where she belongs. Over there, she will talk to the ancient rocks and evergreen trees, lizards with heads like crocodiles, and red sun spiders. Over there, she will bring us answers about our land that the Europeans took from us so easily."

"Oh, Mkhize, you are beginning to sound like Musa," Khulu squeaked as she returned home.

Kükuchi asked her where she had been. Khulu told her she had been out getting fresh air.

"I know where you went. I didn't know Papa Mkhize had fresh air in his kraal, Khulu."

"You don't have to be sarcastic. Yes, Mkhize has plenty of fresh air, and he says the fresh air tells him you must be a *Sangoma*."

"A *Sangoma*! Why?"

"Because you will tell us how to get back the land stolen by White people."

"What? Why doesn't he tell Mrs Posa to promote me? I am the brightest in that class. I beat them in arithmetic, even in English."

"You want Posa to promote you so you can be a *Sangoma*?"

"She has Apartheid, Khulu. You should have seen her promote two boys and leave me behind, even though I'm the cleverest. I outsmarted them all. My teacher tells the principal that I refuse to follow her instructions. When the principal comes to promote students, she tells my teacher she can't promote me because I can't see the writing on the blackboard. She says she wants me to sit in the front row, like all children with albinism do. These people are jealous. I refuse to sit in front."

"You must learn to respect teachers because they know better than you."

CHAPTER 3

'Mixed Race'

Toby's mother was Mrs Karel Owen. The single mother and her daughter were classified as 'coloured' by the apartheid government. A few coloured families lived among 'blacks' in White City. The regulated spatial distribution of the population ensured that coloured communities had their townships away from black Africans. However, occasionally, the apartheid technology, known as the 'pencil test,' malfunctioned and failed to detect activities and movements that interfered with their interracial family policy. As a result, dozens of 'coloureds' became 'white' and moved into white spaces. A few unlucky ones sank to the lowly 'African' existence at the stroke of a pencil. The rest remained 'coloured,' bearing all the benefits and hardships associated with skin colour under the apartheid masters.

Toby endured schoolyard taunts as people used hurtful terms to refer to her. While Mrs Owen ignored it all, she seethed with rage one day when her daughter complained to her about abuse at school. Karel hastened to Donaldson to demand that the principal stop it, explaining at length in her impeccable Tswana language that her father was a Tswana-speaking man from Phokeng.

Not unlike many black women, Karel worked as a 'domestic' for a white family in Johannesburg. She spent her days, often weekends, caring for a white family, initially from Greece. In addition to the couple, Karel took care of their elderly relative, as well as two toddlers and two teenagers. As a result, she could not pay enough attention to her pretty Toby, who made unilateral decisions regarding her daily and nightly activities, including where to go and whom to be with when she was away. Needless to say, Toby went anywhere, sometimes to school until morning break, and most times caught a train to Hillbrow, where she spent her nights with strange men who showered her with attention and some money.

Toby was one of the prettiest girls in White-City. Kükuchi could not help but dote on her endlessly. Her smile had once earned her a spot in Drum Magazine's Perfect Smile competition. She had also won the Miss Donaldson Primary School Beauty pageant for three years. Following Toby's sizeable portfolio of crowns, Mrs Posa entered her name for the Rosettenville-based contest called 'Missy Elegance'. Rosettenville was a white suburb in the central business district of Johannesburg.

After waiting expectantly for a week, Owen and Posa received a rejection note. Toby did not meet all the requirements to enter the white Teen beauty contest. The school officials stated that they had identified specific issues in her application, which disqualified her from participating in the pageant. When Posa demanded a more straightforward explanation, the organizers pointed out that the applicant was not a white girl but a coloured girl living among the 'Bantu.' Mrs Posa responded immediately and sought an audience with her counterpart at the Rosettenville School.

Ignoring her request, the school explained that, according to police, they did not acknowledge 'non-white' beauty contests, and that hosting a mixed-race contest was illegal.

White-City was outraged. The *African National Congress* Women's League (ANCWL) took up the cudgels on behalf of Toby. Karel became embroiled in the controversy while the media peddled fiction by embellishing her plight to create hype.

Through *Township News*, Karel expressed her indignation, saying, 'Everyone in White-City knows Toby is prettier than white girls in Johannesburg. I have often been to Rosettenville; that place smells like a trash dump. How can they do this to my child?'

After the African newspaper published her angry reaction on the front page, Toby's mother lost her job where she had worked for five years. But that was not the end of her problems. Later that week, she hosted three security officers at her two-room house. The sight of white police officers in White City was always an ominous sign. Curious neighbours would rush to watch everything happening at Karel's house from safe spots behind their picket fences.

The white officers went directly to the point. Their leader, Captain Venter, who bore a resemblance to a pastor more than a detective, requested to see her daughter.

"She went out to play."

"We asked your neighbours, and they said she ran away. Any idea where she is?"

"No, she did not run away."

"Did she sleep here last night?"

"No, I don't remember. I'll ask her when she comes back."

When they asked if she was a member of the ANC, Karel told the officers that she had heard of the church but that she was not a member. The younger officer chortled. The other officer, who looked quite edgy, said, "Well, are you a member of the ANC Women's League, then? You do know them, don't you, girl?"

Karel hesitated a bit, trying to figure out the best way out of her predicament.

"My girl, do you know you can go to jail for insulting Europeans? When did you smell a bad smell in Rosettenville?" said the third officer.

Venter said, "We know everything about you and your beauty queen daughter: where you go and who you speak to. Beware of mothers who go around telling you to stop sending your child to a legal school like Donaldson. I am talking about those communists who say, 'Take your children to Mayibuye!' That is a communist school. Do you want your pretty child to be a communist like that woman called Musa?"

"No, Baas. I don't want Toby to be a communist."

"Did Musa tell you what to say to the communist newspaper? Did she tell you to say Rosettenville has a bad smell?"

"No, Baas, I don't speak to Musa."

"You do well. And beware of that girl living with albinism. She will poison your child's mind."

After threatening to return soon, the three officers left, and the neighbours disappeared. Though she was crying, Karel breathed a sigh of relief. While she was deciding about her future, one of the officers came back and asked, "Why are you here in this Bantu place? You must go to your people?"

The white men drove out of the White City. Once the coast had cleared, the neighbours promptly re-emerged and dashed to Karel's place to find out about the raid. Karel told her incredulous neighbours that the police suspected her of being a communist. Karel remained alone and wept until the tears ran dry.

***

Toby and I grew to depend on each other to make decisions and to feel appreciated. The harsh truth was that many African children had little to eat. We faced struggles together, fought, and hugged, but fate ultimately decided our destinies. Although I secretly admired Toby's good looks, her shy nature constantly frustrated me. When two boys attacked her outside the school gate one day, accusing her of being coloured, I seized the opportunity to awaken her 'sense of feminine duty' following Musa's coaching. The first boy threw Toby to the ground while the second shouted insults at her. Toby screamed helplessly, got to her feet, and tried to run away. The third boy slapped her across the face, and she dropped like a sack of potatoes. Rushing to rescue her, I threw my arms around her and then grabbed one of the bullies by his forearm, telling Toby to 'fix' the other one. Terrified of approaching the second boy, Toby whined pitifully. I yelled at Toby, threatening to slap her myself if she didn't stop crying. Toby suddenly lunged at the boy. The crowd of spectators and street fighters, which had gathered around, suddenly spilled out of the school and nearby houses, clapping as the bully's nose turned red within seconds.

When the perpetrators fled toward Jabavu, a vigilante student group was hot on their heels. Toby and her mother visited Khulu to thank me for helping Toby stand up to the bullies of White-City. Although disturbed by what she was hearing, Khulu listened patiently as Karel recounted the sordid details of the encounter. Khulu expressed clear disapproval of our actions. From that moment on, Toby's attitude and behaviour changed. Her trail of destruction, which she was about to leave everywhere she went, had just begun. I even started to worry about her antics because people began calling us the wild white girls of White-City.

***

Khulu, often called her younger sister, the 'chicken-pie farmer.' Kükuchi found Khulu's annoyance at hearing Salu's name quite confusing, given that they were siblings.

Salu's name was Ntombiphelele. She was a regal woman with a petite frame but a commanding presence. She had earned respect within her family and the Hlubi clan a few years before the National Party rose to power in 1948, when she received her British Royal-accredited Standard Six certificate. Following that achievement, the family celebrated her as if she were a princess. They slaughtered at least three cows for dozens of guests from as far away as Lusikisiki, Gcuwa, and Vrystaat. King Hadebe of the Hlubi praised Salu for her outstanding accomplishment.

Salu later taught English at Draycott Primary and became popular in the Midlands for her impeccable use of the English language. Her charges included both white and African children from the farming community. Before her employment, the school had a complement of four white teachers, including the principal, Miss Rhona McLeod. Six months after taking up her post, Salu found herself embroiled in a dispute involving the new Apartheid Department of Education and Rhona McLeod. The young school head, originally from Glasgow, had defied directives from the Department several times. There

~ 17 ~

had been complaints that McLeod had dared to put Salu in charge of an English class for white children. While parents had been outraged, the children themselves held different views. They loved Salu because she was 'so funny… she makes us understand better and doesn't use a cane…'.

The final straw for the white government officials was a letter from McLeod, in which she declared they had no right to interfere in the affairs of her private school. Seizing the opportunity, the officials pounced on her.

After a long struggle, the Department sent an army of inspectors to fire Rhona and her protégé. They revoked their right to teach anywhere in the country because of their 'meddling in politics'. Although the two continued to support each other for a while, they eventually went their separate ways. Miss McLeod turned her back on Africa and settled among the aborigines of Australia.

After her misfortune, Salu returned to her neglected family land and began farming a modest poultry farm. Within a year, she became a recognized farmer in the Midlands. She raised hundreds of chickens and boasted nonstop about her best chicken sandwiches in the area: "I supply my birds with fortified feed, and that is a good beginning, and I compete with the best white farmers," she crowed endlessly.

Kükuchi was too young to make any sense of it all, but smart enough to see something unsettling about the relationship between her two grannies. To her young mind, there appeared to be unfinished business from their distant past. This riddle increasingly occupied her thoughts as she navigated the maze of her dysfunctional family. Behind their cheerful façade, the elderly siblings hid all traces of bad blood. However, every conversation is an emotional trigger, all set to cause an explosion. In the company of people, they remained decorous, Salu referring to Khulu as Ntombizakhona, her given name. At the same time, Khulu addressed Salu as 'my father's child'.

Although the grannies looked so identical that one could mistake them for twins, their personalities were poles apart. Salu was an overbearing extrovert with an acerbic tongue, while Khulu matched her with a heart as soft as *tofu*. Despite Salu's patronizing attitude to Khulu, she could hardly resist expressing her admiration for her fluency in Afrikaans.

One day, Salu said, "Khulu is always playing the fool, but one can't speak Afrikaans like her without a big brain the size of an elephant. She always plays dumb because she plots something terrible inside her heart against me. Even the Syrians played dumb until they pounced on the Jews and enslaved them because the Jews thought they were untouchable."

Despite her everlasting smile, Khulu hid nothing but the hardships of her township life. Her daily routine started at first light, caring for Kükuchi, then going door-to-door to sell pinafores. She spent the rest of her day humming while sewing on her Singer machine and keeping a watchful eye on her mischievous granddaughter as best she could. Khulu held a special place in Kükuchi's heart. They lived together in a small house, solving riddles, arguing over trivial matters, and wiping each other's tears. Since Khulu couldn't read, all the letters went to Kükuchi. She eagerly waited for the mail carrier, knowing Khulu's secrets were inside. Kükuchi read each letter aloud multiple times, struggling with some words. Recently, in desperation, Khulu dabbed Kükuchi's eyes with a mysterious black mud from Mr Mkhize, a man from Zululand who said it came from a creek near

Mtubatuba. Kükuchi insisted her eye was fine, but it twitched, stressing her out.

Khulu was not home when I returned from school. After digging into the pots on the cold stove and scraping our leftover samp and spinach from the previous day, I rushed out to meet my friends under the school's Yellowwoods. In the past, we used to wander the streets barefoot, with our dresses tucked awkwardly into our underwear. Life had changed somewhat, and our interests shifted in various directions. The meeting spot under the trees provided us with refuge, where salty language flowed freely and family secrets were spilled unexpectedly. As winter approached, bright yellow leaves replaced the deep green of summer. My friends and I took advantage of the remaining natural cover to exaggerate the latest gossip, some of us even revealing stories of abusive episodes at home. Meanwhile, others boasted about their pickpocketing escapades at the taxi ranks in town.

However, attention had recently shifted to the mysterious disappearances of young local girls, some of whom I knew. Fear and paranoia had begun to grip entire communities, from White City to Moroka, Jabavu, and even Orlando. Rumours about sightings of a mysterious, tall Black man in Pimville sent chills down parents' spines. Nobody seemed to know what was happening. Parents would send little girls to local shops and dairies, never to see them again. Some Sangoma practitioners and church prophets sent distressed parents on a wild goose chase after collecting their usual takings. Others, like Mkhize, noted each case and checked with the police regularly.

For us girls, 'after school' meant home, not roaming the streets.

I stayed seated under the Yellowwoods for a long time. When the howling winds signalled an impending storm, my patience turned into intense rage. I touched my chest and felt my heart pounding like a cowhide drum. Salu often said that waiting and a guilty conscience are twin sisters. I began blaming everyone, including God, for my situation. A lone billboard on the dirt road, near the trees, showing a large picture of a white man promoting Cavalla cigarettes, looked out of place amid the cluttered scene of poverty.

Sister Mohale suddenly appeared, disrupting my reverie. She was from Tatenda's shop. Mohale held a newspaper under her arm, with a loaf of bread in one hand and a bottle of paraffin in the other. She struggled to tame her dress, which billowed in the wind until she took shelter under the trees.

"You were trying to hide from me. I saw you."

"Me? No, Auntie."

Olga placed her bottle of paraffin on the grass and moaned about the rebellious boys and naughty township girls.

"You girls enjoy dark spots under these trees!" she puffed. "Nothing good goes on here except gossip about boys and things. What are you doing here, sitting alone like this? Are you inviting boys to come and rape you? Don't you know many children are missing from White-City?"

"How are you, Auntie?"

"Forget about me. The question is: how are you with your family, Kükuchi?"

"We are fine. Did you return Khulu's money, that five bob you borrowed long ago?"

"Money?" Mohale squeaked awkwardly like a duck. "I have my own money and the biggest house here in White City. Have you become a slave to money? Do you know your brother, Dodo, is in the habit of asking for train fare from me each time he comes here from his Wemmer hostel?"

"And you give him, Mama Mohale…?"

"Yes, I know a lot about your family; your mischievous friendship with Toby, that so-called beauty queen." Then Mohale whispered hoarsely, "Did you know she is *coloured*?"

"Oh, Auntie!"

"Yes, look at her and her mother. She has European blood in her veins."

"Her veins?"

Mohale added, "I am not a racist. I am Christian."

"You love Europeans, Auntie?"

"Pray for your enemies and don't lie. That's what the bible says."

"Khulu said you still owe her five shillings."

"You and money! Do you know why Judas Iscariot betrayed Jesus?"

"Iscariot borrowed one pound ten from Jesus and later returned it," Musa told me.

"Yes, Kükuchi! About Musa, your so-called sister. There is something I want to ask you," Mohale lowered her voice to a whisper and said, "I suspect Khulu never told you this, but do you know who Musa is? Do you know she is your real mother?"

The windswept haven under the trees had become uncomfortable for me. Olga maintained a cautious smile of expectation with the impending rain. While I wanted Olga to leave me alone, I was deeply absorbed in what she revealed about my sister, Musa.

She balanced herself on the rock and continued, "Kükuchi, let me teach you a lesson. I know you are a very bright child, and never mind about your white skin; that's why I am giving you my old newspapers to read and medication for your skin. Don't worry, everything is skin deep. As for you, learn to read between the lines. Yes, read people so they do not treat you like a sucker. You are a big girl, Kükuchi. You should be familiar with such things by now. Big girls of your age know about their mothers."

"What do you mean, Auntie? Musa is not my mother."

"That one! I doubt she even let you suckle from her breast…"

"And why not?"

"One day, you will learn something about Musa; never mind her roaming the streets, teaching political stuff to law-abiding mothers."

Mohale picked up her small grocery and stepped back from the woods, smiling warmly like a grandmother and whispering, "Musa is still your mother, but don't tell Khulu you heard all this from me. I don't like township gossip. Ask her. She will tell you everything."

Sista Mohale toddled off and disappeared. My eyes remained fixed on the massive Yellowwood tree trunks that had failed to shield me from her.

CHAPTER 4

A shining Golden Star

Kükuchi's mind drifted toward Priscilla's world. Priscilla was a white girl who lived in Mayfair. A few weeks after her fruitless visit with Musa near the Drakensberg, she passed Priscilla's home. Priscilla's mother had given Kükuchi a new white doll to play with. Kükuchi had been so excited that she even forgot that Musa had said white people were settlers who stole the land. She could not wait to show the doll to her grandmother.

Khulu told Kükuchi, "We must hide your doll..."

"Why?"

"It's because..."

Musa suddenly appeared. When she saw the blonde doll, Musa yelled, "Whose *doll* is this?"

Khulu hesitated, pulled the doll, and fondled her before she said, "Kükuchi likes her *doll* very much."

"You bought Kükuchi a European *doll*?"

"She's just a child, Musa. She doesn't care; it's a European doll."

"Throw this rubbish away..."

Kükuchi broke her silence and suddenly confronted Musa, who angrily told her, "You must throw this thing away."

"She's not a thing. That's my Blossom..."

"Kükuchi's lovely *doll* is Blossom because she likes her," Khulu tried.

Without hesitation, Musa grabbed Blossom from Khulu's safe embrace, held her mockingly by one leg, and stressed, "This *doll* is for white girls. You are a black girl."

"I like Blossom. Bring back my Blossom."

Musa was not about to hand Kükuchi's Blossom back to her. Instead, she snapped open the stove plate and tossed Blossom into the fire. Khulu's screams echoed through the neighbourhood as Kükuchi tried frantically to rescue her Blossom from the consuming fire, and Khulu rushed frantically to save her granddaughter from hurting herself.

It would take some doing for Musa to undo the damage caused by her tactless act of tossing Kükuchi's Blossom into the scorching fire. Kükuchi's loathing for Musa had reached a new low. She swore she would kill her one day.

After waiting forever under the trees for my girlfriends, Toby returned, carrying a plastic container with a birthday cake inside. This act touched my heart.

"I met Sister Mohale on my way here. She told me you don't know your mother..."

"And what did you say to her?"

"I said, Khulu is your mother... I see you are alone. Where are the other girls? Didn't you invite them...?"

"No one else came, Toby. But I am happy you are here."

"It doesn't matter that no one else came. I brought you a cake from my mother. Sorry, I only have one candle. I know it's long overdue, but better late than never."

Toby struck her match, and the candle glowed like a shining golden star on a clear day. As Toby chanted a lone, 'Happy Birthday, Kũkuchi Girl,' the winds grew stronger, and the rain began smashing down. The candle kept burning despite the wind and the shower, and I cried, saying, "I love you, Toby."

"I love you too, Faty, with all my heart. I'll never love anyone else the way I love you."

A Settler at Wemmer Hostel

When she reached home, Kũkuchi winched her ears like a gazelle, eager for a plausible explanation from her grandmother. She reluctantly accepted that something must be wrong with her since most of her friends knew their mothers and, at times, their fathers. No one at her home had ever breathed a word about her father.

The wind picked up speed, and Kũkuchi saw black clouds gather and swirl in an alarming fury. She started to think it was a tornado. Alone in the house, her mind raced back to the day she lost her innocence, thanks to her uncle's evil deed. Dodo was a municipal police officer and a settler at Wemmer Hostel in Johannesburg. Wemmer, one of ten African hostels spread across Johannesburg, stood at the corner of Eloff and Loveday Streets. One defining feature of South African society was the coexistence of white wealth and black poverty. However, no amount of poverty could better illustrate the level of indignity black people endured than the hostel system. From the outside, Wemmer had a stern, military appearance, but inside, he contained human suffering that only the victims could describe. The hostels served as labour pools for white companies that needed 'reliable and loyal' African men from tribal reservations. They also housed municipal police, known as the 'Blackjacks.' Apartheid prevented rural African women and children from joining their partners and fathers. While the system systematically destroyed African families, the material comfort of white men and their families improved more than ever before.

Dodo visited White-City more often than Kũkuchi considered necessary. While at it, he now and then called on 'Queen' Victoria, a local traditional healer, who dabbled in clairvoyance and ran a Shebeen on the side. Upon visiting them, Dodo would regularly bring groceries and clothing from town. He would sometimes take Kũkuchi on enjoyable joyrides by tram. They would then sneak into the Empire Theatre or the Colosseum in Commissioner Street. At that time, Kũkuchi was eternally grateful to Dodo as she thought he was great fun.

However, one afternoon in June, Dodo forces me into the bedroom and rapes me. It happens so quickly that my mind cannot keep up with what is happening to my body. When he first walks into the house, he carries a heavy cardboard carton full of groceries. He opens the carton, pulls out a packet of candies, and gives it to me.

"You enjoyed the film we watched at the Colosseum last time, not so, Kũkuchi? I liked it too. Do you want us to dance like Fred Astaire and Ginger Rogers?"

"No, I can't dance."

"Let's try. I know you can dance."

"I don't want to dance, Dodo."

That's when he overpowers me. Dodo later tries to sweet-talk his way out by telling me how nice a girl I am and that he will provide us with more groceries every week. He asked if I wanted him to take me to the Colosseum Bioscope again to watch nice things. I am upset and shocked, but he does not seem bothered. Instead, he says, "Kükuchi, no one should know what happened here today, right? You know I care for you, but you are a woman now, and you tempted me because you wanted to dance like Ginger Rogers..."

Dodo perches himself on the bench in the 'dining room,' close to his gramophone, and starts reading aloud from his night-school textbook. He is doing Matric at Mayibuye Night School. He sits there while I remain paralyzed on the bed that I share with Khulu. Then I hear the kitchen door unlock and shut. I stand up and find Dodo gone.

When the sun goes down, I drag myself out of the house and stumble over to Mkhize's place. I go in without knocking, and the man from Mtubatuba is working on his muti and bones. I barely get a chance to speak and share my ordeal when Mkhize says, "Go, my child. Go to Mohale. My bones have let me see horrible things before you came. My ancestors are crying tears of blood. Go to Mohale. I can't talk to you right now."

I walk into Mohale's house. She is cooking a meal for herself and her son, Bobby. She says, "You can't lie to me. You have been crying. Who made you cry, Kükuchi?"

I carefully consider what I am about to tell Nurse Mohale. Still, I can't string a thought together to make her believe I did not want to dance like Ginger Rogers. Before I can utter a word, Sister Mohale launches a tirade about the appalling state of affairs in White-City and the discrimination she faces at work as a black nurse. With an ironic smile, her mind wanders off, "I hear the *Boers* are helping themselves with all the farms owned by Africans. Have they said anything to your Salu yet?"

"About what?"

"Her large chicken farm, she's always blowing her own trumpet about."

"No. Why should the government take Salu's farm?"

"The *Boers* take anything they like, and there's nothing you can do about it."

I step back and observe Bobby's profile. He is sitting at the dining room table, reading intensely. Bobby is a clerk for Bantu Affairs at 80 Albert Street. This time, he is under investigation for allegedly interfering with the duties of the 'blackjacks' where he works.

In those days, every African man living in South Africa was required to carry a pass. However, the process included forced vaccinations of all African men against unspecified diseases. The practice of using unqualified African municipal police (the blackjacks) to vaccinate thousands of African men, often with questionable vaccines in unhygienic conditions, prompts Bobby to take action. What irritated Bobby most was the policy of genital inspections of African men by white officials with questionable medical training. Bobby complained to his father that the practice was demeaning. His initial concern in his precinct was about the system, which seemed to care little about individual health conditions before vaccination. He also criticized the use of unsterilized equipment, where one needle was used to inject over fifty unsuspecting African men without regard for disease transmission.

A Jewish businessman, Mr Orlin, learned about this practice through his black employees. His investigation revealed that young black women going through the health system unwittingly became victims of contraceptives.

Their men faced similar challenges at 80 Albert Street, all stemming from the ongoing situation the Jewish man described as covert genocide against Africans. Orlin's murder remained a mystery and happened after he took orders from Soweto distributors.

The police detain Mr Mohale, Bobby's father, after he complains to *Township News* about his son's harassment by 80 Albert Street. The story never sees the light of day because the Apartheid operatives gag the newspaper. Bobby finally vacates his job.

***

In my free time, I usually hide my secret thoughts and stash my worn-out diary in a crack in Khulu's wardrobe. Inside, I vent about my highs, lows, and scores to settle with my enemies. At home, I take out my diary and express my feelings across five pages. Dodo shows up and offers me an apology wrapped in a shiny package. He asks me to open the gift and try on the dress so he can see how I look. I say no. After he leaves, I tear open the box and find a beautifully designed red-and-white outfit. I quickly try it on, but it feels quite dirty. So, I have to hide it from Khulu.

When I got home from school one afternoon, I found Khulu sitting on our bed with my attractive dress next to her. I told Khulu that a hawker had left it for her to check and decide whether to buy it. Khulu asked me to put on the dress before she made any decisions because she wanted to speak with the hawker herself. After I put on the dress, Khulu looked at me strangely.

"What, Khulu?"

Khulu's face retreats to a frown, and she orders me to take off the dress and sit next to her as she has something important to say to me. I panic. It's not every day that I find myself seated next to her like that. She does not believe my story about the dress, a tissue of ridiculous lies. Khulu starts counselling me on how a girl of my age should react if boys want to touch me. She says I must refuse to be alone with any boy, as they always get girls into trouble. Then she asks if I have ever been alone with a boy. I say no. The following day, I returned early from school to hand the dress to my coloured friend to sell. Rummaging through the bedroom, I found that my dress was missing. Then I walked to the garden where Khulu typically buries her African brew from the police. My gear was missing.

When she returned, Khulu stayed silent about it. After two days, I asked her to tell me what she did with the dress. Khulu ignored me.

The Lusikisiki Visitors

Two strange, hungry-looking men arrive, one clutching a heavy portmanteau and the other smiling broadly. They claim to be relatives of Khulu from Lusikisiki in the Eastern Cape Province. I have never heard of such relatives, and they look suspicious, with their jackets frayed and rucked up at the back, and their lips reflecting a hard life like the men who build roads.

I have always associated Lusikisiki with a well-known multi-man known as Khotso Sethunya, who was reputed to own an assortment of snakes on his farm, which helped boost his healing powers and wealth. I choose to keep a safe distance between the two strangers and myself. Extended family members from the outskirts of Johannesburg often cause endless traffic to my home, mostly at night. More than that, I resent my grandma's unbridled generosity; 'No one with a grain of conscience would dream of driving them out into the cold night', Khulu often preached.

The older man says, "There will always be enough bird holes to hide one's head."

I realized that the two men come from a land far away, beyond Lusikisiki. Worse, they are Khulu's relatives looking for a place to stay. I know I must do something before Khulu returns. The two men keep smiling, their lips stretched like a tortoise's beak because of hunger. Trying to charm me, the elderly man says, "I am Khanyile. This boy here is Zazi. You look big, and if you were a man, you would play rugby like my boy here," he says, pointing at Zazi, who winks mischievously at me before puffing out his chest proudly like a turkey. I feel hurt by Khanyile's inapt compliment, implying I should play rugby.

Without any further ado, I throw the men out, claiming to be alone in the house and that Khulu cautioned me against entertaining strangers. Despite Khanyile's frantic pleading, I stand my ground. My eyes accompany them toward Jabavu until the smoke-filled afternoon of the township swallows them up.

Khulu's outrage at the terrible episode shook the entire house. She threatened to send Kükuchi packing to the same Lusikisiki, where girls fetch water from a distant stream and gather firewood from a dark, treacherous forest. Kükuchi laughed, but her conscience shook increasingly to breaking point with time. One day, as night descended, Kükuchi walked to Toby's place and related the story of the men from Lusikisiki. Toby's reaction shocked Kükuchi.

"Lusikisiki? Do you know that place? That's far, Kükuchi, in the Cape Province. Where do you think all those girls who have disappeared have gone?"

"Girls?"

"Yes, those girls... all of them. They disappeared from White-City and Jabavu."

"I don't understand you, Toby."

"My mother is worried, and people are saying things about you and your people, especially your uncle, who stays in that men's hostel. And now you say you have relatives from Lusikisiki?"

"I don't even know them, Toby..."

"Yes, come to think of it, why do you always insist on us meeting inside the dark school yard or under the Yellowwoods? My uncle warned me long ago to avoid touching people like you..."

"Your uncle? What did he mean by 'avoid touching people like me'?"

"You know what he meant, Kükuchi. We are all suspicious of you. Now you tell me about Lusikisiki? Can you swear your relatives have nothing to do with the missing girls?"

CHAPTER 5

African girls can't do javelin.

Then there was Dassie, my half-brother. Dassie was the biggest annoyance in my life. Every time he visited us from Mayfair, where he stayed with Musa, I would pray for the ground to swallow me up forever.

However, Dassie blended into the shady world of White City like mist. His friends admired him because he could speak English like a white boy.

One night, while visiting, Dassie and I sat on the *stoep* outside, having supper. Dassie asked me, "Are you and Mendi... together now?"

"Mind your own business, you."

"He says he likes you. I told him you said you liked him too."

"What did you say that for?"

Later that night, I thought about Dassie's story-making habit. Anxiety turned into panic. What if Dassie lied?

Mendi was the only boy in White City whom I would never dare to hassle. Like us, Mendi came from a poor household. He took his name from SS Mendi, the steamship that sank in the English Channel in 1917 while on its way to France, killing many black soldiers. When his grandmother, Mrs Gasa, named him 'Mendi', she prayed for good luck, hoping he would later lift their family out of poverty and become a truck driver. However, Mendi, the bane of his teachers' existence, had other plans. Many township parents used his name as a bogeyman to scare their kids into line. Posa, the principal, had a soft spot for Mendi's grandmother. As for Diale, Mendi's biological mother, she started drinking long before her husband died. Mendi's granny took care of his school fees despite the small amount given to elders in the African community. Kūkuchi was eager to clear her name with Mendi. But when the chance came, the unexpected happened; Kūkuchi and Mendi shared a few smiles and became inseparable.

The Mayfair thing

Before returning to White City, Musa and Dassie lived in the servants' quarters in Mayfair, south of Johannesburg. She worked there for Mr Grant as a house cleaner and spent most of her time caring for his elderly mother. Musa often told people that Mrs Grant was the only white person because she once saved her life. I visited Musa whenever Khulu ran out of money and meat. The passenger train trip usually took a depressing hour between two extremes: one wickedly affluent and the other deeply hurting Africans. My frequent trips between Pimville and Mayfair helped me understand the contrasting settings.

Yet behind the opulence and serenity of Mayfair lurked menacing signs of a time bomb waiting to explode. I looked upon the wealthy white families with jealous admiration. Priscilla's home in the sleepy white suburb was as large as a smallholding, many times the size of our tiny semi-detached block in White-City. My state of poverty was a noose that strangled my spirit. Many township dwellers blamed the white government for their plight, and Musa often cursed openly, 'Verwoerd will roast in hell'. Musa hated Verwoerd from the day he abolished feeding schemes in all African schools. As Minister of Native Affairs, he had introduced a quota system in which he automatically excluded African children who walked long distances to school. This misguided ruling had a profoundly detrimental effect on the progress of children of farm workers. Musa participated with enthusiasm in women's militant activities against the government. Mrs Sally Motlana, a militant educationist, called for the school boycott to run until the reinstatement of the feeding scheme. Addressing a gathering of angry women at Donaldson one day, she told them that children need a balanced meal daily. She said children who did not get good food could not develop properly. Their conscience dies slowly and they become criminals, murderers and rapists.

We reluctantly went back to Sunday school. One day, I asked Musa if it was true that a particular doctor named Hendrik Verwoerd refused to give African children good food at school because they would become as smart as white children.

Musa retorted in her typically detached manner, addressing both Khulu and me, "Don't worry about that European immigrant. The African women, our League, will soon bring the Apartheid government to a standstill. Kükuchi must stop going to that colonial school called Donaldson. The mothers... we are planning to open our private schools for African children all over the country. We started with Mayibuye School, which will now be a day school."

Greeting Musa's grand plan with scepticism, Khulu said, "You need a lot of money to build a school, Musa. How much money does your Women's League have? You can't even support us here with the little money you get every week."

After supper, I asked Khulu to explain Musa's plan. Khulu took my question seriously for a change. She whispered, "Kükuchi, be patient with Musa. She was once bitten by a rattlesnake near the 'Devil's Tooth' in the Drakensberg, and maybe a drop of poison reached her brain."

I took a train to Mayfair again to visit Musa. Since we didn't usually talk much, I decided not to ask many questions when I reached Mayfair. Instead, I said, "Musa, Khulu needs money. She is short."

Without hesitation, Musa placed ten shillings in my hand and said, "Tell Khulu I don't have enough. I'll bring more next time. I will be coming home soon."

I was not impressed. How could I travel from White-City to Mayfair only to collect ten shillings? Without warning, Musa breathed heavily, violently shaking her head and body as if in a trance. I panicked. When the strange vibration eased off, Musa declared, "Don't worry, Kükuchi. One day, the Africans will own the whole of Mayfair and all of Johannesburg, and these white people will run back to Europe. You and Khulu will never be short of money again."

I looked at Musa in disbelief. My head spun as I remembered what she told me the day we stood near the clouds in the Drakensberg. I was young then and confused. Musa had said to me that white settlers stole our land, but one day I would get it back. I noticed then that Musa called me by my name for the first time, which meant a lot to me. I fought back tears because of the lump in my throat when I heard Musa say 'Kükuchi' so warmly. I held onto the happy moment in my heart.

On returning home, Kükuchi's excitement fluctuated like a hesitant tidal wave. She rested her forehead on the whispering window of the speeding train coach, her eyes capturing snapshots of isolated vegetation on deserted white land; concrete blocks and glossy gold mine dumps of Johannesburg, all rushing past like a dream. Musa's strange words about Mayfair consumed Kükuchi's mind so she could hardly wait to tell Khulu. In her mind, the idea of taking over Mayfair sounded much more exciting than Musa's offer to stop the Apartheid government. However, once she got home, Khulu's cynical look reminded Kükuchi of the snake poison in Musa's brain. So, she changed her mind. After giving the ten shillings, Kükuchi thought that maybe her twitching eye meant that Mayfair white people would soon go back to Europe.

Kükuchi's attitude changed, and she became so cheerful that she started attending Sunday school again. They usually held sessions on the veranda of Miss Lumka's parents' house, weather permitting. When it was too hot, the children and their teacher would gather in the shade under a tree away from the house. There were fun moments, such as birthday celebrations, exchanging gifts like toothpaste, soap, and Nestlé's chocolate bars, and playing games like sack races and cat's cradle. Pinki's sister Niki beat everyone at the cat's cradle game. She always brought her string to Sunday school and played throughout the lessons, much to Lumka's despair. That was Sunday school.

The only downside was Miss Lumka's habit of telling stories filled with thorns and thistles, which made Kükuchi nervous. Kükuchi kept imagining many things about the Mayfair incident. One Sunday morning, she asked Miss Lumka why the Africans took so long to drive out all the Europeans.

Lumka's response was disappointing, according to Kükuchi. Lumka said, "Why are you asking me such a stupid question? Do you think Africans can run the country like Europeans? Can you make cars? Can you make airplanes? Can you make a *rediffusion*? Where have you ever seen an African build anything? Listen, you, Kükuchi; don't let Musa fill your head with funny political stuff."

Kükuchi was furious. She asked Miss Lumka, "Was Jesus an African or a European?"

Miss Lumka hesitated and said, "You are asking too many questions and disturbing my lesson."

"Of course, Jesus was a European and the devil is an African man," said Toby.

"Is that true, Miss Lumka?" Vovo, a quiet, reflective boy from Jabavu, asked.

"Tell me, you Toby; do you know Israel is in Europe?" Kenny, Dr Komane's son and Sandy's brother, asked.

"It's overseas somewhere. Is that not Europe?" Toby answered.

Kenny said, "I know overseas because my father is a rich doctor…"

"Yes, we fly overseas every year…" Sandy confirmed.

Kükuchi asked, "You say we can't build airplanes, so why didn't Jesus build an airplane instead of using a cloud to fly back to heaven?"

Vovo said, "My uncle says Jesus knew that clouds do not have accidents and crash like aeroplanes. But let me tell you about Jesus; he was a Palestinian."

"So, he was not a European like Rosemarie and Priscilla?" Kükuchi put it triumphantly.

Miss Lumka was now fuming, "Listen to me, you Kükuchi. I don't want people to think I am too harsh on children like you. God made you like this for a reason. Remember this: the day you die, you will enter a waiting room where you will see a bioscope of your entire life. If you are a sinner, you will go straight to hell."

Lumka's words were accompanied by noise, and the children were arguing with each other so much that insults erupted. She finally ordered everyone to stand and sing, 'Jesus loves me'.

As the class began singing, Toby said, "Let's go, Kükuchi."

Kükuchi and Toby stopped attending Sunday school, much to Khulu's despair. Sandy and Kenny told Lumka they would no longer be attending because their parents disliked Kükuchi and Toby.

In the dead of night, Khulu questioned her granddaughter about Sunday school, "Why, Kükuchi? I thought you were becoming a Christian girl. That Lumka angel wants you to stop your bad manners."

"Kükuchi explained to Khulu that Lumka is always talking about thorns and thistles and death, and threatening them with hell."

"Yes, both of you will go to hell."

***

Kükuchi got up to sweep the yard in the fresh morning breeze. She looked toward Toby's home and wondered how they would free themselves from Papi's crafty clutches. She thought hard, and her mind went in circles. Then, she returned to the same conclusion that their source of income, thanks to Papi, had brought them significant relief, despite its dark side.

As she continued, she recalled the day Toby first introduced her to Papi, "Do you want to make money, Kükuchi?'"

"Money? How do you mean?"

"Papi... he is Mendi's friend from Alexandra. He says they can supply us with things to sell and make money; Earrings, watches, cameras, shoes... many things."

"Where do they get those things from?"

"Do you want money or not? They supply, we find people. Papi calls it the market."

Kükuchi's attention shifted back to comparing the poverty in White-City with the wealth in European areas. The idea of Africans taking control of the country had become more appealing to her than anything Musa had ever mentioned. She smiled widely, then carried her smile as she returned to the kitchen.

Khulu was on her feet, adding the last touches to one of her pinafores, when she looked up and saw what she thought was Kükuchi's forced smile.

"I can see you are up to your mischief this morning. I don't want to talk, and I don't want anyone to talk to me. I am working." Khulu turned her back and walked to the bedroom.

Kükuchi followed Khulu and sat on the bed. She said thoughtfully, "Khulu. I want to ask you a question about Mayfair."

Khulu froze as if posing for a portrait of her. "I'm waiting," she said.

Kükuchi began with the state of the economy in the African townships, "Black children in White-City are poor and white children in Mayfair are rich and enjoy a good life. I no longer want to live in the township because we are poor here."

"I hope you did not drink Dodo's European beer last night. Children who dodge Sunday school drink in Shebeens and their tongues start to talk rubbish."

Kükuchi felt let down by Khulu's contribution to the Mayfair question.

Khulu continued, "Sometimes I forget I am speaking to an oversized tot called Kükuchi. I long for good conversation. Only Salu gives me good conversation; never mind that it is always full of heat and noise."

"What do you mean, Khulu? Doesn't Musa give you good conversation?"

"No. Only your Salu is an open book, not Musa. You cannot read a closed book. Musa is like a dog that doesn't bark. It stays angry. The day it barks, that's when it bites your nose off."

"So, Musa is a dog...?"

"Musa is a closed book."

"And you like Salu because she gives you good conversation?"

"She is a noisy brazier. That's what your grandmother is to me."

Kükuchi kept working on Musa's tempting puzzle about Mayfair. Yet, she agreed with Khulu's vague description of Musa and the suspected poison in her mind. Sometimes, Musa did say intriguing things.

***

Kükuchi took another trip to Mayfair. Tissues of morning mist escorted her along the tree-lined avenue of the white suburb until she came across Pricilla and Rosemarie. The two sisters were on their way to school; Priscilla to help Rosemarie with her practice on the tracks. When they were younger, Kükuchi visited Musa more regularly. Priscilla would often catch a whiff of her from a distance, and the concrete walkway of the girl's home would come alive with hopscotch-square markings and a low-profile racial contest. As a poor child, Kükuchi endured the game because Priscilla's mother gave her plenty of second-hand clothing and some cash. Rosemarie occupied herself with her looks and never played hopscotch when Kükuchi was around. However, Kükuchi stopped visiting Priscilla's home the day Rosemarie shouted from the window of her bedroom upstairs, 'Priscilla, stop playing that stuff with the white *Kaffir* girl'. Kükuchi's little fortune from Priscilla's mother came to an abrupt end that day.

Rosemarie was pretty but arrogant. She wore her blonde hair in various styles; sometimes letting it cascade down her shoulders. And at other times, she transformed into a variety of brunette looks, all of which made her appear like a mischievous girl who was always scheming. Sometimes Rosemarie looked stylish and mature, mostly when they went to church. When Kükuchi last saw her, Rosemarie had formed her hair into smart bunches, held it in place with a motley set of hairpins, and wore adult perfume with expensive fragrances long after she had gone past.

Rosemarie had changed little, and Kükuchi found her demeanour at odds with her athletics pursuits, given that she had become one of the most popular javelin throwers in the country. To Kükuchi, Rosemarie represented something she deeply resented about white people, a presumption of indelible superiority and an abundance of material possessions to prove the point.

Rosemarie said, "Here comes the *Native* that's trying to be a European. Yes, you white monkey! What are you doing here? Don't you know Mayfair is a place for real white people?"

"Hey, Kükuchi," Priscilla said, "are we playing today?"

"No, I am going back home."

"How come you never play with me anymore?"

"I don't have time."

"Dassie said you want to be a javelin thrower like Rosemarie here," continued Priscilla.

"What! When did he say that?"

"I told Dassie." Rosemarie said, "I have never seen any girl in athletics. African girls can't do javelin. Stick to hopscotch in your township. That's what Mother told Dassie."

The white girls cackled and went their way.

Kükuchi was boiling with anger. In White-City, no girl dared to challenge her like the white girls did, but she knew she would pay if she tried to confront them. She carried her heavy heart back home. Khulu was peeling potatoes and singing her favourite tune.

"She called me a *native*, Khulu."

"Yes? You know them, Kükuchi; they call us names. Don't take it personally."

Khulu withdrew from the conversation and carried on working.

"They are harassing us, Khulu. I must take revenge like Musa said..."

"Stop listening to Musa. She will push you down a donga... and they will hang you for taking revenge against a white girl."

The white girl's snide remarks had cut deeply into Kükuchi. Gradually, her perspective on herself and her relationship with white people took on a determined, vengeful shape. When she met three of her friends one evening, she hurried to share her story about the white girls. Her three, stony-faced friends appeared uncomfortable. One of them, a girl named Niki, who was addicted to the cat's cradle, bravely said, "How do we know this is not a trap? My mother says I must not talk to you about white people and politics."

Kükuchi looked desperate, "I can't set a trap for you, Niki. I heard Rosemarie and Priscilla with my ears. They said African girls can't run like white girls. They said Africans can't throw the javelin like white girls..."

Kükuchi's voice had risen to a piercing screech, her lips shivering with rage. She could not understand why such hurtful words from the white girls hardly triggered outrage here.

The friends remained mum as Niki said, "How do we know you are not a spy?"

"A spy? Listen, you, Niki; maybe you are the spy. I don't trust you. Tell us about that white Superintendent. What was he doing at your house Saturday night?"

"Saturday night?" Niki repeated.

"I saw his blue car parked outside your house, and I stood under the tree until I saw you, Pinki, and your father escort him to his car."

Niki slipped away instantly. Kükuchi waited expectantly for someone else to say something about Rosemarie.

Without warning, the woods echoed with Tina's voice, "Me and my father and mother and I went to see King Kong..."

Tina Tatenda, named by her Rhodesian parents after Albertina Sisulu, was a fun-loving shopkeeper's daughter who often doled out biscuits and chocolate she pilfered from her parents' shop to supply to her friends. The little girl enjoyed telling fairy tales about the spooks and the living. She was about to thoroughly review *King Kong* when Kükuchi said, "Shut up, Tina," before she walked away in a huff.

Dassie and Tina were fond of each other. However, the day her mother stumbled upon the friendship, she blew her top while Mr Tatenda, who was soft-spoken, used diplomatic language to deal with the serious matter. His wife bluntly told everyone concerned to stop it, telling Khulu directly to keep her 'English-speaking dog called Dassie on a tight leash'.

***

Something was brewing in the townships, with sporadic incidents of violence flaring up within local branches of political parties. In White-City, Musa had become a prominent voice of opposition to the ANC *Charter*. The controversial part of the document was the opening sentence that read:

> 'We, the people of South Africa, declare for all our country and the world to know: that South Africa belongs to all who live in it, black and white, and that no government can justly claim authority unless it is based on the will of all the people.'

Salu quickly wrote an angry letter accusing Musa of being unwell upstairs for opposing the Charter. Musa responded immediately, calling Salu a brainwashed woman under the spell of her white friend, Miss McLeod.

Kükuchi found the exchange disturbing. She asked Musa about Rhona McLeod. Musa responded, "Stay away from smiling white people. They will grin and say things in broken Zulu, and you will smile back thinking they are angels..."

Kükuchi shouted, "Just tell me about McLeod."

Musa ignored her. Kükuchi swiftly drew her attention to what the children at school were saying about her political activities. As usual, Musa concealed her feelings behind her silence.

"What about our teachers... all the neighbours? They are always saying things about us. I don't like it. Why can't you spend more time here, helping Khulu when you take a day off? She is coughing. She goes out into the cold to sell pinafores the whole day, and you are always away in Mayfair or busy with the Charter."

A heavy scowl visited Musa's face. She continued ironing while Kükuchi's resentment towards her continued heating up.

"Another thing, I asked Khulu, and she said only you know whether you are my mother."

"When did she say that?"

"You can tell me, 'Yes' or 'No'; who is my real mother and where is she?"

When Kükuchi looked at Musa's eyes again, she saw them glisten with tears. She decided to switch to something political, a pastime of Musa's.

"Musa, one day, Sister Mohale said the Boer government wants to take all the farms owned by Africans by force and give them to white people. Is it true?"

Musa placed the cooling iron on the stove, plucked the hot one, and wiped some soot off with a rag. Kükuchi followed Musa's every move, wondering if she had paid attention to her question. Then Musa looked Kükuchi in the eye and said with a determined voice, "The white people stole our country. We must get our country back."

"I am not talking about your country," Kükuchi shouted. "Sister Mohale said they want to take Salu's house. Can they do that? Can they chase her away from her place?"

"This is our country," Musa repeated expressively, as she wheeled round, back to her ironing task.

Kükuchi found Musa's response depressing. So, a few days later, she tried Khulu once more.

"Khulu, Sister Mohale once told me the *Boers* will take Salu's farm because Africans should not own farms. The *Boers* can't do that, can they?"

Khulu rested her arms on her hips and said, "Why does Sister Mohale repeat such things to you?"

"They won't do it, then?"

"Whatever they do, they will reap what they sow. Forget about Salu's farm. Dassie is coming soon. We must prepare food and his sleeping space. He will be here for good."

***

The idea of Dassie and Musa coming to live with us permanently depressed me. I therefore resigned myself to more depression, which made me consider running off to Salu's Estcourt farm again.

"What are you going to do, Khulu? You can't let Dassie stay here with us. He calls me 'Ugly', and I'll kill him."

"He is your brother. When he says 'Ugly, ' he likes you."

"If he is my brother, how come he knows that his father is dead? Do we share the same dead father?"

Khulu's smile caved in like a squashed accordion, and she breathed heavily. But I was determined to get something about my birth mother out of the way.

"Khulu, is Musa my mother?"

"Ask her. Ask her nicely. Say to her, 'Musa, 'I'm happy you will live with us here in White-City. Are you my mother?"

"I won't ask that woman. Tell me, Khulu, is it because I lack melanin? Is that why she hates me so much?"

"One day your filthy mouth will make the sky fall on your head, and on that day, you will forget the colour of your skin…but remember Kükuchi, now that your brother is coming here, you can't use the 'dining room' anymore because that's where he lays his mattress to sleep."

"Why can't he sleep in the kitchen?"

I resumed my space in Khulu's bed that night. Late into the night, I nudged slowly on Khulu's side and said, "Khulu, are you awake?"

"*Voetsak*! I am not awake, Kükuchi. And you are not awake either."

"Khulu, I want to tell you something that happened on this bed one day, but you must tell the truth first; how come you never visit Salu in Draycott? Do you also think she is a dog, like that woman called Musa describes her?"

"That woman is… Musa never said that, Kükuchi."

"She also says Salu is a slithering snake."

Khulu got up and sat straight before she said, "Almighty! Do you know what time it is, Kükuchi?"

"And as for Salu, when I asked her about what Musa said, do you know what she said?"

"You told your Salu Musa that she is a snake?"

No, I asked her about my father. I asked her, I said, 'Gogo, who is my father?' All she said was, 'All men are snakes, including my father."

Khulu said, "I lose sleep over you because it's impossible to tell you and your Salu apart. It's hereditary. Our grandmother, Bashaye… she was an uncontrollable buffalo. All the women in this family are chaotic. We are all cursed."

"Let's get some sleep, Khulu. You scare me now…"

CHAPTER 6

Women go to Pretoria.

This is no ordinary Sunday because we have to welcome Dassie home. Everything needs to look perfect, but every moment feels like throbbing pain to me. Based on how Khulu has been since sunrise, I bet Khulu will say that Dassie is an angel from paradise.

The air feels cold. Thick smog from coal fires worsens various illnesses in the community. I see Mrs Posa with her twin daughters, Tilly and Babe, rushing to their morning church service beyond the woods.

Dassie and Dodo arrive without Musa. Dassie stands outside on the *stoep* as if reassessing his options in life. The black cap he is wearing heightens the menacing grimace on his face. I hesitate to ask about Musa's whereabouts. Dodo quickly heads to the 'dining room' to play his favourite Spokes Mashiane's music from his 78rpm. Our neighbours quietly emerge from their homes to take a look. Pretty Tina is dressed in a white skirt, a blue blouse, and a broad smile. In good time, Tina and Dassie will be strolling down the dusty street, hand-in-hand toward Moroka.

Something about Tina often brought a smile to Musa's dour face. As for Salu, she once teased Tina's hair, saying, 'I will take you to Draycott one day and show you how to carry a bundle of firewood on your head and brew African beer.' Tina giggled and said that when her mother was young back in Rhodesia, she used to carry firewood and a pail of water on her head.

"Your mother is smart. She knows where the African woman comes from,' Salu said."

While Dassie gnashes his teeth at the thought of living in White-City, seeing Tina warms his heart. We settle down for lunch. Dassie grabs his plate and sits on the porch. After hurriedly eating some of his food, he walks to the kitchen and leans awkwardly against the table next to me. Still pulling a face, he says, "Ugly, do you know what happened to Musa?"

Khulu quickly says, "No, Dassie, we will tell Kükuchi after we finish eating. Go back and finish your food."

"Why don't you tell me, Dassie? I can't finish this food. I have lost my appetite. What happened to Musa?"

"She is in jail. The police arrested her."

"Why? What has she done?"

The penny finally drops.

"Aren't you happy Dassie is here? He is your brother."

"No. Dassie is a liar. He lied about me and said I wanted to compete with Rosemarie."

"Listen, Kükuchi, forget about the white girls. Musa is in jail, and the Boers say she's a communist. That's what they say."

"She is not a communist," Dodo yells from the other room. "She goes to church sometimes. Doesn't she, Mama?"

"Sometimes? Maybe that's why they arrested her. Now you see, even these children, Kükuchi and Toby, they dodge Sunday school because of you and Musa."

I once visited Musa's church, and the women screamed at me when they were filled with spirits," Dodo says.

"What do you expect them to do when they see an evil sinner?"

"Dassie, where were you when they arrested Musa?" I ask.

"The police arrest people at night. I don't know."

Musa's arrest affected Khulu's health. Three weeks later, Musa unexpectedly showed up. She declined to comment on the reasons for her detention or her experiences. However, she was about to learn that Dassie was being trained in township life and spending time with shady characters like Mendi.

***

One day in 1956, thousands of women gathered in Pretoria. On that historic morning, Kūkuchi awoke to the whispering sounds in the kitchen. Musa explained to a discouraged Khulu why she needed to go to Pretoria. She said, "We are going to the Union Buildings to talk to Strydom, the Prime Minister."

Despite her efforts to dissuade her, Musa left. Soon after, Kūkuchi heard rattling sounds coming from the kitchen. She padded softly through Dassie's makeshift bedroom. The Last Supper on the wall hung precariously from its tack, and Kūkuchi stood dreamily near the doorway to the kitchen. Khulu was furiously knocking things about, accusing Musa of going to Pretoria. Khulu stopped knocking things around when she saw Kūkuchi, half-naked, near the doorway.

A little later, Khulu asked Kūkuchi and Dassie to sit down so she could tell them about Musa's trip to Pretoria. After dishing up, she sat calmly in her usual corner, a safe distance from the stove's heat. The two waited eagerly for Khulu to share something amazing about Musa's journey. Kūkuchi said, "Khulu, you can tell us. Has Musa died?"

"*Voetsak*, you!" shouted Khulu. "Do you want to invite bad luck?"

Dassie remained as quiet as a kudu, clearly bored. Khulu took a deep breath and sighed as if she had given up hope. Kūkuchi handed Khulu a mug of water. Even though she was no longer angry, a discouraged tone was still evident in Khulu's voice. She finally spoke slowly for Kūkuchi and Dassie to understand, "All the mothers, including Musa, went with Mama Ngoyi to the Union Building in Pretoria. They went to visit the Prime Minister, Baas Strydom."

"Visit the *Boers*?" Kūkuchi howled. "How can she...?"

Dassie cleared his throat and sleepily interrupted, "The mothers have gone to Pretoria to give the Boers a letter because they don't want to carry passes. That's why."

An uneasy silence settled. Kūkuchi felt overwhelmed by her declining self-esteem every time Dassie spoke to her. After a long pause, she asked, "How do you know all that, Dassie?"

"Musa told me. She said they are carrying a petition."

"And she told you? How come she didn't tell me too?"

"Maybe she forgot," said Khulu.

"And what is a petrition?" asked Kūkuchi, more despondent and feeling deep hatred for her clever brother.

"Musa will explain all that when she comes back," Khulu put it feebly.

Dassie walked out. Khulu hummed her favourite tune. Kükuchi stayed standing like Lot's wife's pillar of salt.

Much later, Kükuchi and Khulu sat down to have a peaceful conversation.

"Khulu, that woman told Dassie everything about Pretoria and left us in the dark like porcupines in the veld. Do you notice how she treats us, Khulu?"

"That Woman? How can you call Musa that woman?"

"What should I call her, Khulu? She is nothing to me. She said nothing to me about the petition. We need to do something, Khulu."

"Something like what, Kuchi?"

"You can hold her tight when I attack with my flick knife. Nobody will find out. We can tell the police that the *Tsotsis* attacked us. I hate her."

In the evening, Khulu and Kükuchi were in the kitchen enjoying soup and dumplings when the door swung open suddenly. Both Khulu and Kükuchi turned around, and there she was—Musa—standing at the door. Kükuchi almost asked if Baas Strydom of Pretoria had given her sandwiches, but she thought better of it.

Breaking the ice, Khulu said, "You are back?"

Musa ignored Khulu and told Kükuchi to bring a bucket of hot water into the bedroom. She wanted to take a bath before going to bed.

"Musa, what is a petition?" Kükuchi asked.

"Just bring me water; I want to bathe."

Musa later appeared, emitting a fresh aroma. She immediately went to her plate to serve herself before telling Kükuchi to go out and bring Dassie home, as she had something important to share with them.

Dassie shouted from the porch, "I am here. I followed you from the bus, Musa."

"Get inside; I have something to tell you about the Union Building."

Kükuchi decided to locate herself outside on the *stoep*. Khulu and Dassie sat silently in the kitchen, facing Musa, who began to recount her trip to Pretoria with meticulous detail that captivated Dassie more than Khulu. According to Musa, over a million mothers had gone to deliver a petition to Strydom.

"What is a bloody petition, Musa?" Kükuchi shouted.

Dassie interrupted, "How big was the petition? Couldn't one mother have delivered it?"

"Shut up, Dassie," shouted Khulu.

"The mothers from all across the country, totalling over two million, were there. And it was frightening…"

"You just said one million…" Dassie observed.

"Shut up, big mouth," Kükuchi yelled.

Musa continued, "Yes, I thought the white police were going to shoot, but we huddled together and kept going. Strydom refused to come out to receive us. So, we dropped the petition at the entrance, and we sang our African National Anthem. Even other women like Helen Joseph and Amina Cachalia were singing. Florence Mkhize shouted, Touch women, you touch a rock, you are dead. Then Lillian Ngoyi chanted and ululated. We sang back home."

Following her unusual energy, Musa went back to the bedroom, singing the whole time. Dassie whistled as he made his way to the *stoep* to join his sister, where he asked for more food, telling Kūkuchi, "Musa's tale about two million women makes my stomach thunder."

Both local and international media extensively covered the Pretoria incident, calling it unprecedented. Over the following weeks, police and soldiers swept through the townships, arresting several women, some of whom had never even been near Pretoria. Musa was unable to escape.

CHAPTER 7

Where is my Elvis?

Three weeks later, Musa returned home unannounced. As usual, she refused to discuss the reasons for her detention, keeping to herself what she experienced during her ordeal. However, upon her release, she found Dassie had become skilled in lawless activities across the township. Within a few months of his stay in White-City, Dassie had broken into the rough woodland areas of the township.

Khulu, Dassie has to stay home," Mkhize said, "Kids on the street corners don't get much rest, and their brains get soggy."

All the African parents held their breaths constantly as their boys found the nights out on the street corners more appealing than their small, uncomfortable living quarters, which were their homes. Mkhize was right. The children of White-City had limited choices because of their conditions of deprivation.

White-City featured rows of dull and monotonous terraced housing, all built according to the same plan designed by the colonial government. In White City, three families shared a communal outdoor toilet that utilized the bucket system. When municipal workers made their undesirable rounds at night, the smell of night soil filled the air like a deadly plague. There was no running water near each household, and showers and bathrooms, essential for personal dignity, were only a distant dream. The colonial authorities designed the small semi-detached blocks so that each had three rooms: a kitchen, a bedroom, and one unspecified extra room. Boys were most affected by this arrangement. In most cases, girls could use the 'unspecified' room at night. Overall, girls tend to be more resilient than boys when facing hardship and distress.

The white supremacist system did not show consideration for individual dignity or respect for African privacy. Instead, it was clear that for Apartheid to succeed, there had to be a strategy to emasculate men considered the heads of their families and to demean women regarded as the mothers of the community. For this programme to work, black fathers and mothers had to have their dignity crushed and their ability to resist destroyed. In such conditions, children were raised by psychologically wounded parents who knew they could never be ideal role models for their children. Many boys raised by fathers who appear weak and powerless develop unchecked anger, which they express at any and every target.

Moreover, the white system of government was to create a pliable workforce for all time. They would reproduce both the parents' way of thinking and squalid living conditions forever. If black people took over power in the future, it would take another hundred years to rebuild proper living accommodation and to recover any sense of self-respect for the majority.

Come bedtime, Dassie would use the dining room as his bedroom, which was a significant source of personal irritation. In Mayfair, he boasted about his small room, which featured a bed and a built-in wardrobe where he stored all his belongings. On his wall was a large poster of Elvis Presley hugging his guitar with confidence. The poster must have meant a lot to Dassie because he showed it off at every chance. In White City, however, Dassie had to adapt quickly since there was no space for extra posters on the wall. Desperate, he decided to tape his prized possession next to Khulu's 'The Last Supper' on the wall.

Once she noticed that Dassie had vandalized her wall, Khulu quickly took the poster down and placed her 'grandfather clock' in the middle, making it hard for Dassie to display his 'Elvis' there. When he returned from his wanderings, Dassie was shocked and desperate, shouting, "Where is my Elvis?"

Khulu asked, "I don't know, Dassie. Where did you put your Elvis?"

"Please, Kükuchi, help me. Where is my Elvis?"

Kükuchi said, "Dassie, leave me alone."

The Land Issue

Although Kükuchi felt sorry for her brother, her ability to help was limited. Dassie consistently sat in his usual spot on the veranda for dinner each night. When the weather was poor, he moved to the corner near the coal stove and often stayed there until everyone went to bed before finally settling down to sleep.

Kükuchi knew it was only a matter of time before Dassie's frustration erupted uncontrollably. The issue was more complex than Dassie's Elvis, however. It was all connected to land, which the white population believed they were divinely entitled to. By the early 1900s, successive white governments had established their economic and political dominance in the region, leading to the 1913 Native Land Act, which reserved only thirteen percent of the land—mostly wasteland—for Africans. According to this racist policy, Africans were no longer permitted to own private land anywhere in the country. When Malan's Herenigde Nasionale Party came to power in 1948, they accelerated the process of expropriating African land without compensation, giving it to white families, including many new immigrants from Europe. Thousands of Black people, displaced by ethnic cleansing, eventually fled to cities like Johannesburg or Durban in search of jobs. Unsurprisingly, due to the breakdown of social cohesion, they were ruthlessly exploited and paid low wages, while the white government failed to address the need for proper housing. Large numbers, mainly men, settled in single-sex hostels.

The squatter movement, led by James Sofasonke Mpanze, affectionately known as 'Magebula', provided Malan with an unexpected answer to the challenge. The flamboyant activist made history by systematically seizing land from white farmers and creating shantytowns for homeless people. He named one of the areas 'Masakeni' because the shacks were made of sheets of sacks. Ironically, the government's security forces ignored the movement's activities, not only because of the sheer number of supporters Sofasonke had, but also because its actions aligned with the broader plan to create a corridor for cheap black labour.

Like Khulu, many people described Mpanza as a man full of worms in his brain for challenging the robust apartheid regime. While some Black political leaders condemned Mpanza for being a lackey of the government, as he was never detained for overt political activities, others secretly applauded his peculiar land invasion techniques. Farming life was slowly coming to a standstill in the south of Johannesburg as the squatter army overran the farmland. Yet, those activities seemed to fit in with the government's ideology of separating residential areas based on race and tribe. They blended well with the plan to forcibly remove all Black families and businesses from Sophiatown and the other regions the regime designated for white occupation.

As it turned out, Sophiatown transformed into an affluent white enclave overnight with the stroke of a pen. With all the 'undesirables' gone, Afrikaner triumph was complete, and Sophiatown could finally be called Triomf. Bobby and his father, Mr Mohale, were among the first exiled to Rockville. Before then, Mohale had operated a successful photographic studio in Sophiatown. He lost all his equipment, materials, and clients' photographs during the forced removal. Later, the Johannesburg City Council named the entire township where Africans were relocated 'Soweto'. It included Meadowlands, Orlando, and Pimville. 'Soweto' (an acronym for South Western Townships) is a collection of large areas previously owned by white farmers.

The farms included Doornkop, Kriel, Vogelstruisfontein, Klipriviersoog, Diepkloof, Albertyne, and Kliptown. The white farmers received substantial, undisclosed compensation.

CHAPTER 8

Mendi's Shady Side

The principal pushed Dassie into standard three, meaning he was close to catching up with Kūkuchi. Like most American schools, Donaldson Primary used the platoon system because of the large number of pupils. Both Standard Three and Four shared the same classroom, with Miss Lumka in charge of the entire group. At Donaldson, she effectively utilized her creativity to coordinate unrelated subjects while addressing overcrowding.

Posa had a low opinion of Lumka's teaching methods. At the start of the year, Lumka divided each large classroom into three groups – Egypt on the far left, Jordan in the middle, and Israel on the right. She believed those in Jordan were average and had great potential. Maybe if they tried hard, they could reach Israel someday. Very few students crossed Jordan from Egypt. Kūkuchi sat in the front seat of Israel, a spot she resented.

However, Dassie's sudden appearance made her forget everything. Instead, she yelled, "What are you doing here, Dassie?"

Lumka said, "What are you doing here, Dassie?"

Posa said, "Yes, Miss Lumka, Dassie is joining this class because he is clever."

Lumka said, "In that case, he must start in Egypt until I assess his progress."

Posa, who did not appreciate being contradicted, asked, "Has this boy demonstrated a good command of English? Have you heard him speak?"

"Lumka said, "I also teach arithmetic. Can he do the twelve times seven?"

While Dassie was settling into his life in Israel, Posa ignored Lumka's protest and went back to her office. Eventually, Dassie joined the boys' army under Mendi's command. The group caused chaos that spread beyond the township.

Gogo Gasa, Mendi's grandmother, was upset with Mendi's street activities and his school performance. Still, Gasa continued to pay his school fees as she tried to encourage him to focus on his studies. At the beginning of the year, she pleaded with the principal to promote him to the next class.

"It's you again, Mrs Gasa."

Yes, Principal. If you let my Mendi go to Standard Six, he will pass. That teacher in his class hates him, which is why she failed him again. In Standard Six, he will pass, you'll see.

"How will that happen, Mrs Gasa?"

"It's because standard six papers are graded in Pretoria."

"Pretoria? Mama, don't you see what else white people are always hoping to see in Pretoria? They're waiting for black boys like Mendi to be handcuffed, put into police vans, and sentenced to death. Have you ever told Mendi that?"

Oh, Principal, that's impossible. Mendi is a self-disciplined, respectful boy. He needs to pass the sixth grade and move on to the next level.

"Mrs Gasa, Mendi probably shouldn't be here this year since he failed. Did you see his report?"

"He told me, but I did not see the report, Principal."

"Now, Mrs Gasa, how do you expect me to promote a child who doesn't even deliver his report to his parents?"

"Maybe he lost it. He will try. I'll help him. I can read. Let me help him..."

"If you insist... I wash my hands like Pontius Pilate. Do you know Pontius Pilate, Mrs Gasa?"

"Of course, I know that man. You know I go to church every Sunday."

***

Strange things happened at Donaldson. Posa saw Mendi during training in the schoolyard. She was so amazed that she immediately became interested in his athletic activities. From that moment, the principal treated Mendi like her own son, much to the teachers' dismay. Despite numerous complaints about his disruptive behaviour, Posa ignored the criticisms and told the teachers to use child psychology. Mendi became the most popular athlete in the townships.

One day, Mendi told Kükuchi about the attack he suffered at the hands of the police and how Musa had saved his life. "They want to arrest me and put me back in Diepkloof. I'm not going there. She told them to leave me alone."

"What did you do?"

"They say I stole money, but that big policeman they call Captain Venter asked the police, 'Where is the money?' So he told them to let me go."

Kükuchi felt a dark cloud cover her after hearing those words from Mendi. She felt that Mendi's lifestyle was dangerous. They often took cover among the flowering shrubs in the schoolyard after school. One day, he took her to Kliptown's Sans Soucie Bioscope to watch Fu Manchu. It became one of the happiest days of Kükuchi's life, and she expressed her gratitude by giving Mendi a necklace and a pat on the cheek.

However, Kükuchi had become aware of the dangerous, shady side of Mendi's lifestyle. One day, she discovered that Mendi was working with a gang from Alexandra that peddled processed marijuana from the Natal Midlands. Reluctantly, she sat inside the school grounds with Mendi, sharing ideas about this and that.

After assuring Kükuchi that he would own a lorry one day, he pulled out a packet of Cavalla cigarettes and gripped one with his teeth. As he struck the match, he asked, "Want one?"

Three men suddenly appeared, smiling at Kükuchi and motioning for Mendi to follow them. Kükuchi was mortified because one of the men was Papi. The other man she did not know told her to stay put and not move. The men used the flower bush to hide what they were doing. Kükuchi ran in the opposite direction and hid behind the corner of the building to listen. Mendi unbuttoned his trousers and pulled out a moneybag. After giving it to Papi, the third man, who didn't trust Mendi, insisted they check the money to be sure. One of the men said the suspicious man was talking nonsense. As the men left, Kükuchi hurried back.

"Who are these men, Mendi?"

"Just friends. Don't worry about them."

"Old people like that are your friends? Tell me the truth about them. I don't like your habit of ducking and dodging when I ask questions."

"What about you? Do you think I don't know?"

"Kükuchi panicked because she was certain Mendi was referring to Dodo."

"What?"

"I know a lot. You think I don't know about Kenny?"

Kükuchi recalled Salu's words in response to Musa's letter, 'Never talk about the rhino where there is no tree nearby'.

"Kenny? What about Kenny?"

"He told me you are his girl."

Kenny was a shy boy with a body as thin as a candlewick. His squeaky voice often sparked humorous jokes that worsened his low self-esteem. As a result, Kenny had no chance against Kükuchi's harsh temperament. Someone must have warned him about the intense hurricane called Kükuchi. He left White City for good and moved to Rockville with his father.

CHAPTER 9

Kükuchi and Toby

Kükuchi and Toby stood outside the school gate, whispering to each other. She shared what she saw while she was with Mendi. She voiced her worries about continuing to sell Papi's 'hot stuff'. However, Toby told Kükuchi about more supplies of bangles and wristwatches.

"Did you hear what I just said, Toby?:

"I heard what you said, Kuchi. In this business, if you get out, you are dead. That's what Papi told me after your secret meeting with him and those guys from Alexandra last week."

"Meeting with Papi? I never had a meeting with Papi."

"I know everything. How can I trust you when you sneak out to have private meetings with Papi's friends in the dark...? Papi told me. If we stop, we are dead. And besides, how do you expect us to make money and support ourselves without him?"

"We can stop him, Toby. We can't let that man control our lives."

"How can we stop him? You are just talking."

Kükuchi spoke gently and slowly, "We can trap him because we are friends. Let's lure him into the veld, beneath the willow trees by the stream. He'll come running when you call because you're pretty. And when he gets there, we box him and stab him until he's dead. Nobody will know."

Toby yelled, "Do you think Captain Venter is a fool? He will find us and arrest us. So many girls are missing here in White City. You talk about willow trees and streams as if you know how everything works. People are talking, Kuchi, and this township is filled with rumours."

"Rumours about what, Toby?"

"Your people, of course. You, your uncle, and your funny family! That Dodo man! Come to think of it, I have never even heard you gossip about him. Are you hiding something? You kept ducking and diving last time I asked you about Lusikisiki."

Kükuchi shoved Toby, and Toby shoved Kükuchi back. It turned into a battle between a lion and a tiger. Kükuchi had to summon hidden reserves to respond, sending Toby howling up the street, shouting invectives.

Posa ordered Kükuchi to her office immediately. This was not the first time Kükuchi found herself in Posa's intimidating office, facing serious misconduct charges. The first time was after she punched a boy in the face, accusing him of pinching her bottom. Then there was an incident of burglary, when she broke into the classroom one night.

When she entered, Posa pointed to the squiggles on a map showing the school for mischievous girls located in Phomolong.

"You are the worst bully I've ever seen in this school," Posa shouted before she tossed a letter to Khulu to get her attention.

***

I knew I was in trouble, so I threw Posa's note into the fire and skipped school for two days, pretending to have a stomach illness. On the third day, when I thought everyone had forgotten, I rubbed my eyes with lemon and hobbled to school. Zondi called me to the office. As Deputy, Zondi would be taking Posa's place for a month. My answers must have upset Zondi because he quickly suspended me.

Khulu was upset, but she couldn't do much about it. The news of my suspension spread rapidly through White City. Some parents came to thank Mr Zondi for his bravery, but not a single parent supported me. I was furious and wished I could disappear. The ANC Women's League questioned Mr Zondi's fairness in expelling only one party. One woman accused Zondi of intolerance toward the disabled.

When she read the story in *Township News*, Salu was in Estcourt, fetching supplies for her farm. She took the overnight Express to Johannesburg, and after picking me up from home, I was there, face-to-face with Zondi again in his office. The stern, colourless Zondi was unmoved by Salu's ranting. He ordered us out of Donaldson, threatening to ban Salu permanently from the school. Salu refused, challenging Zondi to call the police. Zondi dared not do that, risking township anger. So, Salu and I spent the entire day inside Zondi's office, dozing off or having brief exchanges. Zondi kept going in and out, eavesdropping on our conversation, occasionally making faces and mockingly clearing his throat.

When Zondi was gone, I asked Salu about our relationship with Khanyile and Zazi, the men from Lusikisiki.

"It's a long story, Kuchi."
"Did you steal the chicken farm from Khulu?"

Losing control, Salu leapt forward like a springbok and shouted angrily at the top of her lungs, accusing me of asking stupid questions.

After a long, awkward silence, Salu took my hand and said, "I am a lady from the Langalibalele stock. A lady does not lose her temper and shout like a hadada. I am sorry Kükuchi..."

The conversation piqued Zondi's interest when he returned, so he eavesdropped.

"Listen, about the farm, the truth will come out someday. You are too young to understand. But as for you... You are an African girl; get an education and keep your eyes sharp like King Shaka's spear. When you reach for the stars one day, ensure your other eye is watching over your soul."

I was confused. Zondi furrowed his eyebrows, then shook his head dismissively before leaving his office. Salu dozed off, and after a while, we were both fast asleep. However, the Drakensberg chicken farm remained a mystery that stayed blurry in my mind for many years to come.

Zondi rudely shook us up, threatening to lock us in for the night since the school was out. Then, unexpectedly, Khulu arrived with Karel. Zondi apologized to Toby's mother for the pain I caused her family.

"However, she has been suspended, as you are aware..."

Karel asked, "Why target Kükuchi? You have no authority to expel her for any reason." My child, Toby, told me she initiated everything. Kuchi defended herself, and she was justified in teaching Toby a lesson. Currently, we don't even know her whereabouts."

"What are you going to do, Mr Zondi? You heard it from her mother. Kükuchi is innocent," said Salu.

After reconsideration, Zondi allowed me back, as long as I stopped threatening other children. However, Salu insisted that Zondi call Toby to his office to get 'the two sinners', as he called them, to shake hands and make peace. Nobody knew where Toby was, especially not her mother. Following a little investigation, a boy from Moroka disclosed Toby's hiding place. Toby and I became good friends again after the hand-shaking ceremony.

***

A day later, Toby called Kükuchi and asked her to visit her house that evening. Kükuchi became suspicious. At sunset, after thinking over the invitation, she concealed her flick-knife in her diary and took a nervous walk to Toby's house. Besides a small wooden bench, two chairs, a little table, and a tiny four-legged stove in the corner, the rest of Toby's home seemed sparse, open, and bare. Toby told Kükuchi she had something important to discuss.

"You openly brew Barberton stuff, Toby? Why?"

"What can we do? We need the money. Forget about that. Oh, Kükuchi, I like your grandmother from Natal."

"Why?"

"She is strong, and that's why. She made us—*you, me, us all—shake hands. Mother once said that all hatred disappears when you shake hands. Don't you think so, Kükuchi?"

"I don't have any hatred."

"You don't hate me after calling bad names...? I'm sorry."

"No, I don't hate you, Toby. You are my friend. I plait your hair, and you plait mine. Other people won't even touch me. I love your mother because she says nice things to me. I love you both with my whole heart. Your mother baked me a birthday cake and even bought a candle. Your mother always kisses my cheeks; you know that. But tell me the truth: are you Mendi's girl?"

"No, Kükuchi, not anymore. I thought you knew. It's all in the past."

"You lie."

"Please, let's not fight over Mendi."

"You said you wanted to see me. What's wrong?"

"Do you remember the day you hit me? I wanted to share the good news with you. Papi has a different line that we can push quickly."

I don't like this. Is this a trap? Are you still mad at me for slapping you?

"I don't have revenge in my heart, Kükuchi."

After a while, Toby murmured, "Can you keep a secret?"

"Yes?"

"My mother is ill. They say she has breast cancer. She doesn't want to go to Bara because she thinks people go there to die."

"So, what is she going to do?"

Mkhize had offered to take Toby's mother to the Tsitsikama Forest. Like many others, Mkhize believed that Tsitsikama harboured a large number of medicinal plants that could cure cancer.

"Look, Kükuchi, at least if I can get enough money to buy her a bed and maybe some furniture, she can die happy. If she dies today, imagine what the mourners coming here will say... empty house, no chairs, no cakes...?" Toby cracked a smile that touched Kükuchi deeply.

"We are all the same in White-City, Toby. We are fine as long as we have bread."

***

From there, I went straight to Tatenda's shop to buy eggs and fat cakes. On my way out, I saw Dassie and Tina holding hands affectionately behind the shop. When they noticed me watching, the two of them quickly let go and parted.

Tina cupped her laughter with both hands and swayed her hips back to her parents' store.

"Do you like Tina?"

"She says she likes me. What can I do?"

"You come here at night to kiss her just because she says she likes you...?"

As we walked home, Dassie said, "I thought you and Toby were enemies."

"No, we are friends, Dassie."

"Do you know your friend pushes stolen watches and bangles? That man, Papi... he is a member of the Alexandra Gang. He killed a man who stabbed his sister. She can't walk now because of the stabbing, and she needs a wheelchair. Mendi told me."

"Papi killed a man? You lie, Dassie. How come he is not in jail"?

"It's a secret. But Papa Mkhize told me the police are still investigating."

When we got home, we sat on the *stoep* and continued talking about Papi, which drew Khulu's interest.

"The police never investigated the murder. The police interrogated Papi for ten minutes, and he was let go."

"No, Khulu. Mendi told me everything. It was Papi's friends who killed the man."

"You are still friends with Mendi? Shouted Khulu, "Hey Kükuchi, where is my bread? I have been waiting to dish up."

"And Khulu, Kükuchi must stop eating fat cakes and Pap," shouted Dassie.

"Why?"

"She can beat Rosemarie. She must do exercises and get a javelin from the principal. Her daughters are lazy, and she is angry with them."

"Tell me about Rosemarie," says Khulu.

"Rosemarie is a javelin thrower. She likes athletics. I asked Rosemarie's mother to buy a javelin for Kükuchi, and do you know what she said?"

"You did what?"

"Rosemarie's mother said getting a javelin for Kükuchi is like giving jewels to a pig..."

"I'll kill that white woman. I'll attack at night, Khulu. The police will never catch me because I am smart. And what did you say to her, Dassie... about jewels and pigs and me?"

"Nothing. She was about to give me nice shoes and that yellow skirt for you..."

"That terylene came from Rosemarie's mother?" Khulu shouted.

"And you said nothing because of the shoes, you fool! You were there when Miss Lumka spoke about people like you, selling their souls to the devil. And this white woman is a mad devil."

"Shut up, Kükuchi," Khulu cried. "And as for you, Dassie, get out."

Dassie walked out and sat on the *stoep*. Khulu continued to dish up as she addressed Kükuchi.

"What do you care about the white girls? You can easily do this yourself, Kükuchi. Dassie is right. You can throw the javelin like a white child because you have a shapely body."

"You mean I'm overweight?"

"I'm trying to say you are well-built and you look good, Kükuchi."

"Great, now I feel better. But Khulu, I don't like Dassie; I don't like Rosemarie; I don't care about the javelin. What does Dassie want in White City? His lies spread like wildfire. He bores me. He told lies about me to those white girls."

"You don't have to be cruel. Dassie is only trying to be friendly..."

"Khulu, do you know what Rosemarie said to me one day? She said African girls are stupid, they can't do anything right."

"Rosemarie was just speaking in code. That's how they communicate among themselves. I know them; I worked for them for ten years in Vrystaat. Sometimes they say things about Africans in your presence, as if you're not there. Maybe she wanted to test if you believed you were stupid and thought you couldn't do anything right. And maybe she is right. You are a stupid boy if you keep roaming the streets with *Tsotsis*."

***

Back on the *stoep* the next night, I sat next to Dassie, feeling sorry for the way Khulu talked to him.

"I'll leave White-City," he said, "I must leave this place for good."

"No, Dassie. Leave us? Don't do that. Khulu will die."

"Khulu will be happy."

Meanwhile, Khulu fiddled with her pinafores and put them away for the night. She then gave me instructions about her stock and customers. I was half listening.

"Khulu, Dassie was crying outside, and he left his food and disappeared."

"Where did he say he was going?"

"To his friends, maybe. He is angry because you yelled at him and told him he is stupid."

"Go find him. You know his friends. Tell him to come back, I'm sorry."

CHAPTER 10

Javelins in Posa's Bedroom.

Posa instructed Mendi to intensify his afternoon training for the Regional Tournament. Mendi once again convinced Kūkuchi to spend her afternoons assisting him with his javelin routines. Kūkuchi admired the dedication Mendi showed to his athletic training and observed his moves with great interest.

Posa emerged from behind the bushes one afternoon, shouting, "Kūkuchi. What are you doing here?"

"I am just watching Mendi throw his javelin. I am going home now."

"Your brother told me about you, that you wanted to be a javelin thrower. Forget it. You can't do it. You have to be fit to be an athlete, like Mendi here."

Kūkuchi walked away silently, convinced that everyone was terrible to her. Still, she continued spending some of her afternoons with Mendi. One day, as she sat among the bushes, she wondered what kept her from doing athletics like Rosemarie. When Mendi took a break, she hesitantly grabbed the javelin off the grass. After some hesitation, she threw it for the first time, then again, making a series of awkward, uneven slices while her legs wobbled. Mendi showed up and burst out laughing. Then he switched to a serious tone and said, "You throw better than most boys here. Did you see where that throw landed? The tip hit the ground... and it was over thirty."

"What is 'over thirty'?"

The principal watched Kūkuchi's spontaneous javelin throw one afternoon. She was left speechless.

All she could whisper was, "You are amazing, child."

The only javelin at the school had seen better days. Athletes, the few with any interest, had to make do with what the school provided.

Mendi visited Kūkuchi at her home. Khulu was trembling with anger despite Mendi's sweet smile. Kūkuchi quickly pulled Mendi away from the house and behind the lavatories.

"Why...? You didn't tell me you were coming."

"Are you afraid I'll find another man with you?"

"Don't talk like that, Mendi. I don't have another man."

Mendi brought good news to Kūkuchi. The school had a new batch of training equipment stored in the principal's office. He revealed a secret: Mrs Posa had sent boys to take some of the equipment and hide it in her bedroom. Kūkuchi was stunned.

When she went back inside, Kūkuchi told Khulu about the set of javelins hidden in Posa's bedroom. "Her twins, Babe and Tilly, received javelins and other items from some white people long ago."

"Yes, answered Khulu, "One of the girls told me she wants to be a nun…"

"A nun? What does she want to be a nun for?"

"I don't know. Some of these educated mothers push their children so hard that the poor children want a peaceful place elsewhere, like a nunnery."

"Oh, Khulu!"

"What do you want to be when you grow up?"

"Would you be happy if I could become a train driver?"

"I would be happy if you could be what you want to be."

"Do you know what Posa is saying now? He says I'm amazing."

"You asked her what she meant by that?"

"Yes, it's because I throw the javelin like a champion, I even outperform the boys."

"Posa won several javelin tournaments across the Transvaal. African records didn't matter. I know these things because I worked for white people in Bloemfontein. Their children enjoyed athletics."

"I enjoy athletics, too, Khulu."

"Maybe I was wrong to encourage you to believe you could be like white girls. It will hurt you if you take it too seriously. Why did Posa say you were amazing when she knew it didn't mean anything for African girls?

"Kükuchi sighed and said, "I reach over 35 meters now, Khulu."

"I don't want to hear anymore. I am a sinner. Forgive me, God."

"Khulu, I can win. Even Mendi says so."

"Mendi? Kükuchi, has it ever occurred to you that Mendi might be a demon from hell? I have been hearing things about you and that boy. And I don't like any of it."

***

Posa orders Kükuchi to her office. She feels like a puppy summoned by its owner, wielding a whip. This time, Posa is all smiles as she pulls out a new javelin from behind her filing cabinet.

"Your brother, Dassie! He can be persuasive, even though I can't stand his big mouth. Do you know what he said to me? 'Where is your husband? How come we never see your husband here?' He is an embarrassment that Dassie boy."

Kükuchi nearly says, 'I've been wondering about your husband myself'.

While she salivates, Posa hands the state-of-the-art javelin to Kükuchi, who is trembling. Kükuchi admires its lightness and durability, and she instinctively knows she is destined to conquer the world.

Kükuchi caresses her javelin like a new outfit. She waddles home like a back-footed penguin on the seashore. She wants to thank her brother, but Dassie's whereabouts have remained a mystery since Khulu told him that he is stupid.

However, in the morning, Kükuchi says, "Khulu, I was thinking about Dassie. Where is he?"

Khulu says, "Dassie is a boy. He feels lonely because there is no man in this house. He will be back because he is clever, like you."

"Do you think Uncle Dodo is a good man, Khulu?"

"No. A man who handcuffs people without their identity papers isn't good."

Where is Dassie?

My mind drifts back to DF Malan's statement, which Dassie and I had memorized at Musa's insistence. Malan was an apartheid Prime Minister from 1948 to 1954. He had been responding to the ANC's demand for the abolition of apartheid. The statement read:

> I believe it is self-contradictory to claim that, as an inherent right of the Bantu, who differ from Europeans in many ways, they should be regarded as not different, especially considering that these differences are permanent and not man-made.

Musa also insisted that we memorize an African response to Malan's assertion:

> M'Afrika, wake up. The white man says you are different, meaning God made you to be second-rate. That is why the white man gives your children a low-grade education and arrests you when you reject it.

I pace back and forth, reciting words and convincing myself I could throw the javelin better than Rosemarie. Khulu's ticking clock reminds me that time is quickly passing. I shiver at the thought that my struggle as an African girl trying to break into the white man's world might end in tears. While Musa's imprisonment worries me, it feels minor compared to Dassie's disappearance. Every evening becomes a nightmare of anxiety, guilt, and distress over how I treated him. I sit on the *stoep* for hours, waiting and gazing beyond the Yellowwoods into the distant Moroka and Jabavu, toward the faint moon, hoping for any sign of Dassie. I go inside, read old newspapers, then return to sit and wait for something to happen.

I am reading a piece about Musa and other detainees when I come across a 1955 photo of Musa from the archives. It was taken when a group of women gathered to discuss the idea of building schools in African communities. The photo surprises me, and I begin to believe that Musa must be an important woman.

There is a knock on the door. I start trembling like a Cape fox. There she is, Musa, silhouetted against the bright moon and looking dazed. Musa squeezes herself through. The cold night breeze follows her inside, and one candle flickers away. I help carry Musa's bag inside, unable to read her emotions as her face remains hidden in our kitchen shadows.

Musa steps closer to the stove to warm her hands and her back. Our rocky relationship continues, and the furnace she now uses to warm her hands makes me think of Blossom, my doll, whom she incinerated during her irrational fury. My anger is boiling over.

"Where's Khulu?
"I don't know."

An image in the newspaper suddenly catches Musa's attention. She quickly snatches the paper, like a forest chameleon's tongue, and sits on the edge of the bench. After reading the article, she carefully folds the paper and gets up.

"Where is Dassie?"
"I don't know."
"Is there anything you know about this house? Call him. It is late now."
"Where do you want me to start?"

"You're a woman now. You know everything. Dassie is your brother. Don't you care?"

"If Dassie is my brother, tell me about our parents?"

Musa heaves a long sigh of fatigue. As always, she keeps her thoughts on awkward questions inside her bosom.

I sit opposite her and quietly repeat my cutting probe, "Who is my father, Musa?"

"Your father?"

"Most children have fathers. Who is my father?"

Musa responds, "Is Dassie with your boyfriend in Jabavu? I saw your last report. Aren't you ashamed?"

"Ashamed of what?"

"That javelin thing won't get you anywhere. Sister Mohale told me, and she's right. It's dangerous for a girl!"

Khulu rushes in like a wildebeest. She drops her pinafore case on the floor and struggles to catch her breath when she sees Musa.

"Oh, Musa, it's so wonderful to see you. Why didn't the Boers tell us they were releasing you? We could have sent Mkhize to pick you up from wherever they were holding you."

Rejecting Khulu's friendly gesture, Musa insists on finding out where Dassie is.

"Khulu is tired," I shout. "Don't you care...?"

"I'm sorry, Musa," Khulu said gently, "I try always to keep Dassie here, but he goes away from time to time."

"Where does he go?"

"Don't answer her, Khulu," I scream. "Musa must stay home and take care of Dassie herself. Why should Khulu always carry your troubles?"

Musa turns to me and insists I go with her to Jabavu. She thinks Dassie is hiding with Mendi.

Khulu cries in desperation, "Why, Musa? Can't it wait until daylight? It's very dark outside, and Jabavu is an evil place at night..."

"Don't worry, Khulu. I'm going nowhere with Musa."

Jabavu is a muddy, dangerous place, full of dark spots even during the day. When the sun slowly rises elsewhere, it remains hidden in Jabavu until it gradually melts away. At night, shadowy figures of men and women, along with little boys and girls with indistinct faces, appear from the edges of the pathways and then slowly vanish, like curious apparitions. The sightings of short men called tokoloshes are not just urban legends in Jabavu.

Khulu rushes out to ask for Mkhize's intervention. Mkhize is not happy, but as usual, he smiles and tells Khulu he will go to Jabavu himself to look for Dassie. Before leaving, he vents his irritation at Musa and blames her for acting like all typical township mothers, who appease their children with sweets and let them do as they please.

Back in Mtubatuba, Mkhize continues, "We have plenty of trees with branches, and our children know there is not much difference between a twig and a switch."

Into the middle of the night, Mkhize's voice cuts through the darkness and echoes across White City, "We are here, Khulu. Dassie is here."

We rush out to see for ourselves what miracle Mkhize has just performed. Six black policemen are accompanying them.

"I found him, Khulu. He was with Mendi the entire time..."

"Yes, Khulu," says Sergeant Sibande. "You people! You let children go to the streets... look at him. Next time, you'll find him covered with newspapers on a cold Johannesburg sidewalk."

"How can you say that, Officer?" Musa snaps angrily.

"And as for you, Miss Women's League, be quiet. You're nothing but trouble. We know all about you. Forget politics. Take my advice—stay at home in the kitchen and cook good food for your husband. Is this your boy? He will die like a dog if you don't make him go to school."

The officers drive away. We go back to Khulu's kitchen to reflect. Mkhize tells Khulu that they found Mendi lying in a pool of blood. The police are searching for his assailants from Alexandra.

"Where is Mendi now?" I ask anxiously.

"In my house. The police left him in my safe custody. I want to apply my potions of Mtubatuba traditional mixture on this boy's brain."

"You are a good boy, Dassie," says Khulu, "but you must return to school. Eat now, and we can talk about school tomorrow."

Mkhize counters angrily, "Dassie, you are not a good boy. You are a troublemaker, just like that stupid Mendi, who is a heartbeat away from Number 4. Stop hanging around with friends who smoke benzene."

"Have you ever seen me smoke benzene?" snaps Dassie.

"Do you smoke benzene, Dassie?" asks Khulu.

"No, he doesn't smoke benzene anymore. That's for little kids. Dassie smokes marijuana with Mendi and their friends. A troublemaker is known by the company he keeps," Mkhize says before marching out angrily.

Deep into the middle of the night, Dassie whispers from his 'makeshift' bedroom, "Kūkuchi, come out here. There's something I want to tell you."

"What is it, Dassie?" Musa hisses.

"Go back to sleep, Dassie. You will tell us in the morning," says Khulu.

"No. I am calling. Come out, Kūkuchi. It is important."

I shuffle angrily toward the edge of Dassie's mattress. "What's the matter? You scared us."

"Let's go outside. I want to tell you something."

Dassie warns me about men from Alexandra who might come looking for me. Two of those men had earlier tried to kill Mendi, but Mkhize and the police arrived in time to save his life. The men said they were from Toby and claimed she had told them Mendi snatched all their takings. I immediately seek refuge with Sister Mohale and ignore Khulu's plea for me to stay put. Taking my knife with me, I tremble as I head to Mohale's house. The elderly nurse is too tired to argue with me, but points at an unoccupied visitors' bedroom with her tiny finger. She then walks back to her bedroom to sleep. In the morning, I head straight to Toby's place. She lets me into her house with all the curtains drawn, then immediately locks the door and starts to tell the story of her lucky escape. According to her, Mendi had earlier told her to hand over all the takings to him. When Papi and his friends heard about this, they demanded their money from Mendi, who started to hesitate. That's when they stormed Mendi's house. When a neighbour heard the commotion, he ran to raise the alarm.

"They want to kill me, Faty," Toby screams.

"Why did you give the money to Mendi? That was not part of the plan?"

"He convinced me they had agreed. I thought he was telling the truth..."

"You and Mendi are back together again, I can see."

"No, Fat; I'm past Mendi now, I told you. Besides, my mother often said he's not on my level."

"Your level? What did she mean?"

"I don't want to talk about Mendi again. He has caused hurt feelings between us. All the remaining goods are at a relative's house, an uncle who is a policeman in Orlando East. I explained everything to him, and I trust him."

"Be careful of uncles... "How is your mother?"

"She is still with a traditional healer in Tsitsikama. She must come back; I can't stay here alone like this."

I realized immediately that we needed to halt our hawking activities. We had already shared over £120 in four months, and I believed that was sufficient.

***

Mendi spent the following weeks with Mkhize. He was so captivated by the re-broadcast at Mkhize's house that he stayed glued to it all day. Mkhize bought him a loaf of bread and eggs, and Khulu contributed a bowl of spinach, sour milk, and chicken pieces every day. Mendi must have taken some heavy knocks on the head because when Kükuchi first came to see him, he looked completely out of it. But Mendi recovered enough to escape from Mkhize's makeshift custody. Mkhize realized the breakout when he returned from a dairy with sour milk for the culprit. His receiver was missing. Furious with rage, Mkhize hurried to Khulu's place; a piece of wire from his receiver was painfully strapped around his shoulder. He darted in and out of the house like a porcupine caught between lightning and thunder in a heavy storm.

When he finally settled down on the kitchen bench, he said softly, "Khulu, I save this thug from the mouth of a lion; I bring him here to repair his damaged brain; I provide him with the hospitality that my ancestors bequeathed to me; and then? He runs away from the Good Samaritan, back to his wayward business."

Kükuchi struggled to suppress her laughter, but Musa, who was just as confused, offered Mkhize a calabash filled with magewu. Still holding his prized piece of wire, Mkhize said, "I am going to shove this thug into Diepkloof jail myself, and he will stay there forever."

"Diepkloof!" Kükuchi wailed.

"Yes Kükuchi, Diepkloof."

If you could make a wish

Dassie sat on the *stoep* and started speaking out of turn as usual, "I read your notebook, the one you hide in the wardrobe."

"Why did you read it? That's my private book. You are not supposed to read private things."

"Dodo is a bad man," Dassie responded.

Dassie tells Kükuchi that he and Mendi once planned to attack Dodo and kill him. Afterward, they would bury his body under the concrete for road construction near Moroka Police Station. However, Mendi got cold feet and said they should wait a bit.

"But Uncle will pay for what he has done to you."

After a moment of silence, Dassie sighed and asked, "Tell me, Ugly, if you could make your wish, what would it be?"

"Dassie, why don't you say what you want to say?"

"Okay, what do you want in life? That policeman, Venter, he said I must tell him my wish."

"What good is a wish if you don't have money? Me? I wish you could stop calling me 'Ugly'. That's my wish. Satisfied?"

Dassie giggled and said, "You spend too much time away these days. I know where you go; doing your javelin because you want to be like Rosemarie. "Do you know what my wish is?"

"Why don't you go ahead and tell me?"

"I wish to be a mathematics teacher when I grow up and to marry Tina someday because Toby doesn't want to be my girlfriend. She says I'm too young for her. That's my wish."

Kükuchi raised her eyebrows, amazed to hear her brother make such a beautiful wish. There was a lump in her throat, and her eyes began to water. She smiled, looking forward to a second chance to share her wish with Dassie. She asked, "And me? Do you want to know my wish?"

Dassie's mind had drifted, and he asked, "Do you know why Musa is happy these days?"

"No, why?"

"Why don't you ask her?"

"I don't care if she's happy or not. Did she tell you she was happy?"

"Sister Mohale told me Musa is your stomach mother. I know you want us to make Dodo suffer. Don't you want something bad to happen to Uncle Dodo?"

Kükuchi thought, 'It is bad to hate one's brother, even if he calls you 'Ugly'.

CHAPTER 11

Musa is Getting Married

Despite dismissing Dassie's insinuation that she wanted to be like Rosemarie, Kükuchi admitted to herself that her brother could read her heart. Lacking confidence in her athletic abilities, Kükuchi intensified her training in preparation for the local schools' tournaments. She focused particularly on her weak spots, her legwork, and speed. Her main challenge remained timing the distance from the start of the runway to the scratch line, which marks the boundary. It is a foul for the competitor to step on or beyond the boundary line of the runway.

Dassie unintentionally worsened things by criticizing her efforts. One afternoon, he watched as Kükuchi tried to perfect her javelin throw. Later, Dassie said, "Your throw is getting worse. Why do you slow down when you approach the final line?"

"Dassie, do you think a javelin is like throwing dice at the corner of Tatenda's shop?"

When Dassie got home from school, he begged Kükuchi to give him plenty of meat because he was tired of beans. Musa was singing Miriam Makeba's tunes at the top of her voice. With Khulu's help, until Kükuchi could see one of the last teeth still hanging in her granny's mouth, the house erupted into song with screams of laughter echoing through the streets. Kükuchi thought the whole thing was silly.

Before they went to bed, Khulu quietly said, Musa is... ahem... getting married."

"What?"

"Don't shout. She will hear you."

In the morning, Khulu's face looked grim as she expressed how unimpressed she had been with the whole idea of Musa getting married. She said the man she wanted to marry was an ex-convict. He had been in and out of jail since 1955, and he was in prison again after the police found him distributing copies of the *Freedom Charter*.

"How could anyone ever want to marry Musa?" Kükuchi asked.

***

In the evening, once everything had settled, Musa's funny side about his looming wedding faded, replaced by deep irritation. Kükuchi asked again, "Khulu, I have grown older now. You can tell me where my father is..."

"Am I responsible for your father's desertion...?"

Much later, Khulu tried to calm Kükuchi by sharing a story about her father. She showed her an old photograph from her shoebox. The man wearing a 'Stetson' hat and a check tie with a sporty knot was relaxing on a braided branch of a tree, with the picturesque waterfalls in the background.

"He was your father," Khulu put it. "Now forget about him."

Kükuchi stayed seated on the mat, trembling as she looked at the photograph. She said, "Khulu, where is he? I want to talk to him."

You can't tell Kuchi that. Musa will get mad at me. She can't know I showed you those pictures.

Khulu was right. That very night, Kükuchi overheard Musa confront Khulu, "I see you have been telling Kükuchi many things about that man, Mama."

Kükuchi instantaneously seized Musa's throat and held her down as if time had stopped.

Musa was choking and couldn't breathe. Kükuchi kept smothering Musa with her jersey, trying to force the air out of her. After a lot of effort, Khulu broke up the fight and handed a glass of water to the coughing Musa.

Khulu sat quietly later, looking more discouraged than Kükuchi had ever seen her. The three women remained in their spots in the small kitchen, in awkward silence, until Kükuchi said firmly, "Never talk to Khulu like that again, Musa."

***

In the morning, a cold wind followed by heavy rain worsened the gloomy mood inside the house. As soon as Musa left, Khulu quietly said, "Kuchi, my child, Musa is your mother. I am sorry she has never acted like one toward you. I should have told you when you were small that she is your mother. She promised long ago, when you climbed Pasiwe, to tell you yourself that she is your mother. Instead, she took you up the mountain to show you the land stolen by Europeans. I begged her many times as you grew up. But I want to talk to you to prevent you from going to jail someday. Your tongue is sharp like a cobra's fang, and your hands are angry. There are things you must never say or do to others, no matter how they upset you. Musa cried all night after you suffocated her. You nearly killed her. I feel sad. Please, Kükuchi, do something about your temper. You need to apologize to Musa when she returns. Tell her, 'Mother Musa, I am sorry for what I did. I was angry. But I shouldn't have done that.' Will you say that, Kuchi?"

"No, Khulu. She needs to apologize first for how she treats you. I will never apologize to her. Maybe I'm an embarrassment to her because of my skin colour. Why is she ashamed to say I am her daughter?"

"Don't start, Kükuchi. She can't be embarrassed?"

Lobola furore

The upcoming wedding did not bring happiness to the family. Kükuchi asked Khulu what she knew about the man Musa wanted to marry. All Khulu knew about the man called Jobe Sithole was that he was an ANC activist. She asked Kükuchi to write a letter to inform Salu about the unhappy situation. Salu's response was quick. She took the overnight Express train from Estcourt and arrived like a hurricane.

Crashing into the kitchen, she demanded, "What is this I hear?"

Khulu said, "We didn't expect you this soon, Ntombiphelele..."

"Forget about me. Musa is getting married? Have you, township folks, turned into Europeans?"

Musa finally agreed to introduce her fiancé to the family next Sunday. Salu was angry and told Musa she didn't need an introduction, but the man first had to send his delegation to ask for Musa's hand. By the end of the day, Salu had relaxed because Dassie kept telling silly jokes that made her laugh.

Jobe Sithole arrives promptly, dressed in a black suit; he seems to be someone heading to preside over a funeral. They all stay seated in Dassie's makeshift bedroom, which doubles as a dining room during the day.

Khulu chats casually with Sithole while Salu remains silently grim, openly eyeing Sithole from head to toe. Surprisingly, Musa looks upbeat and carefree after the family meeting with Sithole. Kükuchi and Khulu start to suspect that Musa might have staged and rehearsed the whole episode with Salu. Musa assures Khulu and Salu that Sithole will be sending his representatives soon to begin the lobola negotiations.

Salu says, "How can he start talking about lobola when our beer is already brewing under the garden? These politicians smoke elephant dung, I'm sure."

***

Final lobola negotiations begin early beneath my orange tree. Several relatives arrive, jostling for space in the house, as Toby comes searching for me, her face moist with tears.

Toby and I step outside and lean against the latrine.

"Something terrible, Kükuchi. Papi is dead..."

Toby's words make my stomach turn, and I feel dizzy.

According to her, the police found Papi's body on the 10th Avenue crossing in Alexandra. Although he had severe stab wounds on his chest, little blood was visible around him. The police think he was killed elsewhere.

"Do they know who was responsible for his death?"

"Maybe they do, but I'm finished with this now. My mother's cousin came to tell me that Mendi is the prime suspect."

"Mendi?"

"Of course. Who else could it possibly be...?"

Papi was a kind man. When he came to deliver bangles and earrings last time, he told me he was still taking care of his disabled sister. He said he loves her, and she will be the first member of his family to pass matric.

"What are we going to do now? The earrings move very quickly. The higher the price, the more people buy."

"Think, Kükuchi. Let's eliminate them and move on completely. You need to axe Mendi. Clear him from your mind. He's trouble, and maybe his hands are covered in blood."

***

When I walk back into the kitchen, I see Salu grumbling, even accusing Khulu of failing to control the 'ill-disciplined' Dassie. The rest of the women in the family listen quietly, their curiosity piqued.

Khulu responds softly in an unclear and unpersuasive way, "I discipline him. I go to his teachers and to the principal. I talk to him and get him to behave."

Salu is not satisfied. She says, "Dassie needs nothing but a firm hand, which only I can provide in Draycott. I'll give him work. My curfew is six to six, not this looseness I see here in your township, with children coming back home at midnight. There are no loitering streets in Draycott."

"Dassie is a good boy," Khulu protests. "It's the township life that's corrupting him..."

"Flies never visit an egg that has no crack," Salu retorts. The rest of the women remain silent spectators to the entertaining little feud between sisters.

Khulu sounds frantic, and with her breathing becoming noticeably strained, she keeps trying, "Dassie has had a tough time. He must be helped to grow..."

"Assisted? You can't help plants grow by pulling them up higher. Do you want to help him end up in jail?"

Khulu comes out the worse for wear after the uneven exchange. My heart grows heavy for her.

***

Salu was eager to finish brewing her African beer when Khulu introduced Jozi to the relatives. Jozi was Sithole's sixteen-year-old daughter, who had come to help out. When Salu saw her, she took a liking to her and quickly called her 'My eager beaver' because of her hard work.

Tina visited Salu to discuss her previous promise to take her to Draycott. Salu was emotional and said she would coordinate with her parents. Tina hesitated about involving her parents in the secret trip, but Salu reassured her that she would figure out the best course of action.

"You promise you won't tell my mother when you come to get me?"

"Promise. We shall go to Draycott, just the two of us."

Five men, including Dodo and my other uncle, Funani, slaughtered a goat and a sheep.

Salu said of Funani, "Like father, like son; Funani's father could talk the hind legs off a donkey."

After the rituals, they began discussions with four delegates from the Sithole family. There were dozens of beer bottles and two calabashes of African brew. The afternoon was advancing, and the women waited eagerly for the results.

Musa told the impatient women, "We should have had at least one teetotaller in there. What's taking them so long?"

"Yes, those men drink like an Arabian camel," added Salu.

Meanwhile, Mkhize stood in his yard, watching the events at Khulu's house with sadness because he hadn't received an invitation.

After sunset, Dodo and Funani entered the vegetable garden where Salu, Khulu, and the rest of the women were waiting for the outcome of the talks.

The decisive moment had arrived! As he unveiled the report, Dodo said, "Regarding the talks about the lobola, we had a lengthy discussion and..."

"Dodo, cut the compost and tell us how many cows these people must give us," shouted Musa.

"Three cows plus £5.10," he said, ablaze with satisfaction.

Musa and the grannies leapt up shouting, "Three cows!"

Musa kept going, "You worthless relatives! How could you agree to sell me for just three cows? Do you realize what I am worth? I told you ten cows. I have a J.C., a Junior Certificate, First Class..."

"Musa, what do you know about culture? Your J.C. means nothing here," Dodo said defiantly.

Supporting Musa, Salu says, "Dodo, we told you; fifteen cows and ten sheep, didn't we?"

Following the lobola controversy, Salu told the relatives to reconvene for new talks in two weeks.

***

After he sobered up a bit, Funani asked me a curious question. He wanted my opinion of Dodo.

"Why are you concerned about Dodo?"

"Answer me, Kūkuchi. What do you think of Dodo?"

Funani's serious tone of voice bothered me a bit. When I shook my head in confusion, he kept going, "You can tell me. I'm your uncle, too. If anyone gives you trouble, come to me."

"Nobody gives me trouble."

"What about Dodo? He's never caused you any trouble, has he? Tell me the truth."

"The truth?" I stammered before turning back to the house. I knew Funani knew more than he was letting on.

Mkhize quickly responded to Khulu's request to lead the new lobola discussions. To everyone's quiet relief, Dodo boycotted the talks, claiming he alone had the final say in family matters.

On the day, Salu arrived unexpectedly.

"Didn't you say you won't come anymore?" Dassie asked Salu.

"I changed my mind. Smart people change their minds. You will realize that fast because you're sharp."

Salu had other plans up her sleeve, as the rest of the family soon discovered. One of the family negotiators she brought with her was Khanyile from Lusikisiki. Since I drove out the grey-haired man and his rugby-playing son on that dry afternoon, I have always felt terrible and scared. Throughout the day, I avoided eye contact with Khanyile. However, my prayers seemed to go unheard. The gentle old man cornered me the next day and said, "You remember Zazi, my son? He is your cousin, you know... or is he your uncle? The Eastern Province selected him, but he can't be a Springbok."

"Why can't he be a Springbok?"

"Because he is African. Only white people can be Springboks. Zazi showed me a paper cutout with a picture of you when you won silver here in Johannesburg. He was bragging in Lusikisiki that you are his cousin and that you might win bronze in the Olympics in the future..."

"Bronze? Just bronze?"

"Remember, international competitions are tough. Do you have a message for him, my child?"

I thought to myself, 'Thank God he did not tell Salu how I kicked them out of the house that lonely afternoon'.

However, just then, Salu appeared and gently told the old man, "Khanyile, you are my cousin. I trust you to teach our traditional ways to these township youngsters. Remember what I said in my letter; at least ten to fifteen cows..."

"Cousin," the regal man replied in his measured tone, "ten cows? That's worth a lot of money these days. Let's settle for five and some spare cash, if possible. That's all."

"No, we shall settle for what we instruct you, Cousin."

"Salu, I think you've lost touch with your culture. Lobola isn't about money or cattle. This is all new to me. That's why we're facing marital problems these days."

"Musa is brilliant, and she passed her Junior Certificate with distinctions. What more do they want? If you don't do what we say, Cousin, I'll toss you out of here like Kūkuchi did when you last came to JoBurg with Zazi. Remember?" I almost wet myself.

Later, Khanyile ordered something strong to drink while he balanced himself on the bench. I hesitated awkwardly before he beamed his quaint smile and said, "If you don't give a calabash of beer to your elders, you will never learn their proverbs."

Although I didn't care much for Khanyile's proverbs, I was willing to offer him as many calabashes as he wanted, anything to soothe my conscience. However, I was curious to find out how Salu had discovered my foolish act, which I had always believed was my well-kept secret. I lacked the courage to ask Khanyile where and how they spent that fateful night.

During a quiet moment, I asked Salu about my silly secret with Khanyile and Zazi. Ignoring my question, Salu said, "We must preserve our ways as Africans. But we must use our heads at the same time."

I felt more insignificant than ever before. One can handle reprimand or punishment, but if people don't even challenge you about your wrongdoings, it makes you feel unimportant.

The talks had barely started when the families agreed on twelve cows. Musa returned, hopping like a darter. Before she left, Salu told Khulu, "I have gloomy feelings about Musa's marriage. Do your thing, but count me out from now on. If they have a big wedding, I won't be there."

Salu's words cut like a dagger through Khulu's heart. She sat down and said, "Why, my mother's child? You cannot abandon me now."

CHAPTER 12

Keep your fish and chips.

Kükuchi grew increasingly paranoid about Mendi's disappearance. She suspected Dassie knew more than he was willing to admit. However, since she was preparing for Provincial field trials, she tried to put Mendi out of her mind. The 'Non-white' body, the South African Sports Association (SASA), had organized the meeting in Orlando East. In contrast, the white body, the South African Athletics Union (SAAU), had scheduled theirs for later in the year. SASA had been in disagreement with the white Union over alleged complicity in the government's discriminatory policies. They also accused the South African Olympic Games Association (SAOGA), an equally all-white body, of duplicity. SASA was enraged that only whites could represent South Africa in international sports like the Commonwealth and Olympic Games, while Black associations remained sidelined.

The Apartheid Interior Minister, Theophilus Dönges, stated that sports in South Africa would continue based on the principles of separate development. He announced his government's sports policy, saying that white and black athletes would participate in individual activities and that laws would prevent any racial mixing. Dönges declared that blacks would not be allowed to compete internationally at the expense of whites.

For Kükuchi, everything seemed like a dead end for African athletes. Although she had been less than convincing in local tournaments, her scores compared favourably with those of the white Provincial records. She consulted Mrs Posa, whose response should have prepared her for the worst. Posa said, "My child, every generation has its problems and struggles, but sometimes many generations get engaged in the same struggles. It is up to one generation to break the back of the problem."

Kükuchi pictured herself as an older adult, telling stories and legends to children around campfires. She wondered if she could pass down wise sayings to future generations, like the cryptic one Mrs Posa shared with her. However, she thought Miss Lumka's constant talks about hell and brimstone were more appealing than Posa's proverbs. The struggle intensified, and the black association worked diligently to ensure that the officials involved included the names of black athletes in the selection process for the South African games. They faced a tough challenge because neither the government nor international organizations recognized black associations. By submitting black names, they hoped to call the white Union's bluff and demonstrate the uselessness of the government's colour-bar policy. Kükuchi was pleased to see her name on the list.

***

Musa was having a lively chat with Dassie on the *stoep* when I reluctantly joined them. Then, the mood shifted. I told Musa about the upcoming tournament at Orlando East and asked her to come with me to see, for the first time, how I threw my javelin. Showing little interest in my activities, Musa glanced at my face, stood up, dusted off her skirt, and strolled away into the night.

Dassie noticed my effort to hold back the tears, although he could hardly see the pain in my heart. He said, "If you want Musa to join you, say to her, 'Musa, I am proud of you. I want you to be proud of me when I throw my javelin. That's what Rosemarie said to her mother. That's when she started attending her tournaments."

"Go away, Dassie."

After Musa's snub, I started thinking about leaving White City for good. Musa came back late at night and set four packets of fish and chips on the kitchen table.

Dassie asked her, "Musa, why did you ignore Kūkuchi when she asked you to accompany her to Orlando? She wanted you to support her like other mothers."

"I can't go there."

I jumped up and confronted Musa, "And why not? Are you ashamed of me because of my lack of melanin? You gave birth to me, remember?"

"You are nasty. That's a horrible thing to say. Why can't you be nice like Toby?"

"Nice! Which Toby are you boasting about? How much do you know about that dagga-sniffing girl?"

"I brought you some fish and chips. Let us dish up and eat."

"Keep your fish and chips, Musa. I don't want fish and chips. You never want to go out with me anywhere. I can't ask Khulu to go with me; she isn't feeling well. Don't you want to see me throw my javelin? I am now competing with the best girls in the country."

Musa hummed an indistinct tune and disappeared into the kitchen to dish up.

"Kūkuchi," Khulu said quietly, "let us eat. We will discuss Orlando High tomorrow. Your principal will be there because she is an official. Maybe that will help."

Dassie sat quietly, lost in his thoughts.

***

Although the officials at Orlando had tried to prepare the grounds for the events, the javelin runway had poorly marked lines, making it difficult even to see the scratch line. When Kūkuchi's regional team arrived, the athletes from Springs jumped off their bus like an ambush to taunt them. Known for their insolent antics, the athletes from Springs continued their theatrics throughout the day. Posa immediately told Kūkuchi's group to ignore the rowdy crowd but focus on their performances.

A large group of coloured people from Kliptown arrived. They had decided to align themselves with the African movement because they saw themselves as Africans. Meanwhile, the rest of the coloureds were still trying to win favour with the white community, who, nonetheless, treated them just as they did anyone they considered non-white.

Disagreements among the officials threatened to scupper the Orlando tournament. One of the hitches related to concerns about the involvement of athletes with 'dubious records', a metaphor for records achieved in the absence of a white presiding official. The umpire disqualified three athletes after they failed to meet the qualification marks. However, a section of the crowd of supporters groaned with anger. Ultimately, sense prevailed, and all athletes participated.

No sooner had the events commenced than two cars, escorted by three marked police vans, made their way toward the makeshift tent for officials. The convoy comprised eleven armed white police and a group of white athletics union representatives who had come to observe the African events on behalf of their white Union. The sudden appearance of whites nearly sparked a riot. The marshals had their hands full, with spectators from Kliptown, Phefeni, and Orlando East surging forward and crowding the field of play. Passions ran high when some regions threatened to withdraw unless all white visitors left the field immediately.

Mrs Posa confidently moved toward the middle of the chaotic field and settled the disturbance. Her words likely made a strong impression, as the crowd swarmed around her, and the contest began. Meanwhile, the white group continued their quiet briefing, examining the field and taking notes in their notebooks.

The sight of Rosemarie among white dignitaries surprised Kükuchi. Carrying her camera and notebook, she appeared like a high-ranking official. Seventeen girls from various parts of the Transvaal had gathered to compete for the javelin crown. Each was given six attempts, according to the rules at the time. While four girls posed intense competition, Kükuchi feared Lesedi the most. She had heard about Lesedi's antics—her flamboyance and gum-slurping from Springs—and secretly dreaded meeting her face-to-face. Though only fifteen, Lesedi looked like she was pushing twenty. Her untidy style and rude attitude made Kükuchi uneasy. Lesedi shot a nostalgic smile in Kükuchi's direction, bringing Tina's cute face to mind. When she wasn't fooling around or throwing the javelin, Lesedi excelled in track and field, especially in the high jump. Only Gemini, a talented coloured high jumper from Kliptown, had beaten her before. Gemini's face looked distressed, and even small disturbances made her cry. She was deeply upset because her family had buried her older brother the week earlier. He had been throwing stones at a police van with some other kids, and the police said they used rubber bullets to disperse them.

Lesedi approached Kükuchi, her wicked smile widening with each trouble-making step. She extended her arm happily, and they shook hands. Then she said, "I heard about you, Kükuchi. They told me you can beat me, but I throw better than you. Everybody knows me."

Kükuchi taunted, "I've never heard of you. Who are you?"

"I'm Lesedi from Springs. Don't you know me?"

"No. Why should I know you?"

"Even I did not know you. I know you because of your colour. That's how I knew it was you."

Khulu's words flashed through Kükuchi's mind, 'Does it bother you if people use insulting names to refer to you?'

Kükuchi retorted, "I see you brought a whole bunch of kitchen-girl maids like you to help you win."

"Who do you call a kitchen girl?" shouted Lesedi as she spat her chewing gum. "Do you know my father has many shops in Springs?"

Kükuchi walked away, sporting a wry smile. A tall young woman who introduced herself as Maluti from the Northern Province immediately greeted her. Maloti was a well-known javelin thrower whose records had caused quite a stir among white athletes.

Lesedi's first attempt was a paltry 37m, and they declared it illegal because the tip of her javelin landed outside an area called 'sector.' However, she kept her usual teasing game, always daring her opponents before she produced her best for the day. After her two hesitant throws, Kükuchi pipped Lesedi at the mark with a surprise 41.3m, but the Springs girl seemed unaffected.

Just then, Rosemarie, accompanied by her sharp body mist, approached the black girls. At over 5'8, she cut an intimidating figure.

"Your throw is weak," she said with a straight face to the African girls. "You have to run faster and time your 'line-and-release.' I saw you girls step over the line time and time again. There are no rules here," she said.

"Who are you?" asked Gloria, one of the coloured girls from Kliptown.

"I am Rosemarie. If you don't know me, you shouldn't be throwing a javelin. You people have a long way to go," Rosemarie added snootily. "And you," meaning Lesedi, "You could do better if you stopped fooling around. As for you," meaning Kükuchi, "what shall I say? Try to run faster than you did last time before each throw. I don't see any competition here."

Kükuchi murmured, 'Run faster than before? This girl is talking nonsense.'

Then Lesedi shouted a township chant, whipping up emotion against the whites, '*Niyabesaba na*?' The field responded with a resounding, '*Hayi asibasabi, siyabafuna'*.

The frightened white convoy rushed out of the grounds in a panic.

After the qualifying heats, only six hopefuls remained. The number continued to shrink with rapid eliminations. Kükuchi took her turn. She paused for a few seconds to gather her nerves as the fear of prying eyes threatened to overtake her. The throw was good but declared 'not legal' because the back tip of the javelin hit the ground first. For the throw to be valid, the javelin must land on its front tip. She tried again, rushing down the runway for her last desperate attempt. She stumbled and nearly fell, screeching to a halt just before her pre-delivery stride. It would have been a poor throw. Luckily, her left foot hadn't touched the ground as she moved to recover. She slowly walked back to try again. With the corner of her eye, she saw an official dart and an eagle staring at her, signalling it was her last chance. This time, her strides from start to finish looked right, and she ran back triumphantly.

***

Kükuchi was satisfied with her performance, especially considering she had to face stiff competition from top rivals. Unable to control herself, she hurried back home to tell his family about her bronze. She found Khulu and Musa sitting there, relaxing. Khulu happily congratulated Kükuchi and said that everyone was proud of her performance. Kükuchi started telling them about the coloured girls. Then suddenly, Dassie appeared, interrupting his sister.

"And Rosemarie was there..." Dassie said. "You didn't see me because I was sitting in the tree."

Musa exclaimed, "What did the white girl want in a black race?"

"She is an officer," said Kükuchi.

"She must be an official for white athletes. Our officials can't attend their white meetings. They would be arrested."

Kükuchi heaved and repeated, "I won bronze, Musa."

Khulu said, "You see now, Musa, Kuchi is doing well. You know my legs are sore; that's why I could not go."

Dassie said, "They robbed her, Khulu. She beat all the girls. Rosemarie was there, but she ran away because Kükuchi was going to beat her."

Kükuchi was proud of her lying brother. The media hopped onto the story, with *Township News* heaping praises on Kükuchi, referring to her as 'a disabled wonder girl'. Kükuchi responded angrily right away, rebutting the insinuation that she was disabled. The newspaper never referred to her as 'disabled' again. A few days later, the security police came to arrest Musa after she organized a boycott of a Chinese outlet opposite Moroka Police Station. They further prohibited newspapers from running the story of her arrest.

But Kükuchi had become a star across African townships.

CHAPTER 13

Deserted Kriel's Farm

Dassie mumbled something in my ear about Mendi requesting to meet me somewhere on the outskirts of the township. I was stunned. Dassie sounded serious because he cautioned, "You don't have to go there, but I know I can't stop you."

"Why tell me if you don't want me to go there?"

Dassie shrugged, and as he walked away, he said, "Remember your flick, Kükuchi."

There was no point reminding me about my flick knife, as it was forever my 'dairy's' portable item. After much hesitation, I sneaked out while Khulu was fiddling with her sewing machine and followed Dassie's complex directions. Mendi's hideaway was a ghostly, dilapidated farmhouse across the Klipspruit stream. The sun was a red ball touching the hill when I reached the ground overlooking the old farm. I had never been that close to the bank of the Klipspruit stream since our townships started losing young girls in numbers. Sofasonke Mpanza and his squatter movement had successfully taken control of Kriel's farm. Before that, the white man and his household owned every part of the land, along with its birds, wild animals, and the stream of pure water flowing down the valley to the Vaal Dam. My eyes scanned across the beautiful land evacuated by the whites, who had no defence against the expanding African shantytown. I wondered how the white family must have felt about losing such pristine property to the Africans they so disliked. The peppers taste the same. I think the whites also tasted the same thing that the Drakensberg people felt when the British invaded and seized their land by force. The difference was that whites always received compensation when they lost land. The local black newspaper called it reparations before the apartheid government banned the article. I only learned the subtle difference between reparation and compensation much later in life. Reparations refer to the policy taken to address historical injustices such as apartheid or colonialism. Compensation refers to financial payments made in response to a specific act of injustice. Cautiously moving along a cluster of willow trees, I slowly stepped forward. A gentle breeze blew, accompanied by the lively sounds of whining crickets and croaking frogs. After crossing the stream, I skirted around the abandoned flowerbed. I took in the sharp scent of the decaying, woody nature. Traces of old rusty wire fences with corroded steel poles were still visible. Meanwhile, the previously lush pastures, which still shone brightly in their scenic green, seemed forlorn and out of place. I had to walk carefully on the abandoned animal grid that marked the entrance in better days. The once-thriving cattle farm had become home to remnants from various rural tribal areas. Kriel's land would soon bustle with activity, cluttered with corrugated shelters and housing destitute mothers with large-bellied children who looked as if they had kwashiorkor. The maize field remained visible, and the new African owners had started cultivating it for survival, using stacks of manure and goat's milk. Sparse bushes sheltered the farm, and the rocky peak extended as far as the eye could see. The imposing farmhouse was hidden from the vantage point of the stream.

Mendi rested on the railing, close to a giant avocado tree, curiously watching me struggle my way up the ill-fated line of trees.

"You're here!" he said mutely.

Aside from his messy hair and dry skin, Mendi appeared neat and attractive. I felt sorry to see him look that vulnerable.

"Mendi, the police are looking for you."

"Why?"

"You know why... because of Mkhize's *rediffusion*. Why did you steal it?"

"It was there when I left his house. Someone went there after me and stole it. What use is that thing to me? Who wants to listen to European violins all day long?"

"But I found you enjoying *'Thoko Shukuma'* last time. Did you think you could steal it and use it without any wires to connect it?"

"Did you hear that Papi is dead?" I asked after a few moments of despair.

"Yes, someone killed him..."

"The police think you know who did. Did you kill Papi?"

"Let us go in there," he pointed at the run-down old house that was once the pride of the white family.

"In there? Why?"

I thought the flick-knife hidden somewhere in my body would come in handy should Mendi start trouble, but I remained uneasy all the same. We hobbled through the neglected lawn toward the building. A young woman with two hungry-looking babies, one on her back and a slightly older boy staggering by her side, eyed me with great suspicion. She was mending old coir mattresses found on the disused farm. A short distance away, two men who took a nervous glance at me were threading wires through the fence as if repairing every broken scrap in sight. The walls inside had graffiti in red reading 'Kaffir Natives.' The Kriel family must have been despondent, having to vacate their mansion to make room for Africans. The empty bathroom had its water taps and bathtub removed, leaving nothing of value behind. Mendi opened one of the doors into his makeshift bedroom. His clean blankets covered the mattress while his personal effects hung on one of the two benches. The bedroom looked too large for one person but aptly sized for one of Kriel's children. Mendi told me with humour and irony that he ejected a man who snored and spoke gibberish in his sleep. The unfortunate man moved to occupy one of the rooms upstairs. Feeling awkward in such an isolated space, I insisted that we go outside.

"Why, you don't want to sleep here with me?"

"No. Khulu will have a heart attack if I'm not home by five."

Mendi took my hand, and we sat under the shade of the avocado tree. The Kriels had many trees, including gum, maple, and pine species, as well as a variety of fruit trees.

"Dassie told me you are still doing your javelin."

"Yes. And you? Why don't you come back and tell the police you know nothing about Papi's death? You must do the javelin again. I can't do the javelin without you."

"It's because of that stupid Papi! He brought three other guys from Alexandra with him to attack me. Why didn't he come alone? He is a coward."

"He is dead now, Mendi. He wanted his money. You stole his money. Why?"

"It was my share. I do things they promise, but they don't pay me. What must I do?"

"You lied to me. You never told me about Toby. Is she still your girl?"

"No. I just went to Toby to get my money from these people."

"What about your granny? She is crying over you. When last did you see her?"

Mendi made a face and looked at the ground. He then lifted his head and stared at the sky as if he were seconds from crying. I put my hand on his shoulder and said, "Go with me. I'll ask Papa Mkhize to hide you in his house again. He knows many things. The police will never find you. Your mother will be happy to see you."

The young mother with a baby on her back and another napping on the concrete floor strolled toward us. She asked for sixpence to buy bread. Mendi gave her one shilling.

"Dassie said you wanted to see me. Why?"

Mendi shook his head and said, "Dassie is a liar. Have you noticed? I don't like what Papi did, dragging you and Toby into selling goods. He did things behind my back. I'm happy Papi is dead. I'll get all my money now. When I grow up, I'll build a big shop and buy a big lorry, and I'll be rich..."

"What if the police arrest you? Your granny comes to Khulu crying every day, and she tells her she is unhappy with your behaviour. Come back to school. Posa will help you. She said you are a great athlete and that one day you will beat the Europeans."

"It is late now, Kũkuchi. I don't want you to walk alone in the dark. Do you agree to put up here till tomorrow?"

If I do, Khulu will tell Mkhize… and who knows what kind of panic the police might trigger?

I stayed with Mendi until early evening and felt sad for him because he had nowhere else to go. Then, I struggled back home.

CHAPTER 14

Papi

When Kükuchi reached her street, two of her girlfriends quickly emerged from the shadows and intercepted her. They were Niki – a cat's cradle enthusiast who once accused Kükuchi of being a spy – and Pinki, her sister. Niki spoke fast, whispering a swarm of words that made no sense. Pinki was not whispering. She was shaking. She told Kükuchi about the presence of some white police officers near her home.

Kükuchi panicked. She started shaking, too.

"What do the white policemen want?"

"How do we know? They start by moving to Toby's house, but they find nothing. Toby sends us here to warn you..."

"But by the time we get here," said Niki, "the police cars are all around your street."

"Where is Toby right now?"

"We don't know. You go to Mkhize. He wants to see you. He is angry with you."

Before the two girls vanished, Kükuchi grabbed the cat's-cradle string from Pinki and said, "I'll bring back your string, Niki."

Kükuchi's body felt like liquid. 'I am cursed,' she said to herself. She finally went to Mkhize's place and opened the door without knocking. Mkhize was furious. He pulled Kükuchi to the corner, slammed the door shut, and locked it.

"Kükuchi, do you want me to go to jail? Why did you send Dassie with this package?"

Dassie had earlier given Mkhize some merchandise from Toby to hide at Mkhize's place.

"Oh, Papa. Maybe Dassie thought it would be safe with you."

"So, he was not lying when he said the stolen goods are yours. Do you know what one of the police officers called me? 'The big fish.'"

"But you know you are not the big fish, Papa."

"So, what should I say to the police about the goods?"

"Papa, please keep them. Hide them under your bed for me. I'll fetch them later. I didn't send Dassie to do this. He always does things, you know him. Just put the package among your muti bones and other stuff from Zululand where the police won't look."

The very idea of standing in front of the white police chilled Kükuchi's body to the bone. She decided to bide her time until the coast cleared. She rushed to the back of Tatenda's shop, where she once stumbled upon Dassie and Tina in a secret embrace. There, she paused for some minutes considering her options. For a fleeting instant, she thought about fleeing to Draycott. However, she felt she would be letting Khulu down. So, she resolved to make her appearance in style. She approached her home, playing her cradle, whistling, and chewing her gum. Three white police officers sat awkwardly in the tiny kitchen, conversing with Khulu in Afrikaans and sipping Rooibos tea. Khulu's linguistic ability was the envy of many. In South Africa, Afrikaans provided easier access to a variety of privileges from white township superintendents, which Khulu exploited whenever possible. Kŭkuchi peeped and noticed Khulu leaning against the kitchen wall. She knew her grandma was tired, but that there was nothing she could do but try to stand on her own two feet when faced with white males. This reminded Kŭkuchi of her class, where students were required to come forward and stand against the wall as part of their punishment. Kŭkuchi stopped whistling but continued playing with her cat's cradle, chewing her gum on the bench.

"Yes, Faty," Captain Venter said, "we have been waiting. Where have you been?"

Kŭkuchi thought the man resembled a picture of one of the kings of England from her history book. However, she hadn't seen the paintings lately, except for that of King Henry VIII, who had married many wives and then founded the Church of England. Kŭkuchi didn't answer but kept chewing her gum, staring at the police as if they weren't there.

"Tell the Baas where you come from, Kuchi," Khulu pleaded.

"Outside."

"Outside? Your granny here tells us she doesn't know where you are, and you say you come from outside? Do you know a man called Papi?"

The question jolted Kŭkuchi, but she survived, thanks to the chewing gum gyrating in her mouth.

"No. Who is Papi?"

The younger white man said, "Papi is the man who once assaulted Mendi. You do know Mendi, don't you?"

"Yes, I know Mendi."

"Aaahh," screeched Venter. "Now, Fat Girl, something terrible happened to Papi. Do you know what happened to Papi?"

"I told you I don't know Papi. How can I know what happened to him?"

"Kŭkuchi!" shouted Khulu.

"Kŭkuchi," said the third officer, "We know you are a good girl. You even swing that javelin thing, and we want to help you, but some people here in White City don't like you because you're different. But we like you because we know you are clever."

"Who are those people? I don't know anyone in White City who doesn't like me."

Venter said, "You have been going around with a man, a criminal. His name is Mendi, and he is a bad man. Can you tell us where Mendi is?"

"I don't know."

"When was the last time you were with him?"

"He was with Papa Mkhize long ago, and he ran away."

"Okay, you say you have been... outside. You didn't happen to meet Mendi anywhere?"

"No."

Venter heaved with impatience and stood up gently, followed by the other two.

"Listen, Fat Girl, when you go outside next time, look around, and if you see Mendi, tell Mr Mkhize or the superintendent. Will you do that?"

The air of apprehension lingered on. Khulu was breathing heavily long after the police had left. She remained seated on the concrete floor, feeling humiliated and tired. Kükuchi helped her to her feet.

"I think I suffered a heart attack, Kükuchi. That's why I don't have the strength to stand up on my own."

"Oh, Khulu! There's nothing wrong with your heart. When a heart stops, you die. You don't have a heart attack, I know."

"Is that what you want, Kükuchi? Do you want to see me dead?"

Kükuchi gave Khulu a glass of cold water from the bucket.

"Please, Kükuchi, stop walking alone when it gets dark."

"What did the police want?"

"They searched everywhere, Kükuchi. They said they were looking for stolen goods."

"But we don't keep stolen goods here, Khulu," Kükuchi responded, her face as straight as a kingfisher's beak.

"Do you know that for sure, Kükuchi? They searched everywhere, and then they found £40 under our mattress."

"What? And what did you say to them?"

"Kükuchi, tell the truth. Where did you get so much money from...?"

"Money...?"

Mkhize budged in, anxious to know what Khulu and Kükuchi had told the police.

"Nothing, Papa," Kükuchi assured him.

"White people are clever beings! I am worried, Khulu. They know something. I suspect they will be back at dawn to bundle me into a cold van like a pocket of potatoes from a farm."

Mkhize dashed out, and Kükuchi raced after him. When they reached a safe distance, she told Mkhize about Mendi's whereabouts.

"Did you tell the police?"

"No, Papa."

"You did well, because I want to catch him myself before the police do, and then I shall strangle him slowly, slowly until he is dead; just like King Dingane did to Ndlela, that conspirator who helped kill King Shaka. I want my *rediffusion* back."

"He said he did not steal it, Papa, but he said he wants to build shops and buy lorries."

"He smokes dagga, Kuchi, my child. That's why he is confused. Many boys are roaming the streets of Johannesburg, stealing and killing. Still, when they kick the bucket, we put them in expensive coffins and read obituaries written by their *Tsotsi* friends."

"Oh, Papa. Mendi does not kill."

"You know that for sure?"

A day later, Mkhize gathered his search party, composed of Zulu men from Pimville Hostel. By the time they reached the dilapidated farm, Mendi had already fled. The squatting community had also escaped, leaving their personal belongings scattered around, along with the food they had been cooking. Only the young mother, accompanied by her two emaciated toddlers, stayed behind. She immediately approached Mkhize and begged him for sixpence to buy bread. Inside the farmhouse, Mkhize searched around and found the remnants of his radio broadcast. He asked the woman about Mendi. She replied, "He's over here or over there, that one. Then, she asked for two shillings to give more details about Mendi. Mkhize handed her two shillings.

The young mother said, "Mendi left with an albino girl, and no one has seen him since. But he will be back with another girl."

Mkhize came back fuming. He went straight to confront Kūkuchi about Mendi's actual whereabouts. Musa was in the house this time. She stood behind Kūkuchi as Mkhize spoke.

"I know you left with him from Kriel's farm. Where did you go from there?"

Khulu said, "Kūkuchi, when the police asked you about Mendi, you said you didn't know where he was. Now we hear you went to the old farm to visit him, and you helped him disappear!"

"The police asked Kūkuchi, and she said nothing to them?" Musa put it calmly.

"She denied everything, and she was lying," Khulu responded angrily.

As soon as Mkhize walked out, Musa slowly pulled the bench, and noticing her ironic smile, she sat down and said, "Well, if Kūkuchi does not know where Mendi is, she can't tell the police where Mendi is. But she can tell us the truth. This is a family matter."

Khulu tut-tuttered with fury, "She must not tell the police? What kind of teaching is that? What if Mendi killed that man from Alexandra?"

"Kūkuchi does not know anything," Musa put it forcefully. "Kūkuchi won't tell the police because she knows nothing."

"Musa, how can you support this child's reckless behaviour? Did you know she had a stash of money hidden under the mattress? Where does she get that much money from?"

"She will tell us about the money, but she does not know Mendi's whereabouts. You will tell us about the money, won't you, Kūkuchi... because this is home?"

"I'm not telling anyone anything."

"Good for you. Tell no one," Musa said triumphantly.

Two weeks later, a black and white police force descended on Kriel's farm. They also searched the previously whites-only cemetery nearby, arrested men, women, and children, and charged them with trespassing. Then, the investigators spent half the day digging up parts of the ground around the willow trees and along the stream. Captain Venter arrived early the next day, accompanied by an army of blackjacks (African municipal police) and sniffer dogs. He placed a ring of black constables around the scene while the detectives, primarily white, examined the ground thoroughly. No sooner had the cadaver dogs started rummaging than they made a gruesome discovery: a shallow grave on the bank of the stream near one of the willow trees. The spot was just a stone's throw from the giant avocado tree that Mendi used for shade against the scorching sun. The unidentified, decomposed body was that of a teenage girl buried with her hands tied behind her back.

Panic erupted when the media got hold of the story. The parents of the other missing girls were distraught and felt powerless. Community leaders blamed the police for incompetence and a lack of effort in investigating cases involving black children. Meanwhile, Venter's team searched thoroughly through the farm, along the stream's banks, and inside abandoned boreholes for several days, looking for more bodies. Rumours spread everywhere, with Mendi the main person of interest. Despite some assurances that the police were following strong leads, Mendi remained at large, and nothing happened for many months. A few weeks later, the townships awoke to shocking headlines from *Township News*, which had uncovered what it called a major scoop based on a tip. The paper reported that during their frantic search on the farm, the police had found a human skeleton deep inside one of the boreholes. The tenants had allegedly stopped construction around that particular borehole. The informant told *Township News* that, according to forensic experts, the remains belonged to a middle-aged Caucasian woman who might have died twenty years earlier. The state promised to release details regarding the borehole case. However, in an ironic twist, the same state raided *Township News*, detained the editor, and banned all media from further reporting on the item. In the African township, residents started spreading rumours that the woman was a victim of a family murder on Kriel's farm.

'Sisi Afrika'

My first day in sixth grade was boring. Mr Zondi looked grumpy. He made me share the rickety desk in the front row with a girl named Sandy. The closest I had sat to her before was in Lumka's Sunday school classes.

Zondi murmured amid the learners' chuckles, "Many are called, but few throw the javelin. My girl," Zondi continued, "standard six is no Dube train to ride in your sleep. If you fail, don't bring your chicken-farm grandmother here to blame me. Ask her to talk to the principal. She's the one who thinks you are Winifred Edgerton."

"And who is that?" I asked amidst a drone of bewilderment.

The class, which had earlier paid little attention to Zondi's dressing-down, whirled around and gazed at me with some interest.

"Never mind about Edgerson..." he said.

Sandy failed to pitch up the following day. In the afternoon, her mother, Mrs Keletso Komane, came driving a new sedan into the schoolyard. She wanted to speak with Mr Zondi. Sandy remained in the posh *Chevrolet* while the adults discussed her situation. Mrs Komane ordered Zondi to relocate her child as she was not comfortable sharing a desk with Kükuchi.

"Why not?"

"Sandy doesn't have to share a desk with Kükuchi because she is rude; she loves to fight, she's not civilized..."

Zondi advised Mrs Komane to teach her daughter good manners, as she was becoming unruly. "If you don't discipline Sandy, you will regret it one day."

Mrs returned to her car, furious.

Two days later, Zondi found Sandy's father at the gate, leaning against his own luxury *Fargo,* waiting for him. Like his sister, Kenny remained fixed in the car.

"Zondi, I am Sandy's father. My wife says you insulted her. Do you know who I am?"

"I know who you are. You just told me you are Sandy's father. What can I do for you?"

"I want you to find another desk... elsewhere in the class, for that white child..."

"We don't have a white child here?"

"I mean Kükuchi. I don't want my daughter sitting next to her. She has bad manners, and she will teach my child to disrespect teachers because she's rude. Sandy told me she was arguing with you about Edgerton on her first day in your class..."

"Is that what your child told you?"

"I don't like arguments. Perhaps you're unfamiliar with my name. I am a doctor... "

" You're a doctor where there are sick people."

"What? I'll speak to the principal."

"Go ahead. If you do not want to teach your child to respect other children, you will cry like a baby tomorrow."

"Do you know the authorities can fire you for contempt, Teacher?"

"I understand your issue, as well as your wife's. Kükuchi's colour isn't a problem because it's not contagious. Bring your child back, and she will learn a lot from Kükuchi because Kükuchi is smart."

***

The identity of the girl found in a shallow grave near the derelict farm remained a mystery. Newspapers drew speculation that she must have been between thirteen and sixteen years old. In such circumstances, if the authorities failed to find her relatives soon, the community would give her a pauper's funeral. Newspapers continued to carry a regular piece about the other missing girls.

Four months later, the Alexandra squad finally found Mendi casually walking with an unidentified girl. After escaping Mkhize's suspicious grip, Mendi had taken refuge with some Alexandra drug lords. The police detained three of his Alexandra gang friends but released them without charging them. Mendi refused to cooperate with the authorities. He admitted to knowing the girl found in the shallow grave, but insisted she was alive when he last saw her. He told the police her name was Sisi. The police couldn't find any more helpful information about Sisi.

Eventually, some women, including Bebe Mothopeng of Phefeni, arranged for a decent funeral for her. The Nightingales Ladies' Choir insisted on giving the unidentified girl a name, and they finally settled on 'Sisi Afrika.' They buried Sisi Afrika amid unprecedented outpourings of outrage and grief in the townships.

During Mendi's trial, *Township News* devoted a page to the proceedings. Whole communities were gnashing their teeth, baying for Mendi's blood. The crowds filled the court precinct at dawn and craned forward to make sure they missed nothing. Political organizations, which had remained silent throughout the ordeal, suddenly made their presence felt, chanting slogans and singing revolutionary songs until their voices cracked.

My Secrets are all Shrouded

Toby and three other girls met Kükuchi inside Donaldson to discuss the missing girls. It turned chaotic there. Toby was not smiling. Returning to her old foul-mouthed ways, she demanded that

Kükuchi explain why she never reported to the police that her uncle had abused her. Toby told the tongue-tied girls that Kükuchi and her family were hiding many secrets from White City.

Kükuchi remained speechless while Toby continued pounding her with questions, accusing her of 'covering up for your uncle Dodo.'

"You can hit me if you like. I'll fight back, and this time, you'll know who I am."

"Who told you about Dodo?"

Toby immediately called for Tina. The girls sat quietly and nervously, wondering what story Tina would tell when she arrived.

Strutting like a supermodel, Tina was all bouncy as she handed out sweets she had stolen from her trusting parents' grocery store. The Yellowwoods' shade kept hiding many secrets.

Toby said, "Forget about the sweets, you, Tina. Tell us what you said the other day about Dodo, Dassie's uncle."

Tina shot a glance at Kükuchi and was left speechless.

Toby said, "Okay, Tina, this means you're a liar. You told us something about Kükuchi and her uncle. Didn't you say Dassie told you Dodo did something bad to Kükuchi?"

Tina darted out of the awkward situation like a cheetah and hurried to her parents' grocery store to hide. Kükuchi felt as exposed as an otter.

***

Back home, I opened the drawer in my wardrobe where I usually hide my things, and pulled out my worn diary to check its contents. The pages where I had carefully described the abuse by Dodo were missing, and on a later page, there was an entry that said:

> *My secrets are all shrouded*
> *And hidden in my soul.*
> *In dimly lit surroundings,*
> *They scald like blazing fire.*
> *With whispers in my left ear,*
> *They taunt and mock, then slither*
> *Like cunning, deadly phantoms.*
> *These silly games must end.*

Feeling so ashamed after the altercation with Toby, I stayed indoors day and night until Toby visited me one morning. She was all smiles and in a playful mood. I expected her to apologize, but she didn't. When Mendi's court case resumed, an extra charge of Papi's murder suddenly appeared on the charge sheet. True to form, Mendi dismissed authority and denied ever killing Papi. His mother, Mrs Diale, was present every day, dressed sharply and sober.

Khulu went over to her on the first day, but she spurned her advances and maintained, "Mendi told me she was in love with Sisi, that decent girl they killed. Kükuchi was jealous. Someone killed Sisi, and Kükuchi knows who did it. Mendi told me. He never killed anyone. He is a nice boy. As for

Kükuchi...!"

On the charge of being an accessory after the fact, the court found Mendi guilty, despite the prosecution's failure to prove beyond a reasonable doubt who murdered Papi. The magistrate, Mr Duvenage, sentenced him to five years in prison at the Diepkloof Youth Detention Centre and ordered him to receive three strokes of the whip each month.

Mendi's grandmother died a few days later. Whatever sparks of hope she may once have nurtured in her bosom for Mendi's bright future flickered and went out before she did. She died a broken woman, mistakenly accounting for her entire life as a failure.

At the funeral, Mkhize said, "All the mothers carry too much pain they should not be carrying."

Mrs Posa, also one of the speakers, said, "Mrs Gasa's seemingly colourless life is a reflection of our society today. African women are swimming against a strong tide because Verwoerd and his government have not only destroyed the feeding scheme in African schools but also undermined African dignity as a whole. Someday, this country will face chaos. It takes time to build a community's conscience. When you remove nutrition from your children, you are like someone trying to build a house using sand as a foundation. I know Mrs Gasa well. Although she never attended school, she understood the value of education and tried her best to educate her grandson. I value her determination despite the many obstacles African women face. When she meets her God, He will understand and say, 'Well done'."

The Department of Bantu Education ordered Posa to report to headquarters, where she stood in a cold corridor for an hour and a half. One of the officials questioned her about what he had said at Gasa's funeral. After threatening to fire her, they forced her to sign an agreement stating that she would never again be involved in politics. When she refused, the threat of firing loomed over her like a Sword of Damocles. Her relatives in Moorstad offered to help her if the Apartheid government carried out its threat to fire her. However, the whole threat fizzled out. After Mendi's imprisonment, an atmosphere of anxiety and resentment took a new turn. Instead of serving as a solution to the disappearance of girls, Mendi's arrest rekindled the complaint that lawmakers did not take the problem seriously. People openly said, without fear, that if one white girl had to disappear, white soldiers would go out on a campaign the very same day. Two more girls disappeared after Mendi's detention.

Kükuchi breezed through with a first-class pass. She asked Khulu to relay the news to Musa.

"I'm sorry, Kuchi, there is no money to buy a cake and Coke; maybe next time."

"Don't worry about cakes, Khulu. I'm going to high school next year, and I am happy."

Late at night, when Dassie came back from his wanderings, Kükuchi whispered, "I have been waiting for you all afternoon. You wander the streets too much, even at night. I don't want someone to abduct you for *muti*. Were you with Tina or your benzine sniffing friends?"

"Who wants to know?"

"Dassie, those friends of yours will get you into trouble one day."

"Everyone is asleep, Kükuchi, and I am hungry. Where's my plate?"

"Before I give you your plate, tell me; in that packet you gave Papa Mkhize a long time ago…

there was £20. Mkize heard I had passed and returned the stuff you left with him, but there was no money inside. I want my money back."

"Did you ask Mkhize?"

"No."

"Why are you asking me, then?"

"Dassie, you are a thief and a liar. I know Mkhize will never steal from me. You are not getting any dish until you tell the truth. I want my £20. I need to buy a tunic and shoes."

Dassie's face fell, and Kükuchi felt sorry for him and left him alone.

Are you Inferior?

Kükuchi registered at Orlando High School, despite Salu's preference for the prestigious St. Peter's, where Oliver Tambo once taught. However, both Khulu and Musa were satisfied with Orlando High.

Musa excitedly showed Kükuchi her J.C. classroom. She said one day, the principal, accompanied by two white police officers, came into her classroom and told her to pack and go because she was a troublemaker. That was her last day at the school. She later wrote as a private candidate and passed with a distinction.

Kükuchi participated in various school activities, earning a range of athletics and debating awards. The reason why Musa was happy with Orlando High was that the school ran political awareness programmes. She encouraged Kükuchi to attend meetings to learn about the topics discussed by the teachers and other students regarding the government. Musa and Kükuchi talked about little else.

The teacher nominated Kükuchi to be her class monitor, which helped catapult her to the position of secretary of the Students' Representative Council. Many Township schools admired Kükuchi for her smooth tongue and fearless attitude.

One morning, Kükuchi asked the principal for permission to speak to the students at the assembly. She was granted thirty seconds. Kükuchi announced that the Prime Minister, Mr Hans Strydom, was dead. A riot of ululating and whistling erupted in response to the announcement, and the school had to disperse immediately. Students from other schools joined the spontaneous protest led by Kükuchi, shouting the Strydom chant, 'Get off Strydom,' until evening.

Following widespread unrest, authorities suspended classes in many townships. Student defiance increased, setting the stage for difficult times ahead in black education. Kükuchi spent a day at the Moroka Police Station and another five days at John Vorster Square, during which she refused to eat. *Township News* featured her story of incarceration alongside their ongoing report on the missing girls of White City.

When Kükuchi finally reached home, she discovered that the police had detained Musa. Surprisingly, when Musa returned three days later, she was in high spirits. After baking a moist fruitcake, she served slices to Mkhize and Sister Mohale. She mentioned they were celebrating Strydom's death, considering it a punishment from the ancestors. However, the celebration ended abruptly when Hendrik Verwoerd was appointed Prime Minister of South Africa, significantly disrupting the political scene. Verwoerd was responsible for ending the feeding schemes in African schools in 1953 and opposed providing African children with better education, believing it would give them access to the same opportunities as European children.

Verwoerd's succession sparked widespread unrest in the townships. People started chanting more militant tunes. One of these was Miriam Makeba's 'Here Comes the Black Man, Verwoerd,' a popular chant written by political activist, Vuyisile Mini.

> *Here comes the black man, Verwoerd.*
> *Beware of the Black man, Verwoerd.*

***

The rioting hurt my javelin training and prospects. School became difficult, and many teachers lost their jobs. In the evening, after Verwoerd's installation, Musa told us she wanted to have an important meeting with us after supper. Musa was no longer smiling as she had been for the past few days. I looked forward to the meeting, hoping Musa would announce her final departure back to Mayfair. Then again, I thought, 'Maybe she is finally getting married.' The invitation piqued our curiosity so much that supper took less than half the usual time. For the first time, we all appeared like a perfect family, gathered in one place under the flickering candlelight that strained our vision. As usual, Khulu wedged herself in her corner behind the door, out of the light's reach. Only her eyes gleamed across the dim kitchen, and her doek made her resemble a crested guinea fowl.

Softly, Musa began to address our wide-eyed family unit. She told us that a dark cloud had descended over South Africa because of the appointment of Verwoerd as Prime Minister. Each time she said 'Verwoerd,' she made a face as if she found the name a challenge to pronounce.

As Musa kept going, my thoughts drifted to her large candlelight shadow, cast like a ghostly caricature on the kitchen wall and stretching up the cylindrical ceiling. The cartoon-like shadow flickered quickly in response to the flickering light. My mind was so drawn to the amusing outline wobbling behind Musa that I struggled to focus on what was truly important in her message.

"You must look after each other, you two," Musa put it.

A careful chortle radiated from the direction of Khulu's dim corner, almost taking away from the solemnity of the occasion. Musa took a quick, unkind glance at the dark spot and then continued, raising her voice an octave higher, "If you don't help each other, the white man will rule over you forever. This Verwoerd man says you are inferior. He says you must get an inferior education because a good education is for their white children. Are you inferior to white people, Dassie?"

"No, Mama. I'm not inferior," Dassie answered, clearly bored with Musa's summit.

"Did you pay attention to what I said, Dassie?"

Dassie giggled absurdly before he leaped out of the house and disappeared into the dark streets of White City.

I sat, holding my thoughts in eager anticipation. An awkward moment of silence followed, however. I was waiting anxiously for Musa to put the same question to me, 'Are you inferior to white people, Kŭkuchi?' Ready with my answer, I took a deep breath and wished Musa would ask me, 'You,

Kükuchi, do you think white people are better than you?" Then, I cleared my throat and prepared my answer. I was also going to repeat what Priscilla and Rosemarie once said about black girls. By then, I was daring to tell Musa and Khulu something better than what Dassie said. I was going to tell them that I was not inferior to white people, but that one day, we shall get back our freedom.

However, Musa did not ask me anything. Instead, she went on to deepen her political education about Verwoerd and the National Party. To me, Musa's voice had begun to sound as if it came from the bottom of Salu's well in Draycott, with empty echoes bubbling to the surface and disappearing into space.

My self-esteem took a heavy knock, and I felt bitter about the way Musa had continued to ignore me, as if I did not exist.

***

The next morning, Funani came gasping for breath. He could hardly greet Khulu but immediately told us that Mendi confessed to the murder of Sisi Afrika. Later that evening, Dassie summoned me into the cover of darkness and gave me a clay-covered sack containing mounds of notes. I was shaking as I counted the money. After a little while, I demanded answers from my brother.

"Let's hide it. Mendi stole it from his Alexandra friends. That's why they beat him up last time and nearly killed him. I helped him hide the bag..."

"Why did you steal Mendi's money?"

"Because he doesn't need it anymore. They will hang him for killing that girl."

I felt my conscience tear my soul into shreds when I recalled how Mendi had boasted about the money he had stashed away, which he was planning to use to build a house for his mother and open shops bigger than Tatenda's, and that he would buy a lorry for his butchery.

"Dassie! What are we going to do with all this money? Mendi might be paroled. He thinks he is rich."

"He won't be released. Do you remember what Miss Lumka once said? 'When you are dead, you don't need money.' If you kill someone, the police hang you or put you in jail, and demolish everything with a bulldozer. Mendi is a dead man..."

Dead! You fool. When did Lumka ever say such nonsense? They don't hang anyone for killing an African. But do you think Mendi killed Sisi Afrika?"

"The day they attacked us in Jabavu, he told me everything."

"Yes? What?"

"I'm not telling because it's a secret."

"Dassie, I am your sister. Tell me what Mendi said about Sisi Afrika. I beg you. I'll ask the principal at Orlando High to recommend you for my class because you are a clever student. Just tell me the truth, please."

I am not Mental, me

Before they went to sleep, the siblings dug a hole in the garden between the orange tree and the lawn and buried Mendi's mealie-meal sack of riches there.

In the morning, Kükuchi thought she heard a motor vehicle screech to a halt outside her home. She craned her neck to investigate and saw a police van. Kükuchi skipped through the window and fled before the police could climb out of their van. Toby was in police custody already. A week later, in the dead of night, Captain Venter and his police located Kükuchi holed up in a house in Moroka. They handcuffed Khulu's church friend and charged her with hiding a fugitive. Venter released Khulu's friend on a warning. Kükuchi spent two days at the Brixton police Station holding cell. On the day of her release, she saw Captain Venter, who gave her a mean look before he disappeared. A few minutes later, a young black female invited her to a sandwich and a piece of chicken.

Kükuchi happily gobbled up the food.

The officer said, "The Captain will take you away because you are 'mental'. He says you have bipolar disorder. You are mental, Kükuchi. Do you know what that is?"

"Mental? I'm not mental, me."

"He feels sorry for you because you are worse than mental. Venter is returning you to Sterkfontein because of your big mouth..."

"Sterkfontein? Again? I have never been to Sterkfontein, me..."

"You see? You've even forgotten. You are a bipolar case mentally. They say you and that coloured girl are hiding big secrets. Did something happen to you when you were young? Maybe a man did something you didn't like?"

"Me? No."

"What about your friend? I have seen her. That girl smokes something: the green stuff or something. I mean, like... some girls are raped by relatives or mistreated by their aunties, and they become criminals. Venter told me everything you said to the doctors in that mental hospital..."

"I have never been to a mental hospital."

"They pump drugs into girls like you, so you can't tell your Sunday from your Tuesday. Venter knows everything. He wants to take you to Sterkfontein, where they'll hypnotize you like they did last time. He wants the truth about the missing girls."

"Please, my sister, policeman. Help me escape. I can't go to Sterkfontein again. They stab people in the stomach with those needles. I have money. My mother told me African police officers earn peanuts. I don't want to be hypnotized and become a zombie."

"You are a very clever liar..."

"Oh, now I am clever? You just said I am mental."

"But you need to be hypnotized. It's good for your mind. Everything you've done and everything people have done to you come rushing back like a flash, and you share it without thinking. Even the day you left your mother's womb, you'll remember..."

"You lie. I said nothing last time the nurses tried their voodoo on me. I am too clever even for the doctors."

The officer hit Kükuchi across the face with a backhand, "You call me a liar? You bloody mental girl..."

Without hesitation, Kükuchi hit back, leaving the young in tears as Kükuchi shouted, "You bloody *skelm* police."

The news of Kükuchi's misdemeanour quickly reached Captain Venter, who ordered her immediate release. Toby was unlucky. After denying she ever worked with Kükuchi, the police charged her with dealing in stolen goods. She spent six months at the Phomolong Reformatory for Girls.

Lebo, My Sister

Mkhize came to inform us about the death of Toby's mother. I was devastated. What a shame that she died before revealing the identity of Dassie's father as promised. Mkhize suspected that Dassie had made up the story. The authorities commuted Toby's sentence so she could attend her mother's funeral. I lacked the courage to help Toby prepare to bury her mother, so I thought it was best to stay away. During my moment of confusion, Dassie stopped me as I was walking to the lavatory and said, "I thought Toby was your friend. How come you don't talk to her about her mother's death?"

"Did she tell you I have not spoken to her?"

"She told me that only Jesus is her friend?"

"Jesus? Why did she say that?"

"You can ask her? She told me her sister will be coming for the funeral."

"Toby hasn't got a sister, you lie."

"You can ask her…"

Curiosity got the better of me, so I finally plucked up the courage and went to Toby's home. My fears turned out to be baseless. I found two black women and one young coloured woman chatting in Tswana. Toby was as healthy as a hippopotamus.

"These are my relatives, my father's sisters, and this is Lebo, my sister from Europe," said Toby excitedly.

They all smiled lazily. Lebo looked bored, which concealed her pretty face a little.

When we finally talked outside, Toby said, "Don't worry, Kükuchi. They will never break us, these police. We have to stick together, even if it costs us."

"Are we still friends, Toby?"

"Of course. Nothing will break our friendship…"

"Dassie told me you said Jesus is your friend."

Toby heaved a sigh of despondency before she said, "Maybe it's because I failed to thank Dassie for visiting me at Phomolong, and you were nowhere to be seen."

"Dassie did?"

"Yes, three times, and he brought me chocolate."

"Did you say that Jesus is your only friend?"

"Yes, Kükuchi, Jesus is our friend. Dassie had sympathy. Do you remember the song we sang at Lumka's Sunday school? Maybe Dassie remembered it. He even said he would marry me."

"Sorry, I did not visit you in prison. I want to be your friend like Jesus."

"All right, Kuchi. I told Dassie about Jesus because I missed you and thought you had abandoned me."

"Tell me about your sister."

"She lives in Europe, a country called Belgium. She was adopted by a European couple when she was two years old. They say she is very clever. She is currently studying at an advanced level and wants to become a psychiatrist. Sometimes people think Lebo is a white girl. That's why they took her."

"They should have adopted you, too. You look so much alike."

Toby shrugged, gulping tears at the same time, and said, "I don't know, Faty."

"Ask Lebo to go with you when she flies back to Europe. Don't you want to go with her, Toby?"

"Oh, I don't know, Kuchi."

CHAPTER 15

On my way to Everton

Dodo brought Khulu a tin of Glenryck pilchards and a bag of samp. He immediately announced that he had some urgent issues to discuss with Musa. He told Musa to consult 'Queen' Victoria to remove bad luck and finalize her wedding.

"Over a year has passed since your wedding plans were made, yet nothing has happened. Our ancestor, Habakkuk, directed me in a dream to give you this message before midnight."

"And your Habakkuk can't speak to me directly? How can he choose a drunkard squatting at Wemmer to deliver messages?"

'Queen' Victoria, a popular traditional healer, had attracted both the ordinary and the elite alike. They consulted her for purging evil spirits or for good fortune. Kükuchi remained too wrapped up in her thoughts about 'Queen' Victoria to say much. Musa remained troubled. After a while, she asked Khulu to tell her something about 'Queen' Victoria. Khulu seemed to know a great deal about the healer. She could trace her roots way back to the days before they settled in White City.

"But you're not consulting her." Khulu tried.

***

While Kükuchi excelled in the combined regional events for juniors, she was unable to secure the top spot provincially. Towards the end of the year, conflict within the ANC had degenerated into name-calling. Mr Mandela, the party's Transvaal President, expelled Mr Potlako Leballo, one of the chief opponents of the ANC's *Freedom Charter*. The split seemed inevitable. It came into reality when a group of stick-wielding ANC loyalists prevented 'Anti-Charterists,' led by Robert Mangaliso Sobukwe, from attending a meeting in Orlando East. The breakaway group held its conference at the Orlando Community Hall, where they formed a new party known as the *Pan Africanist Congress* (PAC) of Azania, with Sobukwe as its first President. Before the end of the conference, the security police had swooped down on the venue and arrested both the leader and the delegate. Musa could not escape.

Salu was seething with anger over Musa's political activities. When she heard of her joining the new party, she wrote Khulu a letter demanding answers. Kükuchi read the letter aloud while Khulu kept shaking her head in disbelief: 'What does Musa know? Has she ever heard of Pixley ka Seme, how he united us? This thing by Sobukwe will divide the Africans further.'

Khulu hid the letter from Musa and said nothing. Salu wrote another letter on the same subject and addressed it to Musa herself. Musa was incensed. Khulu pleaded with her to ignore Salu's comments for the sake of family peace.

I stayed awake all night thinking about my family and future. The house was never peaceful; there was always arguing. In the quiet of the night, I decided to search for my father. After Khulu left on her errands, I turned over the mattress, hoping to find some of her cash. There was nothing. Then I approached the wardrobe and opened it. Lo and behold, there it was—a one-dollar note folded neatly inside. I was heading to Evaton, despite being disappointed that I hadn't found my father. A woman wearing a black doek directed me into a lavishly decorated kitchen. The small, light-skinned, pretty woman with bronzed spots on her face was Mrs Noni Ramola, my father's ex-wife. She was chanting, 'Sinners shall never go to heaven,' as I settled into her grand lounge, which reminded me of Priscilla's beautiful home in Mayfair.

After their divorce, Ramola went his merry way and settled down with a young chief's daughter in Phokeng. Mrs Ramola was kind enough to accommodate Kükuchi for two nights. During that time, she gathered all she needed to know about her father, including tall tales from Mrs Ramola.

I began to appreciate the adage that goes, 'Chasing after a father who deserted you as an infant is like trying to catch a mirage'.

Tina is Missing

A few days later, Kükuchi took a third-class train home and couldn't wait to share how she had found her father's location. However, she didn't realize that since she left, a shadow of anxiety had settled over White City. As she neared, Dassie hurried toward her and shouted, "Kükuchi, where have you been? Khulu has been crying since you disappeared with Tina..."

"With Tina?"

"Yes. Where is Tina? You mean you did not go with her? We thought you went to Estcourt to see Salu. Tina disappeared at the same time. Where have you been? Why didn't you tell me? Even Toby didn't know..."

Kükuchi's body froze, and her throat became so dry that her voice crackled. Khulu hurried out to meet her. The neighbours rushed out and gathered around Khulu's house. When it became clear to the neighbours that Kükuchi had no idea where Tina had gone, a dark cloud of gloom and despair fell over White City. The level of fear and hopelessness among parents with girl children grew more intense.

An overwhelming sense of anguish filled Khulu's house as the family gathered for supper, mulling over their increasing problems. Neither Khulu nor Musa dared to ask why Kükuchi had slipped away without warning anyone. Kükuchi chose to stall as her mind raced through the roller coaster of the past week. Dassie kept going on about Tina's disappearance. Still, everyone seemed to be hiding behind the shadows of suspicion toward Kükuchi.

Dassie persisted, "Kükuchi, when last did you see Tina? What happened after I gave you the money...?"

"You gave Kükuchi money?" Khulu screamed, "Where did you get the money...?"

Musa spoke softly, "Why don't you tell us where you come from, Kükuchi? Mrs Tatenda thinks you went away with Tina to Draycott. What are we going to say to her and the people of White City? They'll think we stole their child and killed her for muti."

Kükuchi's eye started twitching again, this time more than ever before.

***

In the 1940s, Tina's parents left Bikita, a small rural village in southern Rhodesia. They decided to move to South Africa and settled in one of the shantytowns built by James Sofasonke Mpanza near Orlando East. Mr Tatenda, a qualified accountant, and his wife, a trained nurse, rented a small shop from the local council and later opened a grocery store in White City. Tina was born in Orlando East and was their only child. Although Tatenda appeared reserved and hesitant to start conversations, the Ndebele-speaking man warmed up to anyone once a discussion began. He enjoyed talking about his village with Khulu and told her he looked forward to taking his family back home someday. However, when asked, Tina would say she does not want to go to Rhodesia because she does not want to die.

The community of White City remains in a dazed state of sadness. Tina's disappearance pushes Dassie to the edge of despair. He retreats into his lonely world, spending hours out in the veld. When he returns, everyone cares for him with warm water and food without question. One evening, Sister Mohale alerts Khulu to a ghostly sight of Tina's mother, who stands stiffly, like a sleepwalker, outside Khulu's yard. Khulu goes out to investigate and asks her what she is doing. She stares at Khulu, makes a face, spits on the ground, and then stomps off.

***

Kükuchi decided to immerse herself in her javelin routines. Inching her way through the difficulties, she sensed progress in her footwork as she maintained her training regime with extra determination. She gained distance every week and continued to lose weight. It was clear to her that to hold her own against the likes of Lesedi, not to mention Rosemarie, she would have to add speed to her repertoire.

Kükuchi asked Khulu if she had ever consulted 'Queen' Victoria.

"No. And you are not going there either. You can go to Mrs Posa. She was looking for you. She said something about Moorstad…"

Kükuchi went out to seek Mkhize's advice about 'Queen' Victoria.

"Papa," she said, "People who consult 'Queen' Victoria… what type of people are they?"

Mkhize hesitated before he said, "All lizards lie flat on their stomachs; how can you tell which has a stomach ache? It's a secret. I don't care what type goes to see Victoria."

"Do you ever consult her?"

"Me? Do you know who I am? I am Khabazela. I speak directly with our ancestors down there. I don't use stars and crystal balls like township charlatans. No eagle takes flying lessons from chickens. Come to me if you need help…"

"I tried long ago, Papa. You sent me away and told me to talk to Sister Mohale?"

Kükuchi voiced her frustration about constantly having to beg for a place to practice and her lack of coaching. Mkhize approached Mrs Posa, who said, "Smooth seas do not make skilful sailors. Kükuchi must use our rough fields here, and she will become better for it."

Mkhize reminded Posa that the rough fields she was referring to do not even have markings to help the thrower time herself. Posa was impressed with Mkhize's wise words. She promised she would continue negotiating for Kükuchi to train at Moorstad High, a school for Whites. To Kükuchi, Posa's words amounted to empty promises.

She decided to join a group of distressed township residents beating a path to 'Queen Victoria's traditional healing home. The double-story mansion in the elite Dube village looked intimidating. Some of the patients looked healthy and prosperous, and Kükuchi wondered what they were doing in such a place when life seemed to be going well for them. She then recalled Mkhize's words, 'All lizards lie flat on their stomachs.'

As she was wondering about lizards, she heard a familiar voice, "What are you doing here, Kuchi?"

It was Jozi, Sithole's daughter, who looked more embarrassed than Kükuchi over their odd encounter.

"Dassie told me you don't like to be hypnotized. What are you doing here, Kükuchi?"

"Does Queen Victoria use hypnotism?"

"What else? She needs to get into your soul. That's why I'm here — to see if my soul aligns with your uncle Funani's."

"What does that mean?"

"It means I don't know what to do. Funani says he loves me. Has he never told you?"

"Is your soul not too young for the soul of Funani?"

"Queen Victoria will prophesy…"

Jozi quickly walked inside for a consultation. Kükuchi looked around and then promptly disappeared from the scene.

***

I could hardly sleep that night. A few minutes before midnight, something made me creep out of the house. I stood in the dark under the orange tree, where an apparition suddenly materialized. It was Tina. Her attire was a glamorous traditional attire I had never seen before. I was not hallucinating because everything was in bright colours. Tina looked beautiful, with a shiny tiara on her plaited hair and a crown of diamonds. Tina said something about 'Busisiwe,' after which her lips moved, but I could hear no sound. I cleared my throat and asked, 'Who is Busisiwe?' but the apparition had disappeared. I went back inside with a heavy heart. When I told Khulu what I saw, she did not respond.

"Did you hear me, Khulu? She said something about Busisiwe…"

"Who is Busisiwe?"

"I don't know."

Khulu sat up and said, "The other night, I went out and also heard a voice. It was Tina's voice, as clear as I know her. The voice said, 'Ask Donald.'"

"Donald? Who is Donald, Khulu?'

"That's Dodo's full name, Kuchi. That's Dodo."

"Really? What do you think, Khulu?"

Khulu took out her Bible and asked me to read Psalm 23 aloud so she could hear God's voice. I read the whole chapter, 'The Lord is my Shepherd…'

Diepkloof Reformatory

A few days later, Dassie asked me to accompany him to Diepkloof to see Mendi.

"They don't allow piccanins in there."

"I always go there. When I get there, I ask older adults to help me. Go with me. They'll agree because you look old."

"And why do you say I look old?"

Weekends and public holidays were visiting days at the Reformatory facility. Although hesitant, I finally relented because I still harboured warm feelings toward Mendi.

Diepkloof Reformatory was a detention centre for young African male offenders, situated in a country-like setting, a stone's throw from Baragwanath Hospital. Barbed wire crowned with iron stanchions fortified the facility. Diepkloof was a ghostly boys' Town tucked away underneath a far-flung forested hummock away from the White City of Johannesburg. The visitors' entrance was a steel gate operated by four warders.

As family members filed slowly through, I caught a glimpse of Mendi's mother from a distance. The thought of returning home crossed my mind. It seemed Mendi's mother had slowed down on drinking, although her animosity towards my family had worsened. Mendi's mother rested on a rock at the inner gate of the main block. She looked lost and exasperated. When our eyes met, she grimaced like a hungry warthog and swiftly looked away.

The official's eyebrows winched up on hearing that Dassie and I were there to see Mendi. The inmates had their midday parade, and we had to wait for an hour. After that, we could only see Mendi outside the Deputy Warden's office, where security was more rigid than in other sections.

Tears rolled down Mendi's face when he saw me. Dassie had disappeared. After inspecting the food parcel in my basket, the two bemused warders settled down to keep an eye on their prisoner while they winched their ears like foxes. Mendi's contagious tears got the better of me, but in a little while, I pulled myself together.

Mendi had become thin, and his confidence was almost gone.

"They want to kill me," he put it. "Tell Mkhize to help me."

I rambled on, promising this and that. Mendi seemed to have developed some mental disturbance. However, I was eager for him to tell me about Sisi Afrika and the other missing girls.

So, I got to the point and asked, "Who killed all those girls, Mendi?"

Mendi looked heavy-eyed. He ranted, blaming everyone, "They say I did things. They must tell me what has happened to Dassie's girl. I was here when they took Tina away. I don't know where she is. Or maybe I know. I was here all the time. Ask the police."

"Maybe you know? Who took Tina away, Mendi?"

"Those guys from Orlando; they know."

"Which guys? Mendi, you need to tell me. Tina's mother spent many weeks in the hospital because of depression. She thinks we turned Tina into a zombie."

"Tell Mkhize to get me out of here. I'll go with friends from Alex to look for Dassie's girl."

"Tell me about the girl you buried near the stream. What was her real name? You told the police her name was Sisi. Please, Mendi, tell me about Sisi."

Without warning, revelations surfaced effortlessly, like a burst boil. Mendi added casually, "I know a lot about those girls, Kuchi... and I'll tell you."

The officers rebuked him and stopped him from talking further.

Tina remained one of the missing African children.

I know that my Redeemer lives.

Early one morning, the school Principal promoted Kükuchi to the next class. Miss Tequane, who was as thrilled as a drowsy deer about the promotion, buried herself behind a mound of her pupils' exercise books and went on impassively, 'If your parents need more information about your promotion, they can speak to your principal. He is the only one making decisions here.' Khulu was delighted, but so was Musa. Mrs Posa visited Khulu to congratulate her on Kükuchi's progress. She told Kükuchi that Mrs Twaai had obtained permission for her to use the training grounds for her javelin at Moorstad High School, with accommodation and meals covered for the whole week. That school had first-class, state-of-the-art facilities for training. Kükuchi's delight at the news knew no bounds.

In the evening, Kükuchi joined Dassie on their favourite *stoep*.

"What do you want, Kuchi?"

"I just want to talk, Dassie. Don't you want to talk to your sister?"

"No. Go back inside and cut me two more slices. I'm hungry."

"We've just had supper. What's the matter with you?"

"And no peanut butter. I hate eating that stuff at night."

"Now, tell me, did you ask Musa again about your father?"

"She said he kicked the bucket long ago."

"You lie, Dassie. Musa will never use such words."

"She said my father went to hell long ago. But Mama Mohale said my father is still alive."

"So, what are you going to do?"

"Salu said Musa will tell me everything when I turn sixteen."

Kükuchi giggled, but Dassie remained stern-faced.

"I should have gone with Tina. She wanted us to run away, but we didn't have enough money!"

"You? Listen, I'm going to Moorstad High School."

"Khulu told me. Go there and show the whites you can beat them. They will accept you into that school because you are the best. And you look like them."

"Don't you talk to me ever again ..."

***

Posa and I arrived at the Twaai family's smallholding early one morning. Moorstad was an ideal place to jog, as the air was fresh and the setting was a quiet farming area. Twaai was a cigarette sales representative for the United Tobacco Company. He was also an official of the Non-whites' Sports Association in the Western Transvaal. Mrs Makhoba, a middle-aged black woman, was cleaning the front patch behind a well-manicured garden as she hummed her tune. Mrs Twaai, a chubby, cheerful coloured woman with an uneven set of teeth and a charming smile, showed us the way to the front *stoep* and served us coffee and homemade fat cakes.

Twaai, who had been out jogging, was covered in sweat. He headed inside for a shower while Posa and Mrs Twaai continued their lively conversation. When he stepped outside again, the grey-haired man was dressed in his short-sleeved khaki Safari suit, prepared to go to work.

"This is the girl?" he asked with little rhetorical emotion.

"This is the girl," Posa responded.

Sipping his coffee with gusto, Mr Twaai focused his attention on Posa, inquiring about her family. I sat awkwardly, listening to the adults exchanging reminiscences, and soon read between the lines that Twaai was Posa's younger brother. Twaai later led me into his 1950 Chrysler Sedan, and aside from a Springbok Radio program, we drove through the woods in silence. The man was reticent about the kind of arrangement he had made with the school authorities.

When we reached the school gate, he gestured for me to exit, and his car screeched off, leaving me there feeling like a confused orphan.

Observing the school for a meaningful minute, I was no longer surprised by the stark contrast between white and black lives in the country.

As I walked along the paved path toward the main buildings, I admired the lush green fields and exercise tracks.

My footpath winded through the tree-lined driveway, feeling despair over Orlando High, a school full of political ideals but struggling with its facilities for learning and play. Although Moorstad High School served only the white constituency, the number of white pupils was dwindling at a fast rate. African shanty settlements were springing up westward from Moroka and Jabavu. White people are generally apprehensive about having African neighbours. As the squatter camps swept the area, whites relocated to other parts of the country. A lot of them left for overseas. The Department of Education had agreed to accommodate what they referred to as 'non-whites.' However, the school did not allow the increasing number of African children. Within the Moorstad premises, coloured pupils occupied old, derelict buildings and were taught primarily by white teachers. Coloured teachers could not cross over to teach white children.

***

Kükuchi stood outside a dilapidated coloured staff room where she waited for Mr Lesandra. It was assembly time, and competing sounds of Christian hymns from each side of the school flooded the frosty woods. The coloured pupils were chanting their emotional hymn, 'I know that my Redeemer lives'. At the same time, the white section resonated with their piano-accompanied 'Onward Christian Soldiers.'

After the ritual of separate assemblies and prayers, the pupils went about their semi-detached routines for the rest of the day, with minimal interaction between them. Only white teachers were allowed to move freely, walking from one section to another without needing approval. The three coloured teachers—one young woman and two men—were restricted to their section, which had a small staff room of its own. One of the men was Mr Lesandra.

While both 'races' could use the same facilities, Coloured learners needed to get permission from the principal to avoid inconveniencing white learners. Students from different communities—namely Coloureds and Europeans—couldn't use the facilities at the same time.

***

Leandra appeared and directed Kūkuchi to the athletic field. With a hint of a smile, Kūkuchi marvelled at the green sports grounds that stretched out as far as the eye could see. The only sounds Kūkuchi could hear, as she enjoyed the lush, glorious fields, were bird calls and the occasional clatter of student laughter echoing to the edges of the woods.

The lawn manicure extended to the threshold of the inner track, with detailed javelin markings that were bold and clear. As for the margin between 'carry' and 'withdrawal,' it was so easy to make out that one could spot the 'scratch line' from a distance with little effort. In the eyes of Kūkuchi, whose face had become wet with tears and craving for a better life, everything looked beautiful. Leandra told her he was going to teach her new tricks. The sports master was not aware that whatever Kūkuchi knew was mainly self-taught; Posa's contribution was limited to 'throw hard' or 'run faster.' The coach took Kūkuchi to the javelin runway and showed her the phases from 'start' through to 'recovery': 'carry', 'withdrawal', 'transition', 'pre-delivery', and 'delivery'. He emphasized the significance of each segment and that Kūkuchi should take time to practice her footwork and speed. In that way, her final throw would be perfect every time. Kūkuchi practiced a series of throws each day. Leandra, who preferred to call them 'flings,' always located himself at the scratch line, scrutinizing her speed along the runway and observing where she finally put her foot before each throw. Although Kūkuchi maximized her marked landings, Lesandra disqualified her several times throughout the week.

During one of the breaks, he divulged to Kūkuchi that he was an immigrant from Egypt, although she thought he looked like a coloured resident of Eldorado Park. On the last day, the coach said, "Go on working. You're on your own now. Avoid stepping out—practice using the scratch line to measure your throws. Set your mind on the Commonwealth and Olympic Games. You're one of the best African throwers I have seen."

Kūkuchi was pleased with her performances on the field, and the media shared her enthusiasm. *Township News* featured a story about the Transvaal African athletes. She found her full-length photo quite striking because she looked much leaner. The paper detailed how she had won several tournaments and also took part in coaching clinics to help younger athletes. Everything appeared to be going smoothly for her until the Afrikaners attacked Africans in Sharpeville.

The Sharpeville Massacre

In February 1960, Harold Macmillan, who was the British Prime Minister, addressed the Apartheid

Parliament. Apartheid was a racially bigoted system created by Europeans against blacks everywhere. In his effort to sensitize the South African white population, Macmillan pointed to 'the winds of change sweeping across Africa.' His visit captured the media's attention, and his fiery speech resonated worldwide. Many countries and political organizations welcomed the address with excitement and hope. The echo was no melody to the mainstream white population, though. The Apartheid government poured scorn on the speech, accusing Macmillan of being uninformed about Africa. Macmillan's prophetic words came true only a few weeks later with the 'Sharpeville Massacre.' The winds of change held deep significance for Kükuchi because she believed that the British, who had once taken the land of the Hlubi and Ngwe by force, had now shifted their support to the Africans. She then gazed at the clear skies and redoubled her training.

Over time, Kükuchi would come to admit her naivety in relying on the British.

Dodo's visit to White City had become more sporadic than before. One evening, he dropped in, lamenting the worsening political situation in the country. He warned about the looming trouble between the PAC and the Apartheid government. Without any further explanation, Dodo bragged to Khulu that the South African Police had employed and promoted him to the position of Sergeant.

"What happened to your supplementary exams? You have been doing Matric since Kükuchi was a baby," sneered Musa.

"Matric is not J.C. It is difficult," he put it. "But, for your information, I passed. I met Mohale near Wemmer last week. Didn't she tell you I passed?"

"It must have slipped her mind," Musa joked.

"She is jealous, that's all. I'm going to earn a lot of money now, Mama. I have registered with the University of South Africa. I aim to be the most educated person in the family. I have advised Musa many times to study and forget about the *Freedom Charter*."

"Let's hope you don't take another ten years to get your degree," said Musa dryly.

"Now that you are such a big policeman, when are you planning on finding Tina?"

"Leave that alone," said Musa. "What have you been saying about the PAC?"

"Yes," Dodo said, "Make sure you keep yourselves indoors tomorrow. The PAC has directed their followers to go out and burn their passes because..."

"Don't come spewing garbage here," Musa shouted. "Who said anything about burning passes...?"

"Let him finish, Musa," Khulu said firmly.

"Yes, let him finish, Gogo. Maybe he will tell us what the police are doing about Tina and the other missing girls," Kükuchi said. "He seems to know more about the PAC burning passes than about arresting criminals who abduct girls."

Ignoring Kükuchi's outbursts, Dodo reached into his pocket and handed a large bundle of crumpled Ten Rand bills to Khulu, who thanked him sincerely and went into the bedroom to count her blessings.

"The storm is coming; make sure the house is protected," Dodo said as he stepped out.

***

Tina's mother continued to menacingly park her car in front of Khulu's house every night. Sometimes, the car would face the front window, with its bright lights flooding Khulu's bedroom. Khulu uttered profanity several times, using her collection of swear words, clicking her tongue, and spewing curses that Kükuchi had never heard before. Sister Mohale visited Khulu's house to confront Dassie about Tina's disappearance. She asked him to confess so he could go to heaven one day.

"I don't want to go to heaven."

"Everybody wants to go to heaven. You are an evil child, Dassie. The weather forecast predicts a storm. Just pray, you Dassie, that lightning does not strike you to hell."

Realizing she wasn't getting any support from Dassie's household, Sister Mohale walked out, shaking her head in frustration.

Khulu asked with concern, "Don't you want to go to heaven, Dassie?"

"Not if Sister Mohale will be there with us."

"You should show respect to Mama Mohale."

"She thinks I know where Tina is. She is mad."

The house remained quiet, but one could hear the approaching storm. As the sun disappeared behind the dark clouds, Dassie and Kükuchi sat on their *stoep*.

"Dassie, you know I am your sister, and you are my brother, right?"

"You're not asking for money again, are you? I only have six shillings."

"No. I am your sister, right? Tell me honestly. Do I look old?"

"Papa Mkhize said you asked him the same question. What's your story?"

"Well, it's because one day, when we went to visit Mendi in Diepkloof, you said I looked old."

"That was long ago. How old do you think you look now?" Dassie chortled.

"Dassie, tell me the truth now. You always call me ugly. Am I?"

"Kükuchi, don't you have something better to do... like dishing up. I'm hungry."

"Do you ever have anything nice to say about me?"

"About you? "

"Yeah. Kükuchi, you are not ugly. You don't look old. When you smile, you remind me of Tina's pretty smile," Dassie lied.

A dash of colour coated Kükuchi's cheeks, and she crowed, "Oh, Dassie! Tina? She's beautiful. I like her braided hair..."

"Do you think she is prettier than Toby? Toby's face is on the cover of Drum."

"Tina is pretty, and she walks pretty, and she wears her strange traditional attire, and she is always number one in her class. Don't you want to be number one in your class, Dassie?"

"Last time, she came out second."

"Yes, she did, because of you, Dassie. You make her stand behind her parents' shop at night, and you keep kissing her instead of giving her time to read her books. You're both too young to be doing such things."

***

Thick clouds gathered force. Dassie told Kükuchi how he wished Tina could come back so they could get married. Kükuchi felt sorry for him but kept the mystic sighting of Tina to herself. She said, "You are too young to be talking about getting married, and Tina will come back. Maybe she did something to upset her mother, and she ran away."

"I think someone buried her near the Klipspruit stream, just like they buried Sisi Afrika," Dassie said unemotionally."

Distant flashes of lightning lit up the sky, accompanied by thunder, as strong winds howled against the tall trees of Donaldson Primary. Kükuchi said, "It looks like a heavy storm. Let's go inside."

As usual, Khulu, Musa, and Kükuchi lay down low in the house, making empty promises to God while Dassie ate his bread and went to sleep. Gusts of wind and peals of thunder released a downpour on the streets of White City and Jabavu.

Khulu said, "I have a hunch because of the fury of this storm; it tells us a lot."

"Like what, Khulu?" asked Musa.

"Sorrow and tears."

"Mama, you feel bad every time there is lightning and thunder," said Musa.

"No, this one is different. You can hear two owls exchanging hoots throughout; one in the east and another in the west."

We had been in the dark about what was brewing in the country. Mangaliso Sobukwe led hundreds of activists to the Orlando police station to hand over their passes. The security police arrested him soon after, and that was to be his last political activity. Other leaders of the PAC led similar marches in their areas throughout the country. In Sharpeville, Nyakane Tsolo led a peaceful protest march to the police station to hand over African passes. The brave man refused to back down, and he paid the ultimate price.

The massacre that followed was worse than the international community had ever expected. There was unprecedented worldwide news coverage and condemnation of police brutality against peaceful African protesters. At dawn, a loud knock and beams of bright lights disturbed the peace in Khulu's house. The police had come to cuff Musa again. The next few hours were marked by nervous movement as people gathered into groups of curious onlookers on street corners. In contrast, others hurried in different directions to find alternative transportation to work. Some angry men and women gathered at intersections and along main roads to Town, blocking traffic and telling people to go home. Many volunteer activists were already working at railway stations, turning commuters back. Later in the day, people began spreading conflicting reports about the Sharpeville shootings. That evening, Mohale arrived gasping for breath and told Khulu about the PAC protest. According to her, the police had shot hundreds of people, killing many. Mohale criticized black political leaders for 'driving innocent people to the slaughterhouse.' After the attacks, white police officers in vans searched the streets of Sharpeville for suspects. In a scene reminiscent of the Midianites and Amalekites, a group of white soldiers descended from the sky like locusts. With the mutilation of their dignity complete, the residents of Sharpeville began to assess the damage caused in the name of European civilization. The air was fresh because of the previous night's downpour, but the fully armed white enemy, spoiling for a confrontation, was right on their doorsteps. The *Rand Daily Mail* portrayed the Sharpeville incident as a bloodbath, commenting on how the wanton massacre was reminiscent of Adolf Hitler's killing fields in Germany. The paper released graphic images: bodies of men and women, hats, shoes, *takkies,* dolls, and a few bicycles with bent spokes strewn across the site. Sixty-nine people died in Sharpeville on the first night of police shootings, and most of the victims had bullet wounds in the back. In the aftermath, widespread social unrest exploded in most African townships. Education for African children became shards of broken pottery. White children and their families were sheltered from the bloodshed, and the shameful accounts of the violence were also hidden from them.

The era of the armed struggle against oppression had begun. Umkhonto we Sizwe (MK) and the Azanian People's Liberation Army (APLA) aimed to strike at the foundations of the apartheid 'Armada'. As a result, the South African defence force launched deadly attacks on neighbouring countries, hunting down anti-apartheid militants and slaughtering local civilians with reckless abandon.

CHAPTER 16

This is our ancestral Land.

I began preparing for the upcoming Commonwealth Games, spending the next few days practicing my javelin techniques and building my endurance. Long-distance walking was relaxing, though I couldn't help but constantly reflect on the devastating effects of Apartheid on my javelin ambitions.

Over twenty Black girls qualified nationwide to participate in the national javelin playoffs. Unfortunately, only white athletes were officially allowed to compete. Nevertheless, I believed that the Black girls could easily outperform some of the white competitors. The vain duplicity displayed by the bodies of white athletes caused me significant anxiety. Still, I was pleased with my progress.

An invitation to run a javelin clinic for schools in the Durban area was a wonderful surprise. After my positive stint as a budding coach, I went to Estcourt to see Salu, reaching Draycott at sunset. I found her out in the kraal, jumping up and down with delight. One of her Holstein-Friesian dairy cows had calved just an hour before, producing two heifers.

Salu shouted, "Faty, it's you? Come over here and look. Now I know who came here to bring me good luck. Look at *Soksie's* babies," she squeaked, with hundreds of chickens chirping noisily in the background.

I joined the celebration, where we chanted, hopped, and skipped the *Buganu* dance, a Swazi women's tradition.

"Oh, Salu, they look so wonderful."

"How right you are, Faty. You don't look bad yourself. What have you done with all that weight? It seems you're aiming for Miss White-City, like Toby. How's your twitching eye?"

"On and off. I thought you would stop calling me 'Faty.' I am a big girl now."

"Don't push it. Let's get inside for your favourite pies."

***

The countryside was always enchanting, and Salu's chicken farm a one-of-a-kind place to see. It nestled among green fields and rolling hills of the Midlands, offering a striking view of the Drakensberg.

I loved watching the sky's dance, where the fog would settle and allow white clouds from the South to puff up with pride before the black clouds carrying the lightning bird moved in, casting displays across the sky. The whole earth would tremble when the black clouds rumbled with a sound louder than a thousand cowhide drums. I loved the spectacle, and when the earth shook, I could feel the thunder roaring inside my chest. When the heavens cover the earth and electrify the basin, Salu would wrap herself in a posture of prayer.

The European *Voortrekkers* had christened the mountain range 'Drakensberg' because to them it looked much like the dragon's back. The escarpment stretches the length of the western boundary of Natal from the Eastern Cape to Limpopo. In winter, a blanket of snow covers the landscape, while for the rest of the year, snatches of shiny grey cut a swathe across the rock faces and ridges. Yet it is to the Africans' countless struggles over centuries that we owe a glimpse of life and activity in the region. The rivers tell stories, not only about the Drakensberg's fierce storms with their irresistible magnetism but also countless tales of fierce events in history. The winds are whispering about the battles of resistance against poisonous cannons on the left hand and a pretty little book on the right. After theft and forced relocations, many hectares of African mud-houses proliferated and straggled across the floor of the mountain like tiny pebbles encased in puddles. Most communities have since struggled to practice their traditional communal life. New settlements have increasingly upset vast tracts of the countryside. The white government had continued uprooting African communities from their ancestral Land, dumping them on rocky desert wastelands of no use to white families and their livestock. In Europe, such undermining of family life by an alien force would be called 'genocide.' Still, in Africa, it is referred to as 'government policy' because the victims are black.

Salu remained unaware of the events that would soon turn her life upside down. The insidious apartheid fraud and corruption were about to engulf her entire life, leaving her paralyzed with despair. The threat of large-scale land seizures by whites, using fraudulent laws that granted them impunity, had not stopped in 1913 or when the British lost control. The brutality with which they carried out forced removals after 1948 revealed the moral bankruptcy of both the British and Afrikaners.

Salu maintained her usual strict rules for farm maintenance. The pathways around the farm buildings looked immaculate, and she used mowers and herbicides to keep weeds down on the roadbeds. She kept the hose bins clean and dry to prevent caking and disease when feeding broilers. From her hatchery, she produced one thousand eggs daily, in addition to raising and preparing broilers for markets in Mooi River, Winterton, Ladysmith, and Estcourt. Always flying her kite, Salu claimed that chicken mortality on her farm was among the lowest in the Natal Midlands.

When we finally settled down for supper, Salu said, "Faty, I see you have become famous. I read your story in *Ilanga*, where you and your high-flying javelin friends decorated the front pages for a week. When I showed my white neighbour the articles about you and told her you were my granddaughter, she snickered with disdain..."

"Why? Is it because of what I think...?"

"What do you think?"

"Why would you boast about a mere girl with no melanin?"

"Is that what you think of yourself? A mere girl?"

"Well...?"

"Stop being prickly. Jealous people snicker at the soft breeze touching their faces. The woman thought I was making small talk, name-dropping. Or maybe she was jealous. You should know that some white people are green with envy when they see a successful black child."

"Yes, even when we beat them at hopscotch."

"So, there. Remember, popularity is cheap, my child. Your family comes first, and your lack of melanin hardly features in our intimate vocabulary."

"Are you angry with me, Gogo?"

"Are you a credit to the family?"

"What do you mean, Salu?"

"I hear you have been chasing after your so-called father. Never judge a book by its cover. Some wealthy people seem decent on the outside, but most of them have feet of clay. That man is up to no good, and he will never be part of this family as long as I live. Life is not a happy place, Faty, but you are my happiness. I am glad you took the trouble to come and see your old Granny. When you were here last, you denied you were pregnant. Come to Salu the day you suspect your period is missing. I'll keep you hidden here until you give me a great-granddaughter."

"No, Salu, I am not pregnant."

"When I was your age, our elders were always curious about our state of virginity. They thought they had the means to unearth the truth, but that was another illusion. The girls who had lost their virginity ended up isolated from other girls, with questionable proof of what they thought they had found. I learned quickly when I became a teacher that culture is an artificial invention, sometimes a crafty device to keep women in their place. Let's leave that alone. Tell me, why are you here?"

"To see you, Salu...and to give you this," Kükuchi handed Salu £15.

"This is a lot of money, Kükuchi. Do you have any change remaining?"

"Of course I do."

"Let's talk more at bedtime. You will sleep in my bedroom, right?"

"I always sleep with you, Salu."

"One never knows as girls grow taller. Don't you want your so-called privacy?"

"You asked me why I am here. Please go with me to Ixopo sometime this week, Salu."

"Ixopo? What have you got buried there?"

I reminded Salu about the story of Sisi Afrika, which Mendi had shared with me during my previous visit to jail. Then, he told me something hard to believe about that girl. Salu jumped to his feet, shouting, 'I must be under Mendi's spell or bewitched.' I told Salu they had convicted him of the crime, and he gave me her name and where she came from. That's all he knew. He said he never told anyone else because he feared her family might use strong muti to bring him even more bad luck.

"Served him right," Salu said as she scoffed at my request. "Do you know how far Ixopo is from anywhere or how large the countryside is? Where shall we start? Did he give you the address of the child's parents?"

We can ask around on the streets. We might find someone who knows a missing girl called Sisi.

"Called Sisi?

I'm not going anywhere near Ixopo, and that's final."

***

In the morning, Kükuchi ventured out to the cold where she saw two herdsmen leading cows out of the kraal, taking advantage of the lactation cycle. She then helped the workers in the hatchery with debeaking, dubbing, and scrubbing. Afterwards, she walked into the vegetation, and when she smelled the lavender, she slowed down and gently chose a pebble to place next to her pillow for a restful night. Ambling around the rock pool, she marvelled at the sight of tadpoles performing various swimming strokes alongside triplefins and spotties. Kükuchi knelt and carefully selected two white water lilies for Salu.

By the time she got back to the house, Salu had changed her tune.

"We leave for Ixopo tomorrow. Today, we're going to the eastern edge of the farm. There's something I want you to see there, besides the white woman next door who thought I was bragging when I showed her your picture in the newspaper. She needs to see you in person."

"Are you okay with a European as a neighbour?"

"Remember, a mile separates us. So, it's not like we have to kiss every morning. You can't be okay with people who look at you and see a maid, even when they know the maid produces abundantly and feeds half the Midlands without subsidy."

"You mean…?"

"White farmers get money from the government that enables them to buy the things we all farmers need, to make things easier during a drought. I get nothing of the sort."

"What do they say when you ask for a subsidy?"

"Do you think they listen? To them, I am just a rural African woman engaged in subsistence activities. Let's forget about subsidies, shall we? My child, some of us do not have long to live. There are things you must know about your family. You were right. We should have told you something about that stupid father of yours when you were eight months old."

The silent burial Place

Salu and Kükuchi walked into the white neighbour's farm and stood a shouting distance away from the entrance. The Forty-something white woman welcomed them in her rotunda. She was all smiles as she hugged Kükuchi like an old friend.

The sun was setting when Kükuchi and Salu walked past a group of sheep grazing on the lush side of the hill. Salu said, "Do you see that flock over there? That's how our family should stay together."

They trekked through the brushy area toward the edge of the hill, continuing despite the discomfort of weaving through dense grass. Since the field was wet, they took small, cautious steps, allowing them to converse as they advanced. The wind whistled melodiously, reminding Salu of the days of her youth. They pressed on along the hill's edge until Kükuchi interrupted the melody.

"Salu," Kükuchi said, "Sister Mohale once said white people want to take over all the farms owned by African farmers. What have they said to you?"

Salu stopped, awkwardly pulling Kükuchi by the arm, and looked blankly at her before saying, "To everything, there is a season, Kuchi."

She started walking, leaving Kükuchi standing still. It was clear to her that her grandmother was dealing with some private trouble. Kükuchi paused for a moment, as Salu continued. Salu kept walking, and Kükuchi finally caught up and faced her confidently.

"What season are you talking about, Salu?"

Salu pulled Kükuchi by the arm again and hugged her. When she let go, Kükuchi saw tears running down her grandmother's face.

"You are crying, Salu. Why?"

They kept walking across the fields. Salu struggled up the steep hill and said apologetically, "It's asthma, my child. I am not tired. I was born right here in the Drakensberg valley on the windy side of Ntabamhlophe. Climbing hills was our daily routine. I'm not over the hill yet," she snorted wittily. "Oh, who am I kidding? Old age never announces itself at the gate of a kraal. I grew up here, an hour's walk from the 'Devil's Tooth,' and we used to run up and down these slopes with Khulu. It feels like yesterday, but somehow, I'm aging and struggling to catch my breath."

"And Musa?"

"Now that you know everything about Musa, that she is your biological mother, you must know something about her deep familiarity with these swampy planes. When she was little, she was special, energetic, and full of fun. She walked barefoot and caught snakes. Young snakes do behave like gentle pets. But snakes do grow big and bigger, and they remain snakes."

Salu went on to tell Kükuchi how Musa once brought a young horned adder, which she had detected on the rock-strewn riverside of Pangweni.

"As its tongue flicked from side to side, Musa crowed, 'I am the best snake catcher this side of the ocean. No one can beat me. She found the whole thing amusing."

"What makes snakes so fascinating?"

"Her mind could be a double-edged sword, a hint of what was to come. Her passion for politics later in life would draw her into activism, a world filled with all sorts of snakes. Then there would be a maverick you, wielding your javelin, something we haven't seen since the death of King Shaka or Langalibalele."

When they reached the brow of the hill, the sky had turned gloomy, the cool breeze suggestive of a downpour before long. Salu pointed at a gully and said despondently, "They want to take our Land. They say this is a European-designated area. Have you ever seen a white area in Africa? Why did God not make an African area in Europe?"

"You must not allow them to take your land."

Salu's breathing became so difficult that Kükuchi began to suspect she might be dying.

"Allow? The Europeans allow themselves because they believe Africa's fruits have been waiting for white children from overseas to come and harvest them freely."

Salu hid her tears by blowing her nose.

"I brought you here to this ditch so you see where Musa and I laid your twin brother to rest. Let's get closer."

"Twin…!"

They walked carefully along the dangerous bank of the stream, one of the small tributaries of the Thukela River. Salu used her forehead to point at a cemetery. The sky released a light rain, but they seemed to be in a bubble.

"This land is sacred. It belongs to our family and holds some of our relatives' remains, which were exhumed from the mountain after the Battle of Langalibalele."

Salu had been in a dispute with the neighbouring white farmers over her family graves. The white farmers claimed that the graves were encroaching on their land. They had already begun cultivating and planting within a few meters of the gravesite.

"The noise caused by a farmer has been increasing recently. When I asked him about it, he responded through his lawyers. The man fails to take seriously our humanity, that this is our ancestral land, a place where our culture must be preserved. Unfortunately, some people dismiss our culture as inferior or nonsense. Imagine if many of us from the Midlands went to their sacred Stratford-upon-Avon and told every English community to relocate Shakespeare's ancient burial site to the wasteland. Do you know what would happen?"

"The European Union would rise against Africa?"

"Let me tell you what happened here, something that will be remembered for generations. Musa was never the same after you were born. Guilt seemed to wrap around her soul like winding thorns. We buried your twin brother among these rocks with part of the umbilical cord still attached."

"How come no one ever told me I had a twin brother?"

"Musa will tell you the rest of this sad story himself one day. The rock on the embankment marks the grave. Nobody touched the stone because African people know this is our family cemetery. We need to get closer, so you touch the ground that covers your brother and then plant a flower."

The colourful, shimmering little stars, along with the yellow tulips, decorated the plants around the old graves. Thorns and thistles grew in the moonlit landscape like cherry blossoms. Kükuchi began to believe that the prickly plants shadowed her like Eve's curse, everywhere she went.

"What was his name, Salu?"

"He died before your mother gave him a name, but you survived."

***

At dawn, Salu tried to sneak out of bed, hoping she wouldn't wake Kükuchi, who chirped, "Out to feed the chickens, Salu?"

"No. I'm going to the kitchen to make coffee to feed my brain. I could not sleep after going through yesterday's ritual."

"As soon as I got into my blankets, I was all gone."

"Yes, you were all gone into your noisy dreams. How I wish I could do something about your sleepwalking and swearing."

"Oh, Salu, swearing?"

"The blood of Bashaye is in your veins, and you can't help it."

"You said you and Musa saved my life, but I believe Musa was trying to kill both me and my twin brother."

"You need a stronger coffee than I do, Faty."

After Kükuchi finished her tasks in the broiler, including removing litter and collecting eggs, Salu told her to prepare for Ixopo early the next day.

CHAPTER 17

Third-Class Coach

We finally caught a slow train that stopped in Estcourt and small villages before taking a break at Ixopo. Two coaches reserved for whites were quiet and nearly empty, while the rest of the train was crowded with Africans traveling from different parts of the country to the Cape Province. African coaches were often lively with music and laughter. At the corner of our coach sat an overweight man, singing and playing a concertina, accompanied by a guitarist strumming a battered guitar with one string missing. Salu dozed off and then slept on my lap. Before long, she was snoring like a piglet.

Halfway through our journey, the musicians got off. By then, the coach was half empty. Salu woke up and said, "Those musical people are gone? Be careful, Kuchi. Spooks haunt all trains, some disguised as musicians or young men or women. When we were young, a long-distance train was a scary place to be in. At the start of each journey, we had to surrender our secrets to God out of fear that we might not reach our destination. Coaches had three classes, ranging from first to third grade. White governments, with their supporters, are the masters of creating conflicting classes and partitions. But when the train begins to brave the mysterious journey, all of us—first class or third, white or black—are tied together as one in a space called anxiety, speculating as to the planet we would end up inhabiting by nightfall. Now, Faty, we still have some distance to cover to Ixopo. The self-righteous people occupying first class think they do not have regrets in their hearts before their God. What about you? Do you have any regrets or secrets that God does not know?"

"Secrets? No, I don't, Salu."

Salu heaved a sigh and turned to look out the window.

She said slowly, "Dassie told me something. Do you want me to repeat what Dassie said?"

"No, Salu. Dassie is a liar."

Salu whirled around, glared at Kükuchi, and said, "We are all fallible, and sometimes we make bad choices, but never use fancy language when someone confronts you with an awkward question. Should I repeat to you what Dassie once said to me?"

"No, please, Gogo."

"Kuchi, don't let your conscience weigh you down. Dassie told me he read your diary one day. Did Dassie read your diary?"

I was so overwhelmed that my head started to spin. It was pretty uncomfortable discussing my diary with my grandmother, but since she wouldn't let it go, I finally said, "Okay, Salu. One day Uncle Dodo raped me."

Salu's extreme shock left me with a dry tongue. She began to sweat and gasp for breath. Two young female passengers in Zionist church uniforms came to our aid. One lifted the coach window for fresh air, while the other fanned Salu's face with her white doek. After a while, one of the women wiped Salu's face and handed her orange juice.

When she recovered, Salu sat back in the seat and said, "Thanks for saving my life, good angels."

The women went back to their seats. Salu rested her head on my lap, and we both drifted off to sleep. When the train stopped on the long Umkhomazi River bridge, I began praying that God would forgive all my past sins, including referring to Mama and Papa Maseko as the greatest liars in White City.

Salu asked, "Where are we?"

"I don't know, Salu. What if this train stops here forever? Can you see the river down there?"

"It will stop forever if you don't start talking. What you told me isn't the story Dassie shared with me. Are you sure you're not trying to accuse Dodo wrongly?"

I felt awkward, knowing I had embarrassed myself in front of Salu by revealing what Uncle Dodo had done to me.

"You are quiet. Is what you told me about Dodo the truth?"

"What I am telling you is true, Gogo. What did Dassie say to you?"

"How old were you when this terrible thing happened to you? Do you remember?"

"I was eleven, Gogo."

"Dassie told me something about you and Toby, involving the peddling of stolen goods at a Johannesburg taxi rank. That's the secret he shared with me. Is Dassie a liar?"

"Oh, Gogo."

"However, there is never a right time to avoid discussing your issue with Dodo. Rape is a serious crime, and those who commit it must face harsh punishment. Your body, your breasts, your nipples, your thighs, and your sovereignty are all your God-given assets. If you'd like, you can have fun and play games with your lover by designing riddles and surprising each other to rekindle your affection. My child, Kükuchi, no child should participate in such complex activities. Do you agree?"

"What, Salu?"

"Having committed such a heinous act, Dodo does not deserve to live. Look me in the eye and tell me that everything you told Salu is true, Kükuchi."

"Yes, Salu."

"I don't suppose you told your Khulu or Musa what you just told me."

"No, Salu. And you're not telling them either, right?"

"Right, Faty. Let's keep this just between us, as our train secret. My sister would be devastated if she ever heard such wickedness, and Musa would kill Dodo with her bare hands. We're not telling them, but I will talk to Funani. He has his methods, my cousin's kid, because he's a professional investigator, trained by Scotland Yard."

***

The train starts moving slowly without waking them. When Kükuchi opens her eyes, it is raining, and the coach windows are foggy.

"Salu, when you told me about my twin, you murdered and buried at night, I wanted to ask you something. Did that twin brother look like me?"

"If he looked like you, his mouth would be cleaner than yours. No one murdered anyone. Yes, to answer your question, your twin had albinism. And that's why that so-called father turned his back on Musa the day she saw you."

At the makeshift police station, three officers briefly looked up when Kükuchi and Salu entered. The seemingly busy officers continued their quiet work. A young officer came out from inside and hurried away. Kükuchi's attempt to stop him was unsuccessful. Twenty minutes later, a Black sergeant called them over to his part of the desk. After begging for help for barely a minute, he told them to go home, saying the station had no resources to chase ghosts. Salu showed a newspaper clipping about Sisi Africa, including images of her burial in Soweto. The officer examined the clipping and then looked at the two white police officers as if seeking their approval. But since the matter wasn't directly related to white children, neither of them showed any interest. Salu and her granddaughter left the station very sad. Kükuchi was crying hard. Salu suggested they return to Drycourt immediately. But their return had to wait until the next day, according to the train schedule. So, Salu and Kükuchi went back to the station and sat on the bronze bench inside the waiting room. As night fell, it got uncomfortably cold, and Salu complained of feeling hungry. Toward midnight, Kükuchi and Salu were abruptly awoken by a young policeman who had earlier ignored them at the station and then quickly left. They were shivering from the cold. The Warrant Officer, Hamilton Bopela, stood somewhat formally in front of them and asked about their purpose in Ixopo. After they explained their mission, he pointed them to a battered van, promising to drive them to a warm bed to sleep. Salu's doubts faded as Kükuchi expressed her gratitude to the officer for his hospitality. In the morning, Bopela took his passengers back to the station and told them to wait outside. Salu looked around the corrugated iron structures and saw two toilets, one for whites and another for Africans.

"They segregate everything, even pit toilets," Salu quipped. "That policeman needs to learn how to greet and acknowledge people. His fidgeting hands and shifty eyes make me feel like he's trying to escape from himself. Maybe he's one of those who think our culture is primitive. What is so primitive about showing respect?"

A Name Greater than all of us

When Hamilton hurried back, he had his jacket on and slung a black bag over his shoulder. He was hiding a new trick up his sleeve.

"I understand what you're looking for. Let's grab a taxi. Too bad about the rain."

Once they were settled in the taxi, Hamilton started blaming Kükuchi for using the whites-only bathroom. Salu apologized, saying she wasn't aware. Kükuchi told Hamilton that her teacher, Mr Zondi, once said that if a black person entered a white bathroom, the sky wouldn't fall. Hamilton warned Kükuchi that what she did was against the law.

More commuters gradually boarded the taxi as it steered down the muddy road. After a long, awkward pause, Hamilton finally began to open up. In his neighborhood, he revealed, a girl from Nyaka had left home years earlier and then disappeared.

"She may have gone to Cape Town, Johannesburg, or even Durban. Our girls here in the rural areas fantasize about the bright lights of the cities, but they are easy targets for city scammers and pimps. But do you think they ever learn?"

"There's nothing here for them, Hamilton," Salu responded.

The light rain continued. Inside the taxi, mist had formed, limiting the driver's visibility. He grabbed his old yellow rag and wiped his side of the windshield, but the rest of the glass stayed foggy.

"The girl who went missing… what was her name, Mr Hamilton?" asked Kükuchi.

"I remember her well because we are neighbours. They have been searching for her for over four years. As she grew up, she sang, danced, and entertained better than any girl I knew here. She delighted the audience at my sister's wedding in Kwa-Makhanya. Her name is still on everyone's lips around my Mahehle area. They referred to her as Sisi, although her real name was Busisiwe Blose."

Kükuchi collapsed, and the taxi driver skilfully guided his vehicle to safety beneath the bridge.

***

Kükuchi later realized how the taxi driver had disgracefully abandoned them; they were now near Mahehle School in Hamilton's hometown. Instead of waiting an hour for the next transport, Hamilton suggested they walk. Kükuchi noticed threatening streaks of lightning on top of the nearby mountains ahead of them. As they drew close to Hamilton's home village, they caught a shabby-looking taxi that had seen worse days than the previous one that dumped them under the bridge. The showers persisted. After struggling up and down the rocky terrain, they circled Creighton and headed down toward the woodlands of Nyaka. Twenty-four hours of continuous, steady rain had made the dirt roads quite dangerous. Near the low bridge, the middle-aged driver wisely stopped. The taxi couldn't cross without the swirling surge pulling it out to sea. The driver made everyone evacuate the cab right at the riverbank, and the battered old vehicle returned to Mahehle for another load of unsuspecting commuters.

With Hamilton's encouragement, the trio waded across. Salu howled, "I wish I could stay here and wrap my head around the fabric of this world's art. Long ago, I dreamed I was here. Maybe it wasn't a dream. Maybe when I was a baby, I was brought here by my birth mother. I tell you, I know these hills and the sugarcane fields and all the shiny houses decorating the hills over there."

The following taxi looked less battered, and Hamilton whistled a cheerful tune. The vehicle moved through a rugged, muddy canyon between Kwa Makhanya and Nyaka. A little more drizzle fell before Hamilton said, "Let's get off. We're almost there."

Salu strolled, admiring the familiar stream flowing over the shiny rocks. Kükuchi and Hamilton distanced themselves from Salu, who kept scratching her head, pondering the land from her dreams. She tried to keep up with the young people who moved like lovers. In this country, black settlements frequently lacked necessities such as running water and electricity. African schools used the bucket system as toilets, a strange shame white children never faced.

The muddy road grew narrower until it turned into a footpath. Hamilton began squeezing Kükuchi's hand warmly, causing Kükuchi's body to go numb.

"This is the first time that I've been this close and talked to a girl like you…"

"A girl like me?"

"You know what I mean."

"Look, Mr Hamilton, my skin colour isn't the core of who I am. I'm a girl. I go to school. I'm the top javelin thrower in the township. You could at least ask me about my recent trip to Durban, where I met some athletes. There's a boy at a school in Glebelands near the hostel. I was relieved to see him throwing a javelin even though he's paralyzed. I spent the day working with him and left him feeling hopeful about his future. So, what do you mean by 'a girl like me'?"

"You're too smart for your age. I have to introduce you to my mother. She will love you a lot because she likes clever kids. She is the principal of Kwa Makhanya Primary, which is where I was born. I am one with this world."

The trio finally stopped near a shrub-lined entrance leading to a colourful homestead made of fancy mud huts and thatched rondavels. At the end were two recently built modern cottages and a kraal, all surrounded by large rocks.

"The people living here must be well-to-do," Salu said.

"He is a headman. The chief's homestead is on the other side of this hillock."

A yellow 1938 pickup, tucked into a wooden shed some distance from the kraal, bloomed out like a delicate rose petal on the forest floor. Kükuchi reflected on the heavy burden on her shoulders as the scene became surreal. She could sense Sisi Afrika's presence as if she were about to step out of one of the huts to greet them. Three young girls played happily with their izingedo pebble game on the porch. Surprised to see strangers, the girls quickly ran to tell their parents.

Hamilton shouted a greeting loudly as per tradition, "Nina bakwa Shinga, Ndelu."

'Shinga' and 'Ndelu' are respected traditional praise names of the Blose clan. Hamilton's work as a police officer raised his status to that of a headman or priest. A middle-aged man with a shaggy beard and a full hairline greeted Hamilton with his praise name of 'Hlomuka' as he approached. Blose invited them inside a visitors' rondavel. Once inside, two girls curtsied before laying out beautifully decorated grass mats. Blose called his three wives and the other family members present to introduce them to the visitors. It was a large household with eleven children, ranging in age from two months to twenty-two years. Only eight children were there. They gathered quietly, eyes wide with anticipation. The formal introductions took quite some time.

Ndelu and the Blose household," Hamilton began, "Mama Mthimkhulu from Bhekuzulu in the land of the Hlubi is here with this maiden from the land of Gold. She is her granddaughter. They have brought news about what I believe to be your child. I will ask our dear mother to tell you everything she knows."

The entire family moved like thatching grass in the breeze, all focusing on Salu. Kükuchi could tell right away who Sisi's biological mother was because a flood of tears started streaming down the young mother's face before Salu said a word. Her name was Bonisa, the youngest among the wives. Busisiwe was the only child she had after years of being insulted as 'barren.'

Salu shared what she knew about Busisiwe's death amid screams of devastation echoing throughout the household. Tholiwe, the second wife, draped a shawl over Bonisa's head and offered her comfort.

***

They settled down for a hearty meal as it started pouring again. Blose expressed relief and happiness about the rain. He hadn't seen anything like it in over 25 years, and he smiled and exclaimed, "This rain will mean plenty of good cattle feed for many months to come. There will be a good yield, and all the hills will produce large potatoes. Good potatoes are beneficial for us because they enable us to send our children to school to receive an education. It will be a glorious season here. The rain is a sign that Busisiwe is pleased with the news you brought today."

When the rain stopped, Bonisa asked, "Her grave... where is my child's grave? How will I find her without her name engraved anywhere?"

"The mothers of White City and Orlando called her Sisi Afrika because nobody knew who she was. They buried her in Nancefield Cemetery," said Kûkuchi.

An uneasy silence settled as everyone tried to come to terms with Sisi Afrika's tragic end. Blose broke the silence with an awkward, low-pitched, peculiar giggle, "Sisi Afrika? How amazing. My child dies a gruesome death at the hands of lowly township jackals and is buried like a beggar, far from her mother at Nyaka. Sisi Afrika! My girl is drawn to a place, a Johannesburg none of us has seen, and she leaves behind such a legacy, a name greater than all of us! 'Sisi Afrika!"

CHAPTER 18

Sister Mohale's Anguish

The warm welcome home touched me, even though I could still feel the lingering gloom over Tina's disappearance. That evening, Khulu reminded everyone about Musa's upcoming wedding day.

Khulu quickly changed the subject, "The newspapers say you made a lot of money in Natal. How much did you get?"

"Twenty pounds," I lied.

"Help Musa. Give her all that money."

"You told me there was a lot of money she hid somewhere only she knew."

"Still, it's good to support her because she loves you. I know they will face struggles after marriage."

"She loves me? Musa?"

***

The disappearance of Bobby, Sister Mohale's son, upset everyone. Sister Mohale became paranoid. When Dassie and I took our spot on the porch, Dassie said, "I know where Bobby has gone. But don't tell anyone."

"You lie."

"He left with the guys from Sharpeville to Bechuanaland. They have gone to get revolvers from Russia to shoot the Boers," explained Dassie.

"Bobby would never tell you something like that. You lie."

"It's true. He told me. Do you know why? He wanted me to go with them. He said, 'Out there in Russia, they give you a gun with real bullets that follow your enemy even when he runs away and turns a corner'."

"Bullets that do what…? Dassie, do you still smoke benzene?"

"Can you keep a secret? Don't tell anyone, not even Khulu. Bobby said the van taking them will come back, and I'll follow them with the other boys."

"Are you mad? You want the white soldiers to kill you, Dassie?"

Rumours about Bobby's disappearance spread throughout the township. However, Mkhize viewed Bobby's actions and disappearance cynically. He told Khulu, "When I last saw Bobby, he was walking smugly like a flap-necked chameleon, with a newspaper tightly clenched under his arm like a Dube tycoon. He hardly responded to my greetings appropriately. One day, I asked him how he was getting along with his schooling. He asked cynically if I paid his fees.

Ten police vehicles converged on White City and parked their vans on both sides of Sister Mohale's house, sending twenty heavily armed white officers to search her home. All but three stayed in their vehicles while the others tore down Sister Mohale's fence, broke into her house, and slashed her sofas in search of something. They were there for four hours and only sped off a few minutes before Sister Mohale returned from work. Her shock at finding her house ransacked and in disarray brought

Mohale to tears. Musa went to visit Sister Mohale to learn about the boys' escape to Bechuanaland and to comfort her. Jozi stayed with Mohale for over a week.

A few days after the unwarranted police search, Sister Mohale made her way to Khulu's house, accompanied by Jozi and her ex-husband, Mr Mohale. Sounding distressed and scared, she whispered, "Khulu, where is Musa? I came to tell her about Bobby. After the dirty police broke into my house while I was away and stole my belongings, they later returned and detained me for three full hours. They asked me about Bobby. How should I know?'

Musa emerged and hugged Mohale and said, "Musa, you need to call a meeting here in White City because our people are upset with the government. How can they treat me like this? They destroyed my furniture, took many of my books, and confiscated my cherished family albums. They even took my private letters from when Mohale and I were dating."

Mr Mohale looked agitated but said little.

"Oh, Musa," Sister Mohale cried. "What should I do? Bobby is my only child."

Mr Mohale said quietly, "This Sharpeville thing, Musa... the white people were just testing a new tactic. Henceforth, the police will employ the same approach against any future protests in the country. Hitler started his slaughter by using stormtroopers against the communists as a warning of what was to come. The Jews were Hitler's main target, and the Holocaust was his ultimate prize. Expect more of the same, if not worse, from the Boers. The security forces and military will be responsible for governing the country. When Hitler killed white people in Europe, the outrage was immediate. But here in Africa, who cares if Africans die like flies? After Sharpeville, the Apartheid government knows that whatever they do, the Western media will shout from the rooftops, but their governments will do little more than look after their own."

"After Sharpeville, Mandela said in his Independent Television News interview:
'Many people believe it is pointless to keep discussing peace and nonviolence against the government, whose response is only brutal attacks on unarmed and defenceless people'."

Sister Mohale cried. "Please try to get information from the people up there. You are well known, and the ANC will tell you about Bobby."

"Musa is a PAC official," Mohale said, "They are against the ANC Charter."

"Why, God of all heavens! Our children are leaving the country in our old age, and we're quibbling over PAC and ANC! Musa, are you saying they won't tell you about my son's whereabouts because you belong to PAC?"

"I'll do my best..."

Bobby's decision to escape into exile filled me with great hope for our chances of participating in the Commonwealth Games. After Musa's inspiring idea about Mayfair all those years ago, I started to believe that Bobby and his friends would do something extraordinary to end Apartheid. That year became especially significant for African athletes. Between August and September, Rome hosted the Olympic Games, where many independent African countries participated. Black people thought that the International Olympic Committee (IOC) would exclude South Africa because of its apartheid policies. However, that was not the case.

A flicker of hope appeared when Abebe Bikila of Ethiopia won the Olympic gold, making him the first African to achieve this. In the same event, the all-white South African team earned one silver and two bronze medals. African countries celebrated the ironic news of South Africa's defeat with joy.

However, Rome marked the last Olympic opportunity for Apartheid South Africa. As expected, many white athletes soon emigrated to other countries, mainly the UK and Australia. Most of them quickly embraced their European roots and criticized Apartheid from a safe distance. Others chose to remain silent out of fear. Regarding Rosemarie, who ended up in Wales, she stayed mum about everything.

During my training, I spent time reading newspapers and doing my schoolwork. I also kept in contact with the people organizing the exhumation of Sisi Afrika's remains from Nancefield. The Nightingales prepared all week for the sombre event. *Township News* featured their story, highlighting previously unseen pictures of Sisi Afrika in her school uniform at Ixopo High. There was also a haunting photo of Tina, captioned, 'Still Missing: Tina, the Rhodesian Grocer's Daughter.'

***

I feared meeting Hamilton because I might have misled him, but I knew I had to clear things up.

"I see you've been avoiding me, Kükuchi."

"Me? No."

"Good. So, it's a date. This sad affair about Sisi Afrika will pass, and we must meet again."

"Sorry, Hamilton. Last time, you asked if there was someone else, and… yes, maybe there is. So, let's forget about the date."

Hamilton was naturally upset.

However, Toby had once made me aware that unrequited love is a part of life, and some people get over it, while others don't.

Before the Blose family left, Mkhize visited Khulu and said something unsettling. As a traditional healer, Mkhize explained, he had tossed his bones from his ancestors in front of the Blose family, and he saw nothing that linked Mendi to Sisi Afrika's murder.

"Mkhize," Khulu said, "Don't you think your ancestors are wrong this time? Remember the day they accidentally swallowed your bones?"

"My ancestors are never mistaken. Those lost bones will return, but as for Mendi…! There is something strange about this case of Sisi Africa. Mendi had nothing to do with it."

"Why did he admit to killing her, then?"

"Remember, they beat African men to a pulp until they confess to something they never did."

CHAPTER 19

A flourish of Confetti

Musa's wedding day finally arrived. In the morning, I went to meet Salu at Johannesburg Park Station. As usual, she brought a large suitcase and a bag full of chicken pies. I later asked why she had come to the wedding despite having sworn she wouldn't. Salu dodged my question by rehashing her old jokes, which only she found funny. Not that she cared. She went on to tell me about a squad of police who came to her farm hoping to see Tina. Tina's mother had filed a charge against her for abduction. She told the police that Salu once threatened to take Tina to her rural kraal so she could carry firewood for her and that she feared Salu had lived up to her threat to turn Tina into a zombie tokoloshe.

"What does the woman think I am? I'm a former English teacher with an education background. What do I know about zombies?"

"In White City, they park in front of our house every night, even now."

"I know. Dassie tells me. Now, let's talk about you. You've been the weirdest one in the family. Whoever thought we could have a successful athlete? But don't get carried away; even Musa believes the Olympics will never happen during Apartheid's lifetime."

"Sometimes, I feel overwhelmed and want to give up. It's really about the politics. I wonder if true cooperation between Africans and whites will ever happen without struggle. Isn't that what Musa always emphasizes—that we may need to stand up and fight for what's right?"

"No, Musa has been saying we should forget about whites and compete among ourselves.

"Yes, this white government is scared you might beat their white athletes and embarrass their racist policies. In 1936, Jesse Owens proved to Hitler and his followers that the white claim of Aryan supremacy was a myth. They know if they give a chance to blacks in any endeavour, they will prove their racist theory wrong."

We got home before the convoy headed to church, and I caught a ride with Funani in his battered car. The 1920 Sedan sped us off while the owner kept talking until we reached the church grounds. Outside the church, Funani whispered, "Yes, Kuchi. Please do me a favour. Please talk to Jozi. Say nice things about me. I want her to be my girlfriend."

"Funani, why don't you tell her yourself?"

"You know how it works. This girl said I am too old. How can she say that?"

"Maybe she prefers younger men."

"It can't be. A man must always be older. Do I look old to you?"

"My name is not Jozi. If Jozi thinks you are too old for her, then you are..."

"Please, Kŭkuchi, say nice things about me..."

"I can't think of one nice thing to say about you."

"Kuchi, we're family, and we need to help each other. One day, you'll need my help. Say something to her; she admires you. You're a woman, and you're popular here."

A medley of choruses went on until the guests filled the pews. Musa wore a dazzling wedding dress, covering her head with an extra-large chiffon scarf. Unable to conceal his irritation at the delay, the young minister rested his listless body on the pulpit and stared indifferently at the excited crowd. An eye-catching bouquet sprays the sculpture of Jesus Christ fixed behind the altar. However, one could not make out from the apex of the crown of thorns if the cross was bronze or gold. Sporting her newly acquired ANC *doek*, Sister Mohale looked like a pompous giraffe amidst a flock of sheep.

With all the key parties seated, the priest began his message by saying that Africans would be the last to enter heaven because they could not keep time. There was a murmur of disapproval, which helped cut short the sermon. The pastor was able to calm tempers by turning to and preaching from John 2:11, in which Jesus turned water into wine at the wedding in Cana, Galilee. The gathering danced their way out of the church as rainbow-coloured confetti floated through the air. The procession wound down toward the porch. Musa cast a curious glance at Kükuchi, whose guilty conscience over her refusal to be one of the bridesmaids refused to let go. Kükuchi immediately knew that this was Musa's happiest day.

The sun was setting, and billows of dark grey smoke were rising from household chimneys as Funani drove Kükuchi to 12 Maile Street, Phefeni, the groom's place.

Funani repeatedly urged Kükuchi to help his cause, saying, "Please, Kükuchi, don't forget about Josefina. I want her to marry me."

"Now you want to marry Jozi? Don't forget to send your people to her people first, and you must pay 25 cows because she is still a virgin."

"A virgin? How do you know that, Kuchi?"

"She whispered to me one day."

By the time the 'reception' festivities started, Maile Street was filled with spectators. The bride's family had brought a bunch of blankets and a striking bedroom set as gifts for the Sithole family. Sofasonke Mpanza, the main speaker from Orlando, called for more invasions of white-owned land across Johannesburg. He said, "Our detractors attack us, yet they are the first to settle on the corner stands of the land we have invaded. You can be assured of it; the day we gain our freedom, our African political brothers will reveal their true colours. We know they are obsessed with Stetson Durangos, open coupé Buicks, and Chevrolet Impalas. They will all rush to occupy white-owned, north-facing corner stands and forget about you."

CHAPTER 20

They found Tina.

Maluti, the girl from Northern Transvaal, was an intimidating field athlete. She achieved almost 50 meters, with all the African javelin girls trailing behind. Celebrations erupted countrywide, and the athlete was fêted like royalty. The Sunday Times published Maluti's achievements on its front page, which threw the white athletics establishment into severe panic and disarray. The international media hailed the success of the black girl, which filled the Apartheid government with uncontrollable jealousy.

Kūkuchi, on the other hand, was so motivated that she spent more time on the pitch, hoping to reach Maluti's level of performance. Macmillan's 'winds of change' projections became ill winds for Kūkuchi because, in 1961, South Africa became a white Republic. Paradoxically, the same year marked the commencement of the construction of the Berlin Wall, a symbol of the Cold War division between East and West. The Afrikaners, who assumed the role of Israelites of the Promised Land, saw themselves as the prototypical representatives of the West in Africa. Not only did they entrench themselves with repressive state apparatuses, but they also used a concoction of Christianity as their state ideology to bolster the Apartheid system. For Kūkuchi, the 'winds of change' amounted to a whirlwind of uncertainty howling on all sides. Hendrik Verwoerd departed for the Conference of Commonwealth Prime Ministers to discuss South Africa's continued membership in the Commonwealth. *Township News* followed the proceedings with keen interest. Verwoerd's insensitive statement to the Commonwealth embarrassed his friends and irked his detractors. He told the meeting that Apartheid was just a policy of good labour practices and good neighbourliness. All anti-Apartheid sports bodies scoffed at the statement, while most member countries threatened to leave the Commonwealth if South Africa remained. Verwoerd withdrew the application for continued membership when he sensed the level of international hostility had increased. This meant that after the country became a Republic, it would cease to be a member of the Commonwealth. White South Africans hailed Verwoerd as a hero. When he returned from his travels, he addressed his audience, comprising both English and Afrikaans supporters, and told them that leaving the Commonwealth was a 'happy day for South Africa.' Ironically, Verwoerd's 'happy day' amounted to an athlete celebrating before reaching the finish line. A flood of applications for permanent residence from white athletes flooded European countries. Many of those athletes had stood silently behind Verwoerd, yet they were now lamenting having to forgo their ambitions for the Commonwealth Games.

Posa remarked, "White South Africans have a knack for wishing to eat their cake and having it. We blacks have no choice but to stay in Africa."

Looking miserable, Kūkuchi heaved a sigh of despair.

Mkhize said, "Those white athletes rushing abroad claiming European ancestry will eventually return here with their families, reclaiming their African roots. The Europeans have perfected deception and the art of chameleon-like adaptation."

Kükuchi said to her brother, "Dassie, you lived for a long time with Europeans. Do you think they will all run back to Europe?"

"You know what, Mohale was saying to me, 'Kükuchi needs a good doctor to examine her head.'"

"You lie, Dassie! Why did she say that?"

"Something to do with Mayfair. She says you have already booked a house in Mayfair because you think the Europeans are about to run to the sea. She says your mouth is big like that of a hippopotamus."

"A hippopotamus! And what did you say to her?"

"Nothing."

"Why do you always say nothing when strangers insult me? I am your sister; you should have protected me. That nurse has a big mouth like a pregnant crocodile! She is always babbling on about Bobby. It's Bobby this, Bobby that. Everything is Bobby. Can you think of anything more boring?"

Kükuchi's opinions about Bobby reached Sister Mohale's ears. When she met Mkhize at Tatenda's shop, Mohale expressed her profound distress at Kükuchi's attitude. Mkhize later took a walk to Khulu's place to confront Kükuchi.

"Kükuchi," Mkhize started shrewdly, "Sister Mohale says everyone in White City hates Bobby. She says Dassie told her. Do you hate Bobby?"

"No, Papa."

"Did you not say Bobby is boring?"

"Dassie was lying."

"Tell me, does Mohale have a mouth as big as a crocodile?"

"She started it. She said I was born with a big mouth like a hippopotamus."

"But Mohale is an elderly person, Kükuchi. If she starts something, you cannot fight back by saying her whole family is boring and that they will all burn in hell. Did you say Mohale must bring back Khulu's money she borrowed when Dassie was still a toddler...?"

Mohale stopped visiting Khulu's home for all of one week. When she reappeared, she ignored both Khulu and Kükuchi but said with sarcasm, "I hear Musa is around today. I know some of us here have had enough of Bobby and his mother. One day, the chickens will come home to roost. Where is Musa?"

Musa appeared, and Mohale said, "Ah, here you are. You will tell me all about your married life sometime. Let's talk about more important things. As a Women's League leader, have you heard anything about Bobby?"

"I am not with the Women's League, but Sister, please keep this to yourself. Bobby is safe. After spending a few weeks in the Soviet Union, he went to Cuba with another group that had recently left the country. One group will be in the military, but another will study other things like political science..."

"Why is the mother always the last to know? You said military? Bobby will not join the military. He is too clever. He must do science. My son cannot be a soldier, please, Musa. Tell your political people he must do science and become a doctor. We are a cultured family. His father is the first African to earn a diploma in Photography and a degree in architecture. Our son must not shoot people with guns."

"It's going to be his decision."

Changing the subject, Mohale said, "And the people! They are gossiping, Musa. They think Dassie and Kŭkuchi know something about Tina's whereabouts. You know me; I don't like gossip."

Ever since Tina's disappearance, White City had become a ghost town, and many children ended up in rural areas across Southern Africa.

When South Africa became a Republic, all major Black sports bodies resolved to take the Apartheid government head-on. The South African Sports Association (SASA) launched the National Athletics Games for Blacks at Coronationville, a township designated for the coloured community. Four provinces took part. A throng of smiling officials flowed out of their brief, coursing down the long-jump runway toward the centre of the field. For the first time, unity among the provinces seemed possible. Although Maluti knew she was the one to beat, the Limpopo girl appeared to be a bundle of nerves when she arrived. But the beauty of her smile hid all signs of excitement. Recent official records hung over other black athletes like a dark cloud. The white media had held up the white records as justification for denying blacks the chance to participate in international activities, arguing that no black had reached an acceptable standard in a significant meeting.

The Coronationville tournament was balanced on a knife's edge. When the number came down to eight, the officials gave each contestant five chances. Crunch time came when four girls remained, each receiving three chances. Maluti sent the entire field into a panic when her two throws landed flat on the ground, which meant 'no marks.' On her last chance, Maluti looked tense, her fingers shaking as she tried to take control of the grip. She held her javelin comically above her head as she often does and sprinted along the runway. Up to that point, Kŭkuchi had the edge overall, having beaten Lesedi into second place. For the first time, four black women had made over 40m in a significant competition. However, Kŭkuchi's spirit sank when Maluti and Lesedi finally relegated her to third place despite her improved performance.

***

As I approach home from the tournament, I spot a police van parked against the Donaldson Primary fence under the tree, one of the spots that Tina's mother often uses when she's on the warpath. There are a few neighbours around, but the silence feels eerie, and I sense something profound in the air. Mkhize, who seems unusually out of it, says, "Kuchi, a blanket of death has covered White City. We are heartbroken, and we are crying..."

Musa remains strait-laced and absorbed in her thoughts. And then she blushes. Dassie's eyes are fixed directly on me. Khulu is seated quietly, holding a damp handkerchief in her hand.

"What is it, Papa?"

"Kŭkuchi, my child, they have found Tina."

"Where is she?"

Mkhize fails to answer. When I turn, I see an ominous dark ring of sadness below Khulu's eyes. Dassie's demeanour remains expressionless as if something inside his soul had died. I am so overwhelmed with emotion that I cry piercingly. Musa cries, and for me, her tears are priceless. I feel an emotional bond like I've never experienced before.

"Tina is no longer with us," Mkhize says pointlessly.

"Who killed her, Papa?"

Dassie says, "If we find him, we'll kill him."

"Why are the police here? What is happening?"

"Certain people have threatened to attack Khulu and burn the house. I called the police," Mkhize said.

"Why? What has Khulu done?"

"Tina's mother has been spreading stories about Khulu, telling people that Khulu and her twin sister, who lives in Natal, are witches."

Luckily, the small crowd disperses by late evening. Three police officers remain parked under the trees. In the middle of the night, Khulu whispers, "Kükuchi, are you asleep?"

"What is it, Khulu?"

"Were you listening when I prayed?"

"No, Khulu, let us sleep. I am tired."

"I prayed for forgiveness. You went to Coronationville, and when you came back, we all forgot to ask you about it. Did you win the athletics?"

"Oh, Khulu. Let us sleep. I'll tell you in the morning."

"Tell me what happened in that coloured township of Coronationville. I was worried because of the wall between the coloureds and us."

"Okay, Khulu. I beat myself, but I still got bronze. Can we sleep now?"

After a few minutes, Khulu whispers, "Kükuchi, you got bronze? We are proud of you. Do you know that you are an asset to this family?"

"Good night, Khulu."

At dawn, I peer through the curtain and see Sergeant Sibande and two constables trying to shake off the cold. I make tea for them. Musa comes to the kitchen and asks if I slept well, an unusual display of decorum by Mother's standards.

The *Pioneer* newspaper describes the Coronationville meeting in contemptible terms as 'a non-white competition of no sporting significance'. I write back to question the editor's integrity. White athletes, I point out, had held a similar contest previously, which the same newspaper described as the 'major South African trials involving the best sportsmen and women in the country'. I ask, 'Do you think we have forgotten what you wrote in your stupid newspaper?'

The Right-wing *Pioneer* responds by inferring that I could not have written the letter 'without the help of my 'Azanian communist sister called Musa.'

For its part, *Township News* features the gruesome discovery on its front page— a picture of a smiling Tina in her brown school uniform, alongside another blurred image of her body covered with a blanket inside a police Black Maria. A deep sense of desolation consumes White City. Musa returns to Phefeni, where she has lived for a while.

I found Dodo at home the next day. There was a mound of porridge and meat in front of him. As he ate, he was busy bragging and telling Khulu to start preparing for his big graduation party. Dodo's insensitivity irritated me so much that I asked, "Dodo, do you know Tina?"

"I am your uncle. Call me uncle. Of course, I know Tina. What's wrong with you?"

"Maybe I should be asking you that question..."

"Kükuchi!" Khulu reprimanded me.

"Now, Uncle, did you hear about Tina that the real police found her decomposed body in the veld near the Klipspruit stream?"

"I know that. I am a policeman," he responded while filling his mouth with porridge.

"One day, Musa asked you what the police were doing about all the missing girls, but you played dumb."

"The case of those girls who ran away from home? It's closed; *finish and Klaar*."

"Ran away from home? Are you mad?" Khulu shouted.

"I asked you about Tina. You show no interest in what happened to her, but all you care about is your stupid party."

Dodo seemed to be feeling the heat. He slipped away, leaving his unfinished porridge and meat on his plate.

Following several uneventful days, the officers under the trees packed their belongings and left. I took advantage of the quiet atmosphere to retrieve the sack of meals containing Mendi's money that Dassie and I had hidden in the garden. In 1961, South Africa adopted a decimal currency, replacing the pound with the Rand. The government made a countywide call for people to surrender their old currency. I had the idea that we could start exchanging the money gradually to avoid suspicion. Late at night, I crept out of the house. As I burrowed through the garden patch, I became suspicious when I felt a patch of loose earth. I was becoming more desperate because there was no sign of Mendi's sack of money. I continued, growing more frantic with each mound of earth I hollowed out. On realizing that someone had removed the sack, I heaved and gazed at the bright stars, imagining the best way to inflict maximum pain on Dassie before 'killing him to death', as we used to say in White City.

I knew that confronting Dassie would yield nothing. Instead of covering the site, I left a gaping hole to observe Dassie's reaction. In the morning, Dassie said nothing, and my rage grew each day. I spent every night cursing the day Dassie became my brother. Still, I kept watching to see how he responded to the mound of earth sticking out where the sack of mealie-meal had once been.

After a week, Dassie said, "I see you removed the bag. Keep the money safe."

"Dassie!" I exploded, "Don't make a fool out of me. Where is the money?"

"Didn't you dig it out and hide it?" he asked nonchalantly.

"There was no money in there, Dassie. Only two people knew about it."

"Maybe someone saw us put it in there, and they stole it."

"I want it back, Dassie, or else you will pay."

After losing the battle and making empty threats, I told Dassie he was a dog and a snake. Our relationship worsened as the country's political situation became more unstable. Sharpeville had ignited deep racial hostility and violence nationwide. The government declared the first State of Emergency and ultimately banned black political parties, detaining many activists.

Meanwhile, the Scandinavian people had nominated Chief Albert Luthuli for the Nobel Prize. Mkhize was still explaining to Khulu what the Nobel Prize meant when Musa burst in with the news of Sister Mohale's arrest.

"What has she done now, poor woman? Have the *Boers* run out of people to arrest?" Mkhize said.

In the early hours, Khulu said, "Wake up, Kuchi. Did you hear that noise?"

"Who could that be?"

"It is cold and raining, and the sun is still far away."

"Maybe it's Tina's mother."

"It's Mendi's mother," Dassie whispered aloud from his makeshift bedroom.

Both Khulu and Kükuchi leaped out of their blankets. Khulu had not seen Mrs Diale since Mendi's detention. Kükuchi was scared, but Khulu was petrified.

Khulu whispered, "Go open, Kükuchi. I don't know what that woman wants here."

"No, Khulu. I think she wants you. Why don't you go open for her?"

Dassie stood up, flicked open the latch, and walked out, leaving the door wide open for Mrs Diale to walk right in.

"Is Khulu in? I want to speak to her."

"Go in. They want to know what you want here."

With great effort, Khulu hobbled to the kitchen and discovered a transformed woman standing comfortably, her smile as if she were settling down on a church pew. She called out her greetings to Khulu, her eyes absolute gardens of godliness. Khulu smelled a rat. Diale took off her 'mac,' revealing her striking new attire: a long black skirt and yellow blouse with flecks of green. She also spotted a green headscarf folded into a triangle over her head. Her composed appearance was hypnotizing, and Khulu's jaw was on her knees.

"I know you are wondering where I have been. When the *Tsotsis* destroyed my house, I went to live with my brother in Krugersdorp."

Khulu said, "They told us you went to live in Sterkfontein."

"My brother forced me to go to a mental clinic. I am not mad. I don't drink anymore. I only went to the asylum because I had no place to live."

Khulu asked her about Mendi. Mrs Diale's soothing face creased up like a dry lake. She let loose a tirade of accusations, "Mendi is carrying other people's sins like Jesus Christ. As for this house, all of you, including Dodo... you are hiding something. And by the way," she continued, wrinkling her nose and sniffling, "I hear Dodo is doing a degree. Mendi told me he also wants to be educated like

Dodo. I told him he must forget about Dodo. I told him, underneath a snail is still a slug, no matter how educated."

"A snail?"

"You and your classy people! Like Doctor Komane and his high-flying wife, Keletso! They slaughter a beast for their ancestors and invite us, saying, 'Come for tea'. Do their ancestors drink tea? Why are they ashamed of their culture?"

"How is Mendi getting on?"

"Mendi has been doing well. You know he has now moved to Number 4. I must thank Dassie because he supplies Mendi with stuff and money every month."

"Money?" Kūkuchi shouted.

"Kūkuchi," Mrs Diale said, "every time I go to see him, he says I must bring you along; otherwise… I must never come to see him again. I lied last time and said you were ill, but he still refused to talk to me. I should never have lied. I am born again now, although I know you have no idea what I am talking about in this house."

"What does Mendi want with Kūkuchi?" Khulu asked.

"He has something important to say to her. Please, Khulu, let me go with her. There are family matters I need to discuss with him, and Kūkuchi will help me arrange a meeting. He takes after his father, stubborn like a mule."

"You said I was a liar. Did Mendi tell you what he did? He is mad if he thinks I'll go see him," Kūkuchi swore.

Kūkuchi and Mrs Diale finally leave without Dassie. Mrs Diale says, "Mohale told me you are rich now because you are a javelin champion. I never knew one could make money by just throwing a spear. The Europeans have been hiding many things from us."

"I help train school athletes and sometimes go on exhibition tours. But I'm not rich."

"Dassie said he got the money from you, and he gave it to Mendi. It was touching that you still cared despite what you did to us."

"We did nothing to you. Stop blaming us for your nothing."

"If you did not put him in jail, we would also be rich because he throws the javelin better than you."

"Mendi went to jail because he killed girls. Did you ask him why he did that?"

"Are you hiding a knife in your pocket? I overheard you tell Khulu you don't trust me. Just because my child is in jail, that doesn't mean I am a murderer. I know you are always armed because you like fighting. I'm not a criminal. All my friends deserted me when the police arrested Mendi. I owe Posa my life. She treated me like her own sister and buried Mendi's grandmother."

When he saw me, Mendi said, "I'm happy you came. The whites are refusing to let me go. Tell Mkhize to forgive me for stealing his *rediffusion*. Tell him to come and talk to the Europeans here. They make us work in the sun. I've been doing many things, and I am reading books..."

Mrs Diale grimaced before telling us to make it snappy, as she had important family matters to discuss with her son. However, Mendi roughly ordered his mother to sit on the bench a few metres away and leave us alone. Once Mendi was satisfied that his mother was out of earshot, he spoke slowly and softly, his voice deep and fully formed.

Mendi shared many things about himself. However, he couldn't express everything that stayed in his heart because a long line of guests was waiting to be greeted by the staff.

Mendi repeatedly insisted on Kükuchi asking Mkhize and Posa to write a letter to the authorities to release him, concluding, "Once I am released, everyone will see that I am a rich businessman. I'm happy you came, and I know you'll ask Posa to write those letters. Now I can talk to my mother."

The story of Mendi's bag of money made me believe I was destined for hell. If only he knew the truth—that he was never going to be rich, ever!

As we said goodbye, tears streamed down his face. He sniffed and turned away without saying another word. My eyes stayed dry because the intense heat of guilt had dried out my soul.

Dassie was seated on their *stoep*, reading a newspaper, when Kükuchi approached.

"You look like a well-behaved boy today, but you ran away from Mrs Diale."

"I don't like her. Did you talk to Mendi?"

"Yes. He wants his money back. He knows you took it. He says when he comes out of jail, he will track you down and kill you."

"You know, Faty, when you lie, you show those lip lines…"

"What are lip lines?"

"I don't know; that's what Rosemarie's mother once said to me."

"Tell me, Dassie, is Rosemarie your girlfriend? Her name is always on your lip lines."

"No, she said her mother would kill her if she dared to have a *kaffir* boyfriend."

"You proposed to a white girl?"

"She said she will think about it when I get educated."

Kükuchi was about to find out that after she left with Mendi's mother, Salu had arrived from Draycott to attend Tina's funeral. Dassie warned Kükuchi about the heated argument in the house. She stood at the closed door, listening to the highly emotional exchange. The noise suddenly stopped when she stepped into the kitchen. It was clear to her that the house had become a powder keg of bitter arguing among the three women, whose chests puffed out like racing ostriches.

"Salu, when did you get here?"

"I was on your heels when you disappeared to jail with the murderer's mother."

"I did not know you were coming. Otherwise, I would have fetched you from Park Station instead of wasting my time with Mendi's mother."

"How did it go with Mendi?" Khulu asked.

"It went well. Am I disturbing something here, Salu?"

After an awkward silence, Salu said, "Sit down, Kükuchi."

The argument resumed. "Ntombiphelele," Khulu said, "Why don't you tell the truth and say what happened between us?"

"Do we have trouble, Salu?" Kükuchi asked.

"Yes, there is trouble," Musa responded. "Salu, tell Kükuchi how the family farm ended up under your sole name..."

"Ask them, Kükuchi. Let them prove what they are saying. We have the courts," shouted Salu as if crazed.

"Kükuchi, your grandmother," Khulu said, "since she was a little girl, she has always rolled herself up into a ball like a hedgehog whenever truth stared her in the face."

The disagreement between her two grannies caused Kükuchi considerable pain.

"What about you, Musa?" Salu screamed. "I stuck up for you when everybody had turned their backs on you. This is how you repay me?"

Musa's forehead furrowed, and her cheeks wrinkled like cup fungi. She stood up and headed for the door, but Kükuchi yanked her back as if caught in a rainstorm and shouted, "Sit down. Salu just asked you if this is how you repay her."

Salu said, "This is about my Draycott farm and..."

"It is about truth," Khulu retorted.

"Let the courts rule. I remained on that land when everybody abandoned us..."

"This is a family matter. No court can bring peace to this family," Khulu said.

Mkhize looked troubled when he accidentally got involved in the dispute, but the noise suddenly stopped. He squinted across the dim kitchen, trying to figure out what was happening.

Khulu stood up, sighed, and said, "My father's child, you know that the court is a friend of the crafty. The outbreak of boils leads back home because tricks lead nowhere. Let it pass, just as all of us will pass from this world. I don't want flowers on my grave, and no one must think something will open my ears when they come to speak to my bones. My God will protect me with clouds."

"What is wrong, Khulu?" Mkhize put it awkwardly.

Khulu covered her face and said, "Oh God, who can fill my empty heart?"

"Khulu?" cried Kükuchi. Please, Khulu."

Following an awkward silence, Khulu said, "Let's have Rooibos so you can rest, my sister. It's been a long journey from Draycott. Tomorrow, we bury Tina, the little girl from Rhodesia."

After the funeral, Salu took Dassie with her to Draycott. A few days later, Tina's devastated parents left their Soweto home and business and began a lonely journey on the South African Rail back to Bikita Village. South Africa, where they had sought refuge from the Rhodesian racial conflict, and which was the only home Tina knew, had become the worst possible choice for her parents.

CHAPTER 21

Kükuchi's Results

My mind drifted toward the Matric results. The structural system always expected an African candidate to behave like a mountain tortoise, forever long-suffering in silence while expecting crumbs from the master. One of the demeaning convictions wedged within the demented psyche of Europeans was that Africans have no feelings worth taking seriously, as Africans have no soul. After twelve years of racial separation, candidates had to take separate exams. The white government staggered the release of results based on race. White candidates received theirs first, always before Christmas, and they often earned the highest grades with many distinctions. African candidates always came last, after coloured and Indian candidates. The results for African candidates were usually announced around the end of January, with consistently very low grades.

The results for white candidates were about to be announced when the government temporarily lifted the restriction order on Albert John Luthuli. Luthuli was a well-known anti-apartheid activist who served as the president-general of the *African National Congress* (ANC). At the time Kükuchi's results were released, Luthuli immediately left for Oslo to accept his Nobel Prize. In his acceptance speech, he said:

> A long time ago, my ancestors extended a hand of friendship to people from
> Europe when they arrived on that continent. What has happened to the extension
> of that hand only history can say, and it is not time to speak about that here. Still,
> I would like to say that as I receive this prize of peace, it is on behalf of all the
> people of South Africa, especially the freedom-loving people, that I accept this
> award and acknowledge this honour. I also take it as an honour, not only for South
> Africa, but also for the whole continent of Africa.

The *Rand Daily Mail* described Luthuli as the most famous contemporary South African. It was also speculated that the world would henceforth view South African political problems differently. However, the Mail's optimism turned out to be a pipe dream. As Luthuli received his Nobel Prize, John Vorster, the Minister of Justice, announced stricter measures to limit political freedom for black people.

My feelings over the future of my javelin pursuit ebbed and flowed like waves as I waited impatiently for my Matric results. Like many other candidates, I arrived at Orlando High School early in the morning to confirm my results. The next stop was Musa's place at Phefeni, where I found her looking miserable in a crumpled shirt with a jagged tear in the sleeve and a rip around the elbow. She was visibly embarrassed to see me arrive unannounced. The kitchen was in a state of disrepair.

"Where is Jozi?"

"Jozi never lives here anymore. She took her things and went to her mother's place."

"Why, Musa? She looks like such a decent girl."

"A lion cub is always tender from a distance. I thought you knew that."

I wondered why it never occurred to Musa that the reason for her loneliness was her habit of rubbing people up the wrong way.

"How is Khulu?" Musa asked.

"She is weak. I think she worries too much. But I came here to tell you I passed, Musa. First class."

"And what are you going to do now?" she put it grimly.

I stared in disbelief at Musa's nonchalant reaction to my school performance. While I knew that my javelin interests meant nothing to her, I had looked forward to achieving a first-class Matric pass, confident that, for once, the person I now knew to be my mother would be happy for me. I began to reflect despondently on Sister Mohale's curious words, 'Musa is your real mother... the one who carried you here for nine months'. I walked to Musa's bedroom, tears forming in my eyes, and I dropped myself on the bed.

The house was clean when I woke up, and a tray of sandwiches and juice lay on the table.

"Sorry you found my place in such a state. I was tired. I could not sleep last night because of worry."

"What do you think of my results?"

"I knew you would pass because you are smart."

"Musa, my father said if I pass, you must let him know because he wants to help with fees at Fort Hare. What are you going to do?"

"When did he say that?"

"Long ago. His wife told me."

"Wife! You can send your results to his wife, and she can pay if she wants to."

I immediately stood up and walked out of Musa's house feeling as empty as shadows. The thought crossed my mind never to have anything to do with her again. Back home, the neighbours greeted me with enthusiastic displays of traditional dance, chanting, and ululating. Mohale, who had pencilled my name on the page of *Township News*, was shuffling around and leading the charge.

Weeping tears of joy, Khulu smiled and said, "God has answered our prayers."

Miss Lumka arrived and gave me a congratulatory hug. The sense of dejection that had earlier followed me out of Phefeni faded away.

Mendi Unleashed

Lumka informed me about a breaking story concerning Mendi's lawyer applying to the High Court not only for his immediate release but also to overturn his original conviction. Judge Nel then stunned the court by ordering Mendi's release, 'when this court adjourns'. The news spread rapidly and sparked unprecedented township anger since 1953, when Verwoerd ended subsidized feeding schemes for African schools. The protests back then gained international backing because it was evident that subsidized feeding programs continued in white schools. After his release, Mendi vanished. Rumours started spreading that he was getting back to criminal activities in White City. Some said they saw him in Krugersdorp with his mother, while others claimed they saw him in

Alexandra. His lawyers later filed a claim for compensation from the government, accusing wrongful imprisonment. Mendi bragged at Township News offices about his future wealth.

One thunderous night, a knock louder than any from the skies jerked us out of sleep. Two or four aggressive men demanding to see Dassie forced Mendi to point to specific locations throughout the night. They threatened to smash the door open if we didn't open and produce Dassie. It was clear to us that Mendi was in serious trouble. Khulu was shivering. The men with indistinct voices accused Dassie of stealing their money. Khulu refused to answer the door but shouted that Bobby's boys had taken Dassie and that they were already in Bechuanaland. Mendi sounded desperate as he begged Khulu to prove that Dassie was not in.

"Dassie stole our money with this man, Khulu. Open the door."

Khulu whispered to me, "This is another of Mendi's ploys. What makes them think Dassie would do such a thing?"

"I don't know, Khulu. I don't know."

"Dassie," shouted Mendi, assuming Dassie was hiding in the house, "you were there and you saw me bury the money near the river. Tell the men you took it."

Then one of the mysterious men said, "Let's go. You are a dead man, Mendi. You're dead. We want our dough..."

The angry voices, along with their footsteps, faded into the distance toward Jabavu. I felt deep in my heart that I would never see Mendi alive again. Guilt gnawed at my conscience, prompting me to peek through the bedroom and kitchen curtains many times throughout the night. Khulu also couldn't sleep, but she found my pacing back and forth more annoying than the men who kept her awake.

At dawn, I heard Khulu sneeze. I whispered, "Khulu, are you asleep?"

"*Voetsak*! Asleep? How can I be asleep, Kükuchi?"

"Please pray, Khulu. There are several police cars near the trees. What are they doing there?"

Khulu jumped, drew the curtain, peered, and whispered, "Looking for Mendi, maybe."

"He should have stayed in jail, Khulu, for his safety. Did you pray... for his safety?"

No. I prayed that your Mendi, who has been unleashed on us by demons, would die and then go to hell forever.

"What if they killed him, Khulu?"

Khulu made for the window again to peek. She then said, "If they killed Mendi, I will cry for his grandmother, who is in heaven. The boy is nothing but trouble."

***

We were seated nervously in the kitchen, drinking tea, when a chilling tap on the door sent us scurrying back to the bedroom.

"It's me, Khulu," whispered Mkhize, who came in puffing excitedly. Salu and I tripped over each other trying to warn Mkhize about Mendi's latest movements in White-City.

"We saw him with our very own eyes," Khulu swore.

Mkhize sat down and said calmly, "Khulu, there is a dead man under the bush... and some police around are there investigating..."

"It must be Mendi, Papa," Kükuchi whispered.

"No, it is not Mendi, unfortunately. But I wouldn't be the slightest bit surprised if we found him with his throat slit one of these days."

"Do the police know who the dead man is?"

"We don't know either. Let's keep it that way. A few hours ago, someone knocked on my door and asked to hide. Can you guess who that was, Kükuchi?"

"Mendi?" Khulu offered.

"Mendi had a stab wound in his back that he got during a fight with his friends from Alexandra."

"Is he still with you?"

"I am treating him in my house, Khulu. I don't know what kind of wickedness I ever committed against my ancestors. I spent my young days as a loyal shepherd in Mtubatuba. Before I came to this glittering Johannesburg, I let my entire clan know I was going to look for work and that I would bring them a lot of money, clothing, and food. My Aunt cried because she did not want me to go to the big city. She told me, 'A walking man builds no kraal'. It was a curse, Khulu. Look at me now. I will spend the rest of my days nursing a stubborn *Tsotsi* who should have been in jail the very day he was born."

"Maybe they should not have released him from jail, Papa," I said.

"Come to think of it, white people enjoy playing riddles. I think releasing him was a good thing. The system does this all the time, Khulu. When the police have had enough, when they want to remove a stubborn *Tsotsi* from the face of the earth, they release him and then supply free marijuana to all his enemies."

"Oh, Mkhize?"

"The police are gone now. So is the black vehicle of death. If they come back, you know what to say, right, Kükuchi? You know nothing."

***

Three police officers came the following afternoon to probe further. One of them was Captain Venter. Kükuchi was on the *stoep* writing something in her diary.

"*Magogo*, I know you make nice Rooibos."

"Yes, Baas, I'll make it just now." Answered Khulu.

Kükuchi was about to walk away when Venter said, "Good, let's sit out here with you, Fat Girl."

"I don't drink Rooibos," Kükuchi said.

"Just sit, I want to ask you about your brother. Where is he?"

"I don't know."

"Tell the Baas the truth, Kükuchi. Dassie is attending school in Zululand."

"Oh! And Fat Girl does not know her brother attends school in Zululand?"

Khulu served tea on a tray for Venter and his officers.

"Thank you, *Magogo*. Now, let me tell you, early this morning, we found a *tsotsi* under the trees over there. He was dead. Did you hear anything?"

"No, Baas," said Khulu.

"And you, Fat Girl?"

"My name is Kükuchi. I am not a Fat girl."

"Kükuchi!" cried Khulu.

"Okay, the neighbours say they heard commotion coming from this house. Did you hear any commotion?"

"No, there was no commotion here," Khulu rushed in.

"Are you sure, Magogo? Your neighbours said they saw about eight men and a light-skinned girl running away from your house here. Did you hear anything, Fat Girl?

"We heard nothing, Baas," said Khulu.

Before midday, Kükuchi walked to Mkhize's place. Mkhize was still fuming and shivering, "Why are you children giving me problems? Just go back home, Kükuchi. They must not find you here. You want to get me arrested?"

"Okay, Papa, I'll go back. Let me talk to Mendi, and then I'll go."

Despite his severe injuries, Mendi staggered through and struggled to say, "They can't kill me. I'm too clever. After this, I received a substantial amount of money from the government because they arrested an innocent man, Kükuchi. I'll be rich. I'll buy my mother furniture and a nice stove..."

"Mendi, did you kill that man they found under the trees?"

Mkhize swiftly jumped up, "Don't answer that, Mendi. Go home, Kükuchi."

"Venter said they saw eight men around here with a woman. Who was the woman, Mendi?"

"There was no woman."

"You know the police like to lie... to trap you," retorted Mkhize. Listen here, Kükuchi, Mendi is confused. Those men hit him on the head with a brick."

After a long, despairing sigh, Kükuchi begged Mr Mkhize to send Mendi to Ixopo to speak with Sisi Afrika's mother before she curses him with bad luck that will last the rest of his life.

CHAPTER 22

Little Mandelas, Little Lillians

Kükuchi could barely sleep. The next day, she boarded a chartered bus heading to Fort Hare from Johannesburg's Park Station. The student passengers with her were as loud and boisterous as the American cheerleaders. A flood of Castle Lager cans and harsh language flowed freely. She saw bits of brandy and whiskey passing from one friend to another. The whole scene left her confused. Several girls were drinking and smoking, and one boy, Jerry, who seemed popular, was seen cozying up passionately with different girls from Fort Hare. The ideal image of the university as a place of elegance and high morals fell apart on that bus trip. Still, the idea of moving into such a respected school made Kükuchi excited.

Fort Hare was a higher education institution for Africans. In 1959, the South African government enacted the Extension of University Education Act, often called 'University Apartheid' by critics. According to the Act, four new universities were to be established: the Western Cape for Coloureds, Westville for Indians, Turfloop for the Sotho, Venda, Tswana, and Tsonga groups, and O'Ngoye for the Nguni people, including Zulu, Ndebele, and Swati. The apartheid government heavily invested in expanding university education for Afrikaners nationwide. Meanwhile, others faced strict monitoring by security police. The government showed little interest in educating anyone other than white, mainly Afrikaans-speaking individuals. Fort Hare, once a prominent and respected university during British colonial times, declined into an ethnic college solely for the Xhosa. The white universities could no longer admit black students without approval from the Minister of Education, in consultation with the security police. Such permission was granted only when the requested courses were unavailable at the ethnic universities. Often, the apartheid government presented black students with options that led them into curricula unrelated to their aspirations. For example, Kükuchi could choose O'Ngoye, using her Hlubi heritage, or Turfloop if she wanted to follow her biological father's tribal group. Interestingly, no one required proof of her ethnicity at the University of Fort Hare. The apartheid education system was still in its early phases.

However, that was soon to change drastically when the Apartheid government unleashed white Afrikaans professors, fresh from the Broederbond initiation school, on all black universities. The government wanted to ensure that black institutions were kept under tight security.

Fort Hare was originally a British fort during the conflicts between the indigenous Xhosa people and British imperialists. This diverse university welcomed students from all over Africa. When Kükuchi stepped onto the campus and saw a 3,000-year-old Baobab, she realized she had entered a sacred place, akin to the tomb of Esther and Mordechai as described by Miss Lumka in their Sunday school. Fort Hare proudly features notable alums. An official led her into Iona Hall. Throughout the hallways, returning students were greeting one another with kisses, hugs, and loud noises.

She was soon going to be with her two roommates. One was Goodenough, a petite Ndebele-speaking Rhodesian who had also enrolled to study law.

"You can call me Goodie," the 16-year-old prodigy told Kükuchi. "My mother, who is a doctor back in Matebeleland, calls me Goodie."

The other was Peta, a Butterworth beauty queen with her hair shaved into a bald head. She had little to say and looked lost in thought most of the time. She watched movements and voices, and seemed interested in other physical expressions. But she mostly kept her opinions to herself.

Besides boasting about her achievements, the small Rhodesian often drank a cocktail of brandy and milk. She was thin and tightly skinned, with quick, bee-like movements. She bragged to the wide-eyed girls about her advanced academic certificates, "I have London 'A' Levels, and I got distinctions in all my subjects."

The sixteen-year-old was so talented that Kükuchi's self-esteem waned, making her question whether she had erred in attending such a prestigious university. She quickly started to dislike the Rhodesian girl and couldn't wait to move to a different room.

Once they got to know each other better, she whispered to Peta, "You know, I don't like this Goofie girl."

Peta said, "Goodie, you mean? She is a baby. Let's look after her."

***

Addressing his new law undergraduates, Professor Smit said, "I have to warn you that only a few of you will pass come year-end. Law is difficult. There is no time for little Mandelas and little Lillians in the Law Faculty. You are either in the so-called struggle or in serious business to get an education. Those who want to be in the struggle, go back to the townships, throw stones at the police, and see where that gets you. You can do your struggle all you like, but this government is not going anywhere."

Kükuchi was livid. Back in their room, she asked Goodie what she thought of the professor's words. Goodie did not want to talk about it at first. Finally, she said, "Professor Smit is right. We must study and forget politics. My mother, who is a doctor back home... she always tells me there are two types of people, the wise and the foolish; wise men learn while foolish men brag..."

"Goodie," said Peta, "where you come from, do people think Ian Smith is a wise man or a foolish man?"

"My lips are sealed."

"Keep them sealed forever, Goofie," re-joined Kükuchi.

"Yes, you got it, Faty..."

Kükuchi leapt up shouting, "You call me Faty again, I'll kick your backside back to Rhodesia."

By that time, Goodie had already bolted out of the room and escaped, leaving Peta amused.

***

Kükuchi gravitated towards a group of athletes on campus. During the year, she collected several field prizes in the Cape Province. Although she rarely exceeded 44.8m, the overwhelming support she was getting on campus helped her in her quest for future international appearances.

Basing their criteria solely on race, white athletic bodies continued to overlook black qualifying records, despite international pressure. The University Athletics Union used the media to keep the

IOC informed about the struggles of black athletes in the country. One of the activists was Gordon Sekonyela, a thirty-year-old coach and low-profile activist from Bisho. He was a junior lecturer in the Department of Music but spent most of his time training field athletes. He later became Kūkuchi's dedicated trainer.

When Kūkuchi first met Sekonyela, he helped her with valuable tips on how to improve her performances. Among other things, he advised Kūkuchi to use weights to help tone her arms, which would also aid in her weight loss. Kūkuchi found the helpful advice, as it helped improve her winning throw rate.

Sekonyela proposed to take Kūkuchi out on a date. She said she was going to think about it, but before she could confirm, she was going out with him on evenings and weekends. The relationship was taking on a distinctly romantic slant, although Kūkuchi did not want to talk about it when the beauty queen of Butterworth warned her about the disaster she was calling for.

After a few pints of beer, Sekonyela would open up and express his views energetically on many issues. Kūkuchi learned from him that his hero was Jan Hendrik Hofmeyr, an Afrikaner politician and intellectual, who, according to him, was the cleverest man in the country because, at the age of thirteen, he had already become a university student. Sekonyela refused to disclose his political affiliations, claiming he was 'not aligned'.

"Is that not a copout? In this country, you're either with the Charter or against it."

"Yes? And which side are you on?" Sekonyela challenged.

"Those who grabbed our land are not on our side. That's which side I'm on."

Sekonyela changed the topic. He asked Kūkuchi to spend time with him at his place to celebrate Africa. When she went back, Kūkuchi asked her two roommates how she should have responded to Sekonyela's advances.

Goodie responded, "You should be careful. Going out at night with that man is dumb. What is wrong with you?"

A few days later, Goodie parked herself against the door to eavesdrop. Kūkuchi said, "Peta, this tiny girl, Goofie from Matebeleland; how old is she?"

"Sixteen. She's brilliant."

"She looks 13 to me. Why does she always blow her own trumpet? Who does she think she is? She talks funny. I asked her to show me her concoction, which she calls a cough mixture. Do you know what she said?"

"Leave her alone, Kuchi. She's just a child with a big mouth."

Goodie suddenly budged in, "Am I interrupting something? I could have sworn I heard voices in here before I opened the door, something about big mouths and tiny Goofie from Matebeleland. Suddenly, it's all quiet. And we all know what that means."

"Yes, we all know this because our friends have lunch every day with families of racist professors," Kūkuchi said.

"Peta, please ask Kūkuchi to stop being mean to me. Otherwise, I'll ask to change rooms. I was there because the professor asked me to come to his office to discuss transferring to the medical faculty. His wife is a medical doctor and a good friend. She knows I am smart. I told her I couldn't do medicine because I hate cadavers. She then called my mother, who was very upset with me... telling me I'll get used to a cadaver."

"I must talk to her, your doctor friend," Kükuchi said. "She might help me switch to medicine. I qualify. It was my second choice. I can't stand that law professor."

"You want to switch to medicine? You can't just do that. Besides, you have to be smart like me. Not every Tom, Dick, and Harry can become a medical doctor."

***

A few days later, Goodie said, "Peta, you know that tall javelin girl from White-City...?"

"You mean Kükuchi, right?"

"Yeah, the big bully. She thinks she's the centre of the universe just because she became a popular athlete on campus. She's been avoiding me. When I try to be friendly, she snubs me. Do you know what a hatred for foreign Africans is called? Afrophobia."

"Did you ask her? Maybe she has problems."

"She has problems, alright, but I can't ask her. I'm scared of these people from Johannesburg. I think a woman who throws a javelin like her has low self-esteem issues. This explains her psychological tendency toward physical violence at the slightest provocation. I saw them break windows and trash garbage bins the other day, demanding their term results. How can the university give them results when they haven't paid?"

"How do you know they were from JoBurg?"

"I know them. They speak *Tsotsi Taal*. Please, Peta, you're the only civilized South African I know. Talk to the xenophobic girl, without mentioning my name, of course. She is so mean to me."

"Okay, Goodie. I'll ask Kükuchi when she comes back."

"Also, you're not going to say I said so, right? She spends way too much time throwing that stupid javelin. I even suspect she has something going on with that music teacher..."

"Sekonyela?"

"She's always on these so-called 'outings', but she struggled to finish her last few assignments. Can you tell me where she is right now?"

"She is a big girl, Goodie."

"Also, tell her to stop referring to me as Goofie. I don't like it a little bit."

***

While Kükuchi was attending an event in Cape Town, two police officers left a message for her to report to the authorities at Alice Police Station on Monday.

When she came back, Kükuchi studied the note and nearly passed out.

"White police?"

"It must be serious," said Peta.

"Don't worry, Kükuchi," Goodie said, "Only the guilty are afraid."

Peta said, "If I were you, I would run away. You can hide in your grandmother's farm and then come back when things cool down a bit."

Apart from the ominous matter with the police, Kükuchi had to finish her Criminal Law assignment. She finished it in the early hours and left Goodie with a request to submit it.

When she entered the police station, the authorities immediately handcuffed her. One African constable led her to her cell. Kükuchi slept like a baby, despite the harsh conditions. The concrete double bunk was without mattresses or pillows. There was a hole on the floor against the wall, which functioned as a toilet. A small basin stood next to it. The latrine stench was an integral part of the cell, and the tiny rusty metal window served no discernible purpose.

In the morning, they slid an enamel plate loaded with porridge through a slot in the steel door. It was porridge from breakfast to supper. Kükuchi could neither eat nor drink.

The African constable was on duty again. After opening the cell door, he spoke softly to Kükuchi, "Those *Boer* police… call them Baas. Don't try to be clever. This is not Johannesburg."

Seven days went by, and the police kept interrogating her. Colonel Peters, a female officer who had recently transferred from South West Africa, pointed at a letter and asked, "Is this your handwriting?"

Kükuchi, weakened by hunger and dehydration, refused to respond.

On the 9th day, Kükuchi faced four highly ranked police officers. She hadn't eaten since her detention and felt dizzy. The leader of the group said, "Stop writing letters to our enemies, otherwise you'll go to jail."

They released her soon after without further interrogation.

Unbeknownst to Kükuchi, her incarceration received widespread media coverage. Because of her javelin activities, Kükuchi's name appeared in headlines across the international press. The Times published the letter Kükuchi wrote to the IOC, which was the basis for her detention. The paper described it as a 'simple cry from the heart'. After her release, Kükuchi returned home, feeling exhausted and unclean. Although Goodie assured Kükuchi she had submitted her assignment, Kükuchi believed she couldn't go home for Easter because she was behind on her projects. Later that day, Kükuchi was horrified to discover her assignment was still in her drawer. Kükuchi was furious. Peta informed Goodie, who immediately searched for alternative accommodations to avoid an approaching hurricane and tried to prevent their paths from crossing.

CHAPTER 23

The dung beetle

I received a telegram from Musa: 'Come home immediately.' The message struck a chill down my spine as I was convinced that Khulu was dead. I packed a few items right away and boarded the overnight train. When I arrived, it was drizzling in Johannesburg, and the wintry morning breeze puffed across my face, adding ice to the frosty condition of my heart. Approaching the township, the sun struggled to emerge from behind the low, dark clouds, and I walked home with a sense of foreboding.

"What is wrong, Khulu? I received a telegram from Musa."

"I told Musa to leave you alone. You must not be disturbed at school," said Khulu.

"And how is Dassie doing?"

Khulu sighed and said, "Oh, that one has sunk deeper into trouble. Only a miracle will save him. His Estcourt school suspended him, but Salu is sorting out the problem."

"What's the matter with him? Why was he suspended?"

"He threatened to stab a female teacher with a knife."

"Dassie can never do that. I swear."

"Yes, he claims the teacher resents the way he asks questions in class."

That was not the reason for the telegram, though. Khulu showed me a letter that Salu had received from the Department of Bantu Affairs. The government was informing her of the rezoning of her farm for white use. She had fourteen days to call on the local office at Wembezi to formalize her relocation. They were giving her £50 as compensation plus a rented four-roomed house at the Wembezi African Township.

I broke down and shouted uncontrollably, "They can't do this, Khulu. Where is Salu now?"

"She is still there, fighting the case, but it's all futile. The *Boers* are the government with stiff necks. You know them. And they own guns and jails and laws."

I could hardly sleep as I remembered Khulu's ominous 'prophecy' of doom she once aimed at Salu. She had been fuming back then, saying to Salu, 'The hours of darkness will lead you back home'. I wondered, unable to tell the difference between a prophecy and a curse.

In the morning, Khulu put it emphatically before I got out of bed, "Ntombiphelele, your grandmother in Draycott, is getting what she deserves. You reap what you sow because God is not a fool."

"You can forgive her now because she has paid for her sins."

"God cannot forgive a sinner who does not sincerely say 'Sorry' from her heart."

***

Jozi accompanied Musa and Kükuchi to Draycott. On their way, the two girls had a chat privately. Kükuchi asked," Jozi, you made peace with Musa?"

"She let me go back. My mother chased me away when I confronted her about her boyfriend. I was stranded."

"No questions asked?"

"Musa said she knew I would come back with my tail between my legs, and then she made me the most sumptuous soup. She asked me no question."

"And where is Funani?"

"He earns a lot of money now. He is upgrading his forensic skills at the Scotland Yard again. They say he is a clever detective. He wants to marry me when he gets back."

"And you are happy with that?"

"Yes, what can I do? Deep down, he is a human being, even though one never knows what he will do next. He is unpredictable in his seriousness."

"He doesn't abuse you; I hope."

"I've never been happier with a man…"

From Estcourt's Harding Street, their dilapidated bus struggled through hazardous loose gravel roads. A ribbon of mist along the riverbank greeted them as they approached Draycott. Near the scheduled stop, the bus laboured up the hill and finally came to a halt. The driver immediately emptied his bus. The three women hiked up the steep incline and slowed down as they approached the entrance to Salu's property. Recently pruned chestnut trees arched over the narrow driveway, leading to the main house. Two tall mahogany trees cast an ominous shadow over the chicken pens.

Salu's eyes appeared hazy up there on the porch. She snuggled up in her shawl on her rocking chair, looking old and defeated. When the three were close enough for Salu to confirm their identities, she flew over the chair and yelped like a desert coyote, "I have been watching you since you got out of that leaking ship of a bus." She laughed so loud the echo floated unsteadily across the Drakensberg valley. This is not Johannesburg, you know!

You brought Jozi along? Oh, my eager beaver! You did well, Kŭkuchi. She must go to the women over there and show them how to tidy up. I hope Funani will treat you well, my child. I don't trust him around girls, never mind that he is a policeman and a relative."

"Oh, Salu. How did you know about Jozi and Funani?" Kŭkuchi asked.

"If you have Dassie, you have a radio and a newspaper and you know everything."

"I want to see *Soksie*," Jozi twittered. "Kŭkuchi told me she had calved and has twins."

"How I wish you could stay here with me, Jozi, to help *Soksie* during this time of lactation."

Dassie was tending flowerbeds on the northern side of the house. On seeing him, Musa's peculiar smile returned instantly. No one made an issue of his expulsion. So, he relaxed and started opening up, but it was clear from his sunken eyes that something had driven him into depression.

***

After lunch, we went to Salu's study. She told us she had hired two Afrikaans-speaking lawyers, hoping she might sway the system and save her farm. However, a letter from a Mr Van der Skoon, a white constituency member of parliament, said, 'The law is the law; there is nothing you can do about the farm'.

Mr Barry, a British recipient of the farm, imported his wife and children to South Africa. Initially, his wife was unhappy about relocating to what she referred to as 'the dark Continent'. After much persuasion, however, she finally agreed and could hardly contain her tears of delight when she set eyes on the large farm, something beyond her fantasies while home in England. Many white immigrants come from the slums of Europe, and their skin colour holds many benefits upon landing on the shores of Africa.

Musa heaved a deep sigh of pain, lips quivering. She asked Salu what she was going to do.

Salu giggled absurdly and said, "The law is the law. What can I do, Musa? The very man called Barry was here a week ago. He did his walkabout on my farm with his family, accompanied by Skoon and two white men. It's as if they own my place already."

"Skoon may be a member of parliament, but his constituency is the same white land grabbers," said Musa.

"Salu, you should have sued Skoon for trespassing," I cried.

"When Africans stray onto their farms, they don't sue but shoot to kill," added Musa.

"You can't sue a white man for trespassing. I learned that lesson when Rhona put me in charge of an English class for white children. White officials from the department came to our school whenever they wanted and rode roughshod over our kindness before they fired me."

"My father is a politician," said Jozi, "When I was young, he told me I'll become a lawyer and then I'll make life a living hell for white people."

Salu said, "I went to my lawyer's office the other day, and the same Parliamentarian was there. My lawyer was trying his best. I asked the Member of Parliament if his ancestors were happy with what he was doing to the African people in Africa. The man told me in the face. He said, *Magogo*, you are tilting at windmills. The lawyer advised me to accept a settlement of £50. When I refused, Skoon said, 'If you keep rolling a rock up the hill, you must be careful where you put your next foot'. Imagine! I said something and he told me to shut up. These whites! Am I a child? I said to him, 'The dung beetle must be careful lest it drops its dung balls it has rolled up'."

Jozi tittered.

"What white arrogance, these whites!" Musa exclaimed.

Salu looked worn to a frazzle, projecting an unusual picture of defeat. She said, "Wherever the white government takes me, I'll have to find space for my rocking chair. There's not enough room for my chair in that Wembezi matchbox house. Oh, my God! What a nightmare."

Salu's eyes travelled across the room, desperately expecting someone to say something. Everyone was tired. At last, we were all fast asleep.

***

Much later, I opened my eyes and watched everyone else continue to snore. I crept, searching for Dassie until I reached his bedroom. There was a collection of large, crumpled posters on the wall, including one of Elvis' Jailhouse Rock. I noticed a newspaper clipping showing Hendrik Verwoerd. Dassie had written 'Kill' in red on the picture. Many other images on the walls were defaced with cruel graffiti, which upset me. Dassie's bedroom had turned into a shrine to his dark world, and I felt sorry for my little brother.

I thought the foggy, rebellious space that Dassie entered would soon lead to Satanism, as is often true for troubled teenagers.

Crying and wiping tears

In the evening, Kūkuchi and Dassie sat on the concrete floor next to Salu's rocking chair, out of their Grandma's sight. Kūkuchi asked Dassie if Salu had ever been in his bedroom, and he replied, "I keep my room locked."

"I went in there and saw all those disturbing things on your walls."

"I forgot to lock... don't tell Salu."

When Kūkuchi asked him why he left school, Dassie responded in his familiar roundabout manner: "The other day, Salu had a meeting with all the workers here. She told them that the *Boers* had taken over the farm and that she was going away to die at Wembezi. Most of them were crying, and it was not nice."

"What did the people say?"

"The people? They sat there silently, crying and wiping tears. Salu told them to pack their belongings and go back to where they came from. As you can see, only a few remain."

Kūkuchi's concern with Dassie's calm demeanour deepened. She feared he might be harbouring terrible thoughts about his school, his teachers, or those who were about to take over Salu's farm.

After supper, Salu was in her white gown as she tucked herself into the comfort of her king-size bed. Leaning on her large pink pillows, she directed everyone to sit on both sides and listen. Kūkuchi thought Salu was about to tell them she was going to heaven. Dassie chose a small bench next to the door, which made him look like a security guard. Salu held a book in her hand titled 'The Politics of Inequality' by G. Carter. When she set it aside, she said, "Kuchi, some time ago, when you were here, I mentioned something to you about the sacred gravesite and what Musa and I did. Do you remember?"

"Yes, Salu."

"Tell Musa what I said."

"Musa, Salu once told me something about you rescuing animals in the middle of a thunderstorm. I did not believe a word she said. I think she was trying to cover up for you... Something nasty that happened here about my twin brother, you and Salu murdered and buried at night near the ravine down there."

Musa was gasping for breath. When you were a little girl, Khulu and I advised you to take action regarding your language. I know Musa has little time, and she can't give you proper discipline. Ladies are cultured and graceful, you know."

Salu fanned her face while the rest remained silent. Musa gulped the water, stood up, and said, "Salu, why did you tell Kūkuchi such things...?"

"Sit down, Musa. Let me tell you in front of these children. Kūkuchi needs you. You have a chance tonight to break free from being a victim and be a mother to your daughter. The bones of your baby boy haven't given me peace since I took Kükuchi to see his final resting place. Look at what has happened to me. Only three people know about the burial, and the third is that man from Pangweni. I should never have let Kükuchi touch the grave. I made a mistake. Please take a look at the trouble we're facing now. My father and mother have turned against me, and they have handed me over to the wolves—the government, a white government at that. Tomorrow, you must go with Kükuchi and follow the traditional custom. Take Kükuchi to his brother and explain everything to him. Promise me you will do as I say."

Kükuchi was pleased to hear Musa say she would think about it overnight. She believed that her family's fortunes would change, and this might save Salu's farm. However, much later, into the depths of the Drakensberg night, Kükuchi sat up on the bed and said, "Salu, earlier you said we are facing so much bitterness because of my brother's grave. I remember one day, Khulu saying about you, 'Your Salu has always rolled herself up into a ball like a hedgehog whenever truth stared her in the face'. Why did she say that?"

Salu jumped out of bed and confronted Kükuchi, "Your Khulu has brainwashed you against me. She had no business saying such things, and you have no business memorising and reciting the words." Salu marched out of the bedroom and disappeared like a spook. Nobody knows where she put up that night.

***

In the morning, Kükuchi is surprised to hear Musa say she won't be taking her to the gravesite.

"But we have to go, Musa. You promised. What about Salu's land, her house, and all the chickens? Do you want bad luck to continue?"

Musa shrugs and says, "I can't. What's the point?"

"Okay, then, tell me his name. What did you name him before you murdered him and buried him in that shallow grave?"

Musa screams in pain. Salu quickly runs over and pulls Musa away. Kükuchi's disgust toward the person she thinks is her mother grows worse.

CHAPTER 24

My soul exposed

Back at Fort Hare, I felt miserable. Everything around me seemed to be disintegrating. To make things worse, Goodie betrayed me by failing to submit my assignment, I thought. After she evaded me for several days, I caught a glimpse of Goodie in one of the lectures. However, the puny little Rhodesian disappeared before the lecture ended.

One day, I stumbled upon my enemy strolling casually in Alice, accompanied by two boyfriends from Northern Rhodesia. When our eyes met, she clenched her teeth in terror, and I met her petrified gaze with a threatening smile.

"You guys go away," I said, "I want to talk to Goofie in private."

"Please, Kükuchi, my Darling, I am sorry."

"You are sorry about what?"

The diminutive girl dipped her hand into her handbag and took a gulp from her bottle of brandy before saying with a broken voice, "I was just joking," she begged. "You are not a communist. I know Peta told you a lot of things. We were having fun..."

"What are you on about?"

"Please, Kükuchi. You are our freedom fighter. I know you are going to liberate our continent from the Europeans like Ian Smith..."

"What about my assignment, you good-for-nothing *Stompie*? Why did you lie to me? I found it still lying there in my drawer when I came back. Why didn't you submit it?"

Goodie let out a deep sigh of relief. Grinning widely, she squeaked, "Peta didn't tell you? I wrote a separate one for you and asked her to transcribe it; for the handwriting, you see... she being in a different faculty. I submitted it myself to the lecturer. While you were away, I read the one you wrote and found it wasn't up to scratch."

"What?"

Goodie had secretly helped me achieve 90%; our lecturer's feedback being a simple, 'quite perceptive'.

Suitably cut to size, I avoided contact with Goodie for many days, and we never discussed the issue afterwards. While the prospects for African athletics were at an all-time low, activities in the Northern Transvaal offered a glimmer of hope. However, I needed to talk to someone about my family and deep personal problems. Depression and confusion overwhelmed me after my visit to Salu.

***

One evening, I told Peta I was dashing out to the administration block. I was in a worse daze as I walked up the flight of stairs to my trainer. Just then, I collided with Jerry, the flamboyant character who appeared popular with most of the girls on my first trip to college.

He took a shifty glance at me, quick steps up, and when he turned back, he said, "I know you're from White-City. Do you remember Kenny, my cousin?"

"Kenny...? Sandy's brother?"

"Yes, he told me you were a scorned lover; that you and Mendi wanted to kill him. That's why he fled to Pimville. He said you were after him."

"Where is Kenny now?"

"Zulu 'Varsity. He is studying something there."

"Zululand? Is he not Sotho speaking?"

"Yes, but his father is a medical doctor..."

"I see. Jerry, your cousin is a liar. Next time you see him, tell him to hide at that Zulu college for good, if he likes his face."

"The more things change..."

"What happened to her sister?"

"Sandy? I don't want to hang our dirty family linen in public, but there is no love lost between Sandy and her mother... my mother's younger sister, for your information."

"Why are you hanging the linen in public then?"

"I'm just giving you an update on your friends."

"Those two were never my friends...."

"I don't want you to go searching for Kenny in Pimville the day you want to sort out his face. You won't find him there. But tell me this: Are you dating your coach? I see your steps taking you in the direction of his office. Is he giving you nice things? He's got a reputation."

"It takes one to recognize one."

"I can't help it if women find me pretty."

Although Sekonyela appeared occupied with something, he cheerfully welcomed me in. Sekonyela apologized for the mess in his office and invited me to his flat, half a kilometre away.

Entering the porch, he plucked a rich red rose, planted the stalk in the palm of my hand, and said, "For the future javelin champion."

The unexpected compliment pleased me, and as we entered, I felt anxious, realizing there was no one else inside at the moment. Still, I noticed hints of feminine qualities and a girlish touch in the choice of curtain colours, a Joybird furniture brand, a Staircase wall painting, an orderly bookcase, and a pink coffee table napkin. My female eyes gave me strange jitters, and I felt stranded as a foreigner in an environment I admired and wished I could design. However, the large, exquisitely crafted portrait of a pretty woman carved into the lounge wall explained everything about this home, so much so that when I looked at it two or three times, my soul trembled with envy.

"Your wife?" I blurted.

"Yes. My marriage has been on the skids for months, and my wife left me for another man."

"Sorry, I shouldn't have bothered you."

"Well, it's one of those things."

"Why did she leave you?"

"This or that."

Sekonyela's elusive smile caused ripples of uneasiness throughout the room. We discussed Salu's farm extensively. He revealed that he was a descendant of a clan in Basotholand that fought against the British colonial leader, John Sprigg, who compelled Africans in the region—through their chiefs—to surrender their guns and ammunition. Sekonyela told me that Sprigg believed gun ownership was reserved for Europeans or whites, as they prefer to be called nowadays.

"We believed otherwise. Sprigg brought his 'squads' from the Cape, and they disarmed us by stealth. We lost our guns plus our land, and we have not recovered since," Sekonyela cackled incongruously.

The conversation veered to current university politics, including the government's plan to entrench racially based institutions. We then talked about the politics of the Olympic Games. The subject resonated deeply, becoming both stimulating and intimate. We relocated to his couch and enjoyed 'Grazing on the Grass' by Hugh Masekela, plus a few glasses of dry wine.

"I like your lips," he said, and that started a slippery slope.

When we start hugging, my feelings seem to split in two; one part on fire and the other stuck in the shadows of White-City with Mendi. I feel uneasy. And I tell him so.

***

I lay dreamily on top of Sekonyela's duvet till morning, my defective soul exposed. Dragging my brain to reflect on the foreign space, another woman's sovereignty that I had invaded, it felt surreal. I recalled Salu's words to me: 'Many girls seem to relish illusion, and when they lose their virginity at a young age, they think it's an achievement.' I cursed myself for my temporary lapse of focus. The shame of raiding someone else's territory so choked me up that I left without touching anything else in the flat.

When I entered our residence, Peta chanted teasingly, 'I am squatting with my lover'. You were with him the whole night...?"

"Never mind."

"Never mind? You don't look happy. And it looks like you need a shower."

***

Five weeks had passed since Kükuchi's night with Sekonyela. Kükuchi learned she was pregnant. The shock hit her so hard she called Peta to a quiet corner of the cafeteria to reveal all.

"I could not talk about this in our room. That little Goofie has a big mouth."

"Aren't you being too harsh on her? By the way, you have not thanked her for rewriting your assignment and getting you an A."

"Thank you, Mom! Look, Peta, this means nothing. Something bad has happened recently. Sekonyela raped me."

"Oh, Kükuchi; How can you say that?"

"It started with us talking about my family's problems, and then suddenly... it happened."

Peta was silent for a long moment.

"You don't believe me, I know."

"No, I don't. And anyone who knows you won't either. Why didn't you go to the police?"

"I wanted to go, but with time, I stopped."

"Why didn't you defend yourself? You've got quite a reputation in Johannesburg. They say you're a street bully. They say you do not stop until the enemy's nose starts bleeding. Why didn't you protect yourself from this man? I do not believe you."

"I don't know, Peta. Everything happened so fast. Why are you blaming me?"

"I can't believe it happened the way you describe it."

"It happened. How can a woman avoid rape? It's like your itching skin. It just happens."

"Tell me about your mother ... I mean, she must be upset about the rape?"

"No one knows, except you."

"Except me? Why?"

"I respect you, Peta. You think before you open your mouth."

"Yes?"

"What are you thinking?"

"Listen, Kükuchi, assuming this was a true story, one day you will find someone you care about, someone who truly loves you. If that happens, do not do anything stupid like opening your mouth and telling him about your rape. I was about to marry the boy of my dreams when I foolishly told him that I was once raped."

"You?"

"I was on my way home after wearing the Miss Butterworth crown. The rapist took me in his car promising to drive me home. Along the way, the respectable man I trusted, pulled a trick on me and raped me. I parted paths with my boyfriend after I refused to divulge the name of the rapist."

"Why did you refuse?"

"It's not easy. Things can get complicated, Kuchi, and sometimes women who harbour dreams and aspirations experience lapses in concentration. Hindsight is twenty-twenty. I should have opened a case against the high-ranking man."

"Like Sekonyela?"

Talking about Sekonyela, he is your coach, and you spend time together. I'm sure you were attracted to him and tempted him..."

"No. I went to him for advice about my grandmother's plight. He kept promising that he would find a way to defend us. But Peta, my problem right now? I'm pregnant."

"No, Kükuchi!"

"I'm thinking of getting rid of it..."

"Not a moment too soon. Do it."

The story of Salu's ill-fated chicken farm reached *Township News*. However, before the editor could publish it, the security police had prohibited it. In terms of section 10 of the Apartheid's Internal Security Act, police could gag a publication deemed subversive or sexually suggestive and detain anyone involved in such activities. While the police kidnapped and murdered many black people, the media could not publish such stories. The only articles permitted were mostly about internecine tribal killings in Natal and the victories of the South African Defence Force against 'terrorists' in Angola,

Mozambique, Rhodesia, and Lesotho. The Fort Hare Students' Representative Council (SRC) circulated copies of the article smuggled from *Township News*. Student activists rallied around and visited Salu's farm as a protest. The SRC came to our residence and asked me to address the student body, to acquaint them with the corrupt practice of expropriation of African land without compensation. After much persuasion, I finally agreed. But I started shaking afterwards, wondering what I was going to say. To avoid fluffing up my lines, I spent two days rehearsing in front of Peta. When the moment came, I mustered up courage, climbed the podium, and stood for a while, almost blanking out. One could hear the birds chirp outside.

'I hope you do not mind a Mlungu addressing you.'

The roof nearly collapsed from applause.

'I won't bore you with a story about myself, but I want to tell you about my grandmother. We call her Salu. She used to be a teacher, but she was forced out of teaching by the government and couldn't teach anywhere in the country. She went back to the land of her ancestors and developed it. We are descendants of the Hlubi under Chief Langalibalele, the first African political prisoner to be incarcerated on Robben Island. But I want to tell you that we, the Hlubi and the Zulu, are united in our demand for the land that the British stole from us. Salu's farm, a large piece of land in Draycott, is now one of the most successful chicken farms in the Natal Midlands. A few months ago, our family lost that farm because the white government took it from us. They said it was in a European area. As we all know, our title to the land comes from the bones and graves of our ancestors. They promised my granny a small four-room house outside Estcourt. They have violated her dignity, and our family is distraught. We call on the students and all forces of democracy to fight for the restoration of our land. This is our land.' A Cheerful clattering, ululating, deafening chanting, and whistling ensued. Some shouted 'Mayibuye! Mayibuye!' While others chanted '*Izwe Lethu*! (Our Land!). Yet, amidst the uproar, I felt as helpless as a pelican in the wilderness without any lake. Inside my body was something I did not know what to do with. I could not remove it for fear I might die in the process. So, I knew very well that one day this something was going to become a baby. I walked back to my seat in tears and silently recited Khulu's prayer, 'Oh God, who can fill my empty heart?' as Peta and the other female students helped me back to my room.

Elsewhere, the Security police were monitoring the gathering closely. By dawn, they had arrested several students, including me. Upon my release, Peta said, "Your *Stompie* took a tot of liquor and then disappeared to ask Professor Smit to stop the government from taking over your grandmother's farm. Goodie was shouting, 'Long Live Castro' when she came back."

"Peta, I think Goofie has become an alcoholic. She needs help."

Alcoholic or not, Goodie was oblivious to the 'Black Prohibition of Interdicts Act', a law that prevented Africans from petitioning the courts against forced removals. The Apartheid parliament had become a sophisticated law unto itself. Yet, more whites continued to vote for the racist national party without losing a smidgen of sleep.

CHAPTER 25

Salu Vacates her Land

Salu quietly left her farm and moved into her assigned four-room house at Wembezi. She took her furniture and books but left her entire stock of animals, including poultry, for which she received only token compensation. The local superintendent refused her request to bring *Soksie* along, but she persisted and made the best of her difficult situation with the twins. Dassie was about to take a long, lonely train journey back to White City. Before leaving, Salu tried to pray for him, but her words remained stuck inside her lips until she finally told Dassie to pray for himself when he boards the train. Dassie showed no emotion when he said goodbye to his grandmother, but her mind raced with haunting images of her and McLeod leaving their tearful primary school children in 1949, flashing through her mind like a frightening dream.

After introducing herself to her new neighbours, Salu realized that she was in for a busy time, more than before, in the poverty-stricken township.

***

My mind kept recreating beautiful scenes of the Olympics. It seemed a long way to catch up with Sue Platt. The perennial uncertainty around the selection of athletes based on race kept my motivation on edge. Alone in the room, guilt wrapped over me like a thorny headscarf, and I began to take seriously the persistent and scary sound of the clock ticking away every second of my life on earth. While it is often easy to conceal one's sins, with time it becomes impossible to do the same with one's pregnancy. The security police stepped up their harassment of campus activists. I had no idea why they always picked on me for detention. In certain instances, they questioned me about events I was unaware of. That went on until I completed my studies at the University of Fort Hare. I continued to do light workouts, refining runway strategies, focusing on speed and footwork, and other weak points, six weeks into my pregnancy. Amazingly, I was able to push boundaries even further, which protected me from wallowing in self-pity. However, I was doing my exercises in the middle of the landing band, with my knees on the ground and my head up high, when I felt dizzy. I regained consciousness at Alice Hospital. The European nursing sister, a nun, was attending to me. She was Sister Abigail, originally from Belgium. She said I was showing signs of a miscarriage. Three days later, I awoke from a deep blackout. Sister Abigail wheeled me into a bare, draughty room they called 'Talk Room'. The airy atmosphere and Sister Abigail's grey lips and melancholy eyes made me feel empty inside. When she told me I had miscarried, I felt numb with no emotion. The reason for the miscarriage had not been apparent, according to her.

"But there are many causes of a miscarriage," she said. "What is critical is to secure the safety and well-being of the mother. Let us pray."

I could hardly close my eyes, let alone pray. Sister Abigail's last line was, 'May its soul rest in peace, ' which sent a freezing sensation down my spine. A few minutes passed, and the nurse sat patiently, genially holding my hand, her dry lips in silent prayer.

Eventually, I said, "Was it a girl or a boy?"

"It was a boy."

"He was only six weeks old, Sister. Do you think he had a soul?"

She shrugged graciously and said, "I don't know, Ms Kūkuchi. I just prayed... just in case. Who knows at what stage the soul finally penetrates the womb to break into the embryo! All I can tell you is that there was once a living being in your body, and it died and went to heaven."

More piercing shrills went down my spine, and I asked stupidly if she could tell whether the foetus was going to live with albinism or not.

"I don't know. But that is not important to me because he was a baby."

'I'm heartbroken for you, my baby-boy, whatever your name would have been. But I admit, my broken heart is also mixed with relief.'

"You can still name him, although your family won't be able to bury him because we treat such babies as waste material here."

"Waste?"

I left Alice Hospital feeling heavy-hearted and troubled in my soul.

I can sleep in the Kitchen.

Meanwhile, Salu was taking it all in her stride, hardly resting from her newly found chores. A few days after settling into her new home, she visited her neighbours to introduce her idea of planting cash crops for profit. Within a year, many women in the area stopped buying vegetables and eggs.

Kūkuchi visited Salu. The local municipality had just allocated a small piece of land to the women in the area where they could set up a cooperative and grow carrots and Brussels sprouts. Kūkuchi was amazed at the level of cooperation that existed between the poor women.

"I am proud of you, Salu. You are doing a lot here..."

"You speak as if I am rich, Faty. I am only rich in spirit."

"I am angry... bitter. What happened to you? Aren't you bitter, Salu?"

"I should be. What the whites have done, trampling over our land with big boots like the marauding Midianites, dancing on the graves of our ancestors in celebration of illegal possession of our heritage, is not easy to forgive."

"Yes, the Jews do not find it easy to forgive Hitler for the Holocaust, either."

"Some people think our case is less severe than that of the Holocaust. Only God can split such hairs."

"Quite. The cows? *Soksie* and the twin calves... You are still keeping them? The piece of land here is too small."

"A piece of land is never a little thing. The space is small, yes, but maybe one day we shall recapture the land of Langaḷibalele. You never know what you have until it's gone. I'm beginning to appreciate little things I had on the farm, like free milk and free freshly-baked bread."

Kūkuchi spent the time venting her frustrations on Salu, mostly about her coach.

Salu said, "I did not expect you to behave like a typical township girl, with low self-esteem issues; otherwise, you wouldn't have settled for the lowlife you call your coach. Does Musa know about your stupid pregnancy? Does your Khulu know?"

"Let's not go there, Salu. As for Khulu, life has dealt her too much of a burden."

***

Kükuchi's time away with Salu proved cathartic. She returned to her routine at Fort Hare with improved vigour. Her body had become so light that she broke several Cape and Natal Provincial javelin records in those days. One day, as she was doing her sit-ups on the runway, she felt a hand come down on her arm. The coach said, "Your improvement is phenomenal."

Kükuchi ignored him.

"Well then, I plead guilty. I'm sorry."

"It's too late, I don't need a coach now. I don't need anyone. Stop it."

"Do not exaggerate. As you know, this is a small campus. I hear from the grapevine you had a miscarriage."

"Like you say, this campus is small."

"My wife and I are reunited... thanks to you."

"That's good."

Trying to milk secrets, he asked, "I also hear rumours you were seen in her company in a café before you were carried to the hospital. You can tell me what you were discussing with her. I'm curious."

"Woman-to-woman stuff? I don't suppose you know anything about that."

"Did you reveal our little tryst to her?"

"Tryst? Why don't you ask her?"

"I'm curious as to how you located her and why you invited her to a restaurant."

"You know, Sekonyela, curiosity caused David, that King of the Jews, to get into trouble with a girl named Bathsheba. Did you ever go to Sunday school when you were a small boy? Bathsheba was taking a bath without realizing that the king kept feeding his prying eyes with her naked body. So, please go away and leave me alone."

As he walked away, Kükuchi said, "You might be interested to know, it's your wife, Bridgette, that invited me to that restaurant."

***

Kükuchi woke up with a twitching eye, so she got out of bed and splashed her face with cold water. The twitching stopped. After dabbing with a towel, she sat down to read. Before she could run down a page, the irritation in her eye had started again. Kükuchi consulted her roommates.

"Many children in Rhodesia who look like you have eye problems. Get your eyes tested regularly. I know these things," boasted Goodie.

At night, severe eye flashes took over, and migraine followed. It was not only her eye that was 'pulling back' but the left side of her face as well. The light on the wall fluttered like her mother's shadow on their home kitchen wall, the night she lectured her and Dassie on the 'evil man' called Verwoerd. After a tormenting night, her left eye could only see a blot of darkness. Kükuchi was now blind in the left eye, but the headache was gone.

Just then, a cold shiver cut through her body when she received a message from Musa that said, 'Come home immediately'.

Kūkuchi said to her roommates, "I must go home. I suspect my granny is dead."

Goodie shot up excitedly and said, "Kūkuchi, go with me. I have never been to Johannesburg. I learn it is a big town, like Bulawayo."

"I don't come from Johannesburg, Goofie. I come from White-City. It is a small village located far from Johannesburg. Ask Peta. White City resembles a rundown military camp in the heart of Vietnam. Have you ever been to the Zimbabwe Ruins?"

"Of course, I've been to the Ruins with my mother. What do you take me for?"

"White-City is worse. We don't even have bathrooms or showers. Our lavatories are outside, fifty meters away, and we use the bucket system. If you have to go at night, forget it because those thugs will be waiting outside to abduct you."

"And worse," Peta teased further, "there are lions there roaming the streets. Aren't you afraid?"

"Please, Kūkuchi, my good sister."

"Besides, there's no space for visitors to sleep," added Kūkuchi for good measure.

"I am no visitor. I can sleep in the kitchen. I'm used to it. At home, I don't have a bedroom of my own. I sleep with my mother. Sometimes when there are important visitors, I sleep on the veranda."

"Veranda? There are no verandas in White-City. Forget it, Goofie."

***

Clouds of smoke billowed from the chimneys of White-City, greeting Kūkuchi and Goodie, who sat uncomfortably in a speeding sedan taxi. Many people were already on their way to work, and children in uniform were clearing off the streets.

Dassie settled on the *stoep* early, a cloud of despair visible on his face. Goodie and Dassie looked at each other carefully, searching for answers. Jozi ran out of the house, happily greeting Kūkuchi and Goodie, saying, "Khulu is inside, with Musa. It's good you came. So, this is Goodie?"

"Yes, she is from Matabeleland. Goodie, this is Jozi, my sister, and that is Dassie... And you? Why are you not at school?"

Goodie said, "At last we have arrived. It's so good to be here to meet your folk! Oh, Dassie, Kūkuchi told me a lot about you."

"A lot?"

"Yes. She said you want to be a mathematics professor when you grow up?"

"Me?"

"If he grows up," murmured Kūkuchi. "Stand up, Dassie, and greet Goodie."

Dassie stood up, dusted the back of his short pants off, and retorted, "Yes, let's take a walk, Goodie. I'll show you around. White-City is a nice place."

"Goodie is tired, Dassie. She must eat first and drink something; not so Goofie?" Kūkuchi pointed out.

"Oh no, I'm not hungry," chirped Goodie. "Let's go, Dassie. I'll tell you all about Matebeleland,"

"Okay, let me introduce you to Khulu and Musa first."

Kükuchi could tell that Khulu was suffering from a serious illness. She said, "Goodie, this is my grandmother. We call her Khulu here. And this is my mother, Musa, she is the one who carried me here." She laughed as she pointed jokingly at her tummy.

Musa smiled shyly and said, "Let me see your eye," Khulu said to Kükuchi.

"There's no pain anymore, Khulu. I am getting along fine with one eye."

"Musa must take you to St. John's. They must check your eyes."

Dassie and Goodie vanished from the streets of White-City.

"Tell me about this child from Matebeleland. Isn't she too young for university?" asked Jozi.

"She's only sixteen, but she talks too much."

"Universities have become primary schools. I must go back to study, you know," Jozi put it cheerily."

"Let's hope she is not nursing ideas about Dassie. I am getting worried now," Kükuchi said.

Jozi stood tall on the *stoep*, cricked her neck, and said, "Oh, Kükuchi, look. These two! I don't think they're talking about Matebeleland at all. Look at how they're holding hands."

Family in Turmoil

Musa ordered everyone to gather in the house for a meeting. In the evening, they quietly congregated in the 'dining room' to hear what Musa had to say. Bunched together like a pack of daisies, they prepared themselves eagerly. Curiously, Musa spoke to Goodie and told her about a girl named Tina. She explained that the police found her body in a shallow grave near a local stream beneath the branches of a willow tree.

Goodie looked upset.

Turning to Kükuchi, Musa said, "I have sad news, Kükuchi. The reason we called you... Dodo, your uncle, was arrested and charged with Tina's murder..."

Kükuchi passed out. Musa sent for Mohale. When she came round, Mohale was fanning her face with a large towel.

Kükuchi was delirious, "Mohale, how are you? Where is Bobby...?"

"I think she is confused," Mohale whispered. "Don't worry, Khulu, I'll give her some sedatives. She'll sleep like a baby the whole night. And the girl from Rhodesia will have to come to my place and put up there. I have enough room in my house."

In the morning, Mohale returned to watch over Kükuchi, who had fully recovered. She motioned her outside and said, "I know you don't know this, but you must know it was Mendi who saw everything..."

"He saw what, Sister Mohale?"

"When your dirty uncle, Dodo... when he buried that child of the shop-keeper, Mendi was there and he saw everything."

"When did he say that to you? Why didn't he tell the police?"

"I asked him the same question, the stupid boy. After they released him, he came to my place and told me he was a rich man. Then he told me the rest of the story about Dodo. He said he did not want the police to arrest Dodo because he was your uncle. He did not want you to be upset because he cared for you."

"Me? Oh, Mendi!"

***

The dark cloud over family honour was worse than anything that Khulu had ever experienced. Newspapers carried disjointed coverage of Dodo's story, making a gratuitous mention of Kükuchi's name as the niece of the perpetrator. Funani was not forthcoming about Dodo's arrest either.

Kükuchi said to him, "I see you are serious about Jozi. Are you in love with her?"

"Of course. She is a fine girl. I should have told you. We plan to get married soon."

"I am happy for you. I like Jozi. She has been good to Khulu. Tell me about Dodo…"

"I can't answer questions about him."

"Why not?

"We are still investigating."

"You are my uncle. You can tell me if he confessed. Did he rape Tina… or are you still investigating that too?"

"I can't tell you, Kuchi. Can you tell me something about you and Uncle Dodo? I suspect something happened to you. Am I wrong?"

Before they left for college, Khulu said a prayer and then addressed Goodie, "You, my child from the land of the Ndebele; I have good feelings about you because you remind me of my great-grandmother, Bashaye…"

"The buffalo," Kükuchi quipped.

"Let me tell you, Child of Mzilikazi; Bashaye gave Durnford's soldiers a run-around before they locked Langalibalele up on Robben Island on trumped-up charges. The British soldiers ran helter-skelter after Bashaye sent them on a wild goose chase. You must return to the Drakensberg, your country, where Mzilikazi Mashobane's navel was buried. We are related to you because we are blood relatives of the Zulu. There must be a good reason why your ancestors sent you to this township of White-City to be with us. Maybe you are the one sent to rescue Kükuchi from herself. That's why you and the Ndebele people have to come back to the Buffalo River Valley."

"Sure, Khulu, you'll see me here again in December."

"In your bloody dreams, Goofie," Kükuchi put it bluntly.

The train to Park Station was almost empty. So, Goodie and I had the compartment to ourselves. I was cautiously hopeful over Dassie's circumstances, as he had seemed adrift before the Goodie whirlwind swept across White-City.

"What have you been saying to Dassie? I see he is raring to go back to school."

Goodie flashed a wicked smile and said, "Nothing."

"You like him, don't you?"

"He's honest, sensitive; I like that in a man. He is fun to be with and I enjoy his company..."

"How many men do you have?"

Goodie reflected a bit before she said, "One or two. What should I say to them now? I wonder."

"Goofie, you're much too young to talk about men. As for Dassie, he is still in high school. He is my brother, and I know him. He is not as mature... as you. Doesn't that bother you?"

"You think I'm mature? He tells me he doesn't know what he would do without you."

"Dassie would never say something like that. Did he tell you about Lesedi?"

"No. Who is Lesedi?

"Lesedi is a girl, Goofie, a pretty javelin girl from Springs. Dassie wants to marry Lesedi and Toby. Do you want to be wife Number three?"

Khulu passes away

Before launching his final year's lecture, Professor Smit excitedly told his African students that the government had issued a 10-year ban on Lillian Ngoyi. As a result, she was confined to her home in Orlando East, Soweto, and the ban prevented her from attending any gatherings, including church services.

After explaining its legal implications, Smit said smugly, "This will teach her to meddle in politics."

Kükuchi raised her hand and said, "Is Lillian Ngoyi the same lady who led one million women to Pretoria in 1956?"

"I'm not sure about one million, but same troublemaker."

"Was it not rude of Strydom to reject a memorandum from the million women?"

There was a furtive murmur of approval to Kükuchi's questions. Smit coughed uneasily and put it, "This is a law class, not township buffoonery. Ask your Lillian Ngoyi if their gathering was illegal or not. Ask her what she thinks now. Let's go on," said Smit, rattling through his lecture papers.

Outside the lecture hall, Smit pointed an admonitory finger at Kükuchi and whispered, "I know all about your communist mother. If you want to get ahead, forget politics."

On their way to their residence, Goodie remonstrated with Kükuchi, "You must stop asking stupid questions, Kükuchi. These lecturers are vindictive; they'll fail you, and you'll end up working as a domestic in Johannesburg. Your first-class Matric certificate means nothing if you are black."

Feeling offended, Kükuchi said, "What do you know about being a domestic?"

"I'm sorry. I shouldn't have said that. Peta told me your mother worked as a maid for white people in Mayfair. I told her my mother was once a girl for a white settler. She advised me never to offend white lecturers because they wield all the power over your future."

"They can't fail me for asking a simple question."

"If they can get rid of Lillian Ngoyi, who do you think you are?"

Khulu's words began to ring in Kükuchi's ears: 'When you deal with these people, Kükuchi, you must use your head'. Kükuchi felt small in the face of Goodie's lofty reproach.

***

The end-of-year break brought relief and excitement. As Kükuchi pondered on what to wear, Goodie tore into her space singing joyfully, "I've finished packing. Ready when you are, Kuchi, my dear sister."

"Ready? Where are you going, Goodie?"

"To JoBurg with you, Kuchi. White-City."

Still holding a grudge over Goodie's impertinence after the Lillian Ngoyi lecture, Kükuchi said, "You never discussed this with me. It's Christmas time. You can go to Rhodesia, your home."

Goodie became desperate. She threw herself on Kükuchi's bed, gulped back her tears, and put it feebly, "Please, Kükuchi, my beautiful sister. I promised Khulu I would come back for her. You also heard her say all the Ndebele people must return to South Africa because we are compatriots. Khulu is expecting me."

"I can't go with you. We don't have space in White-City, I told you last time."

Goodie stood up, darted from one corner to the next like a bumblebee attracted by the flower's scent. She rummaged through her bag to produce her bottle of 'cough remedy'. After tilting a nip, she said, "Please, Kuchi, Khulu relies on me. You heard her. I have to go with you to look after her."

"You can't fool me. It's not about Dassie, is it?"

"Pardon?"

***

A grumble of thunder and flashes of lightning greeted us as we entered the muddy streets of White-City.

Goodie blurted out, "Last time I was here, nobody told me there was lightning here in Johannesburg. At home, the weather kills people, and they accuse old women of witchcraft. Is there any witchcraft here in White-City?"

"Ten times more than in Rhodesia. That's why you have to stop coming here. This is the last time, right, Goodie?"

"Do you think you can buy me by calling me Goody and not using that offensive name. Only Musa, Jozi, and Khulu love me, but one person in the whole world treats me with contempt."

"Maybe I'm bewitched. Otherwise, why does a *Stompie* keep following me?"

"Bewitched? My mother, who is a doctor at home, says witchcraft is the opium of the black masses. Do you know what that means, Kükuchi?"

"It means you have to stop sipping alcohol in dark corners and stop following me to White-City."

***

We visited Khulu. She was sound asleep, but out of the Intensive Care Unit. Dodo's arrest had taken a heavy toll on her health. After a long while, she lifted her head and then smiled a blissful smile. She touched Goodie and mumbled through in her bristly voice, "I dream beautiful dreams these days," she gasped, displaying a huge gap where a set of teeth once stood.

We had a good time cracking jokes and telling Khulu about Fort Hare.

"You did well, coming today, Kükuchi, and you, my child from the land of the Ndebele; please help Kükuchi to deal with her anger so she can look after her uncle. He is family. Whatever we may have against him, we should not let private shame spill over into public view. He needs our help. Am I wrong, my girl from Matebeleland?"

"No, Khulu. You are right. My mother, who is a doctor back home, always says, 'It is wrong to hang your dirty linen in public'."

"Kükuchi, another thing, always visit Salu. It is not easy for her, either. To lose your home and become a pauper overnight is difficult to cope with. I pray for her every day."

We took a walk to Toby's home. Toby felt ill at ease because the whole room heaved under stolen merchandise, not excluding pairs of shoes and colourful costumes.

"This must be the girl from Rhodesia."

"What's all this, Toby?" I asked, quite agitated at the sight of the stashes.

"I didn't know what to do, Kükuchi. Mendi came here early the other day; it was still dark, and he offloaded the stuff. He promised to fetch it later."

"And you want me to believe that? You promised..."

"How are you, Goodie? Papa Mkhize has been bragging about you. I am serious about going back to school again, you know. I want to be a social worker. I'll attend night school to complete my matric. They say you are a very bright girl, Goodie."

"Very. I did my A Level..."

"Okay, okay," Kükuchi butted in. "Look, Toby; you'll never be a social worker if you continue seeing Mendi and fraternizing with those men from Alexandra."

"No, Kuchi. S'true. You can have Mendi. He came unexpectedly with his friends. He doesn't want to go to jail again. We all went together to see Khulu."

"Do you sleep with Mendi?"

"Me? Of course not."

"I have something for you. You remember how you saved my skin... going to jail and protecting me? Here, take this. It's part of the money I saved after Papi died. I still have a mother, and you don't."

"What a lot of money, Kükuchi. I couldn't even afford bread today. Oh, Goodie! I must thank you too. Dassie sure likes you. I've never seen him this happy since... long ago? But you must be careful; he goes back to his *Tsotsi* ways when you are gone."

When we reached home, we sat on the *stoep*. Goodie said, "Did you have to ask Toby if she slept with Mendi?"

"I wanted to know."

"That's childish. But tell me about Mendi. He was in jail? What was he in for?"

"You don't want to know."

"All of you folks, everything about White-City seems filled with skeletons."

"Don't you have skeletons and secrets where you come from, Goofie?"

Dassie entered, appearing taller and more confident. Goodie leapt into Dassie's arms. After a brief moment of greetings, Dassie's posture softened, and his face seemed to scorch. He said, "I brought you sad news. I left Musa and Mr Mohale in the hospital. Khulu has passed away."

***

Khulu had lost the will to live the very moment she heard of Dodo's murderous activities. She had taken the blame on her shoulders as if she had failed as a mother. I trembled when I recalled Mkhize's words, 'All our mothers carry too much pain, even extra pain they should not be carrying'.

Goodie withered and appeared disconnected from anything around. Her sniffling went on until she stumbled toward Sister Mohale's place to sleep.

Musa and I remained dry-eyed throughout. In the morning, Musa ordered us to a meeting to discuss funeral arrangements. Musa appeared relaxed and in charge. After the meeting, she thanked the two of us for our understanding. I had never seen Musa so cool and cultured before. However, without warning, Musa began to scream in a loud voice as if she had just received the news of Khulu's death. I stretched out my arms to comfort her. After a few minutes, Musa wiped her face and said, "Dassie, you see your sister here, you must respect her. You two must love and protect each other."

Musa's strange performance reminded me of the night she addressed us all those years before, about the appointment of Hendrik Verwoerd as Prime Minister. I stared at my lonely mother and felt deeply sad for her. However, I suddenly recalled a question she never asked me that night, a question that had left a deep wound in my spirit. I felt the urge to ask, despite feeling down about the state of our family. While I had earlier decided to accept her as a lonely and private individual, it was always hard for me to deal with such unresolved sticking points from our past. The question she never asked me that night leapt out and engulfed my soul. I gazed at Khulu's favourite spot, but Khulu's glistening eyes were no longer there to watch over the proceedings in her kitchen.

I said, "Musa, do you remember the night you asked Dassie if he was inferior; that day you were telling us about Verwoerd?"

"No, when was that?" Musa said amidst her sorrowful snuffling.

I could feel my heart pound against my chest again, and I said, "You were telling us, Dassie and me, what that man Verwoerd said about the Africans; that they were inferior and that African children did not deserve the greener pastures of white education. Don't you remember?"

"Yes, I remember now."

"You never asked me. Why did you not ask me too?"

"I never ask you what, Kūkuchi?"

"You did not ask if I thought I was inferior. You only asked Dassie, but you did not ask me?"

"Oh, Kūkuchi. You are a strong girl. You are not inferior, and you know that."

"You only asked Dassie. Why didn't you ask me too? I also wanted to tell you something."

Musa puckered her brow and squeaked, "What can I say, Kuchi, my child? I didn't think it was important to you because you are different, and... maybe I was afraid to ask."

"Different, Musa? Is that why you did not ask me, because I am different from all of you...?"

More tears now streamed down Musa's face. She said, "I mean you are different because you are a strong girl, Kūkuchi…because..." Musa paused and looked toward Khulu's dimly lit corner. Khulu was no longer there to rescue anyone from sticky situations..."I don't know what to say."

Musa wiped her face. Dassie handed Musa a handkerchief and said, "Why don't you ask Kükuchi the question, Musa?"

"What should I say, Dassie?" Musa put it clumsily.

"No, Musa, forget it. Musa is our mother, and we love her."

After the awkward episode, I felt relieved that I had lanced the boil, though I was sad to see Musa upset. Dassie walked out, leaving an uneasy emptiness in the kitchen. Musa and I stayed there, unable to think of what to say to each other next.

Jozi arrived the following morning, followed shortly by Salu, who was fuming, "I had to read it in the newspapers that my sister was ill."

Salu turned down Jozi's offer of tea. Instead, she instructed Musa and me to accompany her to the mortuary.

I began considering ways to evade Salu's planned trip to the mortuary. "Salu," I said, "I can't go to the funeral people. I have a visitor, all the way from Rhodesia, and I must look after her."

"There's no visitor here. I heard about your friend. She cannot be white; otherwise, the superintendent would not have given her an overnight permit here. She must be an African, and she can't be a visitor in a bereaved family."

Goodie was whistling as she walked in. She held a jug of sour milk from the dairy in her hand. White-City had become her home turf.

"Salu, this is Goodie, the visitor I was telling you about. Goofie, meet Salu, my granny."

Goodie grabbed Salu's arm like an old friend, "Salu! Oh, Salu! I've heard so much about you. At Fort Hare, everyone moaned the loss of your farm..."

"So, you see, Salu. That's why I can't go with you to the mortuary."

"We are getting to the mortuary?" Goodie exclaimed. "Oh, Kükuchi, I've been to the mortuary to do the ritual stuff and things on our bereaved relatives back home. Now they rely on me whenever a relative crosses the River Jordan. I want to go, Salu. It makes me feel peaceful and very close to the heavenly spirits from Paradise."

I got mad. After pulling Goodie by the arm, I dragged her outside, all the way to the tree behind the lavatory.

"What's wrong, Kükuchi. My hair? You're hurting me."

"Up there in Matebeleland, do people enjoy visiting mortuaries?"

"Why, no!"

"Goofie, you just told Salu you like dead people because they cause you to be with the spirits in Paradise."

"Please, Kükuchi, you are causing pain to my arm."

"Now listen, you *Stompie*; I don't like mortuaries and I don't like dead people because they cause me to dream bad dreams. So, go back there and tell Salu you have changed your mind and that you don't think visiting people who go through Jordan is such a good idea. Say you want to remain here with me. Otherwise…!"

I let Goodie loose, and she squeaked, "You are the cruellest person I have ever seen."

"And you are a liar. Back there at Iona, you told us you could not be a doctor because you hate cadavers. Now you say the dead remind you of Paradise?"

"How can you even think of our beloved Khulu as a cadaver?"

***

On the wake, Khulu's home became a hive of activity from early morning; neighbours and relatives at hand, helping with various chores in preparation. Salu and two women had taken their spot on the mattress. As soon as the men left the room, Salu winched her body forward, came within reach of the coffin, and cried so loud the whole house stood still: '

'Ntombizakhona, they told me what you said about me, that I don't give you conversation, that I am a noisy brazier. Well, I am here to provide you with more heat than you ever got when you were still breathing air from the fog of the Drakensberg. I heard mysterious voices whisper in my ear. Those voices said you said I should not attend your funeral. Now, tell me, my father's child, what are you going to do about it? Here I am. How can you say I, your baby sister, your flesh and blood... that I should not bury you? You, who survived on a trickle and left me a stream from our mother's breast, because after you had been born, you were trapped in the deep by the descendants of the Gordon Highlanders; I know your past as if it were today. Our folk tales are awash with blood and riddled with painful memories, but your leaving me behind fills my existence with floods of tears. I am the only one surviving to show all of them the very smudge of earth where Mother Buthelezi, our dear mother, interred your umbilical cord among the roots of the apple tree. I scooped out the world and brought it along to plant your seed to restore your ties with Mother. You will rise above the stars and be a beacon to your descendants today, tomorrow, and every day.

A long silence followed; a lull before Salu broke down uncontrollably over her sister's death. Her excruciating scream was brief but intense. Women and girls cried in sympathy. Goodie covered Salu's head with a chiffon to calm her down. Salu settled on the mattress and dozed off.

Goodie, who seemed to have forgotten about our earlier spat, said, "Kükuchi, did Khulu tell Salu not to attend her funeral?"

"Who told you that?"

"Salu said things to Khulu in there, as if she were still alive."

"Have you been drinking your cough mixture the whole day?"

***

My eyes had remained dry throughout. The setting at the cemetery resembled a murky landscape, with mourners and the dead appearing as floating apparitions, making indistinct groaning sounds. My head was spinning, and I could see the old dead standing over their graves, staring at me.

But by the time I came forward to sprinkle white rose petals over Khulu's coffin in her grave, my mind had cleared, and I said, "Khulu, I will bring Salu so you can have a good conversation together. I promise."

On our way back to the vehicles, Salu said, "Here's your so-called father. Tell him to go away; otherwise, I will give him a bit of my..."

"My father?"

"How are you?" Ramola greeted us.

He was tall but disappointing because he was aging and looked frail. The image of him that I had built in my head over the years suddenly faded in the blink of an eye.

"You are my father?"

"Yes, I'll call and invite you to my home near Rustenburg."

"Funny you never cared for her before she got a distinction in Matric and is now finishing law at University," railed Salu. "Let's go, Kuchi. Let's go to our car."

After the mourners had left, Funani and I sat in the shade of the peach tree. Funani said, "It's a lovely dress you're wearing, and you look great in it."

"Oh, thanks, Funani. But a funeral dress is not supposed to be something to look great in. Tell me, is it a sin not to cry after losing someone you love dearly?"

"The spring of tears is never dry, Kuchi, but nature helps us to hold back. Otherwise, we wallow in our sorrows until we drown in our ocean of tears. You spoke well during the service. Tears would have interfered with your eulogy."

"What did I say? Remind me."

"What can I remember? You said Khulu taught you that the currency of integrity is truth. You said more, of course. You also said Khulu was always a shoulder to cry on. So, next time you need a shoulder to cry on, you know where to find me."

"Oh, Funani; where have you ever seen anyone cry on a policeman's shoulder?"

"I am an uncle to you, not a policeman."

Funani told me about Dodo's confession, revealing his sexual assault on Tina before strangling her to death. Funani revealed that he advised him to plead guilty to receive a reduction in sentence. This disappointed me.

"Do you want his sentence reduced? Why?"

"Perhaps the judge will consider the significance of new findings in his disclosure."

"Funani, tell me out loud why you want the judge to make life for this person easier."

"Sometimes when we investigate the actions of suspects, we get them to cut a deal to get at the truth. Besides, psychopaths will find ways of dragging the case, frustrating the legal process."

"What deal did you strike with Dodo?"

"Twenty years... hard labour."

"And then he gets paroled after five?"

"Maybe. That's the law."

"You know, Funani, Tina chose the wrong skin. She should have chosen a white skin and blue eyes, just like Rosemarie's. Tina would still be alive today because Dodo would never have crossed the line and got to the European side looking for a white girl to rape and strangle. Dodo would know he would hang; no twenty-year deals and no mercy. All men the world over, think twice before raping a white woman but when it comes to black women, all men feel entitled because judges give them bail before they slap them on the wrist. Next time you see Dodo, ask him what he did to me one day when he found me alone in the house. Treating Dodo with kid gloves is like letting the chickens out of their pens where there is a skulk of foxes around.

"Oh, Kükuchi, you're crying! I had no idea you could cry. I knew there was a soft side to those eyes that burn like a coal fire. I heard many stories about Bashaye, our ancestor. You are her reincarnation…"

"*Ag,* Please!"

"Kükuchi, we are relatives. When we were growing up, our grandmothers would share with us their deep oral histories. Some people believe that Bashaye was cursed because she gave birth to white girls and only a sprinkling of black boys. Lazy people are always looking for an explanation for everything they don't understand, like a curse or witchcraft."

"Tell the truth, Funani. If you look at me, what do you think of me?"

"The truth? Would you like to be treated differently from other girls?"

"Stop beating about the bush and answer my question."

"Oh well. You are a self-confident woman, but I sometimes see some weakness in you. You should stop fishing for other people's opinions about you, as that reflects low self-esteem. You are smart and crafty, but you lack confidence where it matters most. And the conflict that you carry makes you angry at times."

"What does that mean, Funani?"

"To you, this world is an enemy because you think humanity owes you something."

"Of course it does."

"The world owes you nothing, you. You must accept that. When you were young at primary school, you refused to sit in front when your teachers tried to help you because of your eyes, which gave you problems."

"It is not good to be treated like a disabled person."

"God made you different, and you had an eye problem. That means you have a disability. But then tell me as your uncle. Do you have love?"

"How"

"Musa. Do you love Musa?"

"I don't know Funani. I've never thought of it that way before."

"You have to think about it that way so you don't miss out on life. Musa is your mother."

"Funani, what are you being taught at your police Academy? Jozi told me you studied in Scotland."

"It's in Scotland Yard, England. There, I learned that morality and ethics are more important than reputation. No matter how famous you may be, if you have never thought of love for your mother, all of that is futile…"

"She must love me first."

"You can't make people love you, but you can love them regardless. Here is something else: do you occasionally have sleepless nights thinking of someone you want to be with?"

I reflected on the question for a moment, not knowing where it was leading. Then I said, "Yes, I do sometimes. I appreciate compliments on my lipstick, my stylishly plaited hair, the colour of my earrings, and the brand of my attire... There are indeed times when I can't sleep, thinking of someone."

"Aha! Now I know that Kükuchi is a girl who cries tears; a fashion-conscious girl, one who spends sleepless nights due to loneliness. Do you remember Hamilton?"

"Who? How do you know him?"

"He is a police officer from Ixopo. After all, even police do exchange secrets about matters of the heart with one another."

"Yes ...?"

"The last time I saw him, Hamilton kept pressuring me, asking me endless questions about you."

"Yes ...? What did you say to him?"

CHAPTER 26

End of an Era

Two weeks after Khulu's funeral, Musa and I went to Wembezi. Goodie and Dassie accompanied us to Park Station. Goodie wore a bangle and a beautiful gold wristwatch. I called her to find out where she got the trinkets from.

"Shush, please, Kükuchi. I don't have the money to buy a wristwatch. I need it to time myself when I study. Besides, my mother, who is a doctor in Matebeleland, always says, 'Those who live in glass houses should never throw stones'. Do you know what that means? Dassie told me lots of things about you and about that bosom friend of yours called Toby."

"Why don't you tell me what Dassie said about my bosom friend?"

"I'd rather not say. But… as for you and Toby? You had an interesting life together, didn't you?" Goodie chuckled.

***

We sought permission from the new farm owner to visit our family burial ground. After making us wait for two hours, Barry said he could only allow one *Kaffir* at a time, as he did not want a crowd on his land. Salu explained that the ritual required the three of us to be together. Two days later, Barry permitted us to visit the site. We slaughtered a goat in preparation. Barry dispatched his tall sixteen-year-old son, who came fully armed with a shotgun, to escort us to the gravesite. We had to walk fast because our marshal kept demanding we 'get moving'. The surreal, callous nature of the whole idea left us numb. It was so sapping on Salu's dignity that she could barely walk. Musa and I had to assist her all the way. When we reached the Eastern elevation along the creek, wild daffodils were nodding in the wind while an ensemble of swallows chirped to the murmurs of the stream. I held Musa by the hand, and Salu joined us to complete the circle. There was no dry eye left. The white boy with a shotgun on his shoulder sniggered and shook his head derisively. The whirlwind of resentment against our oppressors intensified. When we reached home, we performed the ceremonial washing of hands, our hearts boiling with disgust.

"This is the worst day of my life," I said.

"Every day is the worst day for African women," Salu said with resignation.

Kükuchi's mind was elsewhere: the IOC's decision regarding South Africa's status in world sport. The Summer Olympics in Tokyo became the focus of international attention. Kükuchi fantasized about being one of the 20 female javelin contestants from 12 countries. A group of sports activists had earlier formed the South African Non-Racial Olympic Committee (SAN-ROC), aimed at ensuring the entry of black sports associations into the IOC. It was also to render invalid IOC's recognition of the all-white SAOGA. As soon as the government smelt a hint that the IOC was discussing with the new body, it accused all concerned of introducing politics into sport, an ironic remark given their relentless tyranny towards black sport. In a remarkable feat of further originality, white sports bodies tried to convince the world that the South African Government sports policy had undergone a significant change; their convoluted explanation being that whites and blacks could compete against one another, if the club facilities were open to the designated race. They insisted, to outside ridicule, that racial discrimination no longer existed.

When the black golfer, Sewsunker Sewgolum, won the SAOGA tournament, he received his prize outside the clubhouse in heavy rain. Gary Player, a prominent golfer, is said to have tried in vain to persuade his white counterparts to understand the folly of their ways, but they ignored his counsel. The extent of the Player's efforts to intervene in the Sewgolum matter has remained a contentious issue.

Kükuchi took the warning signs with trepidation. Most of her peers had abandoned athletics to pursue other interests. Despite feeling lonely, she pressed on nonetheless.

***

A few weeks later, Khanyile and Zazi attended a family cleansing ceremony after Khulu's departure. Zazi was wearing a blue shirt, light-coloured trousers, and a tattered straw hat, which reflected the hardships that had persisted in his family. Kükuchi was touched.

"Remember me?" he said. "I came here long ago with my father."

How could Kükuchi forget him? Her troubled conscience made her squirm.

"We are sorry about Khulu, but life goes on," he said solemnly. "We can learn from our old people, though. They did well, they did badly. Let's choose the good. As a family, we must pull together. I learn that Salu did not attend Khulu's funeral."

"Who told you that?"

"Well, did she?"

"Go on."

"You see? How can she not attend her own sister's funeral over something that happened when they were small girls?"

"What happened when they were small girls?"

Zazi went on to divulge a strange tale to Kükuchi about Khulu and Salu. In their young days, when they were fourteen and eleven respectively, Salu did something to Khulu for which she refused to apologize. It was all about a heifer. Salu allegedly lied about Khulu to their cruel father, saying that Khulu had thrust the calf down a gorge in anger. Because Khulu, an introvert, was forever the victim of her father's rage, she suffered further humiliation at the hands of her household. Salu gave Khulu the brush-off when she asked her to tell the truth. The wound never healed, even as they grew older. At their father's deathbed, Khulu begged Salu to tell the truth, to no avail. They finally went their separate ways.

"Fifty years is a long time for sisters to keep up that kind of relationship," said Zazi sullenly.

"How do you know all of this?"

"It's a well-known family history. I visited Salu after she moved to Wembezi, and she half admitted it with a wry smile, but no mask of smiles could ever hide a guilty conscience."

Kükuchi exhaled and said, "Salu did attend the funeral, if you wish to know."

"Oh? Something else surprised me when I went to Wembezi. Do you know the name of the heifer that was thrown down the ravine, allegedly by Khulu?"

"Tell me."

"*Soksie.*"

"Oh!"

"A sign of remorse, maybe? She should have said 'sorry' while Khulu was still alive. You know Salu; there's not an ounce of remorse in her blood. But, Kükuchi, let's leave the old tales alone and talk about you and me."

"What for?"

"I checked with some elders and they said we can get together, you and me..."

"Elders? Why should we get together?"

"Because we care for each other, Kükuchi. I want to take a walk with you, and I know you'll enjoy it too. I love you to the moon and back."

"Sorry, you're not my type. Besides, what makes you think relatives should love each other to the moon and back?"

"I'm sorry if I seem to be coming on to you too strongly. I know you have struggled. We have all struggled."

"You don't know the half of it, Zazi. But since you know so much about our past, can you tell me about Salu's history? How did she 'happen' upon the farm?"

I found Zazi's story too bizarre to believe, yet eye-opening. Khulu had two brothers (Jantshi and Nico) and one sister (Salu). Their mother's family owned a piece of land, which they bequeathed to the four on an equal basis. However, there was no love lost between the siblings. Khulu and the brothers decided to put aside their differences. The three worked on the land, planting mealies, cauliflower, and peanuts.

During that time, Salu was away getting an education and later working as an English teacher. Despite the low-intensity sibling rivalry, this could not compare with the resentment they all harboured towards Salu. When she lost her job as a teacher, they celebrated by slaughtering a lamb. However, the party was short-lived because Salu was about to throw the cat among the pigeons. One day, she stepped into the farm unannounced, telling everyone that she had moved house and was returning home. Jantshi welcomed Salu with open arms, arguing that she would be of great use to them due to her education and skills. After a month, Khulu and Nico had deserted the land. Salu and Jantshi made the best of the dire situation until he died in a tragic accident in Estcourt. Nico ran for the hills, and nobody knows what happened to him.

Khulu trekked to Bloemfontein, where she worked for a white family for many years, during which time she raised an orphan she had found in the area. His name was Donald. Khulu called him Dodo.

"You're serious, right?"

"Ask Salu, if you're bold enough. She will confirm the story about."

The court found Dodo guilty of Tina Tatenda's murder. Salu, Musa, Dassie, and Kükuchi later sat dejectedly on the *stoep*. Dassie disappeared two days after. Kükuchi and Musa searched all over for him. Two months later, Funani, their only source inside the police, told them about Dassie, who had arrived in Bechuanaland together with a group of boys and girls from Meadowlands and Rockville. Most of the youngsters were children or descendants of the families forcefully removed from Sophiatown, a settlement later called *Triomf* by the Apartheid regime.

Dassie's disappearance caused Kükuchi to fall into a deep depression, as she believed she would never see him again.

***

In Switzerland, meanwhile, the IOC demanded that South African sports authorities end Apartheid in sport by the end of August of that year. South Africa responded by announcing the inclusion of seven 'non-whites' in their team that consisted of over 60 whites, something that angered the IOC and isolated South Africa even further. The World waited in great anticipation for the IOC's final decision, specifically whether to ban South Africa from participating in the Tokyo Olympic Games. The ban would effectively bring to an end South Africa's participation in any further Olympic Games. For Kükuchi, that would mean an end to her Olympic dreams.

At Fort Hare, students huddled up around wireless gadgets, most of them praying for the total expulsion of South Africa. As for Kükuchi, she remained tense in her room, Goodie by her side.

Kükuchi said to Goodie, "My grandmother once told me that one evening in 1948, their community sat around the fire, waiting for the results of the elections. Some prayed for the defeat of Jan Smuts, the man who had made empty promises to the Africans. Others felt Malan's victory would spell doom for the Africans. Many Africans thought Malan would be their saviour."

"Did your Granny support Malan or Jan Smuts?"

"She said, 'When it comes to the crunch, the European community in Africa will always build a wagon circle. '"

"What did she mean?"

"She meant that white people did what Africans are struggling with, and that is to be united. Do you know Jan Smuts lost the elections, even lost his seat?"

"Served him right."

"I wish the IOC could consider our plight. We don't make laws in this country. Why should African athletes suffer? Do they know what that means to me?"

When the International Olympic Committee announced the expulsion of South Africa, the University of Fort Hare erupted into a frenzy of chanting. Tears fell like rain down Kükuchi's face. Goodie dabbed her friend's cheeks with her doek. She then handed over her bottle of liquor, which Kükuchi quickly accepted and drank, not leaving a drop.

Then they slept soundly, despite the noise of celebrations outside. In the morning, Goodie shook Kükuchi and said, "Wake up. Who is Hamilton?"

"What Hamilton?"

"I don't know. You're the one who's been calling his name in your dream."

"Leave me alone, Goofie. My head is beating like a cowhide drum because of your alcohol."

"Here, sip a tot for a hangover. It helps. We shall drink coffee and forget about suffering. The Olympics are a dead dream, Kuchi. My mother, who is a doctor back home, says, 'It doesn't help to cry over milk spilled on sand'. So, forget about the Javelin and move on. Let's do our best now so we can become good, prominent attorneys."

"Yeah?"

Another year had passed. Back in White-City, where our home was turning into a ruin, with our lawn and trees unattended, I sat alone during the holidays, waiting for something to happen, anything to interrupt my monotonous time in my desolate White-City. Every sound, silence, lightning, thunder, and the hooting of a taxi brought back haunting recollections of my challenging and fun days in the township. I longed for Dassie's theatrical company and wondered how Goodie was doing in Matebeleland. As I wallowed in self-pity, I heard muffled voices and footsteps, followed by a hard, agitated knock on the door. Before I could open my mouth, Sister Mohale and Mr Mohale, her ex-husband, were already inside. My mouth puckered up when I saw Mr and Mrs Maseko on tow. A sombre expression of grief was visible on the faces of the older adults. They pulled the benches and sat down in silence as my mind began to race in infinite directions.

Breaking the silence, Sister Mohale said, "We have lost the war."

"Why, Auntie? What war?" I began to shake because my sixth sense told me something terrible about Dassie. Many boys who left the country to fight against the government ended up dying like flies.

"I know you cared for him," said Mohale, "and he cared for you too..."

"Who, Auntie?"

"Mendi was shot dead in Pretoria," Mr Mohale put it bravely.

I screamed and passed out. Sister Mohale used her nursing skills to resuscitate me. The screams had echoed through the neighbourhood. Within a few minutes, Mkhize and five women had squeezed themselves inside the tiny kitchen.

Sister Mohale related the story of Mendi's death, going over it as our inquisitive neighbours streamed inside Khulu's space. "It was an armed robbery that went wrong. A white woman was killed, and the husband shot both Mendi and his friend who came from Alexandra."

There was groaning and sobbing.

Mkhize, who took the news with a despairing sigh, said, "Mohale, many African young men are either dead or in jail, all because they wanted quick money so they could shine in White-City. That is township life."

"It must be heavy on you, Mkhize," said Sister Mohale, "because you did everything for Mendi and even hid him in your house after he killed that man from Alexandra."

Sister Mohale's faux pas sent the kitchen reeling into palpable silence. Mkhize wrinkled his nose clumsily and stroked his hairline. He did not take kindly to Sister Mohale's blunder about his secret activities with Mendi. When he finally recovered, he smiled wryly as Mr Mohale said, "Yes, Mkhize, we are proud of you. Our boys end up doing time because they think crime is a sign of masculinity."

"Yes," said Papa Maseko, "when they get back from jail, everybody treats them like celebrities."

"As for me, Mohale, I am going back to Mtubatuba to die there," said Mkhize. "Perhaps one can still find a trace of *Ubuntu* in my village. Living in White-City has been a long nightmare, with serpents and cheats nipping at my heels. It has been the superintendent and security police on this side and gangsters on the other. Maybe when we get freedom, black people will treat each other with respect, and there won't be gangsters preying on other poor Africans."

"Without hope, we are dead, but with such an oppressive government, there are few prospects for the future of our children," said Mr Mohale. "Quite depressing the way they killed those two boys; one of them, the one from Alexandra, he died instantly. They say Mendi begged for his life. They deliberately left him on the pavement's edge near the stormwater drain as a pedestrian spectacle, where he squirmed and bled to death in the sweltering Pretoria sun."

Kükuchi rose with great effort and thanked the elders for informing her of Mendi's death, saying that her spirit was broken as she loved him dearly.

"Another thing," said Sister Mohale, "your friend Toby..." she paused, as if listening and waiting for a pin to drop...

Mr Mohale took over and said, "Yes, Kükuchi, Toby, she was with Mendi, together with the men from Alexandra when they did their armed robbery. The police arrested her."

"Toby! Are you sure, Papa Mohale?"

"I know. Of course I know. Toby is lucky to be alive."

"Oh, Toby!" Kükuchi cupped her face while the women wailed, "If only she had died too," Kükuchi finally whispered. "How will she ever cope with life in jail again? She wanted to be a beauty queen. That's all she wanted, but the white principal at Rosettenville prevented her from entering the contest because she was a coloured. That broke her heart and crushed her spirit against competing."

"I remember well," said Mr Mohale. "That white school turned down her entry, thereby depriving Toby of her humanity... and got her disconnected from her femininity that she was entitled and proud to flaunt."

"To them, she was not a woman seeking to create and perform in a great theatre but a redundant extra in their theatre of bigotry," said Kükuchi, quoting Drum Magazine.

"She is in jail as we speak, all by herself... awaiting her fate. White people do not take kindly to having fellow whites murdered by so-called non-whites. To them, such a murder is an act of treason. Toby will hang, or get life if lucky," Mkhize added.

"Oh, Toby, my dear friend! I am fully responsible. We promised each other long ago never to peddle stolen goods again! But temptation...! She promised to go back to school and learn so she could become a social worker. Maybe she tried, but I was always there, speaking in forked tongues and pushing her in the wrong direction. I am so sad about Toby."

Mohale said, "Toby was pretty and lovable, but she could never discover herself and understand how her beauty, such as she had, her loveliness, and appealing smile, had failed to get her anywhere and why Kükuchi had seemed to achieve everything. Toby was distraught when she told me about herself once, about her ambition to become a social worker. She told me that she found learning, reading, and concentrating difficult to sustain because she struggled to understand many things. And worst still, the teachers made fun of her, often referring to her as 'a dumb beauty queen'. We all saw her sister, who lives in Belgium, beautiful and bright."

"Yes, she studies at a university in Belgium. Soon she will graduate."

"Toby was an actor, a stage entertainer. She should not have tried to compete with anyone. We all admired her charm and elegance," Mr Mohale said.

***

Toby had remained inside for several years, with undefined parole possibilities, when Kūkuchi decided to visit her. Following many weeks of introspection, Kūkuchi went to the prison. The female section had a bleak appearance on the outside. However, more apprehension quickly took over as soon as she walked inside. Nothing could cover up the stench of torture and suffering seeping through its hidden crevices. There was a chilly squeakiness in the foyer, shiny polished floors, and intimidating faces of white officials who swaggered about as if they owned the Continent of Africa. Indeed, they owned the world. The environment was much worse than anything that Kūkuchi had seen in Diepkloof Prison or anywhere else. Before then, she had envisioned the female section as situated in a serene, home-like environment, featuring a playground for children and a library available for use by all inmates. The image of bee-alluring flowers and currents of fragrances all around was all in her fantasies. What she found made her so weak that she could hardly twitch her big toe.

Toby's face looked parched, her eyes sunken, and her lips lined with cracks, like a peeling-off potato skin. Only her magazine cover smile had endured all her tribulations.

Toby jumped up and paced up and down in shock and joy. With tears streaming down her cheeks, she shouted, "Kuchi, you are my first visitor here. All my friends and relatives have abandoned me. Someone came here to brag and ended up telling me he read in a newspaper that you were blind, saying that it was because of our bad ways when we were young that God had struck us in this way."

"Sies! Who was that?"

"Pastor Gumede of Moroka..."

"Bandile Gumede? Do you know that he avoided me and did not even want to touch me at his church?"

"I know, they told me. Maybe he thought albinism was contagious. How are your eyes now?"

"Only one eye can see."

"I feel sorry for you, Faty. How do you cope?"

"One gets used to it. What bothers me is headaches. Gumede was right. This is a curse."

"You'll never know what it means to me... your being here, I mean. It is so easy for people outside to avoid a prisoner. But I knew one day you would come because you are my true friend."

The childhood friends embraced each other as if it were forever. Inside her heart, Kūkuchi had taken personal culpability for Toby's circumstances, having been with her in the trenches of delinquency in White-City, yet never having to suffer the consequences.

Under normal circumstances, visitors and inmates were not allowed to touch each other. Toby considered herself lucky, knowing the warders let it happen in her case because they felt sorry for them.

"You saved my life, Toby? I am not sure what I would have done if I had been the one jailed in the first place. You stuck up for me and missed many things in life. How can I ever repay you...?"

"Oh, Kuchi, you can repay me. Please bring me *snoekfish*, achaar, and, maybe, a cake for Christmas. Also," Toby whispered, "Please, Faty, bring me a packet of *Cavalla* and hide it inside the cake."

"You never stopped smoking, Toby?"

"If I don't smoke, my head goes bumpy as if I am travelling on the back of a lorry along the streets of Jabavu. I get some *boxes* from the warders. But I need a big favour..."

"I'll do anything for you."

"Please, Kükuchi, let us sing that Sunday school song... remember the one Miss Lumka used to make us sing?" "Jesus loves me?"

"Yes...?"

"Can we sing it together, like we did with Miss Lumka...?"

Kükuchi decided it was best not to spoil her friend's joyful moment by reminding her of the past. The friends started singing softly, tears rolling down their faces.

Jesus loves me, this I know,

Yes, Jesus loves me

For the bible tells me so...

Toby spoke softly about their former Sunday School friends. Sandy has twins, and Vovo is the father. But Sandy's Dad said Vovo would marry his daughter over his dead body. And Kenny joined Mandela's MK army.

"Are you sure, Toby?"

"I know things. Prison is a place where secrets whizz like fresh air. Kenny bombed part of the West Street Magistrate's Court, maiming an African Tembisa girl in the process," said Toby. "Please, don't repeat this. I tell you because you are my friend. I know because I withheld some crucial evidence that the police don't have."

"How?"

Kenny and Toby once spent two 'romantic' days together at the Carlton Hotel. One night, Toby heard Kenny slip out of the blankets like an eel, disappearing from the room for a while. After waiting a long time for him to return, Toby got out of bed and walked over to Kenny's clothes. When she found a small file and a large amount of money in his wallet, Toby began to suspect that Kenny had deceptively invited the pretty woman as a decoy to avoid suspicion. Toby, a street-smart girl, took the money and file and immediately left the Carlton Hotel.

"I robbed him of everything and ran away with a large sum of money to my uncle's place. People often think you are unintelligent if you have limited education. He looked for me everywhere with his friends until he gave up. He could not find me because I dyed my hair yellow to look like yours and made up my face to look like you ..."

"Ha! What happened to those papers?"

"At home... somewhere. I dug a hole... like the Barberton hovel where nobody could find it. But let's leave Kenny alone, Faty. I want to ask you for a big favour. Please go to my mother's grave in Nancefield. Tell her I am sorry for everything I have done..."

Kükuchi was stunned.

"I swore before she died and repeated promises on her grave."

"What did you promise her?"

"That I would go to school and stop hanging out with dangerous men like Mendi. I promised her with all my heart I would read just like you and pass Matric. But it was challenging for me, Kuchi, because when we took exams, my mind went blank and I couldn't recall many things. I wish I could be as clever as you. I left school and followed the bad crowd. Will you do that for me, Faty?"

"I don't know, Toby. What are you asking me to do…?"

"You are my only family. Please help me. My mother is angry with me. That's why I've been having such bad luck. Just tell her I am sorry."

After a long pause, Kükuchi sighed, "Okay."

"And another thing, you remember the man who died under the Yellowwood tree opposite your house, the man from Alexandra? Everyone thought Mendi had killed him. No one was caught because why?"

"Yes?"

Toby whispered, "I'm the one. Not Mendi. I did it after he stabbed Mendi in the back. While we were there, we heard strange voices—like children screaming, shouting, and crying. Nobody knew what was going on. As you know, we've always suspected that spot to be an old children's graveyard. With the noise and the demonic cries, I got the chance to stab the man."

"So, Toby, you are the girl who was with Mendi that night?"

"Yes, sorry, Kükuchi. I could not help myself."

"How did you feel about Mendi? Tell me the truth."

"I didn't have any feelings for him. He was just there when I had nobody else to turn to. You know how all the girls felt about Mendi..."

"You betrayed me, Toby, when I trusted you."

"It's all history now. Mendi is dead. When you go to my mother's grave, tell her I was protecting Mendi. That's why I stabbed that man. Ask my mother to help me remove that man's blood from my hands. When you stab a man to death, the blood sinks to the ground and back into your own body, and his spirit gives you no rest. I am suffering."

***

I had never stopped pondering the unsolved murders in White City, including those of Papi, Sisi Afrika, and an unknown number of girls. Toby kept me guessing, even though she begged to visit her mother's grave, because I recognized a half-truth when I heard one. The true details of the murder of that mysterious man from Alexandra had yet to be uncovered.

"Tell me, Toby, how much did you hear about Tina's death?"

"You should know better, Kükuchi. It was your uncle. Maybe I should not tell you this, but one day your uncle came to my house and nearly… he could have raped me. Papi saved me. Before that, Dodo pretended he was there to check how I was doing. Then he started looking at me funny and touching my bum. He dragged me by force to the bedroom. Fortunately, Papi showed up. He was there to fetch his money, and they went out together. I know your uncle bribed Papi to shut him up. But Papi, too, was smart, and he worshipped money. I think he forced Dodo to pay every month to silence him… "

"What makes you think that?"

"I don't think, I know. Papi used to visit Dodo every month's end. So, when I heard that Papi had been found dead near the bridge, it became as clear as day, very clear to me what happened. Your uncle killed Papi because of extortion. He could easily hide the evidence because he was a policeman."

***

Being haunted by a guilty conscience, I began confessing my sins to Toby by explaining the theft of Mendi's sack of money, which had been buried near the tree. I had to bare my soul and admit that Dassie was the one who dug out the bag and took it home. As I related my story, Toby slowly got to her feet, her face tightening and her eyes flashing with threatening reactions. Kükuchi curled up as if watching a ghost. Toby forced a smile, her radiant face shining through the desolate space of her jail. She gritted her teeth and gave a single, shocked clap. A flood of tears began to flow down her face.

She then looked Kükuchi straight in the eye and said, "Oh, Kükuchi! Mendi searched everywhere for his money. Everywhere, especially over there along the bank of the fountain. I was with him when he cut weeds with a grass cutter. And together, we were shovelling crabs and frogs away with our fingers, sifting through the cold water, hoping to find something. We searched along the trees at night but found nothing. One night, it rained heavily and Mendi cried like a baby. I went with him many times, exploring the ground, but to no avail. I slept with him right there under the willow tree… to help him feel the warmth of a woman's body so he could forget about the money…"

"Toby…!"

"He told me all his secrets."

"What did he say?"

That's none of your business, Kükuchi. He was whispering to me because I was the only woman who could give him warmth when everyone else had left him out in the cold.

At that moment, Toby looked completely exhausted, as if she had been searching deep inside her soul. Her laboured breathing grew heavier, and her disdain for Kükuchi became even stronger. She fired her question, each syllable pounding like a drumbeat: "Why did… you… steal… Mendi's… money?"

"I would have returned it, I swear."

Toby went on, more brusquely this time, her voice echoing throughout the prison-yard, "Mendi knew Dassie could not be trusted because he was always snooping around and shadowing him. Everybody said nasty stuff about you and that spooky tree at Donaldson, that you prayed to demons in the dark. Look now, Mendi is dead because of you and your Dassie."

"Did Mendi tell you anything about 'Sisi Afrika'?" Kükuchi put it awkwardly.

Toby began to create further physical distance between herself and her friend, "Who wants to talk about Sisi Afrika? I don't even know your Sisi Afrika," Toby snarled like an injured tigress as she began to walk away. "You can go now. Please don't bother to go to my mother's grave. You and

Dassie… a web of lies! And your blind eye? Maybe it's God's punishment."

Kūkuchi cried, "Sorry, Toby. Can't you forgive me? That night, you brought me a birthday cake, and you said you loved me with all your heart. It meant everything to me. Even now, Toby, I love you more than anything in this world."

Kūkuchi watched with deep sadness as Toby walked away and disappeared, leaving the shiny hallway empty, along with a sharp pain from a gaping hole in her heart.

The jail episode tore me apart, and the sad breakup between friends revealed the shadow of growing up in a deprived and leaderless environment. I staggered toward Johannesburg Park Station to catch the Pimville train. There, I sat on a concrete slab in a dimly lit area of the platform behind old, mouldy pillars, hiding my drenched face from prying eyes. When I finally stopped crying, I moved away from the dark shadows and sat on a worn-out bench once designated for 'Europeans only'. Whites had a new set of benches placed farther away from black spaces. The loud, screeching crashes and rustles—from braking train wheels, opening and closing doors, and passengers rushing in all directions—could not stop me from scribbling a few clumsy lines in my diary. I stopped writing when I felt an itch at the back of my blind eye. Instinctively, I removed my reading glasses and tried to wink away the itch. Soft light seeped into my troubled eye. As in a dream, the faint light exploded like distant thunderbolts, gradually clearing my vision so that the entire platform became brighter. I shielded my eye with a tissue, protecting it like a precious blue diamond. Suddenly, I could see clearly.

Back home, all alone with no Dassie to shout at, or Khulu to defy, I patched myself on the desolate *stoep* in the gaze of the full moon and placed a packet of milk chocolate on my lap. The Milky Way was as clear as both my eyes could now allow, and I knew then that beyond the stars, someone had been looking into my heart and listening as the truth finally came out of my lips about Mendi's bag of money. For a few moments, it felt as if Dassie was sitting next to me and that Khulu was inside, dishing up so we could enjoy our favourite dish of sour milk and sorghum.

Yet, nothing could ever fuel my anger against the white government more than Dassie's disappearance. If it had not been for Apartheid, I reckoned, Dassie would still be with me, irritating me no end. I gnashed my teeth; for the end of an era that most people had hoped for had remained as elusive as ever. My entire being had become engulfed in toxic bitterness against supporters of Apartheid. Far from abandoning Mayfair, white people had firmly entrenched themselves behind high walls, while black leaders were left to rot in prison. The chains of Apartheid were tightening, and white people had settled confidently in an African country they had made their own. It was the right moment to admit to myself that my javelin aspirations had been a pipedream from the beginning. I snapped open my chocolate box and nibbled away dreamily; deep inside my world of fantasy, all over again, nestling on the misty Drakensberg in dread of black clouds on the horizon. When I finally accepted that the childhood friendship between Toby and me was over, I got up from the lonely *stoep* of dreams and trudged into the empty bedroom I once shared with Khulu. I slowly pulled back the curtain and saw that Donaldson Primary sat quietly in the dark like a spooky graveyard. Deep sleep eased my heavy heart.

CHAPTER 27

White South Africa in turmoil

Kükuchi searched for Jerry around campus until she found him with Neima, a Tanzanian student doing Honours in Chemistry. Bottles of liquor and tins of beer were strewn throughout the room, competing with textbooks and clothing. Kükuchi asked Jerry to come outside for a private chat. Devouring Kükuchi with her eyes, Neima insisted on her discussing with Jerry in her presence.

"Why?"

"Why? Because I want to hear, that's why."

Jerry gave a side shake of his shoulder and said, "You can talk. Neima is my friend…"

"I am his fiancée. You can talk," she clarified with emphasis on fiancée.

"Okay. Jerry, please give me Kenny's contact information."

"Kenny? I thought that guy was your arch enemy."

"Give me Kenny's numbers, please. I want to talk to him."

"You want to go and rearrange his face like you vowed you would?"

"Is Kenny her boyfriend?" said Neima.

"Please shut up. I am talking to Jerry."

"What cheek! This is my room. Who are you?"

Jerry swiftly scribbled Kenny's number on a piece of paper and said, "Here… don't tell him I gave you his number, right?"

***

Dimitri Tsafendas, a parliamentary messenger, stabbed Hendrik Verwoerd to death. Tsafendas later said he committed the act because 'Verwoerd was an immoral man'. Verwoerd was the man who had forcefully halted the state-sponsored feeding scheme for African pupils.

Kükuchi smiled as she recalled how Verwoerd had brought Musa extreme grief and wondered if she would bake fruitcake ever again. John Vorster, the man who threatened to limit the movement of agitators the very day that Luthuli received his Nobel Prize, took over as Prime Minister. Musa was angry. She told Kükuchi that the time had come for blacks in the townships to make South Africa ungovernable. Kükuchi told Musa she was happy because she could see that the Afrikaners were squeezing even tighter. She said Mkhize was right when he said the more they squeeze, the less they have. To Kükuchi's frustration, Musa was not impressed, arguing that it was up to the oppressed to squeeze tighter by fighting with guns.

Vorster was an unsmiling, angry white man. Salu once quipped, 'People who can't smile often crack jokes which boomerang on their stiff faces'.

She was right. Vorster started a joke around Basil D'Oliveira, a 'coloured' cricketer and anti-Apartheid activist. After he frustrated D'Oliveira's efforts to represent South Africa, Vorster thought the joke was funny because white South Africa seemed amused. The joke was on Vorster and his racist followers, though, because D'Oliveira so excelled overseas that England selected him for the 1968 tour of South Africa. However, the grim-faced prime minister refused D'Oliveira permission to play on South African soil during that tour, adding, 'We will not accept a team chosen, not by the Marylebone Cricket Club (MCC), but by our political enemies'.

Henry Wadsworth Longfellow once put it, 'Whom the gods would destroy, they first make mad…'

***

A flood of Invitations for coaching clinics continued. I had my stint in two Provincial Departments. Some local newspapers covered the story of the invitations and my activities there.

Just then, the state released Dodo on parole. Many people were outraged. My anger soon gave way to deep concern that he might launch his revenge against all his enemies, including me. Dodo went underground, and I feared for my life. I visited the Moroka police station to raise my concerns. This was the same station where Mrs Maseko once opened a fabricated case against me for burglary and attempted murder. After trying to explain my situation for over an hour, it became clear that Dodo was the only party getting protection from the police station.

***

On their graduation day, Goodie and Kükuchi introduced friends and family and shared pleasantries. It was a pleasure to finally meet Goodie's mother, a doctor from Matebeleland, who was as petite as her daughter. One of their guests was Mrs Maseko, the older woman who often lent them her kitchen stove for Kükuchi to cook supper. Maseko expressed her deep gratitude to Kükuchi for inviting her to the graduation. She was in tears when she told them she would die happy, having personally witnessed a graduation ceremony for the first time in her life. Sadly, her husband, Papa Maseko, had died a year earlier.

Following her graduation, Kükuchi confirmed what she had always suspected about the plight of a black woman in the South African workplace. She went round in circles for months across the racist and patriarchal alleyways of her legal profession, looking for a job as an articled clerk. One day, she forced her way into a firm on the 20th Floor of the Universal Building in Jubilee Street. One of the partners appeared sympathetic. He offered to register her as an articled clerk, which was what she had been seeking. The medium-sized firm had seven partners, six managers, and twenty articled clerks at various levels of seniority. There were three white men and a white woman at the management level. Kükuchi became the first African articled clerk in the firm, joining the bottom rung, which consisted of black cleaners and messengers.

Kükuchi encountered debilitating discrimination from the beginning. One of the managers came to her desk and asked how she managed to pass a law degree. Kükuchi responded, 'How do people pass a law degree?' Later that day, the same manager stood patronizingly in front of her desk and told her to use the 'African toilet' on the ground floor, the one used by other Africans. On top of that, Kükuchi was soon to discover that, despite being an articled clerk, her tacit job description entailed interpreting for African clients, making photocopies for everyone, and serving as a glorified general messenger. She also had to make her tea because Lulu could not countenance the idea of making tea for whites and then for her as well. For Kükuchi, the reason for Lulu's resentment was that she was a black woman, just like her. However, Lulu's difficulty – she confessed afterwards – lay in her prejudice towards people living with albinism.

Kükuchi decided to bring her utensils, make her tea, and defy petty Apartheid instructions about the use of segregated toilet facilities.

***

White South Africa was in turmoil. Abraham Tiro, a former student leader at the University of the North (Turfloop), spoke at the graduation ceremony. The speech, known as the 'Turfloop Testimony', sparked protests across the country, and international media quickly spread the speech. The testimony so angered the government that the university agreed to the government's order to expel Tiro.

At that time, a young Black woman named Rosina Sedibane made a name for herself in South Africa by becoming the first Black athlete allowed to compete in a racially mixed tournament. During one of the meetings in Orlando, Tiro spoke about the level of discrimination Sedibane faced under the Apartheid regime, which was supported and enabled by the white Sports federation.

After his expulsion from the University, Tiro became involved in politics, prompting the Government to bar him from enrolling in any educational institution. He eventually sought refuge at Morris Isaacson, where he taught amidst the chaos in black education that culminated in the 1976 riots. Tiro's ideas flourished in Kükuchi's heart.

One day, she attended a student meeting organized by Tiro in Orlando, near the police station where Kükuchi had once been detained as a high school pupil. After the meeting, the State Security police arrested most of those who had attended. Kükuchi herself was kept at John Vorster's Square for ten days. When she was released, she received a one-line letter from her law firm, informing her of her dismissal. Following directives from the security police, Tiro also lost his teaching job at Morris Isaacson. He then moved to Botswana, where a bomb posted by the Apartheid security forces killed him. When Kükuchi risked her life, attending Tiro's funeral in Botswana, she fortuitously came across an Indian stranger, Bharat Chetty, who quickly prepared the way for her to complete her studies as an articled clerk. The Indian company was in Mayfair. How ironic! It was located next to Priscilla and Rosemarie's old home. Out of curiosity, Kükuchi took a walk one morning around the home of the white girls she grew up with. She smiled when she saw the red oak tree blossom in purple, as she had known it to do all those days before. The whole family had left the continent and headed for Britain, where greener pastures suitable for jittery whites flourished.

Kükuchi completed her articles and established her legal suite in the Central Business District of Johannesburg. Because her heart was no longer in the profession, she quickly vacated the offices with little fanfare, turning her back on the profession for which she had trained so hard.

CHAPTER 28

Burn down the Draycott Farmhouse.

The Johannesburg City Council exhumed dozens of skeletal remains, ostensibly to make way for the upgrade of the Old Potchefstroom Road in Soweto. The women of White City gathered and claimed the bodies of Khulu and Tina. Kükuchi made a frantic search for the whereabouts of Tina's parents. Kükuchi eventually located the elderly couple in Rhodesia's Bikita Village. Kükuchi arranged for the repatriation of their daughter's remains, including raising funds from the people she knew. Tina's father had once told Mkhize, 'One day Zimbabwe shall be free and Tina will see the hills and streams of her beautiful ancestral village back home'. Tina found her final resting place in her village of Bikita, among her loved ones and ancestors. The family and town of Bikita expressed their deep appreciation to Kükuchi.

Tina's mother held Kükuchi by the hand and hugged her before she said, "You are a wonderful human being, Fatty…"

The reburial of Khulu's remains took place at Wembezi Township. At that time, Robert Mugabe was leading Rhodesia to independence from Britain, and thunderous celebrations echoed throughout the African Diaspora. In South Africa, security police were running around, breaking up joyful gatherings, arresting, and shooting many militants seen celebrating Zimbabwe's independence. Among the casualties was Sithole, Musa's husband. He was shot dead while trying to escape a police roadblock near Sasolburg. Inside his van, authorities found stacks of ANC propaganda material. After collecting the boxes, the police drove Sithole's vehicle into a ditch and set it on fire with Sithole inside.

Goodie went on to study for a Master's degree at Essex University. After joining MK, Dassie studied privately with the University of South Africa and completed a Bachelor of Science in Mathematics. He taught briefly at the Solomon Mahlangu Freedom College (SOMAFCO) in Tanzania. Dassie and Goodie were married in a secret location in the United Kingdom. Because Goodie was less enthusiastic about Zimbabwe than the couple, they relocated to Swaziland. Deep down, Kükuchi remained grateful to Goodie for having rescued her brother from the slippery slope of White-City township life.

Bobby had become an enigmatic figure, reviled by the white media, yet celebrated in song by African communities across the country. Amidst the political and economic turmoil in South Africa, PW Botha, who succeeded John Vorster, went to Durban to deliver what analysts dubbed 'the Rubicon Speech'. There was heightened hope that Botha would make a world-shattering announcement to abolish Apartheid. At that time, rebel sports tours had snowballed despite opposition by the United Democratic Front (UDF). South Africa had become a playground for opportunists in the arts and sport. Kükuchi was on tiptoe of expectation for something to happen after Botha's Rubicon speech. Despite all that had happened, she hung on to the hope that South Africa would soon be free. On this, Musa said, "Don't hold your breath. No dictator has ever relinquished power out of the kindness of his heart."

South Africa missed their opportunity because Botha failed to cross the Rubicon. Out of frustration, Kükuchi called Kenny's number, which Jerry had given her.

***

My workout routines and coaching clinics across provinces kept me occupied and happy. When I realized that things were not going well, I sold my legal practice for a song. Stepping out of my office, I didn't know whether to turn left or right. However, I needed a sturdy shoulder to cry on – Salu, my grandmother. On my way, driving slowly and taking numerous breaks in between many miles of white-owned farms, what stood out like a sore thumb were African schools with shaky, crumbling walls, broken windows, and dilapidated African living compounds punctuated by immaculate marble homes owned by whites. The Apartheid landscape so suffocated my soul that I cried all the way.

In Ladysmith, I saw a newspaper headline titled: 'MK Chief killed in Angola'. Since many freedom fighters had been murdered across neighbouring countries, the headline didn't affect me. I only read the story when I reached Wembezi, where I saw, to my horror, what I feared. The MK chief in question was Bobby Mohale. The newspaper article provided little information about Bobby's death, and I would have to rely on my sources to find out what happened.

The embarrassing news of my failed law practice did not go down well with Salu.

"I'm here to stay with you for good, Salu. Long ago, you said, 'It is not good for one to be stuck in the same place for too long because that causes lice'. Do you remember?"

"Stop misquoting me. Tell me the truth. Why are you here?"

"Let me tell you the truth, Salu. I left my practice. My office is officially closed."

"You worked hard to become an advocate. How can you throw it all away when our people need you? You are a lawyer."

"I've heard enough from these people! I don't even know why I call them our people. Who are they? Where are they? To me, the future looks bleak because the legal profession has become more of a celebrity scene with little focus on uplifting low-income communities. Maybe I'm not considered a Black person in their eyes; otherwise, they wouldn't treat me like a puppy in need of sympathy. As soon as they see I have a white face and funny-looking hair, they all rush out, bumping into each other at the exit as they usually do. Then they disappear. A well-known Black couple examined my certificates hanging on my office wall. The long minutes they spent perusing my certificates were the last straw. The man shook his head, eyeing me with suspicion, while the woman, wearing a tight-fitting outfit, asked brazenly if those certificates belonged to me. When she realized I wasn't going to answer, she nudged her friend with her elbow, and they left. That's why I will stay with you, and we will plant vegetables in our garden."

Living with my grandmother in Wembezi Township became the most enjoyable part of my life.

***

One day, I sneaked out of Wembezi and drove to Johannesburg. After a brief search, I finally tracked Kenny down in Pimville. Approaching his house, I noticed three portable toilets outside their high walls near the sidewalk. Kenny was about to drive away. We had a quick chat near the electric gate. Kenny told me he had just buried his mother the day before. As we talked, Sandy came out of the house. She stood at the entrance for a moment, watching us with a stern look.

Kenny pulled to the pavement and got out of the car. He looked different, and my knees buckled. Apart from showing a sizable weight gain, his sharp eyes, along with a bit of public opinion, added to his elegance. I could not help but recall a thin chicken that once ran away from Donaldson Primary to seek refuge at his parents' home in Pimville. This time, Kenny exuded confidence with a tinge of self-importance. I was so impressed with Kenny that I immediately wanted to know more about his activities from those young days in White City.

"I can tell you don't want Sandy to see me pay you a visit."

"Visit? Faty, I don't know why you are here."

"In earlier days, you were chasing after me, or was it the other way around? Now, here I am, Kenny."

"Look, Faty, I have an important appointment."

"So, you haven't changed. You still hate people with albinism? I told you when I called that I wanted to speak to you about something important, too."

"My mother died recently, and I am sorting out some things. What do you want to talk about?"

"I learn some people have been setting off bombs in the city centre. Do you have any idea what's been going on?"

"What's that to you? Bombs explode all the time."

"There are rumours that a Tembisa girl was seriously injured after you caused an explosion outside the court precincts. Did you know you've been the person of interest since?"

"Who told you that?"

"Never mind who told me. I want you to do some work for me if you don't want your name to be splashed across TV and newspapers for maiming an African girl child."

Kenny's face shrivelled.

"Is it your policeman uncle who told you this lie? These people have been grasping at straws because they have no scrap of evidence."

I do have evidence, and it's more than a mere piece. The evidence I possess is from the Carlton Hotel. Once you do what I ask, you'll receive all your hidden Carlton evidence back.

Kenny's lips started shaking, and he ranted, "My father warned me against you. He told me you people, your grandmother was a wizard..."

After breathing heavily with rage for more than a few seconds, I said, "Okay, Kenny. Let's forget about the whole thing. You've crossed the line by insulting my grandmother. We shall see what happens after this."

***

After my failed rendezvous with Kenny, I started to focus on international athletics events and reflected on the ironic state of recent history. In the 1980s, the Cold War between the East and the

West gradually waned. In November 1989, the Berlin Wall fell amid widespread celebrations, as citizens from both sides of the wall danced together to mark the beginning of a new era. This signalled the inevitable end of the Apartheid regime. Soon after, in February 1990, FW de Klerk, the last Apartheid President, lifted the ban on black political activity and released political prisoners. It was only a matter of time before the first democratic elections took place. However, the period in between was marked by bloodshed. Many black people lost their lives because powerful right-wing forces opposed democracy and justice for Africans.

Amidst the chaos, an unexpected call from Kenny gave me quite a jolt. He wanted to meet me to discuss the Carlton papers. I agreed to meet him at Donaldson Primary, where I knew I would feel safe. And we sat on the veranda close to the classroom where Sandy, his sister, once refused to sit next to me. Kenny produced a gadget, the type of which I had never seen before, and brushed it over my body.

"What are you doing?"

"Just checking if you are not wired."

"Sies! What do you take me for? A bloody spy?"

"Your uncle is a policeman, and I know you two are very close."

"Are you done? Am I wired?"

"One can't be too careful. You can see the Boers continue to kill our people. Do you still hold grudges for the mistake we made, injuring that girl from Tembisa?"

"This has nothing to do with grudges. As a bomb expert, I have an assignment for you. Please go and bomb a farmhouse in Draycott. It was previously owned by my grandmother, one of your wizards, and they stole it from her. Can you do that?"

After giving me an incredulous gaze, Kenny said, "You know, Jerry told me about the speech you delivered on campus at Fort Hare. But... are you serious about bombing that farm?"

"Yes. I'll give you the date, but it will have to be nighttime."

"Faty, do you know what you're asking me to do?"

"Listen, Kenny, Toby is like a sister to me. You took advantage of her at the Carlton, all because she was an easy target, being poor and an outcast in White-City. I'm not asking you..."

"You are entering a dangerous minefield. How do you know you'll get out of all this alive?"

"Perish your silly thoughts, Kenny. I have friends too. If you are smart, you'll keep me alive until you blow up that house."

Kenny ordered me to step back, saying he wanted to make sure no one was eavesdropping. We took a quick walk to the Yellowwood trees. The rocky woods brought back memories of old days when my friends and I used to hold our small conferences.

"Are you satisfied, Kenny?"

"Okay, I'll get my guys to reconnoitre. I don't do such things alone. But what guarantee do I have that I'll get my files back after putting my head on the block to get your stupid plan going? Can you guarantee you won't spread the stories you heard about me or come back to me for something else?"

"Guarantee? Kenny, you and I are like chalk and cheese. You were born with custard and ice cream in your mouth because your parents were doctors. I grew up in dire poverty with Toby, the girl you took advantage of in that hotel. Toby is my friend. Where we come from, we do not betray friends. This is the guarantee you will get from me."

"Alright. Next time, leave a message with Sandy. Don't call me directly."

"The Apartheid government sponsored hundreds of murders against black people. It was like killing flies with a can of spray. When one kills flies, one hardly takes a tally. How many black people did you kill during your anti-Apartheid operations?"

"Go, I'll meet you in Draycott, Faty."

CHAPTER 29

I voted, we're Free!

As polling day for the first democratic elections drew closer, Kükuchi drove home to where Musa lived alone to assist her, as promised. She found Musa in a weak state of health, but still spitting her brand of political fire. They sat on the comfortable chairs and reminisced about the recent past.

"I see your whites-only sports organizations are now pretending to be good citizens. Do you remember how they organized Apartheid-sponsored rebel tours and dispatched their security police to arrest us for resisting? Even the West Indians, who are Black like us, sold us out, yet they have shown no remorse to this day. What an embarrassment it was to see Blacks sell each other to the highest bidder."

Kükuchi asked Musa, "I heard strange stories from Zazi. Please tell me about your brother, Dodo."

"My brother? What must I tell you about him?"

"Zazi said Khulu adopted Dodo. Is that true?"

Musa's demeanour changed, and she bent to hide her face in her lap. After a short minute, she stood up and walked to her bedroom. Kükuchi made tea for both of them and took the tray to the bedroom. Musa lay in bed, as if in deep thought. Her face was wet with tears.

"Here's tea. Where do you keep your biscuits?"

"Sit. I want to ask you something. What did Zazi tell you about Dodo?"

"That he was adopted and registered as Khulu's son..."

Breathing heavily, Musa stood up and said, "I'll get the scorns I baked yesterday. Khulu has gone to heaven. Let's forget about Dodo."

"Can you confirm he is not your biological brother?"

"Let Khulu rest in peace, Kuchi. Please, I beg you."

South African voters flooded the polls to cast their votes. I put on my bottle-green beret and went to help my mother fulfil her lifelong dream of voting. The beret made her smile.

"This beret! You are still keeping it?"

"For you, Mama. It always reminds me of you."

Her enigmatic smile returned. Many people we knew had moved out of the township. Sadly, others, like Mkhize and Sister Mohale, had died. However, to me, the mystery surrounding Bobby's death remained as unbearable as the lies told by the Apartheid government about many deaths in detention. Every time someone mentioned Bobby's name in South Africa, words such as 'Angola,' 'Quadro,' or 'Imbokodo' appeared in dark corners and quickly faded away like the spirits of Jabavu.

Musa's breathing had become heavy and concerning, yet she went on harking back inaptly, "What a shame!" She heaved her words with difficulty, "Mohale would have been excited about voting. What I see is exiles and others who now claim to have been in the struggle, positioning themselves to get into the white man's shoes. The only people who were in the struggle were those women who took the petition to Strydom in 1956. Some of them are dead now, but I was there." Musa grimaced and continued, "Women like Mohale and Sally Motlana will soon be forgotten because certain people feel entitled to jump the gravy queue."

"Musa, things will change..." I said reflexively.

"No, these white people will be telling us to be grateful to them because they gave us civilization and allowed us to vote, never mind the suffering they brought to Africa, the misery that began centuries ago and continues to hover over our daily existence. Luthuli died in vain."

My heart began to bleed over my mother, and I cried.

"Why, Kükuchi? Why are you crying now?"

"Mother," I said, "we are free now. We can go to vote. Doesn't that mean anything to you? Why are you so full of anger in your heart? It will kill you. I love you. I don't want you to die, please, Mama. I want to take care of you in your old age. Funani made me see I have to fill my heart with love, especially for you. The day we get our family farm back, I'll fetch you so we all stay together. I promise. I'll fight for the land they stole just like you asked me to promise when we climbed Pasiwe many years ago, remember?"

Musa smiled shyly as she brushed her greying hair, her lips cracking, and her face showing unfamiliar wrinkles on her forehead. She said, "I love you more, Kükuchi. You are my blessing. Sorry, I never mentioned it when you were small."

A warm feeling washed over me as I watched Musa enter the voting booth, her mysterious smile hiding her pain and secrets. In truth, it was heartbreaking to see my mother walk in there alone. I had had a mother all my life only in name, and my efforts had been like trying to connect with a stranger in my own home. Watching her walk in alone like a penguin without a family made me feel sorry for her. She had spent most of her life confined in her self-made little worlds of loneliness. I wondered if our new political climate would let her relax and enjoy her twilight years.

I called Kenny and provided him with details about the farm, including the date and time for the deed to be executed. Although I felt uneasy, my sense of justice reassured me that the white people deserved what was coming to them.

Musa emerged wearing the broadest smile ever, and she crowed, "I voted! I finally voted," she squeaked amidst ululating all around. Raising her arms delightedly, she repeated, "I voted. We are free. I am happy, Kükuchi. I love you."

Musa's words warmed my heart. I led her outside the voting classroom, and we sat down in the shade. It turned out to be a heart-to-heart with a surprising impact.

"I am happy to be here with you, Musa. But I must confess I am sorry for what I did to you long ago. I was angry, and I did something I wasn't supposed to do. Please forgive me for nearly choking you to death that day, remember? I was wrong to do that."

Musa giggled curiously and said, "Oh, how can I forget? But listen; if you fight for truth, never apologize. You were right to throttle me because I was wrong. I'm the one who should apologize to you. One day, you came to my house to tell me you passed..."

"Matric?"

"I was too ashamed to say I contributed nothing to your first-class pass, and that I could not afford to pay your university fees. After they fired me as a domestic, I could not get a job anywhere. Imagine struggling to get a job as a maid," she cackled.

"Musa, does Dassie know his father?"

"Dassie? Please promise me... swear by Khulu's name, that you will never tell Dassie."

"I swear, Musa."

"Dassie doesn't know his father because I don't know him either."

"How come?"

"Dassie was given to me by the nurses at the Estcourt clinic. He had been dumped on the station deck by someone unknown. Then I applied to register him as my child."

"You adopted Dassie? Oh Musa...!"

"It was the right thing to do..."

My heart went out to Musa, and I said, "I am proud of you, Mother... more than ever."

A Fatal Tease

Musa kissed me on the lips for the first time in my life. Then I teased her, saying, "Why did you hate my doll so much... the one I called Blossom? Do you remember my *doll*?"

The tease became fatal; Musa suddenly convulsed and developed a strange squint. Uttering words I could not make out, she began to breathe heavily. Her mouth foamed, and she tumbled over, and her limp body rested on my shoulder.

A matron at Baragwanath Hospital told me that Musa had suffered a heart attack. The shock so gravely affected me that my eyesight became erratic again. Musa died a day later. Salu boarded a Johannesburg train to bury yet another relative.

Musa's moment of dying has weighed heavily on Kükuchi's conscience ever since. There are many ways of killing a human being.

Dodo appeared a few days before Musa's funeral, a shock to the family, given his release from custody without serving his complete sentence. Some angry family members and neighbours, especially women, confronted him about the missing girls from White-City and Jabavu. Kükuchi approached and started choking him. Funani, Kükuchi's uncle, suddenly showed up and pushed the crowd aside, insisting that Kükuchi step back.

The mourners were shocked to learn that Dodo had voluntarily turned himself in to the police in exchange for a lighter sentence. Funani shared details of Dodo's confession, revealing the number of adolescent and teenage girls he had murdered and buried at various spots around the township. As expected, these included Tina and Sisi Afrika. There was also Nomvula, Mimi's daughter.

Mimi was outraged to hear that Dodo had buried her child in a shallow grave beneath the Mlamlankunzi railway bridge, and that the police never bothered to investigate the area. Nomvula had gone missing between Ematsheni Primary School in Orlando and her home near the railway station.

Dodo had a habit of exploiting young girls who knew and trusted him. Police exhumed Nomvula's skeletal remains a few days after his latest admission.

What caused even more outrage was Dodo's smug admission to Funani that he was solely responsible for killing Papi, the man who cared for his disabled sister. Dodo mocked what he called the police's nonchalant attitude toward the various White City and Jabavu cases.

***

Dassie and Goodie arrived in the morning with their daughter, Tombana. Kūkuchi was meeting Tombana for the first time, and they clicked immediately.

"Oh, Khulu, it's so nice to see you. I've heard a lot about you," said Tombana.

"A lot? What did you hear about me, Tombana?"

"That you went with your friend to sell stolen goods on train coaches."

"Is that what your dad told you?"

"No, mother told me. She said you fought for the land and you always hid your knife in your chest..."

"When did your mother see a knife in my chest?"

"No, that's Father who said that."

"Listen, Tombana, you are an African girl; get an education and let your eyes be sharp like King Shaka's spear, and when you touch the stars one day, make sure your other eye is watching over your soul."

"You reckon?"

"Yes."

"I'll ask Mother what you mean. She's a brilliant advocate. Did you know that?"

Later, Kūkuchi confronted Goodie heatedly and asked, "Goodie, who taught Tombana to refer to me as Khulu?"

Goodie crumpled up in embarrassment and fluttered her eyelashes before she cheerfully said, "But you are her Khulu."

"In Matabeleland, not here. She must address me correctly. I am her Auntie."

"What are we going to do? We can't change now. It will confuse the child," said Goodie, dejectedly.

After much urging, Kūkuchi finally relented and became Khulu to Tombana.

Mendi's stash of money had left obvious loose ends that refused to be tied up. We sat on the porch like we used to, and I said, "Dassie, I have a surprise for you. Remember your Elvis poster?"

"Where is it? I knew you did something with it."

"Me? Listen, I found it among Khulu's stuff after her funeral. Before I return it, Dassie, I want the truth from you. All these years, I kept thinking about the sack full of money we hid here in the garden. It has caused me a lot of distress because Toby blamed me for stealing it. She has not forgiven me even today, and that's why evil spirits haunt us. What happened to Mendi's money? Please tell the truth, for Tombana's sake."

"Tombana's sake?"

"Yes, Dassie, the truth."

The spectre of lies and secrecy within the family refused to leave us. Dassie said, "I did not tell you, right? I thought you would be angry with me. I dug it out and gave the money to Tina's parents just before they went back to Rhodesia."

"You lie, Dassie. All that money? I don't believe you."

Mendi's sack of misfortunes remains one of the most unsolved family mysteries. Sadly, the dark shadow still haunts us whenever we gather as a family. I told Dassie that because Mendi's sack of mealies was missing, he would never see his Elvis again. And I meant it, because I threw the poster into Khulu's stove like Musa did to my 'doll'.

During the funeral proceedings, Kükuchi spotted Toby from a distance. Kükuchi dribbled past her several times, but later, when she thought she had got away with it, there she was, Toby, right in front of her! The two erstwhile friends remained gazing at each other for a long moment of awkward silence. Toby made the first move, hugging Kükuchi passionately. She said uneasily, "Oh Kükuchi. I know why you are looking at me like this. My uncle in Eldos says, 'even a lily that blooms has its seasons and it withers and finally dies'."

Kükuchi ran her fingers through Toby's hair, and Toby responded in kind. They both shed tears over their inability to break free from their generational cycle of hardship.

"I am happy you are out of jail, Toby."

"It's been years, Faty. I heard from my uncle, the police officer, that you went with him to my mother's grave after visiting me. He told me what you said to her, begging on my behalf for forgiveness. Prison life was a nightmare. I used to see shadows and hear voices at night, and I would hear fellow female inmates scream as if the demons were messing with their bodies. Jail is hell, Kuchi. You can visit all those smiling faces during the day, but if you want to see reality, come during the heat of midnight when evil spirits rise from the depths of the earth to harm women and twist their minds."

"We are all in jail, Toby, and we all have demons that abuse us."

"You don't know, Faty. The ghosts of murdered people appear on the anniversary of their death to demand blood from their killers. Once every year, I hear voices and smell the damp odour of the Yellowwoods. The date of that man's death brings heavy rain in my dreams. In the morning, I can tell demonic forces have had their way while I slept because my body is soaked with sweat. And now and then, the warders would pump my body with a sleeping injection and leave me there for two or three days and nights."

"I am so sorry, Toby. Can we be friends again?"

"Kükuchi, it's hard for me to forgive you. What you did, stealing Mendi's money?"

"Maybe one day you will forgive me, Toby…"

"Anyway, listen, Faty; for his sake, I must pass on to you the message Mendi gives me as he lies on the hot Pretoria pavement, waiting for an African ambulance. No, I should say, 'waiting for his slow death' because no ambulance can save him. The white ambulance arrives first. They carry the white woman away and leave Mendi handcuffed, his eyes and groaning fading in front of me. Mendi pleads with the black policemen to give him water. The police handcuff me and leave me lying in the blood next to him. The pedestrians and women in church uniforms stand there watching the scene, waiting for the next act in the sad episode. Others look briefly and then go on their way. Schoolgirls and boys in uniform walk by, chanting their Chris Hani struggle tune. Mendi says something. I must tell you because I can't keep the words of a dead man inside me and invite more bad luck. He asks me to say to you… to tell you he has never stopped loving you, but he wants to be rich before he shows you his heart… that he is serious."

Kükuchi cried, "Oh, Mendi! It did not matter to me that you were not rich."

"That's what he says. I'm glad I've now shared his exact words with you."

"Mendi went to jail for a crime he didn't commit. Is there any greater love?"

"Yes, I believed him because, one night when I was with him during those dark hours of searching for the money you stole, he revealed that the necklace he was wearing was a gift from you. Even on the day he died, that necklace slipped off his neck, and the gemstones sparkled like a thousand stars, something I had never seen before."

"We are still good friends, then, Toby. I want us to be friends again because you are the only one I have in this world."

"Oh, Faty, I don't know. I don't know."

CHAPTER 30

He haunts the Drakensberg.

The ANC secured a landslide victory. Nelson Mandela became the first democratically elected president of South Africa.

Back in Wembezi, Kükuchi received a call in the early hours of the morning. Mr Mohale told Kükuchi that Dodo had hanged himself. Kükuchi sat up. Salu said, "I can feel it in my bones. That is a message of death. Where does it come from, Kükuchi?"

Kükuchi recalled the words often quoted by her Sunday school teacher to scare them into line with, 'The day you die, you will go to a waiting room where you will watch a bioscope about your entire life.'

***

I was more determined than ever to fight for our family farm. However, deep down, I knew I had to get the full story from Salu herself, for her to bare her breast and allow me to move forward with confidence.

After the illegal act of expropriation without compensation, the Apartheid government handed the land directly to Toby Barry's family.

One afternoon, on the day I was supposed to meet Kenny, I climbed over the fence to the farm and hid behind some bushes to watch Salu's doomed house for the last time. I was determined to see the white people who stole our land experience what Africans had been enduring for centuries. Suddenly, a German Shepherd appeared, closely followed by a blonde little girl with hair flowing in the wind. I was terrified.

When she laid her eyes on me, she smiled innocently and said, "Who are you?"

"Don't worry, I am waiting for my friend. What's your name?"

"I am Patricia Barry."

"Barry? What are you doing walking alone like this?"

"I am walking my dog. I feel safe with her around."

"Where are your parents, Patricia?"

"You can call me Trish. Everyone calls me Trish. My parents have gone to Cape Town."

"So, you're alone in the house with your brother?"

"How do you know?"

"I know. Never walk your dog alone, Trish. Ask your brother to accompany you because he has a gun."

"What?"

When Patricia and I parted, I immediately called Kenny and told him to hold fire.

"What do you mean, Faty? Our boys are already at a hotel in Estcourt."

"Go back home, Kenny. Tell your boys to go back to where they came from..."

"What about my papers?"

"Go home, Kenny. You'll get your papers as I promised."

As she made her way through the labyrinth of the new government's bureaucracy, Kūkuchi capitalized on the chaos among the officials.

She filed a complaint against the government for expropriating her family's property without compensation. The farmer's lawyers objected to Salu's claim because, under the 1913 Land Act, she could not hold title to any land in the country. Additionally, they used emotional blackmail by bringing Barry's wife and two young children before the biased court. While awaiting the verdict, Kūkuchi continued to coach young athletes across Natal. After three months, the court produced a ruling in favour of Barry. Salu collapsed. Kūkuchi appealed the decision, a longer process with little chance of success.

A drive with Hamilton

During that time, I experienced a mental breakdown. I was walking along Estcourt's busy De Waal Drive when my phone rang. Hamilton was on his way to Estcourt and urgently needed to talk to me. By late afternoon, I was in Hamilton's semi-luxury car, far from anywhere, moving around, stopping, and executing dangerous U-turns. When we found ourselves cruising along Kemp's Road, I insisted that we make a stop at the Fort Durnford Museum. Though reluctant, Hamilton turned towards the Museum and stopped in front of it. The tall grass whistled, and there was no soul around. After briefly relating to him the awkward relationship that Durnford had with Bishop Colenso's family, he switched off the engine. I went on to tell him about the horrific role that Durnford played in the illegal deposing of the Hlubi King, together with the decimation of his kingdom.

He got out of the car. I followed suit. He whispered, "I know of Durnford's involvement in the war of Isandlwana."

I walked around and stood next to him. He seemed to be gazing beyond the Victorian Frontier, still haunting the soul of the African. I touched his shoulder, and he slowly turned toward me. When we kissed, he ruffled my frizzy hair as our bodies pressed together.

When we parted, reluctantly, I said, "Yes, the ultimate goal of Anthony Durnford and his fellow conspirators, such as Benjamin Pine, Theophilus Shepstone, and John Macfarlane, was to conspire for the British theft of the rich African land in the entire Drakensberg valley."

Hamilton walked me around and opened my door. I felt like a princess. We drove off in silence for a while. I did not know what occupied his mind during that time, but after ten minutes, I asked him if he was not impressed with my lecture on Durnford. He said he was angry with himself and embarrassed that he knew nothing about the love affair between Bishop Colenso's daughter and Durnford. I said nothing.

"I am joking, Kūkuchi."

"The love affair between the Europeans is of no consequence to our history."

"Are you always this serious?

"Where did you get my number?"

"I have my ways and my contacts, Kükuchi."

"What a scary surprise! I was not expecting you. Now that I know you have your ways and contacts, do you know that we lost the case against the government?"

"Funani told me..."

"So, you're here to commiserate?"

"I'm here to talk to you and to see your grandmother's farm."

"I see. Did Funani direct you to the location of my Wembezi hiding hole as well?"

"No, I asked him if you are now married."

"He explained that I was, of course."

"Funani would have warned me if the situation had taken that turn."

"Listen to this, Hamilton; while Funani is my uncle, he doesn't know everything about my ups and downs."

"He is my friend. We gossip and share stories..."

"Do not let him be the source of your gossip about me."

"He told me that Kükuchi has love."

"What love? Anyway, forget about love. You said you wish to see the place that once belonged to my family. We're almost there."

We gradually made our way across the hills and stopped near the Bhekuzulu Palace.

"It's good you're here. I want you to understand that our land is under the rule of our King, Langalibalele, and that the ghost of Durnford still haunts the Drakensberg basin. I'll show you Salu's old chicken farm."

When Hamilton stopped the car next to the land once owned by Salu, we climbed the fence and trespassed inside until we stopped a short distance from my twin brother's desecrated grave. Hamilton saw the length and breadth of the farm and said, "All this place? You must release it, give it up because white people in this country will never let go of such large and fertile land without a fight."

"I have no intention of giving up the land of my ancestors without a fight, either. What makes you think whites have the monopoly where the struggle for land is concerned? A man steals our land, and then we give him the Constitution, which he uses to refuse to bring our property back? Who is the victim here? June Jordan once wrote, 'The notion that you can invade the country of another people, kill them, mine the waters, burn the earth, and then claim equal rights of self-defence if and when the indigenous survivors retaliate, derives from a mentality so hideous, so self-absorbed, as to stagger my mind completely'."

"Yes...?"

"Yes, that was June Jordan, a black American activist and feminist. My mother made me cram for all of that a long time ago. We must fight for what is rightfully ours. Once I get my grandmother's farm back, I'll fight for equality in sports. There must be reparations because the white racist government ignored black athletes and invested in white children only."

"I'm worried about you because I can see you're as stubborn as a mule. Can I call you Faty?"

"As you wish."

"Yes, that's what your uncle calls you. If you want to fight for your land, I will be with you all the way."

"You will be with me? Where will you be with me? The last time we met, you were a policeman in Ixopo. Now you are talking about being with me, fighting for my land?"

"Okay, I have to go now because I have an appointment in Durban."

"I see."

"I have spoken to my people at home. I told them again about you. I told my mother first because I respect her judgment. She thinks you are a special girl because of your javelin hobby..."

"Hobby? It's more than just a hobby. Throwing dice is a hobby, but field athletics is a serious pursuit that requires skill and effort."

"Right. Mother thinks you are special. I've been saving newspaper clippings about you since you nearly died under the bridge that rainy day at Ixopo. You're also special because you made the effort to come all the way to tell the Blose family about Busisiwe."

"You say you have a meeting in Durban. Let's go. You can drop me off at Wembezi."

Facing the Drakensberg skies, Hamilton pulled out a diamond ring and said, "Marry me, Kŭkuchi."

My stomach started to churn because of mixed emotions as Hamilton knelt in front of me, sliding his exceptional ring onto my finger inside my stolen ancestral land. I stared with extreme fondness at my hand that had suddenly transformed my rank in society, wondering if Funani had not gone babbling about my skeletons strewn around my lavatory. In my mind's eye, I saw the face of Peta, our roommate at university, who once said to me, '...one day you will find someone you care about, someone who truly loves you. If that happens, don't ruin things by opening your mouth and telling him about the abuse you suffered. '

In my confusion, I asked him, "What did you say to your whole family about the ring you just put on my finger?" Did you hint that the girl you want to marry lacks melanin?"

"I told them I met a girl. I fell in love with this girl and I want to marry her."

"I hear. And my grandmother? You will have to talk to my family... your people must come and open the way according to culture."

"So, I take it's a 'Yes'."

"You must first take me on a hiking trail until we reach the Devil's Tooth, then I'll take you to the Fort Durnford Museum and the Luthuli Museum. Remember, an hour ago, we merely stood outside Fort Durnford, but we did not go in to reflect on our history. I also want you to see the whole of the Midlands the way my mother showed it to me when I was a small girl. I want you to see the rich land under continued European occupation. Then I'll set a date for your people to meet with my family. Right?"

Later that night, I drove back alone to the farm and stood at the spot where some of our ancestors' graves had been desecrated, to assure the spirits of my ancestors and to the Khoi and the San, who were once buried there, that I was determined to reclaim that land. I also wanted to speak to the spirit of my twin brother, to tell him that Hamilton Bopela wants to marry me and that I think it's a good idea. While my mission exposed me to grave danger because of the trespassing laws targeted at

Africans, it felt safe to proceed under the moonlight. In the company of chirping crickets and distant mooing sounds of cows, I remained immobile for a while when I stopped on the spot where Hamilton had earlier propositioned me. Luckily, Trish was nowhere in sight. Scaling the farm's concrete wall and hiking the rising hill toward the gorge, I saw shadowy movements that disturbed me a little. My hair stood on end when I began to focus on the burial site that had remained lodged in my memory since my evening outing with Salu. Now, what remained of my twin brother's grave was a whispering wind rippling through the surface of the water. Blood-like streaks lined the wrinkling reflections of the multi-coloured moon. I knew then that my brother's remains, whom I had never known, were scattered somewhere in the vast waters between the Thukela River and the sea. I sat on the rock and reflected on my Sunday school story of Jacob, who was so troubled and scared he had to use a boulder for a pillow and watch the mysterious sky. I imagined how the sight of the Milky Way must have made him dream of a better life; a stairway leading to the heavens, with angelic beings walking up and down. When we were toddlers, Miss Lumka taught us that God was both above the stars and underneath that rock Jacob used as his pillow. Our class spent the whole session arguing about such a scenario, until Sandy said, 'My father is waiting; I must go,' and Toby said, 'Yes, let's go, Sandy.' As I reflected on our plight, the water in front of me formed ripples that began to flow across the edges as if reacting to a pebble dropped from heaven. On reaching Wembezi, I saw a car parked ominously on the grassy pavement. As it was dark, I could neither determine its make nor stay to see if anyone was hiding inside. I switched off my lights and quickly made my way inside. While I had Salu's 22 at the ready, I was shaking and half-listening to neighbourhood dogs howling and barking. After a long while, the strange car flooded our house with blinding headlights before it screeched off into the night. I kept mum about the intimidating invasion because I did not want to cause Salu more distress. Uppermost in my thoughts were the eerie images of the moon's reflection on display in the land of my ancestors. I received a letter of encouragement from Mrs Posa, who told me that she and Twaai had successfully reclaimed their family farm in Limpopo. Posa warned me to be cautious when dealing with officials of the new government, as they had become sneakier than those from the past era. Encouraged by Posa's support, I went to the Land Claims Court to challenge the Commission's decision. The appeal drew both local and international media attention, with one article beginning with my struggles to become a javelin champion.

The appeal hearing became a farce. After listening to my testimony, the judge described the Apartheid expropriation of Salu's property as a gluttonous sleight of hand. She then ordered the parties to negotiate with Salu and come back to court within 48 hours for her final decision. Salu alerted me to two ever-present white men outside the courtyard. The elder one, using an embroidered walking stick, was Van der Skoon, who had been a member of the Apartheid Parliament.

"The other one," Salu said, "he wants to speak to you."

"Me? Why?"

"His name is Venter. He says he was once in the police force in Johannesburg, and is now a dairy-farmer in Harrismith. Do you know any policeman by that name?"

"Oh no, it can't be!"

CHAPTER 31

You got your Land back.

A long wait for the verdict had started. We exchanged a few words at dinner, apart from Salu's long prayer for Africa.

"Why are you not eating?"

"Salu, I was expecting you to say grace for my nice meal I cooked."

"I said a prayer for the country, and that includes the delicious food you cooked."

We could barely sleep. After midnight, Salu whispered, "Kükuchi, are you asleep?"

I almost repeated Khulu's signature retort, 'Voetsak, how can I be asleep?' Instead, I asked Salu for her thoughts on Tsafendas, the man who stabbed Verwoerd to death.

Tsafendas did what he was supposed to do. We all have our assigned responsibilities on earth before we depart. Forget about Tsafendas. Today is D-Day. If it doesn't go well... I mean, if we don't regain our land... promise me one thing.

"That I should perform my responsibility to a Catholic monastery and become a nun?"

"I'm talking about marriage. You don't want to spend the rest of your life without a man, do you?"

"Oh, Salu!"

***

Outside the courtyard, Kükuchi's heart was skipping furiously. Salu was in an even worse state. Kükuchi helped fan her grandmother's face, which was dripping with sweat. Inside, Patricia sat on her mother's lap, with her brother standing next to an angry-looking father. Kükuchi's eyes met Patricia's smile, and they exchanged friendly waves.

The judge said it with little emotion, "Miss Salu Hadebe, you got your land back. The papers have been prepared, and you and your lawyer, Miss Kükuchi Hadebe, will have to sign."

The judge had already spoken privately with the Barry family, who promised to vacate the property within seven days. Although Salu remained somewhat sceptical, tears of joy began to flow down her face.

As they exited, Patricia approached Kükuchi and said, "I remember you."

"Yes, Trish. I remember you, too. How is your dog doing?"

"She's doing fine, but mother said we are giving her away because the *kaffirs* will be living in our house."

The media captured images of Kükuchi with Patricia, both smiling and hugging. Then Rita, a woman in her thirties with a sizable build and full lips, jumped out of a luxury car and asked if she could speak with Kükuchi and Salu under a tree. Wearing a short, tight red dress with matching high heels, her round eyes looked hesitant, as if she were about to burst into tears. She must have been crying all night, Kükuchi thought. A wooden crucifix hanging from her neck spoke volumes about what was going on inside of her.

The conversation was polite but awkward as it went on.

"My name is Rita Hadebe. I've been following this case with interest because we are relatives. My grandfather was Nico. Do you know Nico, Gogo?"

"Nico? Of course, I know Nico. He's my brother," Salu whispered, wrapping her arms around Rita. "You're my brother's granddaughter? Where is he?"

Rita saw her grandfather for the first time at her father's funeral. Her parents had separated when she was a toddler. By the time she tracked down her father, he was dying. Hence, she knew little about the family until she learned more when she met her grandfather. Even then, what she heard from him was wrapped in cryptic language that made little sense.

"I was impressed with Kükuchi's excellent testimony, which made me proud because it shared with us the history of my clan and the Hlubi nation, about which we knew little. Kükuchi and I are sisters."

Salu's heart was pounding again. After Kükuchi's effort to reclaim their land, a strange woman suddenly emerges, claiming to be a relative. Salu began to think that the ghosts of her past had come back.

"You say you've been following this case; what do you think of the verdict?" Kükuchi asked.

"It was nice to get our land again. I hope we shall sit down soon to discuss its future."

"Do you accept that the judge handed back the title to Gogo Salu..."

"I know. But the judge isn't family. That's why I want everyone to discuss it without mentioning the judge or her verdict."

Kükuchi felt so weak she could barely think. Salu nervously licked her lips, waiting for something meaningful to come from Kükuchi's lips.

"If you would like to speak with the family, I will arrange for us to do so in the judge's chambers. You can invite the entire family. I have a brother who teaches mathematics in Swaziland. I will ask his wife, who is a lawyer, to be present. We shall all be there..."

"No, I was not suggesting we follow the legal route..."

"But the judge has already issued a ruling. How can we bypass the legal process?"

Without another word, Rita swirled and broke into a well of tears that Kükuchi had earlier suspected had been building inside. Kükuchi attended to her.

After apologizing for making a fool of herself that way, Rita told them she was going through a messy divorce, which explained her sense of hopelessness. Rita owns a smallholding at Mooi River, where she lives with her 16-year-old daughter.

"Her name is Zakhona, and she looks just like you, Kükuchi."

"Albinism, you mean?"

"Yes, she often jokes that she is the only European in the family. My older sister and I have been at odds since high school. She accused me of stealing her boyfriend. Recently, she has formed a sinister friendship with Zakhona and her boyfriend."

Kükuchi asked, "When did the friendship with your daughter begin?"

"It started recently, after we heard something about the case. That's why I want us all to sit down under a neutral tree that will help us resolve the matter once and for all. If necessary, we will enlist the help of our king or his headmen to oversee the matter."

Bless you, Mr Venter

When we reached the exit, Captain Venter was leaning against the wooden gate, his expression filled with a mysterious power, yet he still maintained his commanding presence. He concealed his piercing eyes behind his white beard, which he unpleasantly brushed and pulled all over the place. But his entire demeanour still evoked menacing memories of our cat-and-mouse games in White City. Salu drifted away.

Venter said, "Things turned out well, Fat Girl. Remember me?"

"Yes, you're Captain Venter. How do you know things turned out well?"

"I was here from the beginning. Besides, we farmers talk to one another. That's how I know, and I'm happy for you. I knew you would make full use of your education…"

"Are you not retired?"

"Not quite. A policeman never truly retires. I believe you understand this because you're a clever lawyer. Veteran police officers often ponder various things, including cold cases. Do you know what worries every detective the most? It's the thought of dying before solving a serious case that leaves communities in shock."

My heart was pounding against my chest. I had just won back a family farm, and here was Rita, who claimed to be my sister, posing riddles and shedding what may well have been crocodile tears. As if that wasn't enough, there is this white man, flashing a sardonic smile as he threatens to crack cold cases at my expense. My stomach ached, and my tongue turned into dry rye.

"What are you doing here, then?"

"Observing. I'm interested in the past and the future. Where is your brother?"

"Dassie? He lives in Swaziland with his family."

"Ah! He didn't come back from the trenches of struggle to ride on the coattails of Mandela's Parliament?" Venter chuckled. "With his clever mind, he could be a Cabinet Minister. I saw your court speech the other day. Of course, I always knew you were sharp. The old nurse you called Sister Mohale? Remember her? She said you had a big mouth."

"She said that to you?"

"Yes, she said, 'One day that Tsotsi girl will be a lawyer because she reads newspapers and she is a clever liar. I hope you don't mind me repeating that."

"No, I miss her. Did you she passed away?"

"No, I did not hear that…I am sorry. His son went to Angola only to be killed by his comrades…"

"Sister Mohale's spirit began to fade the day her son left the country, the same day the police raided her home without regard for her feelings as a grieving mother. Mrs Mohale was a God-fearing woman who respected the law, but all I remember about the law is how the police ransacked her home and humiliated her as a single Black mother."

"Yes, it was a tough time. Things are different now. Still, I remain curious. Tell me about that man we found under the trees near your house when you were young. Do you have any idea who he was or who might have killed him?"

"Man under the trees? It's all history, Mr Venter. Nobody remembers that man."

"I'm sure he would have liked to vote, but unfortunately, he died near your house."

"I know nothing about the man."

"Yes indeed. What is your *Tsotsi* brother doing in Swaziland?"

"Dassie teaches Maths at a Swazi College. He's not a *Tsotsi* anymore."

"When you see Dassie again, ask him about Papi. He will remember him… that boy from Alexandra. His sister had paraplegia. When I found Papi on the side of the bridge with six stab wounds, he was still alive. Do you know whose name he kept repeating before he died?"

"People hallucinate when they are dying, Mr Venter."

"Quite. I am happy for you. But I will only rest when I find and lock up the man who murdered Papi. What do you think, Fat Girl?"

This time, I was angry, not with being referred to as 'Fat Girl,' but with the realization that Venter was diligent in persistently reviving the case in which Dassie would be the person of interest. What made the white man so tenacious in the face of the political turmoil that ensued after the release of Nelson Mandela? Thousands of blacks have died at the hands of the enemies of black liberation, but here was this man, smiling in my face while threatening to destroy my brother.

In anger, I asked Venter how many girls ended up missing in White City and Jabavu and whether the police eventually found out how many had been killed by Dodo. Venter stated that investigators were involved in the incidents, but he was unaware of their involvement. I told Venter that in White City, people said black girls disappeared in large numbers, but the police could not find the source of the crime. White City residents believed that the disappearance of one white girl would have sparked such white outrage that detectives from as far as the Cape would have flooded Johannesburg.

"But your uncle was arrested."

"My uncle? Yes, Mr Venter, but you released him from prison on parole as if he had killed a fly."

"It's all over now…"

"No. When I was young, I used to keep a diary where I wrote my secret thoughts. I want to investigate this matter and write about it."

Venter pulled a face.

"Furthermore, I intend to utilize a newspaper article for a documentary or a book. It was an item published in a newspaper that led to the imprisonment of the editor and two reporters. Do you remember that story, Mr Venter?"

"A lot was going on those days."

"It was an article about a white woman's skeleton found buried inside a well. Did the police investigate the Kriel family on this matter before they let them leave for Australia?"

Pulling his beard, Venter said, "I hope you don't intend to write anything about that incident!"

"I will investigate the source to find peace of mind. I don't believe I can rest until I know the outcome of the sad story. Rumour has it that the white woman's skeleton was that of a 17-year-old girl called Jane Doe by the newspapers."

Venter gazed awkwardly at the sky, and when he turned back to me, he said, "You're right, Fat Girl. Let's forget about the past. That Zulu man, Mkhize, your neighbour? I once asked him about you and your coloured friend... what was her name?"

"Toby..."

"Yes, Toby. Mkhize told me the name meant humble and pleasant to behold. Indeed, she was pretty. He said to me in his beautiful language from Zululand, 'Give these children a chance because any wretched particle of ash may contain smouldering remnants, too small to see, buried somewhere inside, yet holding on for a puff of air'. I jotted it down verbatim and asked my wife to translate it for me. As a Hlubi, I know you love your sour milk. I have an original San jug waiting for you in Harrismith. When you come over, we shall talk about your beauty-queen friend but not about dead people."

"We can join forces and collaborate in the interest of justice for Jane Doe. Are you not curious, Mr Venter? This case might be a ticking time bomb because the press will never leave it alone."

"You are not the press, Fat Girl, so avoid skating on thin ice. Trust me. I care for you."

"Okay, Mr Venter. From now on, we are going to discuss the javelin...?"

"Come to Harrismith. There must be a reason why White-City and Jabavu brought us together. My wife has always been looking forward to meeting you because she doesn't believe the stories being told about you."

"Right, but I prefer sour milk served with our traditional pure sorghum, ground a little coarsely. Tell your wife, that's my kind of Hlubi snack. If you promise to forget about the past — about Papi — I'll hold off on my investigation into Jane Doe. I shall come over to meet you and your wife in Harrismith to celebrate our victory and to talk about your farm and our future as farmers."

"I look forward to it. It's great to see an educated woman from White City joining us to become a farmer. Farming is more art than science. I'm glad I took Mkhize's advice. Dassie must continue to be a good citizen and teach Mathematics. No more cold cases for me."

I could not help but gulp tears of eternal relief.

"Do you believe in God, Mr Venter?"

"You know what my German mother used to say, Fat Girl? She always said, 'Whether you believe in God or not, he is still up there in the sky'. "

"May the God who is up there in the sky bless you, Mr Venter!"

An Approaching Hurricane

The democratic government awarded Barry two million Rand in exchange for Salu's farm. Kükuchi recalled Mkhize's wise words, 'a white man will never lose in Africa'.

Throughout Barry's occupation of Salu's farm, the property slowly turned into a playground for international tourists. Little farming took place there, and only two broiler cages remained as remnants of the past. Three sheep shearers from Bhekuzulu had made use of the abandoned kraal to do their work. Not worried that their business might soon end, one of them said, 'Welcome to our kraal…' and they continued shearing.

"Leave them alone. They'll soon realize they are under new management."

"Where do we start? The impostors ruined your chicken business, Salu…"

"And messed up my rock-pool; it's swarming with decaying wood and sheets of mould. My lively colony of frogs and shoal of fish have been wiped out. No yellow ducklings trailing their odd black mom."

"All the water lilies have died."

"But don't worry about the rock-pool. A queen's rebuilt palace is always more beautiful than the one the enemy destroyed. You will see what Israel will look like after the real Black Jesus comes back for his own."

"Yes, but how will the queen bring back her fine-looking thatched *rondavels* when someone turned one into a lumber room and sealed up the other with a pile of rocks?"

"The dirty hand that drove away all the horses also stripped the paddock bare."

"Yes, Salu," I moaned. "A naked paddock is of no use to us now."

"We can get a few ponies from Mooi River. Then again, we could keep the paddock as a memorial to Apartheid."

"Yes! Ponies, Salu! You got something there: a colt and three fillies. Give it a few months, and you'll be showing them off at the Ladysmith Show Grounds."

"For sure, but first things first… We'll have to empty the white man's pool and restore our sacred burial ground."

***

As I contemplate the damaged plants and mortar, I start to understand the depth of Salu's pain over the wanton mutilation of her farm.

All the same, we celebrate the return of Salu's farm in style, and the day is filled with activity. Rita arrives with Zakhona, her 'European' daughter, who stays glum until she leaves. This makes me want to understand the source of her resentment.

The next group of guests is Jozi and Funani, accompanied by their daughter, Anna. Then comes a bus full of Wembezi residents of all walks of life, followed by a convoy of luxury cars from all over the country. Hamilton swoops in like a vulture, accompanied by two mini-buses, friends, and relatives from Ixopo.

Hamilton and I hide ourselves in the brush on the edge of Salu's ruined pond for a private conversation. Hamilton says, "I don't see my ring on your finger. What happened?"

"Your ring? You gave me that ring."

"Look, in our rush, we left out some issues…"

"The only issue is about a meeting between families."

"I brought my relatives to introduce them to your grandmother. It is best to schedule a follow-up discussion if you intend to proceed. But you have to show your intentions clearly by wearing the ring."

"That's not how it works for me."

When Salu saw the ring for the first time, she described it as a diamond fit for a princess. That hardly clarified her views on marriage.

***

A few days later, Kükuchi left early to confront her anxieties, especially those related to Rita's disguised threats. She also felt uncertain about her relationship with Hamilton. As she passed through Bergville and Winterton, she remembered the morning Musa took her climbing Pasiwe Hill and how she declared, 'This beautiful land you see on the far side of Moyeni and Maqabaqabeni was stolen from the Africans by white settlers. They destroyed our Kingdoms and allotted themselves fertile land...'

All the while, Kükuchi was unaware of her trembling lips and face, with tears streaming from her eyes. She stopped at the foot of Pasiwe Hill, looking at the home where she and her mother had rested and enjoyed chicken pies and tap water. It became clearer than before that her mother might have been excited about voting, but by observing her surroundings, nothing much had changed because white people still controlled that land. Meanwhile, younger Black generations worked on it as indentured labourers, just like their mothers and ancestors before them. Kükuchi looked around and saw that the farmland her mother showed her when she was seven still belonged to white people who felt entitled by divine right, while Black folks remained in barren wilderness.

Kükuchi realized that her mother's wisdom extended beyond bricks and mortar, reaching the vast farmlands that Europeans had seized. What Musa showed her when she was seven served as a metaphor for the arduous journey Kükuchi would face, dealing with her family's long history of conflict. It was a challenge that Kükuchi discovered she had to confront.

Kükuchi was driving slowly along the rural Estcourt road when she started thinking about how everything in life is connected. She reflected on the strong link between her struggle to reclaim Salu's land and the importance of exploring her ancestors' role and impact on their descendants' futures.

***

Kükuchi and Salu are in a casual chat. Salu whispered, "Remember what I said about this property; it will be registered in your name. We get up tomorrow to set the process moving…"

"Are you sure you'll be doing the right thing, Salu?"

"Yes. That girl, Rita, seems to be a real storm brewing. But once she gets to know that the farm is yours, she and her people will think twice before they start trouble."

"I am uneasy about this whole thing because they are family..."

"This land belongs to me. I will be transferring ownership to you because that's my wish regarding my property. After that, you can develop it further or throw it away to opportunists called family."

"Why? You seem intent on losing everything, including family, for my sake?"

"Yes, losing everything is a blessing because that's the only time one gets to search one's heart. I learned that lesson when I was forcefully exiled to Wembezi."

"What are you saying, Salu?"

"When the government took my land and banished me to Wembezi, I felt like a girl drowning in the Buffalo River, with my entire life flashing before my eyes like a horror movie. When God wants to deal with you, he allows even his enemies to do it for him. That's what the book of Habakkuk teaches us. The Apartheid government was God's enemy, and he allowed them to mess up my life to help me look inside myself."

"What did you find when you looked?"

"Things..."

"Like *Soksie*?"

Salu winced uncomfortably and remained silent.

"Salu, when you looked inside of yourself, did you not find somewhere that losing family is worse than losing property?"

"I understand what you're saying. But someday you'll realize that keeping people close just because they're family is as harmful to you as it is to them. I'm not willing to accommodate family members who believe land ownership is a status symbol rather than a result of hard work."

Changing the subject, Kükuchi said, "Salu, since you don't want to talk to me about *Soksie*, let's talk about the man who wants to marry me. About the ring, you said it is nice and fit for a princess. But there is a problem. I don't feel like a princess at all. Hamilton wants me to stay at his Ixopo home as a traditional wife once we get married. I told him that it would never happen as I have this farm to look after."

"You seem to have wrapped yourself up in a tangled web. Communication is key before lobola. It would be a shame if you were to be forced to choose between this farm and Hamilton."

"Yes, Salu. It would truly be a shame. Communication is also essential for our family. That's why I focus on using the top of Pasiwe Hill for observation. We all have something to gain as descendants of Bashaye if we share and support each other."

***

In the silence of the Drakensberg night, my sleepy ears caught a distant purring sound like that of an approaching hurricane. I quickly slid out of bed onto the porch to investigate. It was a strange car whose bright headlights flooded the house. However, when the lights went off, my hair stood on end upon becoming aware that I was looking at the same car that had parked ominously outside our Wembezi home one night. As before, I could hardly make out the number of occupants, let alone their identity. I rushed inside to alert Salu, who promptly came out to the porch, wielding a shotgun I knew nothing about.

Pointing the muzzle at the car, Salu shouted, "Get out of the car!"

The doors swung open, and two people stepped outside. One was a tall man with dreadlocks, while the other was Zakhona, Rita's daughter, who has albinism.

"It's me, Grandma Salu. I am Zakhona with Viki. We want to talk."

I had a nervous hunch about the pair's visit. So, I tried to read their emotions as they walked in. Viki swaggered with his hands securely tucked into his Bermuda shorts pockets, while Zakhona was skittish and visibly shaking. What the pair had to say was about to set the cat among the pigeons.

Zakhona spoke plainly, though with an irritatingly shrill voice, telling Salu that the land she was occupying belonged to the family and that Salu was a bully. Well-informed about the family's history, Zakhona mentioned Ntombizakhona, Nico, and Jantshi as Salu's three siblings who had been forced off the land by Salu herself.

Throughout that time, Viki agreed with Zakhona's tirade with one lazy nod after another. My mouth had become so dry I could hardly speak. A long-standing sibling rivalry had returned to haunt us.

Viki said in a deep voice, "It is only fair that this whole thing gets corrected without resorting to the courts…"

I responded, "I understand Zakhona is a member of this family. And who are you?"

"Viki is my fiancée."

"Your fiancé isn't family here," said Salu. "Has Rita, your mother, given you permission to say all these things to your fiancé?"

"My mother does not have to know everything about me. I am an adult."

"Your mother is an adult, and you will be an adult the day you turn twenty-one."

Viki said, "We have come here to have a decent discussion…"

"Listen, Viki; Salu just told you to shut up because you don't have the right to talk about matters that don't concern you. As for you, Zakhona, I will discuss your unruly behaviour with your mother. I'll ask her if she knows whether you and your boyfriend came to intimidate us one night at Wembezi. Do you remember that? I know how to file a criminal charge with the police, and I know how to put young criminals in that Winterton jail."

After reflecting on Zakhona's rude words, I realized new conflicts had arisen. On second thought, I suspected she might have been sent by her mother to test the waters. Whatever the case, Zakhona's presence was so intimidating that I started seeing flickering lights around me. The saying 'the enemy is always parked at the gate' seemed accurate. Just when Salu and I thought everything was in place, when we believed we had won the most significant legal battle of our lives, a ghost from the past threatened to tear this family apart even more.

By the Creator's providence, the Drakensberg roars with fury, rivers burst their banks, homes and fields are destroyed, and many lives are lost. How can we ease God's wrath now?

***

Later in the day, Rita welcomed me into her private office, where I discovered she was a neurologist.

"I wasn't aware you were a medical doctor."

"Yes, a doctor in need of getting my own broken heart healed."

"I'm sorry. Do you mind discussing your broken heart? I'll discuss mine."

"There is not much to discuss, except that it's about my divorce. The whole episode is not amicable. He is my second, you know. When a woman divorces, even her colleagues think there is something wrong with her. Imagine what they say behind my back now that he is the second! Yes, we can talk about my problems. When you made your presentation in court that day, I said to myself, here is a woman I can trust. I wish I had met you long before this as my lawyer."

"It's never too late. Please tell me what you know about our story... our ancestors' story. I beg you."

"Kükuchi, you know our history better than I do. The whole thing is depressing because I can't cope with so much on my plate."

"What will you do regarding Granny Salu and the farm? We know that the land has been a source of dispute for decades..."

"Now that I have met her and you, I hope Salu and our ancestors can rest peacefully. It is through God's grace that things have turned out this way. We should be grateful that a miracle has happened, giving our family the chance to be together again."

"Do you foresee such a chance?"

"Nothing is impossible."

"Tell me about Zakhona..."

"Zakhona has been a troublemaker, a complicated teenager. Her semi-literate boyfriend led my daughter into doing unimaginable things, including dropping out of high school. One day, she came to me claiming to be pregnant. I have been waiting for months for the pregnancy to show, but nothing has happened. Her father blames everything on me."

"What does she say happened to the pregnancy?"

"She came to me demanding that I do the abortion. When I ignored her, she winced, shrugged, dusted her skirt as usual, and walked away. I have failed as a mother. When a daughter falls pregnant, it is always the mother's fault; you know that."

"Can you arrange for me to meet her privately?"

"That one! The sky can fall on our heads. Zakhona is on a slippery slope to a ditch. What can you do about a girl who squats with an unemployed boy just because he has a car?"

"Let's not give up on Zakhona. Salu and I will be visiting Khulu's gravesite next Saturday. Please join us. And make an effort to bring Zakhona along. No elephant has been weighed down by its trunk. I'm happy to hear that you want us to be a family again. Can you assure me that you have no plans to challenge Salu's ownership of the land?"

"I can't speak for others, such as my older sister and my ex-husband. My sister was in court during your testimony, but she disappeared afterward."

"When last did you speak to your sister?"

"Ten... twelve years, maybe?"

"What is her name? I want to contact her. You just said we have a chance to be a family again."

"Bashaye. That's her full name. We all call her Bashi."

"That name? Do you know where it came from?"

"Our grandfather named her Bashaye. She's always looking for a fight, and the name fits her temperament perfectly."

We had a lot to talk about with Rita.

CHAPTER 32

Epilogue

We wake up early for our first trip to Khulu's grave, feeling nervous. We all wear our elegant Hlubi traditional clothing. I cover my messy hair with my bottle-green beret, which Salu finds funny. And we're on our way.

Despite my excitement, the shadow of the family curse still looms over us. I remain uneasy about the two sisters, Bashi and Rita, who haven't spoken to each other in ten years. Above the Drakensberg summit, a clash of grey and black clouds forms and moves forcefully as the fog lifts. Scarlet rays from the morning sun burst forth like distant brush fires.

"The sky is fighting against me, Kükuchi."

"What do you mean, Salu?"

"I can't continue with this. Do you see the threatening clouds? That's my sister. She said it aloud, 'No one must come to speak to my bones. My God will protect me with clouds."

"Khulu was mad because you showed no remorse. You need to talk to your sister, who will look into your heart and see the humility inside you. But let's be clear, Salu, if you can't speak to your sister today, I'll pack my things and drive back to Johannesburg…"

Salu begins to wail, "Please, Kükuchi, don't you care about my feelings?"

"I mean it, Gogo."

"What about Zakhona and that boy with eyes like a giant spider. How are we supposed to deal with Zakhona? The demons are surrounding me in my old age."

"Please don't feel sorry for yourself. You're not a victim here, Salu. You have to take responsibility in your old age for the weaknesses of your youth."

"Do you believe your legal knowledge can safeguard my farm?"

"Salu, if they want to take the legal route, their ancient legend will end up in the Drakensberg cave because I know the law. Also, I have Goodie on my side. But I think we'll need to find another way with Zakhona and Rita's sister. That will be my burden to bear."

***

Dassie and Goodie took an overnight trip from Manzini to Wembezi and arrived in their new German car at the same time as Zakhona and Viki. When he saw them, Zakhona got out of Viki's car and took a curious look at the strangers. Zakhona was inappropriately dressed in a tight black skirt and a red shirt, along with black socks featuring a fishy tail on her head. Viki stayed in the car listening to reggae. When Zakhona saw Kükuchi and Salu greet Dassie and Goodie, she walked over and sat on a rock near the gate, watching what seemed to be an enticing spectacle.

"Dassie," whispered Salu, "do you see that skimpily dressed girl seated over there? Her name is Zakhona. Please fetch her. I want her to meet with you."

"She looks like Kükuchi."

"Shut up, Dassie," chides Goodie.

"The girl is our blood relative., Explains Kükuchi. She is actively drawing a noose around our necks. She and her boyfriend have hatched a scheme to destroy us."

"How interesting it is to see you shaking with fear for once. The only girl who came close to doing that was Toby," he laughs. "You say this girl wants to destroy you?"

"I said 'us'. She wants the farm, which she claims was stolen from them by Salu."

"Are you preparing to waste time fighting this stubborn girl?"

"Yes, Dassie. And I know Goodie will help because she is an intelligent advocate. I know I can't rely on you because you're only good at stealing bundles of money hidden in Barberton pits."

"Salu wants me to talk to Zakhona. Let me go to her."

Although hesitant, Dassie approached Zakhona, who slowly stood up and subtly brushed her skirt with the back of her left hand – a clear signal for him to leave her alone.

"My name is Dassie. I want to talk to you because you are beautiful, just like my sister."

"Who is your sister?"

"Kükuchi. They told me you are Zakhona. Do you do athletics?"

"Why?"

"Kükuchi will train you to be a track athlete. She is a star. One day, you will compete for South Africa. Don't you think, Zakhona?"

"Me?"

"Let's go. I'll introduce you to Goodie. She is an advocate. Shall we go?"

"No."

***

On the tombstone, there is neither history nor a display of colours showing Khulu's glorious days as a woman with struggle credentials. After placing bouquets, the family quietly settles on grass mats. Countless thoughts cross Kükuchi's mind, but only one stays; Khulu pouring out her frustrations on Salu one day, saying, 'No one must think I will open my ears when they speak to my bones'.

Bashaye arrives and hugs everyone with a smile. Zakhona sits between Kükuchi and Rita.

Kükuchi says, "You can get closer now, Salu. We are here with you. Khulu will open her ears because God is listening."

"Yes, Faty. I am getting closer."

The sombreness around Khulu's gravesite deepens when Salu rests her hand upon the headstone. She holds her breath for a while and then says, "Thank you, Faty. Now I will speak to my Dear Sister. Ntombizakhona ka Langalibalele, I am here with the young generation of our clan. We are also with Goodie, our granddaughter from the land of Mzilikazi.

"My Father's Child, I pray your prayer, 'Oh God, search my heart and help me not to worry. Amen'. Tell Father what Ntombiphelele says. *Soksie* fell down the ravine by accident because of hail. Tell all our mothers, sisters, and brothers that Ntombizakhona risked her life all night trying to rescue *Soksie*. Ask our God Almighty to be merciful to me, a sinner. Amen."

Kūkuchi leaps high into the air. She bounces and circles Khulu's grave like a peacock. Goodie follows suit, ululating and twirling to her Ndebele tune, 'Gwabi, Gwabi'. Dassie parks himself a few steps away, leaving all the women hopping, skipping, and dancing their staccato ballets, with their toes barely touching the ground.

After the impromptu celebration, Kūkuchi shouts, "We can go now. Let's go home to eat, drink, and have fun on this happy day."

***

We reaffirmed our bond with Hamilton a few months later, despite the uncertain outlook. Eventually, we held our semi-traditional ceremony on top of Pasiwe Hill, where spring waters still nourish a group of joyful monkeys. Then a surprise that touched deep into my soul! Toby appeared. Next to her was her smiling adolescent daughter. Although I felt uneasy about my decision to hatch with Hamilton, Musa's ironic reassurance to me, '…you are different because you are a strong girl…' quietly echoed in my heart.

~ *End* ~